PENGUIN CLASSICS

THE POWER OF SYMPATHY

and

THE COQUETTE

William Hill Brown (1765–93) was best known durin̲ day as a witty poet and political essayist. For readers today, Brown's fame rests upon his novel *The Power of Sympathy* (1789). He was born in Boston, Massachusetts, to clock-maker Gawen Brown and Elizabeth Hill Adams Brown, Gawen Brown's third wife. Brown's publishing career seems to have begun in 1787, when his verse epistle "Shays to Shattuck" was printed in the *Massachusetts Centinel*. His poems and political essays brought him much acclaim, even before he published a ballad opera called *The Better Sort: Or, The Girl of Spirit, An Operatical, Comical Farce*, in the same year that *The Power of Sympathy* appeared. In 1792, Brown moved from his New England home to that of his sister, Elizabeth Brown Hinchborne, in Murfreesborough, North Carolina, where he began to study law with Gen. William Richardson Davie of the Town of Halifax. Brown seems never to have married. He died in North Carolina, probably a victim of the malaria that swept through the area in 1793. His (now lost) play, *West Point Preserved: Or, The Treason of Arnold*, was performed in Boston in 1797 and 1800, and a second novel, *Ira and Isabella: Or, The Natural Children*, was published in 1807.

Hannah Webster Foster (1758–1840) wrote a great deal during her lifetime, but she remains best known for having published *The Coquette*, a novel of enduring fame from her day to our own. She was born in Salisbury, Massachusetts, to Hannah Wainwright Webster and Grant Webster, a prosperous merchant. After her mother died, Hannah Webster was sent to a boarding school in 1762. Her first publications, on political issues, started appearing in Boston papers in the 1780s. She married Rev. John Foster, pastor of the First Church in Brighton, Massachusetts, in 1785, and between 1786 and 1796 bore six children, five of whom survived to adulthood. Hannah Fos-

ter anonymously published *The Coquette*, her first novel, in 1797. Her second novel, *The Boarding School: Or, Lessons of a Preceptress to Her Pupils* (1798), never attained the success of her first, although it seems to have been widely read for its advice about women's reading, needlework, writing, dance, and singing. In the early part of the nineteenth century, Foster contributed to the Federalist publication *The Monthly Anthology or Magazine of Polite Literature*, which later became the *North American Review*. She would live to see *The Coquette* reprinted several times before she died in 1840.

Carla Mulford is an associate professor of English at the Pennsylvania State University. In addition to numerous essays in early American studies, she has published *John Leacock's First Book of the American Chronicles of the Times, 1774–1775* (1987), a critical edition of an American revolutionary-era satire, and *Only for the Eyes of a Friend: The Poems of Annis Boudinot Stockton* (1995), a critical edition that sets the canon of a famed eighteenth-century poet. She served as the early Americanist editor of the two-volume multicultural anthology *The Heath Anthology of American Literature* (1990; 2d ed., 1993).

THE POWER OF SYMPATHY

WILLIAM HILL BROWN

and

THE COQUETTE

HANNAH WEBSTER FOSTER

WITH AN INTRODUCTION AND NOTES BY
CARLA MULFORD

PENGUIN BOOKS

PENGUIN BOOKS
Published by the Penguin Group
Penguin Books USA Inc., 375 Hudson Street, New York, New York 10014, U.S.A.
Penguin Books Ltd, 27 Wrights Lane, London W8 5TZ, England
Penguin Books Australia Ltd, Ringwood, Victoria, Australia
Penguin Books Canada Ltd, 10 Alcorn Avenue, Toronto, Ontario, Canada M4V 3B2
Penguin Books (N.Z.) Ltd, 182–190 Wairau Road, Auckland 10, New Zealand

Penguin Books Ltd, Registered Offices: Harmondsworth, Middlesex, England

The Power of Sympathy first published in the United States of America
by Isaiah Thomas 1789
The Coquette first published in the United States of America
by Samuel Etheridge for E. Larkin 1797
This edition with an introduction and notes by Carla Mulford published in
Penguin Books 1996

1 3 5 7 9 10 8 6 4 2

Introduction and notes copyright © Carla Mulford, 1996
All rights reserved

LIBRARY OF CONGRESS CATALOGING IN PUBLICATION DATA
Brown, William Hill, 1765–1793.
The power of sympathy / by William Hill Brown. And The coquette / by Hannah
Webster Foster ; [both] edited with an introduction and notes by Carla Mulford.
p. cm. — (Penguin classics)
Includes bibliographical references.
ISBN 0 14 04.3468 2 (hardbound)
1. American fiction—18th century. 2. Whitman, Elizabeth, 1752–1788—
Fiction. 3. Man-woman relationships—Fiction. 4. Didactic fiction, American.
5. Women—Fiction. I. Foster, Hannah (Webster) 1758–1840. Coquette.
II. Mulford, Carla, 1955–. III. Title. IV. Series.
PS715.B6P6 1996
813'.2—dc20 96–5347

Printed in the United States of America
Set in Sabon

EDITOR'S NOTE

My Penn State colleague Wendell Harris was the first to point me in the direction of *The Advice of a Lady of Quality to Her Children*. I'd like to thank him for the reference, and I'd like to thank Angela Vietto, who kindly created for me an initial transcription of that text. While he was an undergraduate at Penn State, Steve Fonash assisted me in compiling the preliminary list of secondary readings on Brown and Foster. The letter Annis Stockton wrote to Julia Stockton Rush appears among the Rush-Biddle Williams family papers at the Rosenbach Library of Philadelphia; it is reprinted here with permission of the Rosenbach. I'd like to thank Amy Winans, who sent me to the Jeremy Belknap letter with which I begin the introduction to this edition. The letter is located at the Historical Society of Pennsylvania, in volume 30 of the Rush papers; the excerpt is printed with the permission of the Historical Society. Finally, I'd like to thank Suzanne Begnoche, who assisted in reading proofs of this text.

CONTENTS

INTRODUCTION

WRITING FROM BOSTON to his friend, the famous physician, moralist, and educator, Dr. Benjamin Rush of Philadelphia, Jeremy Belknap reported on August 16, 1788, "In one of our papers there is an account from Danvers of a Woman who died at an Inn of a puerperal fever—a Stranger—supposed to be from Connecticut." It was surprising news, useful to moralists, and it was being printed in newspapers throughout New England. The story Belknap repeated involved a woman who, having borne a child out of wedlock, died soon thereafter from the fever she developed while giving birth. The tale had all the ingredients of a suspenseful mystery, one that Belknap thought Rush might use "in some of your moral Lectures to young Ladies." Expecting that Rush would "doubtless see" the story reprinted in the Philadelphia papers, Belknap nonetheless sketched out what he considered the most important details:

> the Lady whose Conduct appeared so mysterious proves to be ye Daughter of a deceased Clergyman in Connecticut. She was handsome genteel & sensible but vain & coquetish[,] a *great reader of Romances*. She refused two as good offers of Marriage as she deserved because she aspired higher than to be a Clergyman's Wife— & having coqueted it till past her bloom, fell into criminal indulgencies, proved *enceinte* [i.e., pregnant] & then eloped, pretending where she lodged & died to be married & carried on ye deception till death—

Tellingly linked here in Belknap's account are the woman's gentility and her sensibility, both of which would seem to have failed her because she was a "great reader of Romances." If a woman *would* read romances and refuse offers of marriage from clergymen, the monitory message ran, she would seem now to have gotten what she "deserved."

This true story about a seduction reveals some of the most crucial cultural fascinations of Belknap and Rush's era. Indeed, the fascinations have continued from their day to our own. Women's bodies and their

behaviors have for centuries been the focus of those who wished to
lecture on morality and the general success or failure of the culture.
Women seem to have become a particular preoccupation during the
eighteenth-century era of Enlightenment, however. Many considered
that the Enlightenment in America, modified as it was by a certain
amount of Christian humanism adapted from the Scottish "Common
Sense" school of philosophers, would produce the world's best system
of government and the best-"enlightened" people the world had ever
seen. Especially as the American Enlightenment was advanced among
elite groups in the Anglo-American colonies and then the new United
States, the era promised a future cleared of the corrupt and evil past of
European monasteries and monarchies, a future that seemed bright with
the possibility of an entirely new and peaceable social order. At least
that is what men like Belknap—a Christian humanist and Quaker ab-
olitionist, who had a sincere belief in social amelioration for all
groups—wanted to imagine. That a woman of some social standing and
seeming moral prominence, a clergyman's daughter no less, could "fall"
in this way, certainly meant that something was amiss in her life: had
her life been better regulated, she would not be dead now, the moral
seemed to be. The scapegoat for the woman's "failure" was her reading
of romances. Her story would serve as an excellent warning for other,
younger women, Belknap thought. And he was not alone in this think-
ing. Both William Hill Brown and Hannah Webster Foster seem to have
agreed wholeheartedly. Ironically, they conveyed the story of the
"stranger" woman, Elizabeth Whitman, in fictions that to some extent
were advantaged by precisely the mode of writing—romances—that
Belknap had deplored to Benjamin Rush.

Brown's *The Power of Sympathy* (1789) and Foster's *The Coquette*
(1797) were two of the first novels published in the United States. Both
novels focused on the social relations between men and women, espe-
cially upon the ways in which women's lives and actions were crucially
centered in the social fabric, and both used real-life circumstances
adapted to the fictional medium. Considered in terms of the *genre* of
novelistic fiction, these two novels were among the first to take part in
the discourse linking women's issues with nationhood. They would
seem, in fact, to have indicated a turning point in Anglo-American
printing culture, for their publication—and their popularity at the
time—marks the beginning of a turn away from the publishing and
distribution of fictional writing in brief or serialized versions in news-
papers to the much more lucrative world of the book. In its very physical

dimensions—small enough to hold nearly covered by one's hand, or tucked away in a vest, sleeve, or pocket of a dress—the book provided for a reader's privacy in reading and thinking. Just as a physical object, the book proved fascinating to readers. Interestingly, novels like Brown's and Foster's were themselves part of a seductive marketplace of culture that was shifting from public consumption of print to private use of it. Increasingly as the eighteenth century turned into the nineteenth century, the market in books served a populace that seems to have had tremendous preoccupation with private activities of people, but especially the private activities—the lives and the bodies—of women.

The *intensity* of the interest in women at the end of the eighteenth century was new, but the appearance of women in fiction in Anglo-America had been occurring for some time. Decades before *The Power of Sympathy* and *The Coquette* were published, readers had been treated to their first newspaper representations of a woman's voice on women's issues in a series of essays written by Benjamin Franklin. "I find it a very difficult Matter," said Franklin's fictional woman character, Silence Dogood, in 1722, "to reprove Women separate from the Men." Between the years 1722 and 1788, it would seem, attitudes did not much change. Silence Dogood's newspaper inquiry into women's situations in the English colonies—published as Dogood essay No. V in the *New-England Courant*, May 28, 1722—revealed the cultural preoccupations of English and Continental readers from at least as early as the sixteenth century. Even the name Franklin chose for his character—"Silence"—implicitly criticized the manner then deemed most suitable for women. When Silence aired her questions about women's place (or lack of place) in the world, she was giving voice to issues that were being addressed again and again by those interested in social and educational theory. She asked, "[W]hat Vice is there in which the Men have not as great a Share as the Women?" To answer herself, she adopted a position commonplace in the more liberal educational tracts of the era: if women were ignorant and fond of luxury, men were accountable for the situation, because men's established social institutions required that women be kept both in ignorance and in ease. Such a situation, Silence attested, enabled men to chastise women for folly, whereas women themselves did not control the situation that produced their supposed ignorance and extravagance.

At the center of this Silence Dogood essay is a remarkable passage Franklin adapted from Daniel Defoe's *An Essay upon Projects* (1697),

where Defoe had called the lack of education for women a "barbarous" custom given the fact that England considered itself "a civiliz'd and Christian Country": "Shall we upbraid Women with Folly, when 'tis only the Error of this inhumane Custom that hindred them being made wiser?" This was a question frequently found in materials on women's status and education in Europe and in England, but a question few seemed to want to ask at that time in the colonies. Yet by the end of the century in the new United States, it became a question that preoccupied citizens.

What *was* the relationship between the reading of romances and women's behavior? people like Belknap seemed to have been asking. Could the education of women improve the overall moral fabric of the nation? A lot of people seem to have thought so. For some who sought "a more perfect union," it seemed that the control of women's bodies would be a crucial step toward the development of a nation free of moral degradation, one that "deserved" to function as a republic. Like the newspaper account that seems to have both titillated and distressed Jeremy Belknap, novels like William Hill Brown's anonymously published *The Power of Sympathy* and Hannah Webster Foster's *The Coquette* indicate the powerful and vexing preoccupations of white citizens in the first decades of U.S. nationhood.

II

What were these citizens like? Several key social concerns seem to have been common to most whites of the laboring, middling, and upper classes in England and Anglo-America during the eighteenth century. One concern, as we've seen, revolved around the relations between the sexes. More to the point, in the English colonies by midcentury, the general population was increasing. "Send your accomplished artisans and craftspeople to the British colonies, for they will find work," Franklin had said again and again in letters and publications sent to England before the Revolution. The population in the British colonies *was* increasing dramatically. Indeed, in the year 1776, when the Declaration of Independence was signed, more than half the white population was sixteen years of age or younger. They were a youthful people who fought the American Revolution and became the first U.S. citizenry. This suggests that women's labor had as much to do with domestic matters—the bearing and rearing of children—as with laboring outside the home. Women would be the mainstay of the new nation.

Another concern common during the century in Europe and the American colonies revolved around the question of what would make a person "valuable" to the community. A man's value was derived from his working life. But what would help determine the value of a woman? It was in the context of this kind of questioning—of issues related to domesticity, labor, and the moral life of the nation—that women's activities were scrutinized and weighed. If women were to be entrusted with the nation's children, then women themselves needed to be educated, it seemed. But how should that education be conducted, and what should it consist of?

While it is true that these cultural preoccupations were not peculiar to the eighteenth century, they did emerge with greater urgency during this era because of a general development of interest in printing and literacy and a concern with the ways in which especially younger people were gaining access to the marketplace, a marketplace both of material goods and of ideas. There was beginning to be a general rise of economic status for those who formerly would have been members of nonliterate laboring groups. In the Anglo-American colonies and the new United States, the reasons for this change in the culture are complicated. At the global level, an increase in international trade (boosted by traffic in slaves) brought greater general wealth—and opportunities for whites— in Anglo-America. More locally, the shift in the power base in England, with more power being wielded by middle-level people, was extended to the English colonies in North America. Generally speaking, for the whites who were in greater numbers learning to read, there began to be more leisure, and more money to be spent, because immigrants were flocking to the colonies, and immigrants provided a cheap labor force. The greater number of laborers in the colonies meant that the costs of labor, to the wealthier, were less, and more people were earning wages (or were enslaved). Cheaper labor meant that more leisure was becoming available for more people of the middling and upper levels. A greater amount of leisure brought more frequent opportunity for reading. Better that women read than they engage in "criminal indulgencies," it would seem—so long as they did not read romances.

The socially mixed and changing nature of the colonial community meant that the situation of women in all aspects of the cultural matrix—their dress, their manners, their labor (or lack of it), their mental and physical abilities, and their chastity (for some women, their only "marketable" commodity)—became centrally important during the latter part of the eighteenth century. It should come as no surprise that by

the end of the century in post-Revolutionary United States culture the scrutiny of women intensified. Gaining the control over women's minds and their bodies, some thought, would provide the key to a successful and virtuous republican government. In the new United States, they argued, books could be the key to developing cultural values appropriate to the commonwealth. That is, if women were going to read books, those books should, of necessity, promote women's moral uprightness and teach them "right" from "wrong." On one level, then, it could be said that it was upon the most youthful and least empowered of United States citizens, the young women, that the expectations for the future glory of the nation were fixed.

III

"Virtue, Virtue alone . . . is the basis of a Republic," declared Dr. Benjamin Rush in Philadelphia in 1778. Yet the meaning of the term *virtue* itself was much contested in the last quarter of the eighteenth century. For some, the term signified a core set of values aligned with broad political and mercantile goals of sincerity and honesty in politics and business, for these attributes would strengthen the commonwealth. For others, the term signaled specific behaviors of citizens, women in particular, whose personal relations should be unquestionably pure in motive and free of lasciviousness. The term floated among groups of people widely disparate in economic means and personal interests. From about 1776 onward, however, it came to be linked with the term *republicanism*—as in Benjamin Rush's comment above—to indicate specific moral goals embedded in a code of nationhood holding that government should be based solely on the consent of the governed.

Yet the word *republicanism* itself was freighted with different meanings for differing groups of people. Generally speaking, for members of the educated elite (the upper-class people who had received formal training), a Republic would develop from an ideal set of circumstances drawn from the admired ancient republics (which were popular governments) of Greece and Rome. For these people (including, for instance, Benjamin Rush and John and Abigail Adams), a successful American Republic would be small in size and homogeneous in population, and it would harbor citizens willing to give up their own private interests for the good of the whole. Such sacrifice of individual gain would be replaced by a security of equal opportunity for all citizens, regardless of wealth. In the minds of these well-read people, whose opinions were drawn from

INTRODUCTION xv

ancient political history and theory, the American Republic could best
be secured in the virtue of its citizens.

Two other approaches drawn from more contemporary theory and
circumstance competed with that of the elite class. One of those ap-
proaches was held not only by some elite people but also by skilled
laborers and members of the middling groups. This second version of
republicanism reflected ideas of government set forth by economic the-
orists like Adam Smith, whose *Wealth of Nations* (1776) allowed for
the rational pursuit of individual self-interest under the assumption that
when an individual assisted himself, he assisted the commonwealth. To
proponents of this sort of republicanism, if individuals were free (as
they had been during the Revolution) to engage in patriotic business
(such as reaping profit from assisting the war effort), the nation would
be enhanced. In this version of a Republic, individual gain was tied
intricately to the nation's gain; by improving their own economic cir-
cumstances, republican citizens were assisting the nation. Thus, for in-
stance, Alexander Hamilton posited in his three reports to Congress—
but especially in his *Report on Manufactures* (1791)—that protecting
individual commerce protected the Republic; the nation could only ben-
efit from aggressive economic expansion implemented by individuals
who were avid for personal gain. Virtue, in this model, resided less in
an individual's moral outlook than in what contributions he (more often
than she) could make to the national economy.

A third concept of republicanism appealed to groups of less literate
and less educated people, those who supported (and were supported by)
the writings of political philosophers like Thomas Paine. These people
believed that a more egalitarian approach to government would make
all members within a commonwealth wish to participate in government
and, as a result of their inclusion, behave virtuously. For these people,
the best government would allow for widespread political participation
based not on wealth or race but on contributions to the commonwealth.
These citizens questioned the ability of members of the gentry and/or
people from cities to think and speak for them in disinterested ways.
They sought wider voting rights and a greater degree of representation
for citizens inhabiting the countryside.

All three versions of republicanism existed in tension with one an-
other during the era of nation-making. Disparate though they might
seem, they nonetheless reflected certain commonly held assumptions
about the new United States. The key assumption was that the United
States, with all its problems, was a virtuous commonwealth (regardless

of whether one considered it an agricultural or industrial common-
wealth) when compared with Europe but especially with England.
"Good" Americans were frequently contrasted with "bad" Europeans
spoiled by luxury, snobbery, and loose sexual behaviors. For the elite,
virtuousness was coded as thrift and self-sacrifice, and for the others,
virtuousness did not conflict with self-interest and "natural" right of
representation.

Evidence of the prevalence of the discourse of republicanism ap-
pears in Brown's *Power of Sympathy* in several places, most notably
in a somewhat minor scene Harrington mentions in a letter to Worthy
(Letter XVII) about a social gathering he attended. The party was
going along very well, until a highly accomplished young woman,
Miss P——, overheard someone whisper about her, in a derogatory
way, that she was "a mechanick's daughter." Miss P—— decided to
leave, and the party came to an abrupt halt. The comment reveals the
contemporary attitudes about class that Brown's novel would, in this
instance, seem to be questioning. In the socially fluid economy of the
new United States, long-standing members of the elite class saw others
—such as workers of the merchant and artisan groups—achieve finan-
cial security and even affluence. Harrington's comment on this
situation—that there really ought be no distinctions of this sort, because
"Inequality . . . is a foe to our happiness"—repeats the "patriotic"
message that such attitudes are unjust and unworthy of an enlightened
people. He goes on to engage another motif common in northerners'
republican discourse, declaiming that habits of haughtiness found in
those of "an aristocratick temper" in the South will be the ruin of the
nation, since such habits are used to keep slaves in subjection. Such
"distinctions," Harrington argues, "are inimical to domestick qui-
etude." Arguments like these were common fare in the newspapers and
in pulpits; they were an innovation in the fictional materials of the era.

If republican principles were to succeed, the theorists argued, they
needed to be inculcated not only at the level of government but also
within the culture as a whole. If the principles were to succeed, too,
they needed to be accessible to women. Painting, architecture, drama,
literature—all, if they were "good," should represent the message of
nationalism and virtue to the public, especially to women. As indicated
in a letter John Adams wrote to Benjamin Rush in 1807, the burden of
the nation's success seems to have rested upon women, both upon wom-
en's minds and their bodies. "I say then that national Morality never
was and never can be preserved without the utmost purity and chastity

in women," Adams wrote. He continued by asserting that "without national Morality a Republican Government cannot be maintained. Therefore my dear Fellow Citizens of America, you must ask leave of your wives and daughters to preserve your Republick."

It was in this context that the education of women became centrally important, for women were perceived as being the instructors of the nation's children. It was in this context, too, that the books women were reading came under increased jealous scrutiny. Good republican mothers were caught in a contradictory bind: in republican theory, a sensible, educated female citizenry would perform the greatest service to the nation by educating its youth; yet domestic tradition condemned the learned woman as a threat to marital and family stability. Women again and again found themselves the central players in a confusing drama in which they were given conflicting stage cues for their actions. Women could read, so long as the works they read were edifying and so long as they continued to perform their household duties. But women dared not become *too* learned; the learned woman would be accused of idleness and of attempting to escape from her "real" work. This was the warning John Ogden mounted in *The Female Guide; or, Thoughts on the Education of That Sex* (1793). Idle women would ruin the nation. According to Ogden, women who merely idle away their time "make bad wives and gay daughters, they make families poor and a country wretched, by circulating scandal and folly, instead of industrious and useful arts, which make us rich and innocent." Even Mercy Otis Warren, a well-known playwright, poet, and historian, warned her niece, Rebecca Otis, against idleness and the reading of fiction. It was not that Rebecca Otis should not read, Warren insisted, but she needed to understand that domestic work was important and that some writings were a waste of time: "As your rank in life has not, nor perhaps ever will set you above an attention to the economy of domestic life; an acquired habit of continual industry will enable you to discharge the duties of prudence, decency and elegance in family affairs, and yet leave you leisure to improve your taste to cultivate your mind, and enlarge your understanding by reading, provided you throw away no part of your time." Rebecca Otis could read, but only to "enlarge [her] understanding," not for mere entertainment. Such advice was common in the era. It was purveyed at social gatherings, in the poetry and drama of the era, in family letters, and in books. Among the elite, there was a decided emphasis on didactic materials from which, it was thought, all citizens, as true patriots, might learn how best to socialize themselves.

IV

"Didactic essays are not always capable of engaging the attention of young ladies," comments Mrs. Holmes to Myra Harrington in *The Power of Sympathy* (Letter XXIX). She goes on to distinguish between essays and novels, with a usefully revealing comment about an implied relationship between "truth" and propriety. "We fly from the labored precepts of the essayist," she says, "to the sprightly narrative of the novelist. Habituate your mind to remark the difference between truth and fiction. You will then always be enabled to judge of the propriety and justness of a thought and never be misled to form wrong opinions by the meretricious dress of a pleasing tale. You will then be most capable of deducing the most profitable lessons of instruction, and the design of your reading will be fully accomplished." "Proper" and "just" thoughts would come from didactic essays, and wrong opinions, from tales that had too "meretricious" a dress.

Yet Mrs. Holmes is not telling Myra to avoid reading fiction. She is saying instead that if Myra can learn to distinguish between a "true" representation and a "false" or overly imaginative one, Myra will be able to learn her lessons well. This was a pretty radical thing for a woman—even a fictional woman—to say in the 1780s. Mrs. Holmes's comments seem to clarify William Hill Brown's position. That is, she seems to be speaking a position articulated throughout the novel: reading fiction, so long as it is not garbed in "meretricious dress," can provide a reader the opportunity "of deducing the most profitable lessons of instruction"—even though the instruction should come from fiction itself. Given what his contemporary generation was saying about novels—that they were terrible, pernicious, even unpatriotic—it should come as no surprise that William Hill Brown might vocalize through Mrs. Holmes an instructive lesson about fiction reading and its potential usefulness. Novels could, Brown's characters Mrs. Holmes and Mr. Worthy tried to suggest, help women develop appropriate social outcomes in their behaviors and attitudes. If women preferred reading novels to reading educational or behavioral tracts, Brown seems to have surmised, then they should be provided with novels that might edify them as to their duty and place in the world.

Perhaps Brown worried about the way his anonymously published novel, the first written by a citizen in British North America and printed in the United States, would be received by readers and moralists. People at the time were continuing to say terrible things about novels. Indeed,

their negative comments did not seem to let up much, even a decade after Brown's novel was published. "Novels not only pollute the imaginations of young women," wrote the editor of the *Weekly Magazine* for March 10, 1798, "but likewise give them false ideas of life, which too often make them act improperly." According to this newspaper editor (who perhaps wished his newspaper to sell as well as novels were selling), the *quality* of reading matter was the all-important issue, and novels could not provide, under any circumstances, high-quality reading: "It is as incumbent a duty to attend to the books a young lady reads as to the company she keeps; for if it is allowed, that the frequent hearing of loose conversation naturally prepares the mind for the admittance of vicious ideas, it cannot be denied that books, in which love is the only theme, and intrigues the sole business of the actors, are more dangerous even than bad company."

Almost as if in answer to charges like these, Brown's *The Power of Sympathy* and Hannah Webster Foster's *The Coquette* included characters who voiced impeccably high-minded and enlightened discourses on customs, manners, and social interaction between the sexes. Both novels involved women characters whose bodies and sexual relations could be considered in a promiscuous light, yet both presented these characters' actions and expressions within a context where characters of "good" virtue and probity surrounded them. Indeed, the novels provide readers an interesting and conflicted interpretive field in the competing representations given to characters' behaviors and attitudes. The characters whose attitudes and behaviors might be labeled "vicious" (in the older sense of the term, as full of vice) are constantly commented upon and surrounded by those who are clearly "virtuous." In theory, it would seem that the ideal republican readers of such novels—especially those young women training to be good republican mothers—were thus given sets of circumstances out of which they could conceivably test their virtuousness without testing their personal chasteness. The reading of these novels might, if only in theory, provide a safe (because vicarious) opportunity for young readers to put themselves in the places of the varying characters in the novels.

It seems that so long as there was a novelistic balance in the story lines between women whose chastity (their badge of virtue) was compromised and those characters whose didactic and admonitory expressions represented standards of probity and moral impeccability, the novel might retain the interest of a reader enough to evade the criticism given didactic essays—that they were boring and uninteresting. In one

sense, then, we can read the epigraph to *The Power of Sympathy* as a comment on the novelist who attempts to win youth to "sentiment and truth" by way of "flowers":

> Fain would he strew Life's thorny Way with Flowers,
> And open to your View Elysian Bowers;
> Catch the warm Passions of the tender Youth,
> And win the Mind to Sentiment and Truth.

Assuming that a mere didactic essay might not be able to "Catch the warm Passions of the tender Youth," this novelist would "fain" create a better vision of "Life's thorny Way." On the level of stated, conscious intent, then, the author of this novel could justly argue in the Preface that his novel *was* "beneficial," because in his novel "the dangerous consequences of seduction are exposed, and the advantages of female education set forth and recommended."

V

The potentially pernicious effects of novel reading were much discussed during the eighteenth century both in Europe and in the Anglo-American colonies. One common theme—as we might have assumed from reading Jeremy Belknap's letter to Benjamin Rush—was the distinction between the novel and the romance. Romances were taken to be the most pernicious of fictions. Romances, it was said, introduced readers to fantastic, unrealistic experiences that would produce excessive influence over the fancy without the corrective influence of rationality and moderation. By pandering to the passions, moralists argued, romances not only depraved readers' imaginations but led them into vicious behavior. What was more, romances fostered in readers a longing for feudal, not "modern" thinking. Anthony Ashley Cooper, third Earl of Shaftesbury, phrased it succinctly in his *Characteristics of Men, Manners, Opinions, Times* (1711) when he announced that romances were "sprung from the mere dregs of chivalry or knight-errantry." Shaftesbury seems to have had a very negative view of romances; he had little better to say about women. According to Shaftesbury, women's only natural cultural capability was in the reading of romances and romantic novels.

As a number of scholars have shown recently and as Shaftesbury's

comment suggests, from a point early in the eighteenth century, fiction —but especially romance—was granted a "female" gender, under the assumption that romances could only properly appeal to women. With the cultural location of romance with women came its relegation (like women) to the status beneath the more "masculine" status of high poetry and serious drama. When, midcentury, writers wanted to improve the reputation of novels and novel reading, they differentiated between the two genres of the romance and the novel in such a way as to suggest that novels could appeal to the (masculinized) rational intellect in surprising ways while romances degraded the intellect by drawing the mind down to the level of mere (feminized) emotionalism.

The overstated evils of romances might be traceable, on the one hand, to chauvinistic English attitudes, in that fictional romances were traditionally credited to Spanish and French authors of the sixteenth and seventeenth centuries. These romances, usually of scenes and incidents remote from ordinary life, featured a class of society (queens, knights, and Catholic ecclesiastics, for instance) that in England, after the peaceable and popular Revolution of 1688, were becoming increasingly held in check by a greater degree of popular sovereignty. By finding ways to praise novels as opposed to romances, in other words, English writers were thus centering themselves in the cultural life of the English nation and supporting an "English" genre of writing. They were also finding an acceptable way to meet the needs of increasing numbers of readers, many of them women.

Yet English and Anglo-American antipathy to the purported extravagance of romance was so strongly argued that other circumstances beyond those related to geopolitics seem to have been influential. Among the cultural values novels were said to promote were rational behavior and "truthful" representation. It has typically been said of American writers that the appeals to "truth" in representation come from the New England Puritan heritage. This seems, however, to reflect a form of American chauvinism. Truthfulness or lifelikeness was the common quality named in order to differentiate between a "useful" or "beneficial" fiction and an extravagant romance. Part of the differentiation seems to have come from the novel's supposed appeal to the reasoning faculty and the romance's supposed contrary appeal to the fancy, or worse, to the passionate emotions. The arousal of the emotions without a consequent directive or outlet for their use in "improving" one's probity and good sense was seen as a false contrivance for no beneficial effect, indeed for harm. Only beneficial effects should occur, it was

thought, especially if the emotions (or sexual passions) were being aroused—whether one was in New England or old.

Multiple sets of theories on emotion and the passions, along with those on the uses of sentiment (also called sympathy), were in conflict during much of the eighteenth century in Europe and the Anglo-American colonies. Earlier in the century it seems that anything having to do with the passions—from emotional or sensual experiences to attitudes connoting desire, even if only of wealth—was condemned as base, beneath the dignity of humane and virtuous consideration. The seeming dualism that equated things emotional or sensual with baseness and things spiritual or rational with beneficial effects has a long history in Western thought, whether one locates the dualistic attitude in Aristotelian logic or in the teachings of Christianity. In either case, women's mental lives and their bodies became central focal points in the discussion, for women, considered subject to their emotions and "faulty" in bodily functioning, were thought to be more subject to errors of passion.

By the end of the eighteenth century, though, a competing (and refuting) attitude was being promulgated, one that found a basis for emotional or sentimental responses in what was considered a natural and pure outcome of environmental stimuli. Sentimental or sympathetic responses, when appropriately aroused, could assist rather than interfere with sociability and culture. Indeed, the development of sympathy was seen as a powerful tool in creating social concern for others in a society increasingly showing signs of individual avarice and desire for personal gain. This was a newer psychoperceptual theory, based on a combination of concepts available in the writings of Sir Isaac Newton and John Locke. The newer theory took psychology away from the realm of what was vaguely considered dark and irrational into a theory of perception that suggested that emotional responses were sense-based responses to outward phenomena. This theory had a materialist orientation; that is, it derived from sensory experience of the material world. It transformed the negative conception that emotions were irrational if not downright devilish, placing emotional responses squarely into the category of the scientifically determinable, probable, and (because scientifically calculable) therefore acceptable. No longer were the emotions denigrated for their unpredictability and their potential for drawing people into irrationality; instead, they were praised because they were seen as occurring within a framework rationalized and scientifically accountable.

The fact that the emotions were brought into a realm theoretically occupied by both men and women indicates the extent to which emo-

tional responses had formerly been associated with women alone. Along with the belletristic writing (poems, plays, novels, and other imaginative works) of the century, scientific writing attempted to work out, by way of a theoretical study of the circulatory and nervous systems, an explanation for the emotional life that would be more gender-neutral and, in effect, more socially responsible as well. George Cheyne, for instance, in discussing the nervous system, attempted to devise a theory compatible with orthodox Christianity that related his "scientific" findings to rational *and* religious impulses, to industriousness *and* the arts. *"Feeling,"* Cheyne wrote in *The English Malady* (1733), "is nothing but the Impulse, Motion, or Action of Bodies, gently or violently impressing the Extremities or Sides of the Nerves, of the Skin, or other Parts of the Body, which by their Structure and *Mechanism*, convey the Motion to the *sentient* Principle in the Brain, or the *Musician*."

"Feeling," in a variety of meanings, became crucial in the newer phrasing of sentimentalism or sensibility (as this psychoperceptual theory came to be called). It was what preoccupied Henry Mackenzie, a Scottish novelist famous in Britain, in his novel *The Man of Feeling* (1771) and in two essays published in *The Lounger* in 1785 and 1786. In defending his own novel writing and his "man of feeling," a businessman, Mackenzie argued that sensibility provided men an elevated or heightened rationalism which enabled them to link their public actions with their private attitudes and needs. "In the more important relations of society, in the closer intercourse of friend, of husband, and of father, that superior delicacy and refinement of feeling which the cultivation of the mind bestows, heighten affection into sentiment and mingle with such connexions a dignity and tenderness which gives its dearest value to our existence." For Mackenzie, superior novels "were meant to convey no bad impressions but, on the contrary, were intended to aid the cause of virtue, and to hold out patterns of the most exalted benevolence." Superior novels belonged to men as well as to women, and they would promote "a certain refinement of mind as part of a moral code including the duty to parents; ties of friendship and of love; the virtues of justice, of prudence, of economy; the exertions of generosity, of benevolence, of compassion." For Mackenzie, poor novels separated out the emotional qualities (such as love, friendship, compassion) in order to show them in a favorable light when contrasted with what we might call the "tougher," more rational and social principles (such as justice, prudence, economy). Superior novels would combine both sets of qualities.

Phrased more generally, superior novels represented viciousness as vice and commended virtue as symbolic of high morals, refinement, social stability, and—in the new United States—patriotism. This was the line of reasoning in which William Hill Brown participated, as evidenced by the words of Mrs. Holmes's father-in-law in Letter XI. "Most of the novels . . . with which our female libraries are overrun," Mr. Holmes says, "are built on a foundation not always placed on strict morality, and in the pursuit of objects not always probable or praiseworthy. Novels, not regulated on the chaste principles of true friendship, rational love, and connubial duty, appear to me totally unfit to form the minds of women, of friends, or of wives." Superior novels, in other words, appealed to the mind, not to the sensual appetite.

Mr. Holmes does not indicate by name the sorts of novels he is condemning, but a number of novels of the era (particularly from the earliest part of the eighteenth century) directly assaulted readers' sensuality. Take, for instance, Eliza Haywood's *Love in Excess: or, The Fatal Enquiry*, published in Dublin in 1724. Haywood, who began her career as a playwright, often developed scenes in which sensuality was exploited to the nearly pornographic, and sexual consummation between the characters only narrowly thwarted. One of many such scenes from Haywood's early novel-writing career occurs in *Love in Excess*:

> she had only a thin Silk Night-Gown on, which flying open as he caught her in his Arms, he found her panting Heart beat Measures of Consent, her heaving Breast swell to be press'd by his, and every Pulse confess a Wish to yield; her Spirits all dissolv'd sunk in a Lethargy of Love; her snowy Arms unknowing grasp'd his Neck . . . : In fine, there was but a Moment betwixt her and Ruin.

Just in time, the two are interrupted, but not before a reader's interest in sexual consummation (or the potential sexual violation of the woman) is piqued well beyond mere curiosity. These sorts of scenes of rather explicit sexuality are frequent in novels by writers like Haywood and her contemporary, Mary Manley, in the earlier part of the century. By the 1740s, though, such explicit representations were less frequent. Indeed, Haywood herself ended her career by writing much more chastened scenes. Yet novels like this became so common (and so well thumbed) that Laurence Sterne could jokingly poke fun at the sort of titillation they provided—especially in the motif of *coitus interruptus*—when he concluded his own books *Tristram Shandy* (1760–67) and *A*

INTRODUCTION xxv

Sentimental Journey through France and Italy (1768), both of which
are mentioned favorably in Brown's *Power of Sympathy*.

Like William Hill Brown, Hannah Webster Foster seems to have con-
sidered that novels should inculcate virtuous behavior. The fictional li-
cense Foster took with the representation of the amorous relationship
between Eliza Wharton and Peter Sanford was amply repaid in the de-
mise and death of Eliza. Foster's interest in didacticism is quite clear
from her other writings, as well. In *The Boarding School: Or, Lessons
of a Preceptress to Her Pupils* (1798), Foster commented on what she
considered the most appropriate aims in educating young women. What
she says is very close to the aims of the didactic novelist of the era:

> to polish the mental part, to call forth the dormant virtues, to unite and
> arrange the charms of person and mind, to inspire a due sense of decorum
> and propriety, and to instill such principles of propriety, morality, benev-
> olence, prudence and economy as might be useful through life.

Surely Hannah Webster Foster would have insisted that her novel *The
Coquette* was aiding the cause of virtue in an effort to "instill . . .
principles of propriety." If in *The Coquette* Eliza Wharton was sup-
posed to represent woman fallen, Julia Granby represented a virtuous
womanly paragon. Julia's comments close the novel with what would
have been considered the appropriate moralistic comment on the scenes
of misfortune the novel offered. "Execrable is the man," Julia concludes
in Letter LXXI, "however arrayed in magnificence, crowned with
wealth, or decorated with the external graces and accomplishments of
fashionable life, who shall presume to display them at the expense of
virtue and innocence." In Julia Granby's dramatically expressed equa-
tion of wealth and grace with vice, literate U.S. citizens could under-
stand that they needn't be wealthy to be virtuous; indeed, wealth and
outward display were rendered suspect if opposed to "virtue and in-
nocence." For readers in the new nation, the great civic equation was
one that put virtue on a par with moderate wealth, even with poverty.

Whether novels aided the cause of virtue was perhaps the most
strongly contested issue novel writers faced during the century. To some
extent, the debate revolved around the question of a given novel's veri-
similitude, its accuracy in representing "real" life. The debate itself was
not resolvable, however, for perceptions of what formed an accurate
representation could shift from reader to reader and year to year. This
was a most troubling issue for readers, for they considered that the cause

of women's virtue was at stake. A tantalizing glimpse of one colonial woman's reading of a novel occurs in the journal of Esther Edwards Burr, daughter of the Great Awakening theologian and philosopher Jonathan Edwards and wife of the minister and College of Princeton president Aaron Burr. Esther Burr's journal entries for March 11–12, 1755, chastise Samuel Richardson, the author of *Pamela* (1740) and *Clarissa Harlowe* (1747–48), for what Burr considered the degradingly unrealistic way in which he represented the virtuous Pamela. For Burr (whose spelling reflects both the cultural instability of orthography in the eighteenth century and the relative lack of education she received in *belles lettres*), Richardson "has degraded our sex most horridly, to go and represent such virtue as Pamela, falling in love with Mr. B. in the midst of such foul and abominable actions." "[H]ow could Pamela forgive Mr. B. all his Devilish conduct so as to consent to marry him?" Burr asks. "Sertainly this does not well agree with so much virtue and piety. Nay I think it a very great defect in the performance, and then is'n't it seting up Riches and honnour as the great essentials of happyness in a married state?"

In Richardson's novel, the character Pamela acts as a sort of redemptive angel to Mr. B., a profligate man who made various attempts to seduce her and then eventually married her. Pamela's piety won Mr. B. to the side of virtue, except for the occasional slip backward, for which Pamela was forgiving. This was not realistic in Burr's mind, evidently, for someone so virtuous as Pamela would not have been interested in someone so vicious as Mr. B., regardless of his wealth or the extent to which his behavior changed as a result of Pamela's influence. In terms of the novel's verisimilitude, then, Burr found *Pamela* lacking in precisely the area in which the novel would seem to have aimed to instruct: if *Pamela* were meant to represent virtuous women, then the title character should have turned away from such viciousness as that represented by Mr. B. For many readers, novels could be instructive only so long as they adhered to principles of "truthful" representation and virtuous action. This was especially so for women readers in British North America, where novels were more costly to come by than in England and where the codes of conduct (especially in Puritan New England and the middle colonies) were more exactingly carried into daily life than in old England. Burr's questions about the validity of Richardson's representation of virtue in *Pamela* suggest the extent to which readers wanted to exact of fiction both a moral code of conduct and a high degree of verisimilitude. The questions also suggest the prom-

inence throughout the century of what I have called the late-century civic equation (registered in Julia Granby's expression of disgust at Sanford in *The Coquette*) between virtue and poverty. "[R]iches and honor" were *not* the essential ingredients in a "good" marriage; virtue on the part of the woman *was* essential.

VI

Novels by English authors achieved tremendous popularity in the Anglo-American colonies. At midcentury, the most popular writer in the colonies was Samuel Richardson, whose two novels (*Pamela* and *Clarissa Harlowe*) featured virtuous women characters (one working class, one upper class) beset by wealthy men who attempted by various means to seduce them into sexual liaisons. The theme of seduction was extremely popular in England and the colonies, especially when the man was a wealthy one, the woman middling or poor. Richardson was of peculiar interest to Puritans in New England probably because the Protestant impulses available in his work appealed to some extent to the ideological underpinnings of elite-class New England society. Richardson was well known in the southern colonies, too, however, which suggests that the values driving his works found broad-based appeal among the colonial readers of the novels.

Interestingly, Richardson's novels held a number of issues in uneasy tension. The fact that *Pamela* and *Clarissa Harlowe* featured women characters who adhered to virtuous behavior would seem to have indicated a high regard for women and a sense that women's actions were of greater importance to the social fabric than men's. The centering of women, in other words, might be read as admiration for their abilities above men's abilities. That Richardson's women were educated, too, suggests a high regard for the then-contested position about women's receiving literate education. Indeed, Richardson's women provided practical illustrations of how women might combine intellectual and domestic accomplishments. These accomplishments were not for their own sake and for the general benefit of women, however. They were accomplishments suitable to men's—especially husbands'—needs, accomplishments considered most crucial to the middle-class woman of the house. In addition, the novels' very featuring of the women's virtue as the corrective to the men's nefarious actions suggests the extent to which eighteenth-century English and Anglo-American culture would hold women accountable for the morality of the men around them and, by

extension, the morality of the nation. Surely Richardson's fictional representations of the relations between men and women found a ready market because they showed the complications most troubling within the current dialogue about the roles of the sexes. The very popularity of Richardson's novels indicates the extent to which the place of women within the social formation was a crucial question during the Enlightenment—especially in the new United States.

Benjamin Franklin was the first printer to print and offer Richardson's *Pamela* for sale in his shop in 1744. Thereafter, printers would print American editions of novels, but probably not as frequently as they advertised British novel imports. Richardson might have been the best-known novelist, but he was not the sole fiction writer of interest to Anglo-American readers. From the time Richardson's *Pamela* was on the market in England in 1740, novels found a steady readership in the colonies. As advertised in printers' lists and newspapers, novels imported and for sale varied to some extent, and they varied from colony to colony along the eastern seaboard, but several novelists from England predominated among those offered.

Richardson was probably favored more in the northern colonies than in the southern, but Richardson sold well everywhere, along with other writers, especially Henry Fielding, whose *Shamela* (1742), *Joseph Andrews* (1742), and *Tom Jones* (1749) served in part as correctives to the Richardsonian representational formula of women of virtue and social aspiration beset by difficulties caused by questionable men. In the Chesapeake area and the southern colonies after midcentury, Tobias Smollett's five novels seem to have been frequently offered. Smollett's work was probably liked for its realism; his novels are picaresque fictions full of adventure, intrigue, and a wide range of social types. Laurence Sterne's multivolume novel, *Tristram Shandy* (1760–67), and his last book, *A Sentimental Journey* (1768), both found a ready reception throughout the colonies. These fictions featured characters representative of the newer theories about psychology and perception generally called theories of "sensibility," so they appealed to readers schooled in Scottish Common Sense philosophy as well as to those with stricter but nonetheless Christian humanist leanings. Indeed, into the early nineteenth century, Sterne's novels were quoted in correspondence and even in courtrooms. Other popular novelists included Daniel Defoe (*Moll Flanders*, 1722, and *Roxana*, 1724), Oliver Goldsmith (*The Vicar of Wakefield*, 1766), Henry Brooke (*The Fool of Quality*, 1760–62), and Henry Mackenzie (*The Man of Feeling*, 1771). Several women novelists

were sought by colonial readers, too. These included Eliza Haywood (*The History of Miss Betsy Thoughtless*, 1751), Charlotte Ramsay Lennox (*The Female Quixote*, 1752), and Fanny Burney (*Evelina*, 1778). Interestingly, in the latter half of the century, those novels that partook of the newer interest in sensibility frequently purveyed commentaries on and representations of it through their admirable characters while placing comments denigrating of women, novels and romances, and sensibility in the mouths and characters of the rakes, libertines, and other ne'er-do-wells. These better-known writers were marketed alongside scores of fictions, whether novels or romances, short fictions or newspaper and magazine stories, that appealed to a broad range of readers.

It is useful to remember that not all readers in the colonies read fiction. Indeed, when considering the literary context of the early American novel, other genres—especially those including advice or conduct books, serious drama, and poetry—are just as important for consideration as the developing genre of the novel. As William Hill Brown's preface to his novel suggests, some thought all novel reading a mark of the devil in the English wilderness, and they frowned on the fiction (whether romances or novels) regularly marketed by the 1780s that featured sentimental tales of seduction, incest, suicide, and painful death. In the eyes of these readers, authors seeking to educate their audiences toward moral behavior should provide their advice in the edifying vehicles that would have no vices depicted in seducingly attractive ways. In other words, authors seeking merely to improve their readers should publish sermons, educational tracts, and/or conduct books. In the colonies as in England, advice books appealed to these readers.

Several sets of advice books were popular alongside the novels available in the colonies. Men readers of secular advice literature following the tradition of Castiglione's Renaissance-era *The Book of the Courtier* tended to find space in their libraries for Chesterfield's *Letters to His Son*. More often, though, the advice books admired in the colonies were ones that aimed to develop in readers qualities of pietism alongside training in social graces. Sometimes they were directed solely to men, but by midcentury and later, advice books more frequently were directed to women readers. The era's cultural preoccupation with women's education and their social behavior and morality was evident, then, not just in the novels of the day but in the masses of books designed for their instruction in conduct.

The sheer number of conduct books available in the colonies suggests that colonial women—and their fathers and husbands—were particu-

larly concerned with women's issues in their mobile and socially fluid
society. The most popular individual volumes included some writings
from the previous century, including George Savile's, the Marquis of
Halifax's *Lady's New Year's Gift; or, Advice to a Daughter* (1688) and
Jonathan Swift's *Letter to a Very Young Lady, on Her Marriage* (1723),
which tended to descant primarily upon the duties of wives. Other vol-
umes published during the middle of the eighteenth century and later
discussed a greater variety of issues regarding women's behavior and
their necessary education in intellectual and moral areas. The more pop-
ular of these volumes in the colonies were Eliza Haywood's *The Female
Spectator* (1744–46) and *Epistles for the Ladies* (1749–50); William
Kenrick's *Whole Duty of Woman* (1753); James Fordyce's *Character
and Conduct of the Female Sex* (1765) and *Sermons to Young Women*
(1766); Hester Mulso Chapone's *Letters on the Improvement of the
Mind* (1772); and Dr. John Gregory's *A Father's Legacy to His Daugh-
ters* (1774). These titles, just a few of the many available in the colonies,
appeared in their British imprints and in American editions alongside
the very popular reprintings in book form and in newspapers of Steele's
and Addison's *Spectator* and *Guardian* essays. By the 1790s, compila-
tions of these and additional titles were being printed in all the English
colonies—a certain indicator of the happy reception such literature was
receiving from early American readers.

The readings offered after 1790 reflected the culture's preoccupation
with women's behavior. All the texts from the eighteenth century named
above, and most others like them, provided colonial women with vari-
eties of advice on similar things: dress and manners when in single- and
mixed-sex company; the raising and educating of children; the duty
owed to parents; the duty of parents to children; and lists of edifying
readings. In most of these books, women were advised in courtly and
enlightened language that men of good sense relied upon women's
greater delicacy in order to assist their becoming more "civilized." The
failure of such "civilizing" would reside in women's errors in manners
and morals, not in men's errors, in other words.

An interesting indication of the influence of advice books in the col-
onies occurs in Brown's *The Power of Sympathy*. In Brown's novel, the
moralistic glossing the book offers on the conduct and education of
women emerges from the cumulative, triangulated voices of Mrs.
Holmes, Mr. Worthy, and the Reverend Mr. Holmes. Rather early in
the novel, Mrs. Holmes recommends to Myra Harrington that she read
A Lady of Quality's Advice to Her Children. Mrs. Holmes suggests that

although this is an English book, it contains useful advice for women. The volume to which Brown is referring, through Mrs. Holmes, is *Advice from a Lady of Quality to Her Children, in the Last Stage of a Lingering Illness*, sometimes subtitled in English "In a Series of Evening-Conferences on the Most Interesting Subjects." Providing chapters that are called "conferences," the book went through several editions in London and Boston beginning in 1778. The *Advice* seems originally to have appeared in French under the title *Derniers adieux de la maréchal de **** a ses enfants*, attributed to Louis-Antoine de Caraccioli (1719–1803); it was translated into English by Samuel Glasse, who dedicated the translation to Queen Charlotte Sophia. Its two volumes offer "conferences" addressed primarily to two sons, yet "Conference X" was directed to a daughter. The book might be a fiction; indeed, its first section, an "autobiography" of the mother who gives the advice, sounds like much fiction of the day. (See Appendix I.) If the book *is* a fiction, it would be an apt example of the ways in which fiction writers "dressed up" information about conduct to appeal to a broad audience. Its appearance within a novel that itself claims to purvey education about conduct provides a doubly intensive strategy by which the reader's concerns about women's issues would be engaged. By providing a layer of text from a popular advice book in the middle of his own novel giving advice, Brown could lay claim to his book's edifying function while providing the very edification he sought to render fictionally. This is a fascinating instance signaling the extent to which authors in the colonies might go in order to create lifelike models for readers. Although such approaches might to us today seem stiff and overly formal (and formulaic), they were, in Brown's day, the mark of a cultured, literate, and enlightened author.

Like advice books, pietistic writings also served colonial readers—and Brown and Hannah Webster Foster—well. The writings of James Hervey, a devotional writer and onetime associate of Methodist John Wesley, for instance, found great popularity in the colonies. Hervey's two-volume series of essays generally called *Meditations and Contemplations* (1746–47) was reprinted again and again in the colonies, frequently with letters and poems testamentary to Hervey's moral excellence and literary elegance. The *Meditations and Contemplations* include a total of six essays: "Meditations among the Tombs," "Reflections on a Flower-Garden," "A Descant upon Creation," "Contemplations on the Night," "Contemplations on the Starry Heavens," and "A Winter-Piece." Using descriptions of the natural world and bor-

rowing heavily from the best-known poets and prose writers of his day, Hervey created what readers must have considered a memorable set of essays that repeatedly and pointedly return to reflections upon the omniscience and divinity of the Christian god, the immensity of the creation, and the inscrutability of the universe.

Foster clearly found Hervey's pietistic "Reflections on a Flower-Garden" appropriate to her character, the Reverend J. Boyer (a sort of "Hervey" in the novel). After surprising Eliza Wharton and Peter Sanford during a compromising evening meeting in a garden, Boyer tells his friend Mr. Selby that with anger but with resignation he broke off his engagement with Eliza Wharton. The letter Boyer writes (Letter XL) includes a passage on resignation drawn from Hervey. Just as Boyer's voicing of his own resignation before "the wise Disposer of all events" forms an apt counterpart to the passage taken from Hervey, the advice Boyer offers Wharton later on in the novel, when she attempts to reconcile with him, are meditationally invigorated by writings like Hervey's. Such meditations typically take individual moments in the day or perceptions of the natural world and use these to expatiate upon the glories of the spiritual world. As Brown used the *Advice of a Lady of Quality to Her Children*, Foster used the writings of James Hervey to reinforce a double message that the sort of resignation figured in the character of Boyer is useful and that the reading of her novel is edifying.

Early American novels, like their English counterparts, constantly borrowed sources and themes common to the novelistic, advice, and pietistic literature of their day. By creating texts that incorporated other writings, especially if those borrowed writings treated similar themes and issues, novel writers created a literate dialogue that could function as a sort of cumulative, inclusive, and metacritical commentary on the actions taking place in their novels. Thus, for instance, Hannah Webster Foster's use of James Hervey suggests that Foster sought from her readers a response to Boyer similar to the one they might have felt toward Hervey. For readers today, the inclusion of Hervey also indicates Foster's contemporary admiration for him and an expectation that her readers might know the source from which she was borrowing. Likewise, Foster's novelistic incorporation of biblical characters and scenes (the Queen of Sheba and Solomon, or Job, for example), of rationalist and/or pietistic poetry (by Alexander Pope, James Thomson, Matthew Prior), and of dramatic references (Joseph Addison's *Cato*, Thomas Otway's *The Orphan*, Nicholas Rowe's *The Fair Penitent*, Shakespeare's *Romeo and Juliet* and *Twelfth Night*)—all indicate her own

literary repertoire. It should be noted that Foster also uses Sterne, Richardson, Cervantes, and Ovid. Taken together, these references present a significant amount of learning on the part of the author, and they indicate as well her expectations about her readers' interests, tastes, and relative familiarity with these works.

As a careful reading of Foster's and Brown's novels attests, these early American novels (and many like them) entered into an engaging dialogue with the literature then considered "high" literature on the issues considered of prime importance in the early Republic. The dialogue they established with these texts served several functions at once, from reminding readers of other important literature on the relevant topics to providing an incorporative framework or a lens through which the current action of the novel could be interpreted. Perhaps in their demonstrable attempts to associate themselves with "high" literature and, so far as drama was concerned, with tragedy, Brown and Foster hoped to achieve for their novels a level of approval that would clearly differentiate their fictions from the "mere" romances of the era. In a sort of literate cultural dialogue, Foster and Brown associated their novels with key examples of pietistic literature, the best-known novels, the most popular dramatists and poets, and the most important classical and biblical writings. In so doing, they conferred upon their own writings a conception of the high seriousness of fiction as a genre.

VII

Like Richardson's novels, both *The Power of Sympathy* and *The Coquette* take an epistolary form; their stories are told in letters sent between the central characters of the tales. Typically, this form enables the reader to enter the action of the narrative to a much fuller extent —because the reader is, in effect, reading over the shoulders of recipients of letters—than the reading of straightforward narration, with some dialogue, might allow. Yet readers of *The Power of Sympathy* have sometimes commented on what they consider to be a stiffness in the language and a relative lack of scrutiny of characters' interior lives, despite the epistolary form. It is true that many epistolary novels do provide for a greater degree of psychological examination of the central characters. *The Power of Sympathy* seems, by comparison, to avoid doing this.

By considering such obvious differences between the writing of Brown and, say, Richardson, we can begin to see the extent to which

the culture of the Republic was attempting to reach for a far more uniform and self-consciously constructed social formation than was ever realized in England. Richardson might have been able to scrutinize his characters in ways approved by English reading audiences. There is no reason for us to expect William Hill Brown to have written "like" Richardson; he was writing for an American audience that had its own expectations and tastes. If in Brown's view (at least according to the preface of the novel) a novel should edify readers, then the function of the novel should be to replicate, with some difference, those texts typically read for edification—such as the advice books and pietistic tracts discussed above, for instance.

Given the eighteenth-century concern about verisimilitude, too, the novel should provide a sort of true-to-life representation. And given the American novelist's particular elite class cultural situation, the novel should aim to inculcate national interests and national goals. In other words, when Brown announced that his novel was dedicated "To the Young Ladies of United Columbia [i.e., the U.S.]" so that they might understand the "specious Causes . . . and fatal Consequences, of Seduction," and when he indicated his wishes "To inspire the Female Mind With a Principle of Self Complacency," he was signaling an awareness of the particular cultural situation in which this novel would be circulating. It was published, as the dedication says, for the "Young Ladies of United Columbia," not for eighteenth-century readers in London or readers today, who might have different tastes.

As we earlier saw in the letter Mercy Otis Warren wrote to her niece, letters during this era in the new United States—particularly letters between women—were often written with an explicit edifying function, telling recipients what they should read, with whom they should associate and for what ends, and how they should behave. The letters do sometimes sound formal and stiff, almost like formal essays and recitations on particular subjects. According to the cultural dictates of the era, letters on behavior *should* sound this way. Take, as another instance, a letter written by New Jersey poet Annis Stockton to her daughter Julia Stockton Rush, wife of Benjamin Rush. Writing on March 22, 1793, Stockton was providing her daughter some reflections on Mary Wollstonecraft's book, *A Vindication of the Rights of Woman* (1792). She began, "I have been engaged these two days with reading the rights of women, which I never could procure before, tho it has been much longer in the neighbourhood." "I wonder you never Sent me your Critique," she observed, before launching into her own evaluation:

I am much pleased with her strength of reasoning, and her sentiment in general[,] but I think that She like many other great geniuses establish[es] an Hypothesis and lay[s] such a weight upon it as to cause the superstructure to destroy the foundation. . . . I have always Contended that the education of women was not made a matter of that importance, which it ought to be—but we see that error daily Correcting—and in this Country, the Empire of reason, is not monopolized by men[.] [T]here is great pains taken to improve our sex, and store their minds with that knowledge best adapted, to make them useful in the situation that their creator has placed them—and we do not often see those efforts opposed by the other sex, but rather disposed to as[s]ist them by every means in their power, and men of sense generally prefer such women, as Companions thro life[.] The state of society may be different in Europe from what it is in America—but from the observation I have been able to make in my own Country, I do not think any of that Slavish obedience exists, that She talks so much of—I think the women have their equal right of every thing, Latin and Greek excepted. [A]nd I believe women of the most exalted minds, and the most improved understanding, will be most likely to practice that Conciliating mode of Conduct, which She seems to Condemn, as blind Obedience, and Slavish Submission, to the Caprice of an arbitrary tyrant, which character she seems to apply to men as a sex.

In writing to a favorite daughter Annis Stockton might have said a number of fond, personal things about the families, the weather, and other familial topics. Instead, the letter provides a useful instance of the ways in which women sought to instruct other women—especially those in their family, but also their friends—about issues crucial during the era. At a time when people placed a high value on didacticism, such instruction was the expected means by which women met their responsibilities to one another. This particular letter's discourse upon a book written by a much-discussed woman in Europe shows the very formal, self-conscious way in which Stockton was meeting her duty as a mother and providing her daughter with the guidance and support she might need to fulfill *her* own duties as a new mother. The issues—women's education and equality of human rights—were of central concern to women of the elite class, who considered themselves the vehicles through which the new nation's morality should be modeled for others. To readers today, these letters might indeed seem a little stiff and formal. They are, nonetheless, representative of the cultural assumptions of that era.

In other words, Brown's novel reflects some of the letter-writing ten-

dencies of his era, and it also indicates some of the cultural expectations placed upon letter writers in general. It is useful to recall that this was an era of performance. Letters—especially letters on edifying themes— were frequently read aloud before an often mixed company of men and women. The expression of sentiment of the author, as well as the expressions given the text by the person reading the letter or other edifying missive aloud, were all-important features within this cultural setting. The rhetorical dimension of public speaking, in other words, was central to the scene. Tone was thus a feature of the text written and a feature of the person reading the text aloud. A rhetorical subjectivity—that is, a development of self to display as subject of the speech act and of the nation—was being fashioned at the time in such a way as to create an equation between what has been called the public virtue of civic humanism and a speaking style at once decorous, governed by strict rules, and inclusive of elite-class markers. The tone might seem overly stiff and lacking in depth to us today, but this is largely because we no longer participate in eighteenth-century American culture's assumptions about "high" diction, personal expression, and performance and the ways in which these interact to form the individual and, by extension, the nation.

VIII

Of course, another less culturally complicated reason might be offered to explain William Hill Brown's diction and rhetorical impulses: he was, first and foremost, a poet and dramatist, not a novelist. Most of the poems in *The Power of Sympathy* were written by Brown. In a tribute to Brown after he died, poet Robert Treat Paine spoke of his friend's poetic inspiration as if it had come from nature itself:

> Yes!—he was doating Nature's favourite son;
> The fostering muses fondly nurs'd the child;
> His infant prattle into numbers run,
> And genius, from his opening eyelids, smil'd.

By implying that Brown's poetic ability was evident in his youth, as if he were born with a natural gift for writing poetry, Paine locates Brown in the mystical realm of authorship of "high" literature, a realm highly esteemed by his literate contemporaries.

 Poetry in the era still was considered by the elite—as it had been in

the Renaissance—the highest form of art, and it was marked by formal
diction and regularity in meter, as these few lines about Brown attest.
Best known in his own day for his verse fables (poetic fables that usually
substituted animals as characters and treated manners, politics, and so
forth), Brown wrote many occasional verses on a number of political
and social issues that received the acclaim of his readers. Indeed, he was
credited in an obituary with having had a "richness of fancy and co-
piousness of expression, which upon all occasions made him serviceable,
not only in a social but civil capacity." The writer of this obituary
published in the *North-Carolina Journal*, September 11, 1793, con-
cluded the statement with a verse epitaph, a genre common at that time:

> Of manners gentle, of affections mild;
> In wit, a man—simplicity, a child:
> With Attic salt, he season'd many a page,
> Form'd to delight at once and lash the age:
>
> A good companion and a faithful friend,
> Unblam'd thro' life, lamented in his *End*.
> Thus say the good and worthy, with a tear,
> Striking their pensive bosoms—
> BROWN *lies here*.

The fact that Brown was well known as a writer suggests the extent to
which writing circles fostered a social network through which writers
became known to one another and their local acquaintances, even
though they frequently published anonymously. Like many of his con-
temporaries, Brown published his poems anonymously or with a num-
ber of different pen names, including "Pollio," "Columbus," and
"Yankee." In this context, it should come as little surprise that Brown
published a novel formal in tone and diction and anonymous in
authorship.

*The Power of Sympathy: Or, The Triumph of Nature, Founded in
Truth*, was published by printer Isaiah Thomas on January 21, 1789. It
is considered the first American novel; that is, it is the first novel by a
native of British North America published in North America. Other
novels might reasonably contend for the distinction of the first novel by
a native North American. Charlotte Ramsay Lennox's *The Life of Har-
riot Stuart* (London, 1751) and Thomas Atwood Digges's *Adventures
of Alonso* (London, 1775) are novels by people born in North America.

xxxviii INTRODUCTION

Both authors emigrated to Europe early, though, and their fictions were published in England. Such a distinction as "first," then, seems to fall to *The Power of Sympathy*, considering that it was written by William Hill Brown, a New Englander, and published in Boston.

Yet Brown's name was not clearly associated with the novel until late in the nineteenth century. Indeed, for much of the nineteenth century (until a niece of Brown presented uncontestable information to the contrary), it was thought that the author of the novel was Sarah Wentworth Apthorp Morton, a poet who usually wrote under the name "Philenia." The confusion occurred because some readers associated Morton, who was well known for her literary ability in her own day, with the episode concerning Ophelia in Brown's novel. This was an easy mistake: Morton's sister, Fanny Apthorp, was, it seems, represented as Ophelia in Brown's fiction. Indeed, Brown took great liberties with his friends the Apthorps and the Mortons when he published their sordid tale before all New England society. Perhaps this was taking verisimilitude a step too far. Frances Theodora Apthorp bore a child whose father, Perez Morton, was married to her sister, the poet Sarah Morton. Charles Apthorp, father of the two women, tried to force a settlement from Perez Morton, and Fanny Apthorp ended her life (in suicide) as a result. Some literary historians have suggested that the Apthorp-Morton families attempted to have the novel's publication suppressed, but there is little evidence to show this for certain; regardless, the Brown family remained friends with the Apthorps and the Mortons even after the novel reached print.

This incident provides a glimpse into a feature of Brown's novel common in many novels of the century. Like many novelists and even more of the dramatists of his day, Brown presented the story line of his novel—the love relationship between young Harrington and Harriot Fawcet—in the context of several subplots that, by way of repetition and reverberation, formed a set of thematic commentaries on the larger story. There are three main subplots in the novel, two of them only incidentally tied to the main action. The first involves Ophelia who, seduced by her sister's husband, ends her life. The second involves a young man who kills himself because his love, Fidelia, was taken up by ruffians just before they were to marry; Fidelia is left ill and unstable from her abduction and her betrothed's suicide, and she is unable to care for her aging father. The third subplot—the history of Maria Fawcet—has greater bearing on the novel's outcome, although it, too, serves as a story of seduction and abandonment in miniature. In this

INTRODUCTION xxxix

subplot lies the crucial information required for the working out of the story between Harriot Fawcet and young Harrington. In addition to these minor stories told within the framing of the letters, the novel also offers an additional story—spoken without pseudonyms—about the life of Elizabeth Whitman, who died shortly after giving birth to a child whose father was unknown. (The Whitman story occupies Hannah Webster Foster in *The Coquette*.) By providing subplots that acted as varying reflections on the themes of the novel, novelists created dramatic intensity while offering additional examples of the problems their novels were interrogating. In its plotted form, then, Brown's novel is much like other novels and dramatic literature of his day.

One of the themes of *The Power of Sympathy* is likewise similar to what was available in contemporary novels and plays. Many novels in Brown's day and even more plays used various means of touching upon the issue of the potentially incestuous consequences of adultery. In many of these novels and dramas, incest is averted by way of accident, such as the discovery of baby switching or the slips of careless nurses. Unacknowledged marriages or changes of name also prevent the threats of incest. Novelists frequently hovered all around the subject, as Brown does, referring to it again and again in a heightening of (usually) the heroine's distress. Even when an incestuous amour cannot be averted, even if consummation does not take place—as is the case with Brown's pair, like many pairs in novels of the latter part of the century—the situation often forms part of an elderly penitent's sorrowful and remorseful history rather than any knowing and willful action on the part of the young people. Given the cultural preoccupation in England and America with women's bodies, such concerns as incest would be accepted, even expected, in fictional representations. The potential for incest occurred in humorous guise in so well-known a novel as Henry Fielding's *Tom Jones* (1749), and in more serious guise in lesser-known novels, such as John Chater's *The History of Tom Rigby* (1773), Henry Mackenzie's *Man of the World* (1773), and Henry Brooke's *Juliet Grenville* (1774). The theme was just as common, if not more common, in Restoration and eighteenth-century tragedies such as Dryden's version of the Oedipus story and Thomas Otway's *The Orphan*, both cited by Hannah Webster Foster in *The Coquette*.

William Hill Brown was probably introduced early to the literary life by a relative, Catharine Byles, who (after Brown died an early death) saw that some of his works were published. Although no exact birth date for Brown is known, his birth probably occurred in late November

1765, for he was christened at the Hollis Street Church, Boston, on December 1, 1765. He was the first child born to Boston clock-maker Gawen Brown and Elizabeth Hill Adams Brown, Gawen's third wife. His youth was probably spent working sometimes in his father's clock-making shop and more often spending his time with books, at the hands of some local schoolmaster and his relative Catharine Byles (half-sister to Gawen Brown's second wife). It is clear from his poetry, drama, and novels that Brown knew most of the then well-known writers of his day in Boston, and he was well read in classical, English, and American writings. It is clear, too, that like many of his generation, Brown wanted the new United States to have a national literature. In *The Power of Sympathy* alone he cited Noah Webster, Joel Barlow, and Timothy Dwight, three of the most admired scholar-poets of his day.

Brown seems to have begun his publishing career in April 1787, with the publication in the *Massachusetts Centinel* of his poem "Shays to Shattuck," a verse epistle supposedly from Daniel Shays regarding his incarceration after he led an attack of farmers upon the government. Brown continued to write and publish poetry and drama throughout his brief life. Indeed, shortly after *The Power of Sympathy* was published in 1789, he printed (also with Isaiah Thomas) a ballad opera called *The Better Sort: Or, The Girl of Spirit, An Operatical, Comical Farce.* The year 1789, then, was probably the high point in his publishing career, but Brown nonetheless continued to write sporadically. He published literary and political essays in Boston's *Columbian Centinel* from September to December 1790, under the title "The Yankee." In 1792, he moved from New England to the home of his married sister, Elizabeth Brown Hinchborne, in Murfreesborough, North Carolina. Although his sister died (from complications in pregnancy) in January 1793, Brown stayed on in North Carolina to study law with Gen. William Richardson Davie in Halifax, North Carolina. Indeed, his last publication—called "Education" and signed "Columbus" in the *North Carolina Journal*, July 10, 1793—supported a movement of which his legal mentor Davie was fond: the establishment of the University of North Carolina. Brown died on September 2, 1793, from an unknown cause, perhaps associated with the malaria epidemic that hit his locale in the fall of that year. It seems that he never married.

At the time he died, Brown left among his papers a number of writings that later saw print and dramatic performance. His play *West-Point Preserved; Or, The Treason of Arnold* (now lost) seems to have been performed in Boston (in 1797 and then again in 1800) to great acclaim.

In addition, Samuel T. Armstrong and Joshua Belcher (Brown's cousin) brought out several of his works between 1805 and 1807, including a number of prose pieces, several poems, and a group of verse fables. These, along with Brown's "Original Maxims," after the manner of Rochefoucault (whom Brown admired and mentioned in *The Power of Sympathy*), brought Brown an audience sufficient to warrant Armstrong's and Belcher's publication of his second novel, *Ira and Isabella: Or, The Natural Children* (1807). The latter was a second try, with a happier ending, on the theme considered in *The Power of Sympathy*. Ironically, the credit Brown received during his lifetime for his wit and his observations about human foibles came from the numerous verses and essays he wrote rather than from his novelistic fiction. Today, however, Brown—who once dubbed himself "a warm, good fed'ralist at heart"—is best known as being the first American novelist.

IX

If there seems to be little known about the life of William Hill Brown, even less is known about Hannah Webster Foster, whose novels *The Coquette* and *The Boarding School* received a great deal of attention in her own day and later. Indeed, *The Coquette* alone went through thirteen editions—and probably thirty printings—before the end of the nineteenth century. Yet Hannah Webster Foster was probably better known among her acquaintance as a well-read woman and an apt conversationalist—an overall "notable woman" (that is, a modest and goodly housewife and mother). These would have been the qualities for which a woman of her class would have wished to remain known. Interestingly, it is for her novels that readers today remember Hannah Webster Foster.

She was born in Salisbury, Massachusetts, on September 10, 1758, to Hannah Wainwright Webster and Grant Webster, a prosperous Boston merchant. In 1762, Hannah Webster was sent to a boarding school, after the death of her mother. Records indicate that in 1771 she was living in Boston; she began publishing political pieces in the newspapers in Boston in the 1780s. In 1785, Hannah Webster married Rev. John Foster, who was four years younger than she, a graduate of Dartmouth College, and pastor of the First Church in Brighton, Massachusetts. The year after she married, Hannah Webster Foster bore her first child, who seems to have died just after birth. Thereafter, between the years 1789 and 1796, she bore five children. Her life must have been tremendously

busy, not only because upon her fell the responsibility of caring for and educating her young children but because, as a minister's wife, she would have been expected to entertain members of the congregation and traveling ministers as well. As Esther Edwards Burr's journal attests, this was exhausting business, for a minister's wife was expected to model for others the Christian and womanly virtues held in high esteem.

Somehow, Hannah Webster Foster found time to write her first novel, *The Coquette; Or, the History of Eliza Wharton; A Novel; Founded on Fact*, published anonymously as written "By a Lady of Massachusetts." It was printed by Samuel Etheridge at Cornhill, Boston, for bookseller Ebenezer Larkin in the year 1797. The novel seems to have been a tremendous success from the time it first appeared. Larkin republished it in 1802, the same year it received a dramatization by J. Horatio Nichols as *The New England Coquette*. On January 29, 1803, the novel's high number of sales was noted in the *Boston Weekly Magazine*. Throughout the nineteenth century, *The Coquette* remained popular; indeed, just between the years 1824 and 1828 the novel was reprinted eight times.

Hannah Foster's second novel, *The Boarding School; Or, Lessons of a Preceptress to Her Pupils*, published in 1798, never achieved the amount of success *The Coquette* realized. The *Columbian Centinel* on September 6, 1797, offered proposals for printing this novel "By a Lady of Massachusetts." Designed to assist in forming the characters and manners of young women, *The Boarding School* is written in the guise of a series of farewell talks—a method used in the *Advice from a Lady of Quality to Her Children*—between a school's teacher and her young women students who will soon leave the school and enter into society. Like most advice books of the day, this one offered advice about needlework, reading, composition, dance, and "sentimental song." Probably the most interesting feature of this book (with regard to a reading of Foster's novel, *The Coquette*) lies in the preceptress's contention that seducers of women should be punished and their victims treated with a greater degree of tolerance.

In the first decade of the nineteenth century, Foster contributed anonymously to *The Monthly Anthology or Magazine of Polite Literature*, a Federalist journal later known as the *North American Review*. She saw two of her children reach their own literary success in the first quarter of the century: daughter Elizabeth Foster (under her married name Eliza Lanesford Cushing) published two novels (in 1824 and 1826) and coedited a monthly magazine in Montreal, Canada, called

The Literary Garland; and daughter Harriet Foster (under her married name Harriet Vaughan Cheney) published two popular books (in 1824 and 1827). Foster had a long life. In her later years, she went to live in Montreal with her daughter Eliza Cushing; she died in Montreal on April 17, 1840. Although she wrote a great deal during her lifetime, she remains best known to literary historians for having published one of the most popular American novels of the eighteenth century.

Part of the popularity of *The Coquette* certainly arose from its interesting use of epistolarity. Foster's characters express their feelings and attitudes much more explicitly than do Brown's. Their letters fictionally indicate a strong sense of the complexities of motivation and sexual attraction. Yet part of the novel's renown is probably also attributable to the story upon which it is indeed "Founded on Fact." Like William Hill Brown, who used a scandalous story of his friends the Mortons only faintly veiled in his novel, Hannah Webster Foster developed her fiction around the story of a woman known to her and known to the family, friends, and acquaintances with whom Foster circulated. By the time Foster wrote her novel, too, the woman was "known" throughout New England from the tremendous publicity her death received. The woman in question, Elizabeth Whitman, was distantly related to Foster's husband. Whitman's story, also referred to in a long note in Brown's novel, became in the last decade of the eighteenth century a centerpiece for lectures upon the morals of young women. Its appearance as slightly stylized "fiction" in Foster's novel surely contributed to the novel's success.

The story of Elizabeth Whitman's life is ultimately an unhappy one. Elizabeth Whitman (1752–88) came from a long line of families prominent in the clergy and in Hartford, Connecticut, society. She was well read in most fields in which women would have sought accomplishment, and she was admired by those who knew her. She had been engaged to Rev. Joseph Howe (1748–75) at the time he moved to Boston (where he died), and she later broke an engagement with Rev. Joseph Buckminster (1751–1812), a man who was held in high esteem by his friends and his Yale colleagues. Quite talented, imaginative, and vivacious, Eliza Whitman was a popular and witty member of a large circle in the Hartford and New Haven areas.

For a time, Whitman was courted by poet Joel Barlow (1754–1812), whose *The Vision of Columbus* was a significant contribution to the poetry of the early Republic. In the years 1778 and 1779, Barlow was courting Ruth Baldwin (1756–1818) at the same time that he was writ-

ing flirtatious letters to Whitman. Barlow's letters to Whitman have
evidently not survived, but her letters to him from that spring of 1779
suggest that she felt for him some degree of attraction. To his first letter
she responded, "What shall I say to all the tender things it [i.e., his
letter] contains but that my heart beats in delightful unison to every
tender sentiment." Her letters written later that spring comment on Bar-
low's "charming last packet" of letters and on what she characterized
to Barlow as "that benevolent heart of yours." One letter attests to the
fact that the two were saying "so many soft things . . . to each other."
Regardless of whatever "soft things" the two said to each other, Joel
Barlow finally married Ruth Baldwin. They had been secretly engaged
for some time, despite the fact that secret engagements were illegal in
Connecticut at the time. Ruth Baldwin was taking quite a risk. So was
Elizabeth Whitman. A fine poet herself, Whitman encouraged Joel Bar-
low in his poetry writing. It was Whitman's guidance, for instance, that
assisted him in beginning to write *The Vision of Columbus*, which is
patriotically mentioned by William Hill Brown in *The Power of Sym-
pathy* and in his early poem, "Shays to Shattuck." Barlow later went
on to become an international diplomat; it should perhaps be noted that
he was already married and abroad when Whitman died of the fever
she developed while giving birth to her dead baby.

Elizabeth Whitman's death was first announced in the July 29, 1788,
issue of the *Salem Mercury*. "Mrs. Walker" had checked in at the Bell
Tavern in Danvers, Massachusetts, and delivered there a stillborn baby.
The *Mercury* reported:

> The circumstances relative to this woman are such as excite curiosity, and
> interest our feelings. She was brought to the Bell in a chaise . . . by a
> young man. . . . She remained at the inn till her death, in expectation of
> the arrival of her husband, whom she expected to come for her, and
> appeared anxious at his delay. She was averse to being interrogated con-
> cerning herself or connexions; and kept much retired to her chamber,
> employed in needlework, writing, etc. . . . Her conversation, her writings
> and her manners, bespoke the advantage of a respectable family and good
> education. Her person was agreeable; her deportment, amiable and en-
> gaging; and, though in a state of anxiety and suspense, she preserved a
> cheerfulness which seemed to be not the effect of insensibility, but of a
> firm and patient temper.

When it became known that the "Mrs. Walker" of this account was
Elizabeth Whitman, the accomplished and well-known woman who de-

scended from several families of the highest respect in colonial New England, the story was picked up, as we have seen, by many New England papers. It took little more than a month before Whitman's hapless story was transformed and redacted into a harshly phrased "moral lecture to young ladies" like the one that appeared in Boston's *Independent Chronicle* on September 11, 1788. According to the *Massachusetts Centinel*, September 20, 1788, this woman reached the end she did because she was a reader of books: "She was a great reader of novels and romances and having imbibed her ideas of *the characters of men*, from those fallacious sources, became vain and coquetish." In his comment to Benjamin Rush from August of 1788, Jeremy Belknap seems to have had ample support for his interpretation of the events.

Whitman's death notices suggest the complicated relationship between fiction and fact. Whereas the "actual" Elizabeth Whitman seems to have comported herself with an agreeable discretion even when she was dying, the woman called "Elizabeth Whitman" whose story was whispered and then touted around the countryside within two months of her death was considered a vain coquette duped by too much reading. In other words, regardless of how discreet and finally unhappy Whitman might have been, her story entered circulation as a monitory one for young women, even in its localized setting of an obituary published shortly after her death. Ten years later, when Foster was writing her fiction "Founded on Fact," then, she was writing within a cultural matrix that had already accepted Whitman as a coquette.

With her story (and its hapless outcome) already known to readers in this way, it should come as little surprise that Eliza Wharton, the central character of *The Coquette*, would from her second letter on sometimes allude to a description of herself as coquettish. Paradoxically, the very wooden and two-dimensional nature of the appellation "coquette" is undercut by the story line of the novel and the range of psychological experiences that Eliza Wharton negotiates. Notably, she has been engaged to one minister, Mr. Haley, whose death is reported in her first letter. She is being sought by another minister, J. Boyer, who seeks her hand in marriage. Were two ministers attracted to Eliza enough to wish to marry her, then she must indeed have been more than the coquette she is sometimes called in the novel, for ministers would have wanted to marry only the most reputable of women. In an unusual twist of the circumstances, Foster created a situation in which Eliza, attempting quite literally to match her inclination with a sense of fair-

ness (attempting, that is, to be truthful to herself and to Boyer), decides
to reject Boyer's importunity and attentions.

The reputation of the Reverend J. Boyer, not just that of Eliza Whar-
ton, is thus what all the fuss is about when it comes to determining
whether or not Eliza Wharton and J. Boyer are "actually" engaged. The
societal strictures of the day called for certain sets of behaviors of
women: if she were engaged to Boyer, Eliza Wharton would not have
been free to attend parties and other social gatherings in his absence.
From Eliza Wharton's perspective, her spoken honesty about her inde-
cision to marry Boyer frees her from the social obligations an engage-
ment to him would create. To her friends (like Mrs. Richman) who want
to insist that the conversation that has passed between the two people
constitutes an engagement, Eliza's behavior is unaccountably coquettish,
and it is unacceptable that Eliza has implicated her suitor's reputation
in her own seemingly poor social behavior.

The novel enables us to take into account the complicated ways in
which language and spoken intents push up against the normative ex-
pectations of society. To Eliza Wharton, speaking her mind constructs
a space for certain freedoms of action; to her friends, Eliza's spoken
thoughts constitute her social self-destruction. Eliza's mistake perhaps
lies in this notion of spoken intents. In her view, her language truthfully
indicates her feelings; she expects that others who deal with her will
likewise be speaking the truth. Yet by the end of the novel, Eliza's lan-
guage has not freed her. Instead, the woman called a coquette through-
out the novel has become one in the eyes of her world: she has engaged
in a relationship with a married man. Most cruelly at the end, too, the
very man whom she wished most to believe, Peter Sanford, having be-
trayed her, says he would not want to marry a woman whose behavior
had been like Eliza's.

Unlike *The Power of Sympathy*, *The Coquette* benefits from the use
of the epistolary mode in terms of its characterization. William Hill
Brown employed multiple points of view—by way of different charac-
ters commenting on the same actions—yet these points of view none-
theless remain fairly consistent across characters. Foster's novel presents
some innovation on this mode of writing in that a greater level of char-
acter differentiation is made available through the sets of characters who
are commenting on the same events, whether it is Eliza Wharton's "en-
gagement" with Boyer or her meetings with Sanford. Foster uses the
epistolary mode to explore to some extent the motivations of the seducer
Peter Sanford and the seduced Eliza Wharton, along with the whole

range of characters whose discourses on the actions of the errant couple
convey the variety of responses culturally appropriate to elite class so-
ciety in the early Republic.

The multiplicity of the points of view has created the possibility for
a number of responses to *The Coquette*. Some have suggested that the
novel's centering on a woman who, though educated and witty, has
little choice in her life but to marry reveals the constraints of the nor-
mative expectations of women in the early Republic. These readers tend
to credit the novel for providing a subversive message about the ways
in which the lives of women even of the elite are subject to narrow
cultural constraints. Eliza Wharton points out in her letters that married
women are confined and their lives not necessarily happy: they give up
their women friends when they marry, she says, and their lives must
needs center on their husbands and children. Within the story line of
the novel, too, it is made abundantly clear that women suffer the pains
of childbirth only to have to face the occasional loss of their babies,
too. Read in this way, the novel does indeed seem to identify women's
lives with personal and social limitations.

On the other hand, other readers have suggested that the novel's
construction of Eliza Wharton as "coquette" is not subversive but in-
structive. Reading the novel within its cultural milieu, these readers tend
to think that, like the cultural space within which Elizabeth Whitman's
story circulated, the novel clearly comes down on the side of the ide-
ology of Republican motherhood and the woman's sphere, a sphere that
celebrated those women who with appropriate sentiment and rationality
accepted their "place" in the world. That Eliza Wharton's friends have
the last say about Eliza's life suggests to these readers that the novel's
outcome—in the death of Eliza—reveals the novelistically construed
"just" punishment for Eliza's transgressive behavior. Clearly, the epis-
tolarity of *The Coquette* makes a variety of viable readings possible.
Indeed, the novel would seem to strike something of a balance between
the two points such that Eliza Wharton can be read as both a victim of
her circumstances *and* a transgressor against them.

The variety of readings *The Coquette* has instigated over the centu-
ries since its publication shows the novel's richness in its delineation of
the era's complicated and conflicted attitudes about women, especially
in their relations with men, and about what should be women's expec-
tations for personal happiness. Much more than a mere novel of seduc-
tion, *The Coquette* examines some of the most difficult questions
uncovered during the era of Enlightenment: What is freedom? What is

the relationship between the individual and the social formation within which she or he circulates? Where does responsibility lie for one's actions? How can the bearers of a nation's children have an equal opportunity for personal happiness? To what extent does language construct us all?

X

As an increasing number of novels reached an ever more avid readership toward the close of the eighteenth century and the turn into the nineteenth, moralists continued their attacks upon novel reading and novel writing. On the one hand, novels seem to have been constructed by their detractors as antigovernment and antisociety in their enabling of young people's independence of thought and imagination. In 1790, for instance, Enos Hitchcock, a Federalist and a church pastor in Rhode Island, claimed in *Memoirs of the Bloomsgrove Family* that "The free access which many young people have to romances, novels, and plays has poisoned the mind and corrupted the morals of many a promising youth; and prevented others from improving their minds in useful knowledge." According to Hitchcock, the young were degenerating in the nation's midst: "How many thousands have, by a free use of such books, corrupted their principles, inflamed their imagination, and vitiated their taste, without balancing the account by any solid advantage?" Linked in Hitchcock's complaint are corrupt principles and an inflamed imagination, and both are set off against their supposed opposite, "solid advantage." Phrased in its extreme form, Hitchcock seemed to claim that imaginative literature would be the downfall of the United States. In 1803, Samuel Miller took a similar position, although Miller's attack was not against the reading of novels but against the writers of them. Miller, a Presbyterian minister and teacher at Princeton, claimed in *A Brief Retrospect of the Eighteenth Century* that in the contemporary novel, "every opportunity is taken to attack some principle of morality under the title of a 'prejudice;' to ridicule the duties of domestic life, as flowing from 'contracted' and 'slavish' views; to deny the sober pursuits of upright industry as 'dull' and 'spiritless;' and, in a word, to frame an apology for suicide, adultery, prostitution, and the indulgence of every propensity for which a corrupt heart can plead an inclination."

Hitchcock's and Miller's comments make explicit connections between novel reading and immorality. They also indicate a largely un-

spoken anxiety about labor. According to both accounts, "useful knowledge" and "solid advantage," "the duties of domestic life" and "the sober pursuits of upright industry" are all being stalled, in fact contradicted, by novels and novel reading. The questions raised about novels and novel reading seem to have involved the extent to which reading—the act in itself—was taking people away from their work in a new nation that conceived itself as a nation of free laborers. We can assume that increased leisure for many of the middling level brought about increased opportunity for reading, but we should assume as well that many readers, taking time away from their potential working time, *made time* for reading, whether or not they were members of the leisure class, because reading proved for them a viable access to "culture."

Some readers probably would have agreed with Jeremy Belknap, Mercy Otis Warren, Enos Hitchcock, and Samuel Miller that novel reading was pernicious because it took people (especially women) away from their "proper" duties. On the other hand, many women and men must have found clear delight and solace in the act of novel reading, not just to escape the stresses of their lives and enter imaginatively into the fictional lives of others but to learn about the constraints and expectations they faced in their social worlds. Particularly for young women—and particularly for women whose families were on the way "up" the social ladder, such as the "mechanick's daughter" featured in Brown's *Power of Sympathy*—the vicarious experience of Eliza Wharton's and Harriot Fawcet's problems might have alleviated to some extent the social isolation they could feel upon entrance into womanhood and initiation into whole areas of social interchange about which they were unknowing. If moralists worried about the nation's potential downfall in its nascent economic relations, these readers individually worried about their own social welfare. For many of these women readers, learning of the attitudes about class—as indicated, for instance, by some of the comments young Harrington and Peter Sanford make—enabled them to figure out ways of negotiating a cultural marketplace in which their increasing wealth brought them into unfamiliar social surroundings.

The novelistic world also provided them an immersion in social values that they could vicariously enjoy even as they learned, literally, the fatal consequences of seduction. Young middling-level women learned from both *The Coquette* and *The Power of Sympathy* that their class of women was particularly subject to the expectations and wiles of

upper-class men. They learned from *The Coquette* as well the alternate
problem of coverture, wherein once women were married, their bodies
and their properties became the possessions of their husbands. For these
readers, Eliza Wharton's careful weighing of her potential future with
Peter Sanford and the Reverend Boyer surely must have counterbalanced
the criticism raging all around Eliza about her so-called "coquettish"
behavior.

For these readers, too, the dashing Sanford, who represented himself
to Eliza as wealthy, *must* have seemed a very attractive alternative to
the Reverend Boyer, who promised stability and societal security but a
rather staid life indeed. In interesting ways, Mrs. Richman's warning to
Eliza early in the novel (a warning that, by the way, uses the language
of Brown's epigraph to *The Power of Sympathy*) surely called up for
most readers, as it did for the fictional Eliza, a desire to rebel. Saying
that no one would wish to deprive Eliza of pleasures, Mrs. Richman
continues: "But beware, Eliza!—Though strowed with flowers, when
contemplated by your lively imagination, it is, after all, a slippery,
thorny path. The round of fashionable dissipation is dangerous. A phan-
tom is often pursued, which leaves its deluded votary the real form of
wretchedness." The course of the novel proves Mrs. Richman's words
here to have been prophetic, just as Eliza herself at this point in the
novel found "Something seemingly prophetic in her looks and expres-
sions." But in a new nation founded on the notion of "freedom," Eliza's
plea that she be taken seriously by her friends must have produced from
many, especially women, a sympathetic acknowledgment. Eliza's ques-
tion of her friend Lucy Freeman Sumner—at a point when the reader
knows of Sanford's duplicity—is a poignant reminder to all women of
the fragility and uncertainty of their lives: "Why should I refuse the
polite attentions of this gentleman? . . . He lives in all the magnificence
of a prince; and why should I, who can doubtless share that magnifi-
cence if I please, forego the advantages and indulgences it offers, merely
to gratify those friends who pretend to be better judges of my happiness
than I am myself" (Letter XLI).

Who *should* judge another's happiness seems to be a question central
to the novel's world. In the novel's conclusion in Eliza Wharton's de-
mise, readers might finally have had to give countenance to the morally
deployed outcome in the destruction of this woman who sought to
challenge societal boundaries. But in giving over to such a conclusion,
readers must also have perceived the bitter message about the costs—
especially to those who did not have power—of belonging to a "free"

society. "Man is born free, but everywhere he is in chains," Jean-Jacques Rousseau had said in 1762. In interesting ways, the novelistic worlds proffered to readers at the turn of the century in the new United States gave them a chance to test their assumptions about the implications and conditions of freedom in an uncertain world.

SUGGESTIONS FOR FURTHER READING

GENERAL STUDIES

Armstrong, Nancy. *Desire and Domestic Fiction: A Political History of the Novel*. New York and Oxford: Oxford University Press, 1987.

Armstrong, Nancy, and Leonard Tennenhouse, eds. *The Ideology of Conduct: Essays on Literature and the History of Sexuality*. New York and London: Methuen, 1987.

Barker-Benfield, G. J. *The Culture of Sensibility: Sex and Society in Eighteenth-Century Britain*. Chicago and London: University of Chicago Press, 1992.

Benson, Mary Sumner. *Women in Eighteenth Century America*. New York: Columbia University Press, 1935.

Bloch, Ruth H. "The Gendered Meanings of Virtue in Revolutionary America." *Signs* 13 (1987): 37–58.

Brown, Herbert Ross. "The Great American Novel." *American Literature* 7 (1935): 1–14.

———. *The Sentimental Novel in America, 1789–1860*. Durham, N.C.: Duke University Press, 1949.

Chambers-Schiller, Lee Virginia. *Liberty, A Better Husband: Single Women in America, the Generations of 1780–1840*. New Haven and London: Yale University Press, 1984.

Cott, Nancy. *The Bonds of Womanhood: "Woman's Sphere" in New England, 1780–1835*. New Haven and London: Yale University Press, 1977.

Dalke, Anne. "Original Vice: The Political Implications of Incest in the Early American Novel." *Early American Literature* 23 (1988): 188–201.

Davidson, Cathy N. "Flirting with Destiny: Ambivalence and Form in the Early American Sentimental Novel." *Studies in American Fiction* 10 (1982): 17–39.

———. *Revolution and the Word: The Rise of the Novel in America*. New York: Oxford University Press, 1986.

————, ed. *Reading in America: Literature and Social History*. Baltimore and London: Johns Hopkins University Press, 1989.

Elliott, Emory. *Revolutionary Writers: Literature and Authority in the New Republic, 1725–1810*. New York and Oxford: Oxford University Press, 1980.

Fliegelman, Jay. *Declaring Independence: Jefferson, Natural Language, and the Culture of Performance*. Stanford, Calif.: Stanford University Press, 1993.

Gilbert, Sandra M., and Susan Gubar. *The Madwoman in the Attic*. New Haven and London: Yale University Press, 1979.

Hansen, Klaus P. "The Sentimental Novel and Its Feminist Critique." *Early American Literature* 26 (1991): 39–54.

Hoffman, Ronald, and Peter J. Albert, eds. *Women in the Age of the American Revolution*. Charlottesville: University Press of Virginia, 1989.

Kerber, Linda K. *Women of the Republic: Intellect and Ideology in Revolutionary America*. Chapel Hill: University of North Carolina Press, 1980.

Lewis, Jan. "The Republican Wife: Virtue and Seduction in the Early Republic." *William and Mary Quarterly*, 3d ser., 44 (1987): 689–721.

Loshe, Lillie Deming. *The Early American Novel*. New York: Columbia University Press, 1907.

McDowell, Tremaine. "Sensibility in the Eighteenth-Century American Novel." *Studies in Philology* 24 (1927): 383–402.

McKeon, Michael. *The Origins of the English Novel, 1600–1740*. Baltimore: Johns Hopkins University Press, 1987.

Matzke, C. K. B. *"The Woman Writes as If the Devil Was in Her": A Rhetorical Approach to Three Early American Novels*. Ph.D. diss., University of Oregon, 1983.

May, Henry F. *The Enlightenment in America*. New York and Oxford: Oxford University Press, 1976.

Mott, Frank Luther. *A History of American Magazines, 1741–1850*. 4 vols. New York: D. Appleton and Company, 1930.

Mulford, Carla, ed. *Only for the Eye of a Friend: The Poems of Annis Boudinot Stockton*. Charlottesville and London: University Press of Virginia, 1995.

Newton, Sarah Emily. "Wise and Foolish Virgins: 'Usable Fiction' and the Early American Conduct Tradition." *Early American Literature* 25 (1990): 139–67.

Norton, Mary Beth. *Liberty's Daughters: The Revolutionary Experience of American Women, 1750–1800*. Boston and Toronto: Little, Brown, 1980.

Orians, G. Harrison. "Censure of Fiction in American Romances and Magazines, 1789–1810." *PMLA* 52 (1937): 195–214.

Parker, Patricia L. *Early American Fiction, A Reference Guide*. Boston: G. K. Hall, 1984.

Pattee, Fred Lewis. *The First Century of American Literature*. New York: Cooper Square Publishers, 1935.

Petter, Henri. *The Early American Novel*. Columbus: Ohio State University Press, 1971.

Quinn, Arthur Hobson. *American Fiction: An Historical and Critical Survey*. New York: D. Appleton-Century, 1936.

Richards, Jeffrey H. *Theatre Enough: American Culture and the Metaphor of the World Stage, 1607–1789*. Durham, N.C., and London: Duke University Press, 1991.

Robson, David W. *Educating Republicans: The College in the Era of the American Revolution, 1750–1800*. Westport, Conn.: Greenwood Press, 1985.

Salmon, Marylynn. *Women and the Law of Property in Early America*. Chapel Hill: University of North Carolina Press, 1986.

Shields, David S. *Oracles of Empire: Poetry, Politics, and Commerce in British America, 1690–1750*. Chicago and London: University of Chicago Press, 1990.

Silverman, Kenneth. *A Cultural History of the American Revolution: Painting, Music, Literature, and the Theatre in the Colonies and the United States from the Treaty of Paris to the Inauguration of George Washington, 1763–1789*. New York: Thomas Y. Crowell, 1976.

Smith-Rosenberg, Carroll. "Domesticating 'Virtue': Coquettes and Revolutionaries in Young America." In *Literature and the Body: Essays on Populations and Persons*, edited by Elaine Scarry. Baltimore and London: Johns Hopkins University Press, 1988.

———. "The Female World of Love and Ritual: Relations between Women in Nineteenth Century America." In *The American Family in Social-Historical Perspective*, edited by Michael Gordon. New York: St. Martin's Press, 1983.

Spacks, Patricia Meyer. "Ev'ry Woman is at Heart a Rake." *Eighteenth Century Studies* 8 (1974): 27–46.

Spengemann, William E. *The Adventurous Muse: The Poetics of American Fiction*. New Haven and London: Yale University Press, 1977.

Stein, Roger B. "Pulled Out of the Bay: American Fiction in the Eighteenth Century." *Studies in American Fiction* 2 (1974): 13–36.

Thompkins, J. M. S. *The Popular Novel in England, 1770–1800*. London: Constable, 1932.

Verhoeven, W. M. "Representation and Resistance in Early American Epistolary Fiction." In *Making America/Making American Literature: Franklin to Cooper*, edited by A. Robert Lee and W. M. Verhoeven. Amsterdam and Atlanta, Ga.: Rodopi, 1996.

Wasserstrom, William. *Heiress of All the Ages: Sex and Sentiment in the Genteel Tradition*. Minneapolis: University of Minnesota Press, 1959.

STUDIES RELATED TO WILLIAM HILL BROWN AND
THE POWER OF SYMPATHY

Arner, Robert D. "Sentiment and Sensibility: The Role of Emotion and William Hill Brown's *The Power of Sympathy*." *Studies in American Fiction* 1 (1973): 121–32.

Bolton, Charles Knowles. "Some Notes on Gawen Brown's Family." *New York Genealogical and Biographical Record* 64 (1933): 318.

Brayley, Arthur W. "The Real Author of *The Power of Sympathy*." *Bostonian* 1, no. 3 (December 1894): 224–33.

Byers, John R., Jr. "Further Verification of the Authorship of *The Power of Sympathy*." *American Literature* 43 (1971): 421–27.

Davidson, Cathy N. "*The Power of Sympathy* Reconsidered: William Hill Brown as Literary Craftsman." *Early American Literature* 10 (1975): 14–29.

Ellis, Milton. "The Author of the First American Novel." *American Literature* 4 (1933): 359–68.

McDowell, Tremaine. "The First American Novel." *American Review* 2 (1933): 73–81.

———. "Last Words of a Sentimental Heroine." *American Literature* 4 (1932): 174–77.

Pendleton, Emily, and Milton Ellis. *Philenia: The Life and Works of Sarah Wentworth Morton, 1759–1846*. Orono: University of Maine Press, 1931.

Walser, Richard. "Boston's Reception of the First American Novel." *Early American Literature* 17 (1982): 65–74.

———. "The Fatal Effects of Seduction (1789)." *Modern Language Notes* 69 (1954): 574–76.

———. "More About the First American Novel." *American Literature* 24 (1952): 352–57.

———. "North Carolina Sojourn of the First American Novelist." *North Carolina Historical Review* 28 (1951): 138–55.

———, ed. *William Hill Brown: Selected Poems and Verse Fables, 1784–1793*. Newark: University of Delaware Press, 1982.

STUDIES RELATED TO HANNAH WEBSTER FOSTER AND *THE COQUETTE*

Bolton, Charles Knowles. *The Elizabeth Whitman Mystery at the Old Bell Tavern in Danvers: A Study of "Eliza Wharton," the Heroine of a Famous New England Romance*. Peabody, Mass.: Peabody Historical Society, 1912.

Cassuto, Leonard. "The Seduction of American Religious Discourse in Foster's *The Coquette*." In *Reform and Counterreform: Dialectics of the Word in Western Christianity Since Luther*. Berlin and New York: Mouton de Gruyter, 1994.

Crawford, Mary Caroline. *The Romance of Old New England Churches*. Boston: L. C. Page and Company, 1903.

Dall, Caroline W. H. *The Romance of the Association; Or, One Last Glimpse of Charlotte Temple and Eliza Wharton. A Curiosity of Literature and Life*. Cambridge, Mass.: Press of John Wilson and Son, 1875.

Hamilton, Kristie. " 'An Assault on the Will': Republican Virtue and the City in Hannah Webster Foster's *The Coquette*." *Early American Literature* 24 (1989): 135–51.

Harris, Sharon M. "Hannah Webster Foster's *The Coquette*: Critiquing Franklin's America." In *Redefining the Political Novel: American Women Writers, 1797–1901*, edited by Sharon M. Harris. Knoxville: University of Tennessee Press, 1995.

Locke, Jane Ermina. Introduction to *The Coquette, or the History of Eliza Wharton, A Novel: Founded on Fact. / By a Lady of Massachusetts*. Boston: W. P. Fetridge and Company, 1855.

Pettengill, Claire C. "Sisterhood in a Separate Sphere: Female Friendship in Hannah Webster Foster's *The Coquette* and *The Boarding School*." *Early American Literature* 27 (1992): 185–203.

Shuffleton, Frank. "Mrs. Foster's *Coquette* and the Decline of the Brotherly Watch." *Studies in Eighteenth-Century Culture* 16 (1986): 211–24.

Okay here is the page:

Shurter, Robert L. "Mrs. Hannah Webster Foster and the Early American Novel." *American Literature* 4 (1932): 306–8.

Waldstreicher, David. " 'Fallen under My Observation': Vision and Virtue in *The Coquette*." *Early American Literature* 27 (1992): 204–18.

Wenska, Walter P., Jr. "*The Coquette* and the American Dream of Freedom." *Early American Literature* 12 (1978): 243–55.

Woodress, James. *A Yankee's Odyssey: The Life of Joel Barlow*. Philadelphia and New York: J. B. Lippincott, 1958.

A NOTE ON THE TEXTS

This edition reproduces the first edition of *The Power of Sympathy* published by Isaiah Thomas in January 1789. The text retains the original spellings, usages, and punctuation, with two exceptions. First, the text prefers modern usage for quotations; that is, whereas in the eighteenth century printers used open quotation marks at the beginning of each line containing quoted material, this edition follows modern usage of using only a single set of open and close quotation marks for each separate quotation. Second, the text uses the modern *s* rather than the eighteenth-century long *s*.

The text of *The Coquette* is likewise that of the first edition printed by Samuel Etheridge for Ebenezer Larkin in 1797. The editorial treatment of this text is like that used for *The Power of Sympathy*, except that minor misprints (e.g., those caused by broken type) have been corrected.

THE

POWER OF SYMPATHY:

OR, THE TRIUMPH OF NATURE.

FOUNDED IN TRUTH.

FAIN would he strew Life's thorny Way with Flowers,
And open to your View Elysian Bowers;
Catch the warm Passions of the tender Youth
And win the Mind to Sentiment and Truth.

The STORY of *OPHELIA*.

Sam: Hill, sc.

"O Fatal! Fatal Poison!"

[FRONTISPIECE TO THE FIRST EDITION OF 1789]

THE

POWER of SYMPATHY:

OR, THE

TRIUMPH of NATURE.

FOUNDED IN *TRUTH.*

IN *TWO* VOLUMES.

VOL. I.

FAIN would he ftrew Life's thorny Way with Flowers,
And open to your View Elyfian Bowers.;
Catch the warm Paffions of the tender Youth
And win the Mind to Sentiment and Truth.

PRINTED at *BOSTON,*
BY ISAIAH THOMAS AND COMPANY.
Sold at their Bookftore, No. 45, NEWBURY STREET.
And at faid Thomas's Bookftore in WORCESTER.
MDCCLXXXIX.

[TITLE PAGE OF THE FIRST EDITION OF 1789]

TO THE

YOUNG LADIES,

OF

United Columbia,

These VOLUMES,

Intended to reprefent the fpecious CAUSES,

AND TO

Expofe the fatal CONSEQUENCES,

OF

SEDUCTION;

To infpire the FEMALE MIND

With a Principle of SELF COMPLACENCY,

AND TO

Promote the ECONOMY of HUMAN LIFE,

Are Infcribed,

With Efteem and Sincerity,

By their

Friend and Humble Servant,

The Author.

BOSTON, *Jan.* 1789.

[DEDICATION PAGE OF THE FIRST EDITION OF 1789]

PREFACE.

NOVELS have ever met with a ready reception into the Libraries of the Ladies, but this species of writing hath not been received with universal approbation: Futility is not the only charge brought against it. Any attempt, therefore, to make these studies more advantageous, has at least a claim upon the patience and candour of the publick.

IN Novels which *expose* no particular Vice, and which *recommend* no particular Virtue, the fair Reader, though she may find amusement, must finish them without being impressed with any particular idea: So that if they are harmless, they are not beneficial.

OF the Letters before us, it is necessary to remark, that this errour on each side has been avoided—the dangerous Consequences of SEDUCTION are exposed, and the Advantages of FEMALE EDUCATION set forth and recommended.

LETTER I.

HARRINGTON *to* WORTHY.

YOU may now felicitate me—I have had an interview with the charmer I informed you of. Alas! where were the thoughtfulness and circumspection of my friend, *Worthy?* I did not possess them, and am graceless enough to acknowledge it. He would have considered the consequences, before he had resolved upon the project. But you call me, with some degree of truth, a strange medley of contradiction—the moralist and the amoroso—the sentiment and the sensibility—are interwoven in my constitution, so that nature and grace are at continual fisticuffs.——— To the point:———

I PURSUED my determination of discovering the dwelling of my charmer, and have at length obtained access. You may behold my Rosebud, but should you presume to place it in your bosom, expect the force of my wrath to be the infallible consequence.

I DECLARED the sincerity of my passion—the warmth of my affection—to the beautiful *Harriot* ——Believe me, *Jack*, she did not seem inattentive. Her mein is elegant—her disposition inclining to the melancholy, and yet her temper is affable, and her manners easy. And as I poured my tender vows into the heart of my beloved, a crimson drop stole across her cheek, and thus I construe it in my own favour, as the sweet messenger of hope:—

"DO not wholly despair, my new friend; excuse the declaration of a poor artless female—you see I am not perfectly contented in my situation——[Observe, *Jack*, I have not the vanity to think this distress *altogether* upon my account]——Time therefore may disclose wonders, and perhaps more to your advantage than you imagine—do not despair then."

SUCH vulgar, uncongenial souls, as that which animates thy clay cold carcase, would have thought this crimson drop nothing more than an ordinary blush! Be far removed from my heart, such sordid, earth-born ideas: But come thou spirit of celestial language, that canst communicate by one affectionate look—one tender glance—more divine information

9

to the soul of sensibility, than can be contained in myriads of volumes!

HAIL gentle God of Love! While thou rivetest the chains of thy *slaves,* how dost thou make them leap for joy, as with delicious *triumph.* Happy enthusiasm! that while it carries us away into captivity, can make the heart to dance as in the bosom of content. Hail gentle God of Love! Encircled as thou art with darts, torments, and ensigns of cruelty, still do we hail thee. How dost thou smooth over the roughness and asperities of present pain, with what thou seest in reversion! Thou banishest the *Stygian* glooms of disquiet and suspense, by the hope of approaching *Elysium*—Blessed infatuation!

I DESIRE you will not hesitate to pronounce an *amen* to my Hymn to Love, as an unequivocal evidence of your wish for my success.

wacky?

LETTER II.

WORTHY *to* HARRINGTON.

NEW YORK.

watch out/ (adealista

"WISH you success!"——In what? Who is this lady of whom you have been talking at such an inconsistent rate? But before you have leisure to reply to these inquiries, you may have forgotten there is such a person, as she whom you call *Harriot*——I have seen many juvenile heroes, during my pilgrimage of two and twenty years, easily inflamed with new objects—agitated and hurried away by the impetuosity of new desires—and at the same time they were by no means famous for solidity of judgment, or remarkable for the permanency of their resolutions. There is such a tumult—such an ebullition of the brain in these paroxisms of passion, that this new object is very superficially examined. These, added to partiality and prepossession, never fail to blind the eyes of the lover. Instead of weighing matters maturely, and stating the evidence fairly on both sides, in order to form a right judgment, every circumstance not perfectly coincident with your particular bias, comes not under consideration, because it does not flatter your vanity. "Ponder and pause" just here, and tell me seriously whether you are in love, and whether you have sufficiently examined your heart to give a just answer.

DO you mean to insinuate that your declaration of love hath attracted

the affection of the pensive *Harriot?* If this should be the case, I wish you would tell me what you design to do with her.

LETTER III.

HARRINGTON *to* WORTHY.

BOSTON.

I CANNOT but laugh at your dull sermons, and yet I find something in them not altogether displeasing; for this reason I permit you to prate on. "Weigh matters maturely!" Ha! ha! why art thou not arrayed in canonicals! "What do I design to do with her?" Upon my word, my sententious friend, you ask mighty odd questions. I see you aim a stroke at the foundation upon which the pillar of my new system is reared— and will you strive to batter down that pillar? If you entertain any idea of executing such a task, I foresee it will never succeed, and advise you timely to desist. What! dost thou think to topple down my scheme of pleasure? Thou mightest as well topple down the pike of *Teneriffe.*

I SUPPOSE you will be ready to ask, why, if I love *Harriot,* I do not marry her—Your monitorial correspondence has so accustomed me to reproof, that I easily anticipate this piece of impertinence—But *who* shall I marry? That is the question. *Harriot* has no father—no mother —neither is there aunt, cousin, or kindred of any degree who claim any kind of relationship to her. She is companion to Mrs. *Francis,* and, as I understand, totally dependent on that lady. Now, Mr. *Worthy,* I must take the liberty to acquaint you, that I am not so much of a republican as formally to wed any person of this class. How laughable would my conduct appear, were I to trace over the same ground marked out by thy immaculate footsteps—To be heard openly acknowledging for my bosom companion, any daughter of the democratick empire of virtue!

TO suppose a smart, beautiful girl, would continue as a companion to the best lady in Christendom, when she could raise herself to a more eligible situation, is to suppose a solecism—She might as well be im- mured in a nunnery. Now, *Jack,* I will shew you my benevolent scheme; it is to take this beautiful sprig, and transplant it to a more favourable soil, where it shall flourish and blossom under my own auspices. In a

word, I mean to remove this fine girl into an elegant apartment, of which she herself is to be the sole mistress. Is not this a proof of my humanity and goodness of heart? But I know the purport of your answer—So pray thee keep thy comments to thyself, and be sparing of your compliments on this part of my conduct—for I do not love flattery. A month has elapsed since my arrival in town. What will the revolution of another moon bring forth?

YOUR &c.

LETTER IV.

Miss HARRIOT FAWCET to
Miss MYRA HARRINGTON.

BOSTON.

I HAVE somehow bewitched a new lover, my dear *Myra*—a smart, clever fellow too—and the youth expresses such fondness and passion that I begin to feel afraid even to pity him—for love will certainly follow. I own to you I *esteem* him very much, but must I go any farther? He is extremely generous—polite—gay—and I believe if you were to see him, your partiality in his favour would exceed mine.

I NEVER saw my poor swain so seemingly disconcerted and abashed as he was a few days ago—he appeared to have something very particular to communicate, but his tongue faultered—ought not one to help out a modest youth in such cases?

YOUR &c.

LETTER V.

Miss MYRA HARRINGTON *to* *Mrs.* HOLMES.

sister

BOSTON.

Are the rural pleasures of *Belleview,* my dear friend, so engaging as to debar us of the pleasure of your company forever? Do your dear groves, and your books, still employ your meditating mind? Serious sentimentalist as you are, let me ask, whether a Ball, a Concert or Serenade, would not afford you the satisfaction of a contemplative walk in your garden, listening to the love tales of the melodious inhabitants of the air?

RAILLERY apart—when shall I take upon myself the honour to wait upon you here?—I want to advise with you on certain points of female conduct, and about my new dress—I have heard you say, lessons to a volatile mind should be fresh and fresh applied, because it either pretends to despise them, or has a tendency to degeneracy—Now you must know I am actually degenerating for want of some of your *Mentor* like lessons of instruction. I have scarcely any opinion of my own, these fashions, changing about so often, are enough to vitiate the best taste in the world.

I FORGOT to tell you my brother has been at home this month; but, from certain indubitable symptoms, I suspect the young man to be in love.

HEIGH HO! what is become of *Worthy?* The time of my liberty steals away, for you know I was to have three or four months of liberty before I gave myself up to his authority, and relinquished all my right and title to the name of

HARRINGTON.

Letter vi.

Harrington *to* Worthy.

BOSTON.

Abashed—confounded—defeated—I waited upon my beloved with my head well furnished with ready made arguments, to prevail on her to acquiesce in my benevolent scheme—she never appeared so amiable—grace accompanied every word she uttered, and every action she performed. "Think, my love," said I, in a tone something between sighing and tears, and took her hand in a very cordial manner—"Think, my love, on your present, unhappy, menial situation, in the family of Mrs. *Francis.*" I enlarged on the violence of my passion—expatiated most metaphysically on our future happiness; and concluded by largely answering objections. "Shall we not," continued I, "obey the dictates of nature, rather than confine ourselves to the forced, unnatural rules of——and—and shall the halcyon days of youth slip through our fingers unenjoyed?"

DO you think, *Worthy*, I said this to *Harriot?*—Not a syllable of it. It was impossible—my heart had the courage to dictate, but my rebellious tongue refused to utter a word—it faultered—stammered—hesitated.——

THERE is a language of the eyes—and we conversed in that language; and though I said not a word with my tongue, she seemed perfectly to understand my meaning—for she *looked*—(and I comprehended it as well as if she had *said*)——"Is the crime of dependence to be expiated by the sacrifice of virtue? And because I am a poor, unfortunate girl, must the little I have be taken from me?" "No, my love," answered I, passionately, "it shall not."

OF all those undescribable things which influence the mind, and which are most apt to persuade—none is so powerful an orator—so feelingly eloquent as beauty—I bow to the all-conquering force of *Harriot*'s eloquence—and what is the consequence?—I am now determined to continue my addresses on a principle the most just, and the most honourable.

HOW amiable is that beauty which has its foundation in goodness! Reason cannot contemplate its power with indifference—Wisdom cannot refrain from enthusiasm—and the sneering exertions of Wit cannot

render it ridiculous. There is a *dignity* in *conscious virtue* that all my impudence cannot bring me to despise—and if it be beauty that subdues my heart, it is *this* that completes the triumph—It is here my pompous parade, and all my flimsy subterfuges, appear to me in their proper light. In fine, I have *weighed matters maturely,* and the alternative is—*Harriot* must be mine, or I miserable without her.—I have so well weighed the matter that even this idea is a *flash* of joy to my heart—But, my friend, *after the lightning comes the thunder*—my father is mortally averse to my making any matrimonial engagement at so early a period—this is a bar in my way, but I must leap over it.

<div align="right">ADIEU!</div>

<div align="center">LETTER VII.</div>

Mrs. HOLMES *to* Miss HARRINGTON.

<div align="right">BELLEVIEW.</div>

ALTHOUGH my attachment to *Belleview* is not so romantick as your airy pen has described it, I think its quiet and amusements infinitely preferable to the bustle and parade with which you are surrounded.

THE improvements made here by my late husband (who inherited the virtues of his parents, who still protect me, and endeavour to console the anguish of his loss by the most tender affection) have rendered the charms of *Belleview* superiour in my estimation to every gilded scene of the gay world.

IT is almost vanity to pretend to give you a description of the beauty of the prospect—the grandeur of the river that rolls through the meadow in front of the house, or any eulogium on rural elegance, because these scenes are common to most places in the country. Nature is every where liberal in dispensing her beauties and her variety—and I pity those who look round and declare they see neither.

A GREAT proportion of our happiness depends on our own choice—it offers itself to our taste, but it is the heart that gives it a relish—what at one time, for instance, we think to be humour, is at another disgustful or insipid—so, unless we carry our appetite with us to the treat, we shall vainly wish to make ourselves happy. "Was I in a desart," says

Sterne, "I would find wherewith in it to call forth my affections—If I could do no better, I would fasten them on some sweet myrtle, or seek some melancholy cypress to connect myself to—I would court their shade and greet them kindly for their protection—If their leaves withered, I would teach myself to mourn, and when they rejoiced, I would rejoice along with them."

I BELIEVE you could hardly find the way to the summer house, where we have enjoyed many happy hours together, and which you used to call "The TEMPLE of *Apollo.*" It is now more elegantly furnished than it formerly was, and is enriched with a considerable addition to the library and musick.

IN front of the avenue that leads to this place, is a figure of CONTENT, pointing with one hand to the Temple, and with the other to an INVITATION, executed in such an antique style, that you would think it done either by the ancient inhabitants of the country, or by the hand of a Fairy—she is very particular in the characters she invites, but those whom she invites she heartily welcomes.

Rural Inscription.

COME YE who loath the horrid crest,
 Who hate the fiery front of MARS;
Who scorn the mean—the sordid breast—
 Who fly AMBITION's guilty cares:
YE who are blest with peaceful souls,
 Rest HERE: Enjoy the pleasures round;
HERE Fairies quaffe their acorn bowls,
 And lightly print the mazy ground.

Thrice welcome to this humble scene—
 (To YE alone such scenes belong)
PEACE smiles upon the fragrant green,
 And HERE the WOODLAND SISTERS throng,
And fair CONTENTMENT's pleasing train,
 Whilst in the Heav'n the stars advance,
With many a maid and many a swain,
 Lead up the jocund, rural dance.

Thrice welcome to our calm retreat,
 Where INNOCENCY oft hath strove,

> With violet blue, and woodbine sweet,
> To form the votive wreath to LOVE:
> O! pardon then, our cautious pride—
> (CAUTION, a virtue rare, I ween)
> For evils with the great abide,
> Which dwell not in our sylvan scene.

THESE are the scenes to which I have chosen to retreat; contented with the suffrage of the virtuous and the good, and inattentive to the contemptuous sneer of the giddy and the futile, for even *these* have the vanity to look with pity on those who voluntarily remove from whatever agrees with *their* ideas of pleasure. He who has no conception of the beauties of the mind, will contemn a person aukward or illfavoured; and one whose store of enjoyment is drawn from affluence and abundance, will be astonished at the conduct of him who finds cause to rejoice, though surrounded with inconvenience and penury. Hence we judge of the happiness of others by the standard of our own conduct and prejudices.

FROM this misjudging race I retire, without a sigh to mingle in their amusements, nor yet disgusted at whatever is thought of sufficient consequence to engage their pursuits. I fly from the tumult of the town—from scenes of boisterous pleasure and riot, to those of quietness and peace, "where every breeze breathes health, and every sound is the echo of tranquillity."—On this subject I give my sentiments to you with freedom, from a conviction that I bear the world no spleen; at the same time with a degree of deference to the judgment of others, from a conviction that I may be a little prejudiced.

I HOPE to be with you soon—in the mean time continue to write.

ELIZA HOLMES.

LETTER VIII.

WORTHY *to* HARRINGTON.

<div align="right">NEW YORK.</div>

I APPLAUD your change of sentiment: *Harriot* is a good girl, and your conduct is extremely praiseworthy and honourable. It is what her virtues incontestibly merit.——But I advise you certainly to gain your father's approbation before you proceed so far as to be unable to return. A contrary step might terminate in the utter ruin of you both.————Direct to me at *Belleview*—for I intend to stop there in my return to *Boston*.

LETTER IX.

HARRINGTON *to* WORTHY.

<div align="right">BOSTON.</div>

I HAVE had a conversation with my father on the subject of early marriages, but to no purpose—I will not be certain whether he understood my drift, but all his arguments are applicable to my situation. One must be an adept to argue with him; and interested as he thinks himself in the result of the debate, he cannot be prevailed upon to relinquish his settled opinion. I am too much chagrined to write you even the heads of our conversation. I now stand upon my old ground.

<div align="right">ADIEU!</div>

Letter x.

WORTHY *to* MYRA.

<div align="right">BELLEVIEW.</div>

I AM very happy at present enjoying the sweets of *Belleview* with our excellent friend Mrs. *Holmes*. To dwell in this delightful retreat, and to be blest with the conversation of this amiable woman, cannot be called solitude. The charms of Nature are here beheld in the most luxuriant variety—it is here, diversified with a beautiful prospect, the late Mr. *Holmes* planned his garden; it is elegant, but simple. My time glides off my hands most happily—I am sometimes indulging my solitary reflections in contemplating the sublimity of the scenes around me—and sometimes in conversation with *Eliza* and the old people.

THE old gentleman is a man of a most benevolent heart; he continues to preach—is assiduous in the duties of his profession, and is the love and admiration of his flock. He prescribes for the health of the body, as well as that of the soul, and settles all the little disputes of his parish. They are contented with his judgment, and he is at once their parson, their lawyer, and their physician.——I often read in the little building that was finished by his son. He was a man of an excellent taste, and I have paid my tribute to his memory—It is the same place that you used to admire, and perhaps I improve more of my time in it on that very account.

<div align="right">ADIEU!</div>

Letter xi.

Mrs. HOLMES *to* MYRA.

<div align="right">BELLEVIEW.</div>

I SIT down to give you, my dear *Myra,* some account of the visitants of today, and their conversation. We are not always *distinguished* by

such company, but perhaps it is sometimes necessary; and as it is a relaxation from thought, it serves to give us more pleasure in returning to the conversation of people of ideas.

MRS. *Bourn* assumes a higher rank in life than she pretended to seven years ago.—She then walked on foot—she now, by good fortune, rides in a chariot. Placed, however, in a situation with which her education does not altogether comport, she has nothing disagreeable but her over assiduity to please—this is sometimes disgusting, for one cannot feast heartily upon honey: It is an errour which a candid mind easily forgives. She sometimes appears solicitous to display her mental accomplishments, and desirous to improve those of her daughter; but it is merely apparent. Notwithstanding a temporary wish may arise towards the attainment of this point, a habitual vacancy nips it in the bud.

MISS *Bourn* is about the age of fourteen—genteel, with a tolerable share of beauty, but not striking—her dress was elegant, but might have been adjusted to more advantage—not altogether aukward in her manners, nor yet can she be called graceful—she has a peculiar air of *drollery* which takes her by fits, and for this reason, perhaps, does not avail herself of every opportunity of displaying the modesty of her sex—she has seen much company, but instead of polishing her manners, it has only increased her assurance.

THUS much of the characters of our *company*. After some small chat which passed as we took a turn in the garden, we entered the Temple.

"WHAT books would you recommend to put into the hands of my daughter?" said Mrs. *Bourn,* as she walked into the library—"it is a matter of some importance." "It is a matter of *more* importance," answered *Worthy,* "than is generally imagined, for unless a proper selection is made, one would do better never to read at all:—Now, Madam, as much depends on the choice of books, care should be taken not to put those in the way of young persons, which might leave on their minds any disagreeable prejudices, or which has a tendency to corrupt their morals."—"As obvious as your remark is," added Mr. *Holmes,* "it is evidently overlooked in the common course of education. We wisely exclude those persons from our conversation, whose characters are bad, whose manners are depraved, or whose morals are impure; but if they are excluded from an apprehension of contaminating our minds, how much more dangerous is the company of those books,

where the strokes aimed at virtue are redoubled, and the poison of vice, by repeatedly reading the same thing, indelibly distains the young mind?"

"WE all agree," rejoined *Worthy,* "that it is as great a matter of virtue and prudence to be circumspect in the selection of our books, as in the choice of our company.—But, Sir, the best things may be subverted to an ill use. Hence we may possibly trace the cause of the ill tendency of many of the Novels extant."

"MOST of the Novels," interrupted my father, "with which our female libraries are overrun, are built on a foundation not always placed on strict morality, and in the pursuit of objects not always probable or praiseworthy.—Novels, not regulated on the chaste principles of true friendship, rational love, and connubial duty, appear to me totally unfit to form the minds of women, of friends, or of wives."

"BUT, as most young people read," says Mrs. *Bourn*—"what rule can be *hit upon* to make study always terminate to advantage?"

"IMPOSSIBLE," cried Miss, "for I read as much as any body, and though it may afford amusement, while I am employed, I do not remember a single word, when I lay down the book."

"THIS confirms what I say of Novels," cried Mr. *Holmes,* addressing *Worthy* in a jocular manner, "just calculated to kill time—to attract the attention of the reader for an hour, but leave not one idea on the mind."

"I AM far from condemning every production in the gross," replied *Worthy;* "general satire against any particular class, or order of men, may be viewed in the same light as a satire against the species— it is the same with books—If there are corrupt or mortified members, it is hardly fair to destroy the whole body. Now I grant some Novels have a bad tendency, yet there are many which contain excellent sentiments—let these receive their deserved reward—let those be discountenanced; and if it is impossible 'to smite them with an apoplexy, there is a moral certainty of their dying of a consumption.'——But, as Mrs. *Bourn* observes, most young persons read, I will therefore recommend to those who wish to mingle instruction with entertainment, method and regularity in reading. To *dip* into *any book* burthens the mind with unnecessary lumber, and may rather be called a disadvantage, than a benefit—The record of memory is so scrawled and blotted with imperfect ideas, that not one legible character can be traced."

book—river/against (margin annotation)

"WERE I to throw my thoughts on this subject," said my good father-in-law, as he began to enter more warmly into the debate—drawing his chair opposite *Worthy,* and raising his hand with a poetical enthusiasm—"Were I to throw my thoughts on this subject into an Allegory, I would describe the human mind as an extensive plain, and knowledge as the river that should water it. If the course of the river be properly directed, the plain will be fertilized and cultivated to advantage; but if books, which are the sources that feed this river, rush into it from every quarter, it will overflow its banks, and the plain will become inundated: When, therefore, knowledge flows on in its proper channel, this extensive and valuable field, the mind, instead of being covered with stagnant waters, is cultivated to the utmost advantage, and blooms luxuriantly into a general efflorescence—for a river properly restricted by high banks, is necessarily progressive."

THE old gentleman brought down his hand with great solemnity, and we complimented him on his poetical exertion. "I cannot comprehend the meaning of this matter," said the penetrative Miss *Bourn.* "I will explain it to you, my little dear," said he, with great good nature—"If you read with any design to improve your mind in virtue and every amiable accomplishment, you should be careful to read methodically, which will enable you to form an estimate of the various topicks discussed in company, and to bear a part in all those conversations which belong to your sex—you see, therefore, how necessary general knowledge is—what would you think of a woman advanced in life, who has no other store of knowledge, than what she has obtained from experience?"

"I THINK she would have a sorry time of it;" answered Miss.

"TO prevent it in yourself," said Mrs. *Bourn* to her daughter, "be assiduous to lay in a good stock of this knowledge, while your mind is yet free from prejudice and care."

"HOW shall I *go to work,* Madam," enquired the delicate daughter.

MRS. *Bourn* turned towards Mr. *Holmes,* which was hint enough for the good old man to proceed.

"THERE is a medium to be observed," continued he, "in a lady's reading; she is not to receive every thing she finds, even in the best books, as invariable lessons of conduct; in books written in an easy, flowing style, which excel in description and the luxuriance of fancy, the imagination is apt to get heated—she ought, therefore, to discern with an eye of judgment, between the superficial and the penetrating—

the elegant and the tawdry—what may be merely amusing, and what may be useful. General reading will not teach her a true knowledge of the world.

"IN books she finds recorded the faithfulness of friendship—the constancy of *true love,* and even that honesty is the best policy. If virtue is represented carrying its reward with it, she too easily persuades herself that mankind have adopted this plan: Thus she finds, when, perhaps, it is too late, that she has entertained wrong notions of human nature; that her friends are deceitful—her lovers false—and that men consult interest oftener than honesty.

"A YOUNG lady who has imbibed her ideas of the world from desultory reading, and placed confidence in the virtue of others, will bring back disappointment, when she expected gratitude. Unsuspicious of deceit, she is easily deceived—from the purity of her own thoughts, she trusts the faith of mankind, until experience convinces her of her errour—she falls a sacrifice to her credulity, and her only consolation is the simplicity and goodness of her heart.

"THE story of Miss *Whitman** is an emphatical illustration of the

* THIS young lady was of a reputable family in *Connecticut.* In her youth she was admired for beauty and good sense. She was a great reader of novels and romances, and having imbibed her ideas of *the characters of men,* from those fallacious sources, became vain and coquetish, and rejected several offers of marriage, in expectation of receiving one more agreeable to her fanciful idea. Disappointed in her *Fairy* hope, and finding her train of admirers less solicitous for the honour of her hand, in proportion as the roses of youth decayed, she was the more easily persuaded to relinquish that *stability* which is the honour and happiness of the sex. The consequences of her amour becoming visible, she acquainted her lover of her situation, and a *husband* was proposed for her, who was to receive a considerable sum for preserving the reputation of the lady; but, having received security for the payment, he immediately withdrew. She then left her friends, and travelled in the stage as far as *Watertown,* where she hired a young man to conduct her in a chaise to *Salem.* Here she wandered alone and friendless, and at length repaired to the *Bell-Tavern,* in *Danvers,* where she was delivered of a lifeless child, and in about a fortnight after (in July, 1788) died of a puerperal fever, aged about 35 years.

Before her death she amused herself with reading, writing and needlework, and though in a state of anxiety, preserved a cheerfulness, not so much the effect of insensibility, as of patience and fortitude. She was sensible of her approaching fate, as appears from the following letter, which was written in characters.

"MUST I die alone? Shall I never see you more? I know that you will come, but you will come too late: This is, I fear, my last ability. Tears fall so, I know not how to write. Why did you leave me in so much distress? But I will not reproach you: All that was dear I left for you; but do not regret it.—May God forgive in both what was amiss: When I go from hence, I will leave you some way to find me; if I die, will you come and drop a tear over my grave?"

In the following Poem, she, like the dying *Swan,* sings her own Elegy, and it is here added, as a sorrowful instance, how often the best, and most pleasing talents, not accompanied by virtue and prudence, operate the destruction of their possessor.

truth of these observations. An inflated fancy, not restricted by judgment, leads too often to *disappointment* and repentance. Such will be the fate of those who become (to use her own words)

The description of her unfortunate passion, will remind the critical reader of the famous ode of *Sappho*. In genius and in misfortune, these poetical ladies were similar.

"DISAPPOINTMENT.["]

"WITH fond impatience all the tedious day
I sigh'd, and wish'd the lingering hours away;
For when bright *Hesper* led the starry train,
My shepherd swore to meet me on the plain;
With eager haste to that dear spot I flew,
And linger'd long, and then with tears withdrew:
Alone, abandon'd to love's tenderest woes,
Down my pale cheeks the tide of sorrow flows;
Dead to all joys that fortune can bestow,
In vain for me her useless bounties flow;
Take back each envied gift, ye pow'rs divine,
And only let me call FIDELIO mine.
 "Ah, wretch! what anguish yet thy soul must prove,
Ere thou canst hope to lose thy care in love;
And when FIDELIO meets thy tearful eye,
Pale fear and cold despair his presence fly;
With pensive steps, I sought thy walks again,
And kiss'd thy token on the verdant plain;
With fondest hope, thro' many a blissful bow'r,
We gave the soul to fancy's pleasing pow'r;
Lost in the magick of that sweet employ,
To build gay scenes, and fashion future joy,
We saw mild peace o'er fair *Canäan* rise,
And show'r her blessings from benignant skies;
On airy hills our happy mansion rose,
Built but for joy, no room for future woes;
Sweet as the sleep of innocence, the day,
(By transports measur'd) lightly danc'd away;
To love, to bliss, the union'd soul was given,
And each! too happy, ask'd no brighter heaven.
 "And must the hours in ceaseless anguish roll?
Will no soft sunshine cheer my clouded soul?
Can this dear earth no transient joy supply?
Is it my doom to hope, despair and die?
Oh! come, once more, with soft endearments come,
Burst the cold prison of the sullen tomb;
Through favour'd walks, thy chosen maid attend,
Where well known shades their pleasing branches bend.
Shed the soft poison from thy speaking eye,
And look those raptures lifeless words deny;
Still be, though late, reheard what ne'er could tire,
But, told each eve, fresh pleasures would inspire;
Still hope those scenes which love and fancy drew;
But, drawn a thousand times, were ever new.
 "Can fancy paint, can words express;
 Can aught on earth my woes redress;
 E'en thy soft smiles can ceaseless prove

'Lost in the magick of that sweet employ,
'To build *gay scenes* and fashion *future joy*.'

"WITH a good heart she possessed a poetical imagination, and an un-
bounded thirst for novelty; but these airy talents, not counterpoised with
judgment, or perhaps serious reflection, instead of adding to her hap-
piness, were the cause of her ruin."

"I CONCLUDE from your reasoning," said I, "and it is, besides, my
own opinion, that many fine girls have been ruined by reading Novels."

"AND I believe," added Mrs. *Bourn*, "we may trace from hence the
causes of spleen in many persons advanced in life."

"YOU mean old maids, Madam," cries the sagacious Miss, "like my
aunt *Deborah*—she calls all the men deceitful, and most women, with
her, are no better than they should be."

"WELL said!" exclaimed *Worthy*, "the recollection of chagrin and
former disappointment, sours one's temper and mortifies the heart—
disappointment will be more or less severe in proportion as we elevate
our expectations; for the most *sanguine tempers* are the soonest dis-
couraged; as the highest building is in the most danger of falling."

"IT appears from what I have said," resumed Mr. *Holmes*, "that
those books which teach us a knowledge of the world are useful to form
the minds of females, and ought therefore to be studied."

I MENTIONED *Rochefoucault's* maxims.—

"DO they not degrade human nature?" enquired my father.

"THIS little book," answered *Worthy*, "contains much truth——and
those short sketches traced by the hand of judgment, present to us the
leading features of mankind." "But," replied my father, "that *interest
should assume all shapes*, is a doctrine, which, in my mind, represents
a caricature rather than a living picture." "It is the duty of a painter to
produce a likeness," said *Worthy*.—"And a skilful one," cried my fa-

Thy truth, thy tenderness and love.
Once thou couldst every bliss inspire,
Transporting JOY, and gay DESIRE:
Now cold DESPAIR her banner rears,
And PLEASURE flies when she appears;
Fond HOPE within my bosom dies,
And AGONY her place supplies:
O, thou! for whose dear sake I bear,
A doom so dreadful, so severe,
May happy fates thy footsteps guide,
And o'er thy *peaceful* home preside;
Nor let ELIZA's early tomb
Infect thee, with its baleful gloom." [Brown's long note.]

ther, continuing the metaphor, "will bring the amiable qualities of the heart to light; and throw those which disgrace humanity into the shade." "I doubt," rejoined *Worthy*, "whether this flattery will answer the purpose you aim to accomplish—You entertain a high opinion of *the dignity of human nature,* and are displeased at the author who advances any thing derogatory to that dignity. *Swift,* in speaking of these maxims, in one of his best poems, affirms,

> 'They argue no corrupted mind
> 'In him——the fault is in mankind.' "

"AS I began this subject," added I, "it shall be ended by one observation—As these maxims give us an idea of the manners and characters of men, among whom a young person is soon to appear; and as it is necessary to her security and happiness that she be made acquainted with them—they may be read to advantage."

"THERE is another medium," said Mr. *Holmes,* assenting to my observation, "to be noticed in the study of a lady—she takes up a book, either for instruction or entertainment; the medium lies in knowing when to put it down. Constant application becomes labour—it sours the temper—gives an air of thoughtfulness, and frequently of absence. By immoderate reading we hoard up opinions and become insensibly attached to them; this miserly conduct sinks us to affectation, and disgustful pedantry; *conversation* only can remedy this dangerous evil, strengthen the judgment, and make reading really useful. They mutually depend upon, and assist each other.

"A KNOWLEDGE of HISTORY which exhibits to us in one view the rise, progress and decay of nations—which points out the advancement of the mind in society, and the improvements in the arts which adorn human nature, comes with propriety under the notice of a lady. To observe the origin of civilization—the gradual progress of society, and the refinements of manners, policy, morality and religion—to observe the progression of mankind from simplicity to luxury, from luxury to effeminacy, and the gradual steps of the decline of empire, and the dissolution of states and kingdoms, must blend that happy union of instruction and entertainment, which never fails to win our attention to the pursuit of all subjects.

"POETRY claims her due from the ladies. POETRY enlarges and strengthens the mind, refines the taste and improves the judgment. It has been asserted that women have no business with *satire*—now satire

is but a branch of poetry. I acknowledge, however, much false wit is sent into the world, under this general title; but no critick with whom I am acquainted ever called satire false wit—for as long as vice and folly continue to predominate in the human heart, the satirist will be considered as a useful member of society. I believe *Addison* calls him an auxiliary to the pulpit. Suffer me to enlarge on this *new idea*. Satire is the correction of the vices and follies of the human heart; a woman may, therefore, read it to advantage. What I mean by enforcing this point, is, to impress the minds of females with a principle of self correction; for among all kinds of knowledge which arise from reading, the duty of self knowledge is a very eminent one; and is at the same time, the most useful and important.

"OUR ordinary intercourse with the world, will present to us in a very clear point of view, the fallacious ideas we sometimes entertain of our own self knowledge.—We are blinded by pride and self love, and will not observe our own imperfections, which we blame with the greatest acrimony in other people, and seem to detest with the greatest abhorrence; so that it often happens, while we are branding our neighbour for some foible, or vanity, we ourselves are equally guilty.

"RIDICULOUS as this conduct must appear in the eyes of all judicious people, it is too frequently practised to escape observation.

"I WILL drop this piece of morality, with a charge to the fair reader, that whenever she discovers a satire, ridiculing or recriminating the follies or crimes of mankind, that she look into her own heart, and compare the strictures on the conduct of others with her own feelings."

LETTER XII.

Mrs. HOLMES *to* MYRA.

In Continuation.

MY good father-in-law being so strenuous in proving the eligibility of reading satire, had spun out, what he called his *new idea,* to such a metaphysical nicety, that he unhappily diminished the number of his hearers; for Mrs. *Bourn,* to whom he directed his discourse, had taken down a book and was reading to herself, and Miss was diverting herself with the cuts in *Gay's* Fables.

A CONSIDERABLE silence ensued, which *Worthy* first broke, by asking Mrs. *Bourn* what book she had in her hand. Every one's attention was alarmed at this important enquiry. Mrs. *Bourn,* with little difficulty, found the title page, and began to read, "*A Sentimental Journey through France and Italy, by Mr.* Yorick."

"I DO not like the *title,*" said Miss *Bourn.*

"WHY, my dear!" apostrophized the mother, "you are mistaken—it is a very famous book."

"WHY, my dear!" retorted the daughter, "It is sentimental—I abominate every thing that is sentimental—it is so unfashionable too."

"I NEVER knew before," said Mr. *Holmes,* "that wit was subject to the caprice of fashion."

"WHY 'Squire *Billy,*" returned Miss, "who is just arrived from the centre of politeness and fashion, says the bettermost genii never read any sentimental books—so you see sentiment is out of date."

THE company rose to go out.——

"SENTIMENT out of date!" cries *Worthy,* repeating the words of Miss *Bourn,* and taking the book from her mother, as she walked towards the door—"Sentiment out of date—alas! poor *Yorick*—may thy pages never be soiled by the fingers of prejudice." He continued his address to the book, as they went out, in the same *Shandean* tone—"These antisentimentalists would banish thee from the society of all books! Unto what a pitiful size are the race of *readers* dwindled! Surely these *antis* have no more to do with thee, than the gods of the *Canaanites*—In character and understanding they are alike—eyes have *they,* but they see not—ears have *they,* but they hear not, neither is there any knowledge to be found in them." "It is hardly worth while to beat it into them," said my father-in-law, "so let us follow the company."

WE did so—they walked towards the house, and *Worthy* and myself brought up the rear.

I COULD not but remark, as we went on, that Miss *Bourn* had spoken the sentiments of many of her sex;—"and whence," said I to *Worthy,* "arises this detestation of books in *some* of us females, and why are *they* enemies to any thing that may be called sentiment and conversation: I grant it often happens there is such rapidity of *speeches* that one may be at a loss to distinguish the speakers; but why is there such a calm silence, should an unfortunate sentiment inadvertantly——"

"I WILL tell you," interrupted he, "You all read, and it is from the books which engage your attention, that you generally imbibe your

ideas of the principal subjects discussed in company—now, the books which employ your hours of study, happen to be Novels; and the *subjects* contained in these Novels are commonly confined to *dress, balls, visiting,* and the like *edifying* topicks; does it not follow, that these must be the subjects of your conversation? I will not dispute whether the Novel makes the woman, or the woman makes the Novel; or whether they are written to engage your attention, or flatter your vanity. I believe the result will shew they depend, in some measure, upon each other; and an uninformed woman, by reading them, only augments the number of her futile ideas. *The female mind,* notwithstanding, *is competent to any task,* and the accomplishments of an elegant woman depend on a proper cultivation of her intelligent powers; a barrenness—a sterility of conversation—immediately discovers where this cultivation is wanting."

"GIVE me leave," answered I, "to espouse the cause of this class of females. Tell me candidly, Mr. *Worthy,* whether that insipid flattery, perhaps sacrificed at the expense of truth, does not misguide many of us into erroneous paths? You declare we are handsome—and your conduct demonstrates you to be more solicitous for the possession of *beautiful,* than of *mental* charms. Hence is the deluded female persuaded of the force of her fascinating powers, and vainly imagines one glance of her eye sufficient to reduce a million of hearts whenever she chooses: Her aims, therefore, are confined to the decoration of her person, and her views centre solely in finishing herself in those attractive, allpowerful graces, with which you declare yourselves to be enchanted. How then are they to be censured for neglecting to improve, and to adorn the mind, when your adulation diverts their attention to an external object?"

"I JOIN with you," replied *Worthy,* "in calling it insipid flattery— and the vain coxcomb, the powdered beau, the insignificant *petit maitre,* are those who make use of it. Will women of real merit, and sound sense, believe, what is said by *them* to be *their* real sentiments?—No— There must be a congeniality in the minds of those who give and receive flattery—Has not the vain coquette as much inclination to be thought a goddess, as the empty admirer to declare her so?

"FLATTERY is become a kind of epidemical distemper; many run into it, perhaps, without designing it, or only through civility. There are some women who expect it—who dress to be admired—and who deem it a mark of impoliteness and rudeness in men, who do not pay them the tribute of compliment and adulation. A man of sense *may* comply with

their expectation—he will still think them agreeable *playthings,* to divert him at an hour of relaxation; but I cannot suppose he will entertain any serious thoughts of *a more permanent connexion.*

"MAY we not conclude these things to be productive of many evils that happen in society—do they not frighten all sentiment from conversation—introduce affectation—pride—envy—clandestine marriages —elopements—division of families—and ultimately terminate in the *ruin* of very many innocent, but inconsiderate females?"

BY this time we had got into the house, and our company soon after departed, leaving us at full leisure to contemplate on the many wrong ideas entertained, and fallacious steps pursued by the generality of mankind, in the sentimental part of female education.

<div align="right">ADIEU!</div>

<div align="center">

LETTER XIII.

WORTHY *to* MYRA.

</div>

<div align="right">BELLEVIEW.</div>

A PEACEFUL, recluse life, is suited to my temper—there is something in the soft breath of Nature—in the delicacy of smiling meadows and cultivated fields—in the sublimity of an aged wood—of broken rocks —of rivers pouring along their lucid waves, to which the heart always gives a ready reception—there is something within us congenial to these scenes; they impress the mind with ideas similar to what we feel in beholding one whom we tenderly esteem.

I WAS making this observation to Mrs. *Holmes,* and she told me I was in love—"These are the very scenes," said she, "which your beloved *Myra* used to praise and admire, and for which you, by a secret sympathy, entertain the same predilection. The piece of embroidery which she worked at an early age, and which ornaments the Temple, I have seen you gaze upon several times—you seem to trace perfection in every part of it, because it was executed by the hand of *Myra.*"

I ACKNOWLEDGE I have often *gazed* upon it (as Mrs. *Holmes* terms it) but did not recollect it to be a piece of your work. I stole an opportunity to revisit it by myself, and I instantly remembered it—I remem-

bered when you finished it, and all the happy, inoffensive scenes of our childhood, returned fresh upon my heart.

IT is the work of *Myra,* said I to myself—Did not her fingers trace these beautiful, expanding flowers?—Did not she give to this carnation its animated glow, and to this opening rose its languishing grace? Removed as I am—continued I in a certain interiour language that every son of nature possesses—Removed as I am, from the amiable object of my tenderest affection, I have nothing to do but to admire this offspring of industry and art—It shall yield more fragrance to my soul than all the *boquets* in the universe.

I DID not care to pursue the thought—it touched a delicate string—at first, however, I flattered myself I should gain some consolation—but I lost in every reflection.

I CONSIDERED the work as coming from your hand, and was delighted the more with it. A piece of steel that has been rubbed with a loadstone, retains the power of attracting small bodies of iron: So the beauties of this embroidery, springing from your hands, continue to draw my attention, and fill the mind with ideas of the artist.

FAREWEL!

LETTER XIV.

HARRINGTON *to* WORTHY.

BOSTON.

How incompetent is the force of words to express some peculiar sensations! Expression is feeble when emotions are exquisite.

I WISH you could be here to see with what ease and dignity every thing comes from the hand of *Harriot*—I cannot give a description equivalent to the great idea I wish to convey—You will tell me I am in love—What is love? I have been trying to investigate its nature—to strip it of its mere term, and consider it as it may be supported by principle —I might as well search for the philosopher's stone.

EVERY one is ready to praise his mistress—she is always described in her "native simplicity," as "an angel" with a "placid mein" "mild, animated" "altogether captivating," and at length the task of description

is given up as altogether "undescribable." Are not all these in themselves bare insignificant words? The world has so long been accustomed to hear the sound of them, that the idea is lost. But to the question—What is love? Unless it is answered now, perhaps it never will be. Is it not an infinitude of graces that accompany every thing said by *Harriot?* That adorn all she does? They must not be taken severally—they cannot be contemplated in the abstract.—If you proceed to a chymical analysis, their tenuous essence will evaporate—they are in themselves nothing, but the aggregate is love.

WHEN an army composed of a great number of men, moves slowly on at a distance, nobody thinks of considering a single soldier.

<div align="right">ADIEU!</div>

LETTER XV.

HARRINGTON *to* WORTHY.

<div align="right">BOSTON.</div>

A M I to believe my eyes—my ears—my heart!—and yet I cannot be deceived.—We are generally most stupid and incredulous in what most materially concerns us. We find the greatest difficulty, in persuading ourselves of the attainment of what we most ardently desire—She loves!—I say to myself, *Harriot* loves me, and I reverence myself.

I THINK I may now take upon me some share of happiness—I may say I have not lived in vain—for all my heart holds dear is mine—joy and love encompass me—peace and tranquillity are before me; the prospect is fair and promising as the gilded dawn of a summer's day—There is none to supplant me in her affection—I dread no rival, for our tempers are similar, and our hearts beat in unison together.

Confident

<div align="right">ADIEU!</div>

LETTER XVI.

HARRINGTON *to* WORTHY.

BOSTON.

LOVE softens and refines the manners—polishes the asperities of auk-wardness, and fits us for the society of gentle beings. It goes further, it mends the heart, and makes us better men—it gives the faint-hearted an extraordinary strength of soul, and renders them equal and frequently superiour to danger and distress.

MY passions you know are quick, my prejudices sometimes obstinate—She tells me these things are wrong—This gentle reprimand is so tempered with love that I think she commends me. I however promise a reform, and am much pleased with my improvement. *Harriot* moulds my heart into what form she chooses.

A LITTLE party is proposed tomorrow evening, and I shall attend *Harriot*. These elegant relaxations prevent the degeneracy of human nature, exhilerate the spirits, and wind up this machine of ours for another revolution of business.

LETTER XVII.

HARRINGTON *to* WORTHY.

BOSTON.

OUR little party was overthrown by a strange piece of folly. A Miss P—— was introduced, a young lady of beauty and elegant accomplishments. The whole company were beginning to be cheerful—business and care were disgusted at the sight of so many happy countenances, and had gone out from among us. Jollity and good humour bade us prepare for the dance—unhappily at this juncture a lady and gentleman were engaged in a conversation concerning Miss P——, and one of them repeated the words "a mechanick's daughter"—it is supposed the word "mechanick" was repeated scornfully—She heard it—thought herself

insulted—and indignantly retired—Disorder and confusion immediately took place, and the amusement was put an end to for the evening.

I WISH people would consider how little time they have to frolick here—that they would improve it to more advantage, and not dispute for any precedence or superiority but in good nature and sociability—"a mechanick"—and pray whence this distinction!

INEQUALITY among mankind is a foe to our happiness—it even affects our little parties of pleasure—Such is the fate of the human race, one order of men lords it over another; but upon what grounds its right is founded I could never yet be satisfied.

FOR this reason, I like a democratical better than any other kind of government; and were I a *Lycurgus* no distinction of rank should be found in my commonwealth.

IN my tour through the United States, I had an opportunity of examining and comparing the different manners and dispositions of the inhabitants of the several republicks. Those of the southern states, accustomed to a habit of domineering over their slaves, are haughtier, more tenacious of honour, and indeed possess more of an aristocratick temper than their sisters of the confederacy. As we travel to the northward, the nature of the constitution seems to operate on the minds of the people—slavery is abolished—all men are declared free and equal, and their tempers are open, generous and communicative. It is the same in all those countries where the people enjoy independence and equal liberty. Why then should those distinctions arise which are inimical to domestick quietude? Or why should the noisy voice of those who seek distinction, so loudly reecho in the ears of peace and jollity, as to deafen the sound of the musick? For while we are disputing who shall lead off the dance, behold! the instrument gets out of tune—a string snaps—and where is our chance for dancing?

ADIEU!

Letter xviii.

Harrington *to* Worthy.

BOSTON.

My beloved has left me for a while—she has attended Mrs. *Francis* in a journey to *Rhodeisland*—and here am I—anxious—solitary—alone!—

NO thoughts, but thoughts of *Harriot,* are permitted to agitate me. She is in my view all the day long, and when I retire to rest my imagination is still possessed with ideas of *Harriot.*

ADIEU!

Letter xix.

Harrington *to* Harriot.

BOSTON.

If a wish, arising from the most tender affection, could transport me to the object of my love, I persuade myself that you would not be troubled with reading this letter.

YOU must expect nothing like wit or humour, or even common sense, from me; wit and humour are flown with you, and your return only can restore them. I am sometimes willing to persuade myself that this is the case—I think I hear the well known voice, I look around me with the ecstacy of *Orpheus,* but that look breaks the charm, I find myself alone, and my *Eurydice* vanished to the shades.

I HOPE you will not permit yourself to grow envious of the beauties of *Rhodeisland.* Of the force of their charms I am experimentally acquainted. Whereever fortune has thrown me, it has been my happiness to imagine myself in love with some divine creature or other; and after all it is but truth to declare that the passion was seated more in fancy than the heart; and it is justice to acknowledge to you that I am now more provident of my passion, and never suffer the excursion of fancy,

except when I am so liberal as to admit the united *beauty* of the *Rhode-island* ladies in competition with yours.

WHERE there are handsome women there will necessarily be fine gentlemen, and should they be smitten with your *external graces,* I cannot but lament their deplorable situation, when they discover how egregiously they have been cheated. What must be his disappointment, who thought himself fascinated by beauty, when he finds he has unknowingly been charmed by reason and virtue!

BUT this you will say contains a sentiment of jealousy, and is but a transcript of my apprehensions and gloomy anxieties: When will your presence, like the return of the sun in the spring, which dispels glooms, and reanimates the face of nature, quiet these apprehensions. If it be not in a short time, I shall proceed on a journey to find you out; until then I commit you to the care of your guardian angel.

LETTER XX.

HARRINGTON *to* HARRIOT.

BOSTON.

LAST night I went on a visit to your house: It was an adventure that would have done honour to the Knight of *La Mancha*. The moon ascended a clear, serene sky, the air was still, the bells sounded the solemn hour of midnight—I sighed—and the reason of it I need not tell you. This was, indeed, a pilgrimage; and no *Musselman* ever travelled barefooted to *Mecca* with more sincere devotion.

YOUR absence would cause an insufferable *ennui* in your friends, were it not for the art we have in making it turn to our amusement. Instead of wishing you were of our party, you are the goddess to whose honour we perform innumerable *Heathenish* rites. Libations of wine are poured out, but not a guest presumes to taste it, until they implore the name of *Harriot*; we hail the new divinity in songs, and strew around the flowers of poetry. You need not, however, take to yourself any extraordinary addition of vanity on this occasion, as your absence will not cause any repining:

"HARRIOT, our goddess and our grief no more."

BUT to give you *my* opinion on this important matter, I must descend to plain truth, and acknowledge I had rather adore you a *present* mortal, than an *absent* divinity; and therefore wish for your return with more religious ardour than a devout disciple of the false prophet for the company of the *Houri.*

THANKS to the power of imagination for one fanciful interview. Methought I somewhere unexpectedly met you—but I was soon undeceived of my imaginary happiness, and I awoke, repeating these verses:—

> THOUGH sleep her sable pinions spread,
> My thoughts still run on you;
> And visions hovering o'er my head,
> Present you to my view.

> By FANCY's magick pencil drest,
> I saw my *Delia* move;
> I clasp'd her to my anxious breast,
> With TEARS of joy and love.

> Methought she said—"Why thus forlorn?—
> Be all thy care resign'd:"——
> I 'woke and found my *Delia* gone,
> But still the TEAR behind.

LETTER XXI.

HARRIOT *to* MYRA.

RHODEISLAND.

WE arrived here in safety, but our journey is not without incident—an incident which exhibits a melancholy picture of the wickedness and depravity of the human heart.

WHEN we came to the house of Mrs. *Martin,* who, I suppose you know is cousin to Mrs. *Francis,* we were not a little astonished at the evident traces of distress in her countenance; all her actions were accompanied with an air of solemnity, and her former gaiety of heart was exchanged for sad, serious thoughtfulness: She, however, put on a face

of vivacity upon our being introduced, but her cheerfulness was foreign to the feelings of her heart.

MR. *Martin* was equally agitated; he endeavoured to dispossess himself of an *uncommon* weight of remorse, but in vain—all his dissimulation could not conceal his emotion, nor his art abate the continual upbradings of conscious guilt.

MRS. *Francis* was anxious to enquire the cause of this extraordinary change, but wisely forebore adding to the distress of her friend, by desiring her to explain it, in a manner too precipitate. She was in a short time made acquainted with the particulars of the story—which is not more melancholy than uncommon.

SOMETIME after the marriage of *Martin,* the beautiful *Ophelia,* sister to Mrs. *Martin,* returned from an *European* visit, to her friends in *Rhodeisland.* Upon her arrival, she received a polite offer from her brother-in-law of an elegant apartment at his house in town, which was cheerfully accepted—Fatal acceptation! He had conceived a passion for *Ophelia* and was plotting to gratify it. By a series of the most artful attentions, suggested by a diabolical appetite, he insinuated himself into her affection—he prevailed upon the heart of the unsuspicious *Ophelia,* and triumphed over her innocence and virtue.

THIS incestuous connexion has secretly subsisted until the present time—it was interrupted by a symptom which rendered it necessary for *Ophelia* to retire into the country, where she was delivered of a child, at once the son and nephew of *Martin.*

THIS event was a severe mortification to the proud spirit of *Shepherd,* the father of *Ophelia.* His resentment to his daughter was implacable, and his revenge of the injury from *Martin* not to be satiated. The blaze of family dispute raged with unquenchable fury—and poor *Ophelia* received other punishment from the hand of a vindictive father than bare recrimination.

THE affection of *Martin* now became changed to the vilest hatred.

THUS doomed to suffer the blackest ingratitude from her seducer on the one hand, and to experience the severity of paternal vengeance on the other—and before her the gloomy prospect of a blasted reputation —what must be the situation of the hapless *Ophelia!* Hope, the last resort of the wretched, was forever shut out. There was no one whom she durst implore by the tender name of father, and he who had seduced her from her duty and her virtue, was the first to brand her with the disgraceful epithets, of undutiful and unchaste.

PERHAPS it was only at this time, that she became fully sensible of

her danger; the flattery and dissimulation of *Martin* might have banished the idea of detection, and glossed over that of criminality; but now she awoke from her dream of insensibility, she was like one who had been deluded by an *ignis fatuus* to the brink of a precipice, and there abandoned to his reflection to contemplate the horrours of the sea beneath him, into which he was about to plunge.

WHETHER from the promises of *Martin,* or the flattery of her own fancy, is unknown, but it is said she expected to become his wife, and made use of many expedients to obtain a divorcement of *Martin* from her sister: But this is the breath of rumour. Allowing it to be truth, it appears to be the last attempt of despair; for such unnatural exertions, with the compunction attending them, represent a gloomy picture of the struggle between sisterly affection and declining honour. They however proved unavailable, and her efforts to that end, may with propriety be deemed a wretched subterfuge.

IN the mean while the rage of *Shepherd* was augmenting. Time, instead of allaying, kindled the flame of revenge in the breast of the old man. A sense of the wounded honour of his family, became every day more exquisite; he resolved to call a meeting of the parties, in which the whole mystery should be developed—that *Ophelia* should confront her seducer, and a thorough enquiry and explication be brought about.

OPHELIA exercised all her powers to prevent it; she intreated her father to consent to her desire, but her tears and intreaties were vain. To this earnest desire of his daughter, *Shepherd* opposed the honour of his family. She replied that such a procedure would publish its disgrace and be subversive of his intention: That she hoped to live retired from the world, and it was in his power to accept her happy repentance: In extenuating, she wished not to vindicate her errours, but declared herself to be penetrated with a melancholy sense of her misconduct, and hoped her penitence might expiate her guilt: She now beheld in the most glaring colours, the dangers to which she had been exposed, and acknowledged the effects of her temerity had impressed her mind with sincere contrition: All persons, continued she, are not blest with the like happiness of resisting temptation; she intreated her father, therefore, to believe her misfortunes proceeded from credulity and not from an abandoned principle—that they arose more from situation than a depraved heart: In asking to be restored to the favour and protection of a parent, she protested she was not influenced by any other motive, than a wish to demonstrate the sincerity of her repentance, and to establish the peace and harmony of the family.

OPHELIA now became melancholy, and her intentions visibly bent on the *manner of her death*. As the time drew nigh, her sensibility became more exquisite: What was before distress, she now averred to be horrour: Her conduct bordered upon insanity.

THE day was appointed to bring to a settlement this unhappy business—the time of hearing arrived—the parties met—the presence of *Ophelia* was necessary—she was missing—the unfortunate *Ophelia* died by her own hand.

MRS. *Shepherd* entered the apartment of her daughter—she beheld her pale and trembling—she saw the vial, and the cup with the remains of the poison—she embraced her lost child—"My *Ophelia!* my daughter! return—return to life."

AT this crisis entered the father—he was mute—he beheld his daughter struggling with the pangs of dissolution—he was dumb with grief and astonishment.

THE dying *Ophelia* was conscious of the distress of her parents, and of her own situation—she clasped her mother's hand, and raising her eye to heaven, was only heard to articulate "LET MY CRIME BE FORGOTTEN WITH MY NAME.—O FATAL! FATAL POISON!"

ADIEU! my dear *Myra*—this unhappy affair has worked me into a fit of melancholy. I can write no more. I will give you a few particulars in my next. It is impossible to behold the effects of this horrid catastrophe and not be impressed with feelings of sympathetick sorrow.

LETTER XXII.

HARRIOT *to* MYRA.

RHODEISLAND.

How frail is the heart! How dim is human foresight! We behold the gilded bait of temptation, and know not until taught by experience, that the admission of one errour is but the introduction of calamity. One mistake imperceptibly leads to another—but the consequences of the whole bursting suddenly on the devoted head of an unfortunate wanderer, becomes intolerable. How acute must be that torture, which seeks an asylum in suicide! O SEDUCTION! how many and how miserable are the victims of thy unrelenting vengeance. Some crimes, indeed, cease to

afflict when they cease to exist, but SEDUCTION opens the door to a dismal train of innumerable miseries.

YOU can better imagine the situation of the friends of the unfortunate *Ophelia* than I can describe it.

THE writings she left were expressive of contrition for her past transaction, and an awful sense of the deed she was about to execute. Her miserable life was insupportable, there was no oblation but in death—she welcomed death, therefore, as the pleasing harbinger of relief to the unfortunate. She remembered her once loved seducer with pity, and bequeathed him her forgiveness—To say she felt no agitation was not just, but that she experienced a calmness unknown to a criminal was certain. She hoped the rashness of her conduct would not be construed to her disadvantage—for she died in charity with the world. She felt like a poor wanderer about to return to a tender parent, and flattered herself with the hopes of a welcome, though unbidden to return. She owned the way was dark and intricate, but lamented she had no friend to enlighten her understanding, or unravel the mysteries of futurity. She knew there was a God who will reward and punish: She acknowledged she had offended him, and confessed her repentance. She expatiated on the miserable life she had *suffered,* not that she feared detection, that was impossible; but that she had been doing an injury to a sister who was all kindness to her; she prayed her sister's forgiveness—even as she herself forgave her seducer; and that her crime might not be called ingratitude, because she was always sensible of her obligation to that sister. She requested her parents to pardon her, and acknowledged she felt the pangs of a bleeding heart at the shock which must be given to the most feeling of mothers. She intreated her sisters to think of her with pity, and died with assurance that her friends would so far revere her memory as to take up one thing or another, and say this belonged to poor *Ophelia*.

O MY friend! what scenes of anguish are here unfolded to the survivours. The unhappy *Shepherd* charged *Martin* with the seduction and murder of his daughter. What the termination of this most horrible affair will be, is not easy to foresee.

ADIEU!

LETTER XXIII.

HARRIOT *to* MYRA.

RHODEISLAND.

WHATEVER may be the other causes (if there were any besides her seduction) which drove the unhappy *Ophelia,* temerariously to end her existence, it certainly becomes us, my dear friend, to attend to them—and to draw such morals and lessons of instruction from each side of the question, as will be a mirrour by which we may regulate our conduct and amend our lives. A prudent pilot will shun those rocks upon which others have been dashed to pieces, and take example from the conduct of others less fortunate than himself: It is the duty of the moralist, then, to deduce his observations from preceding facts in such a manner as may directly improve the mind and promote the economy of human life.

THIS may be an apology for sending you the arguments of *Martin* in answer to *Shepherd,* who in his rage and grief had called him the murderer of his child.

HE reminded *Shepherd* of his obstinacy in *persisting* in an explanatory meeting, and refusing to grant *Ophelia*'s request in suffering the affair to subside—"Your proud spirit," said he, "would not hearken to the gentle remonstrance of your daughter—your heart was closed to every conciliatory proposition. Though she expressed a propensity to fly from the eye of the world, she had hitherto appeared lulled in a kind of happy insensibility; yet the approaching time of explanation was terrible, it renewed the story and torture of all her misfortunes, and the idea filled her with grief and dismay. Had you been as willing to receive her, as she to return to you, happy would it have been for both; but your pride was the cause of additional calamities—when the time arrived—But why shall we harrow up our souls with the reiteration of her sorrowful exit?——

"FROM these circumstances," said *Martin,* "you cannot accuse me as the *immediate* cause of *Ophelia*'s death; the facts are as I have stated them—and thus was a straying, but penitent child, driven to despair and suicide by a severe use of paternal power, and a vain attempt to resent an injury, for which it was impossible the accused party could make compensation."

NOTWITHSTANDING the plausibility of *Martin*'s plea, I have little hes-

itation in my mind to charge him with the *remote cause* of the miserable end of *Ophelia*.

HOW far parental authority may be extended, is a question which I shall not determine; I must however think it depends upon the combination of circumstances. The duty of a child to her parents will be in proportion to the attention paid to her education. If, instead of the usual pains bestowed by many partial parents, upon the vain parade of forming the manners of a child, and burthening the mind with the *necessity* of the douceurs and the graces, would it not often be happier for both, to take a small share of thought to kindle *one spark of grace* in the heart?

HAPPY the parents, who have bestowed upon their children such an education, as will enable them, by a principle of mediocrity, to govern them without extorting obedience, and to reclaim them without exercising severity.

FAREWEL!

LETTER XXIV.

HARRIOT *to* MYRA.

RHODEISLAND.

MRS. *Francis* is not altogether satisfied with her journey to this part of the country—She does not delight to brood over sorrow—She flies from the house of mourning, to scenes of dissipation, congenial to her temper and disposition—and, like the rest of the world, bears the misfortunes of her friends with a most christian fortitude: The melancholy aspect of affairs here, will therefore shorten our visit—so you may expect us at *Boston* in a few days.

MY faithful lover (with whom I will certainly make you acquainted in a short time) continues to write to me in very passionate and sentimental strains. His last letter proves him to be a *tolerable maker of rhymes,* and I inclose it* for your *entertainment*.

I am, my dear,

YOUR MOST AFFECTIONATE FRIEND.

* See Letter XX. [Brown's note.]

<center>Letter xxv.</center>

<center># Myra to Harriot.</center>

<center>(Written before she had received the preceding.)</center>

<div align="right">BOSTON.</div>

Your sorrowful little history has infected me with grief. Surely there is no human vice of so black a die—so fatal in its consequences—or which causes a more general calamity, than that of *seducing* a female from the path of honour. This idea has been improved by my brother, on the hint of your favour—as an acknowledgment for which I inclose you his production.

<center>[The Inclosed.]</center>

<center>*The Court of Vice.*</center>

<center>An APOLOGUE.</center>

VICE "on a solemn night of state,
In all her pomp of terrour sate,"
Her voice in deep, tremendous tone,
Thus issu'd from her ebon throne:
'This night at our infernal court,
'Let all our ministers resort;
'Who most annoys the human race,
'At our right hand shall take his place,
'Rais'd on a throne—advanc'd in fame—
'Ye crimes now vindicate your claim.'

Eager for praise, the hideous host,
All spake, aspiring to the post.

PRIDE said, to gain his private ends,
He sacrific'd his dearest friends;
Insulted all with manners rude,
And introduc'd ingratitude.
'Twas he infus'd *domestick* hate,
And party spirit in the *state;*

Hop'd they'd observe his mystick plan,
Destroy'd all confidence in man;
And justify'd his high pretentions,
By causing envy and dissentions.

INTEMP'RANCE loud, demands the place,
He'd long deceiv'd the human race;
None could such right as he maintain,
Disease and death were in his train.

THEFT next appears to claim the station,
E'er constant in his dark vocation;
He thought the place might well repay,
The *crime* who labour'd night and day.

FRAUD own'd (tho' loth to speak his praise)
He gain'd his point by secret ways;
His voice in cities had been heard,
And oft in senates been preferr'd!
Yet much derision had he borne,
Treated by honest fools with scorn;
His influence on the western shore
Was not so great as heretofore:
He own'd each side alike assail'd,
Complain'd how sadly he was rail'd,
Curst by the name in ev'ry street,
Of Paper, Tendry, Rogue and Cheat:
Yet if some honour should requite
His labour—things might still go right.

MURDER before the footstool stood,
With tatter'd robe distain'd in blood.
'And who,' he cry'd, with daring face,
'Denies my title to the place?
'My watchful eyes mankind survey,
'And single out the midnight prey;
'Not cowardlike I meet the foe,
'With footsteps insecure and slow,
'Or cause his death by languid strife—
'Boldly this dagger ends his life.

'Give back, ye CRIMES, your claims resign,
'For I demand the post as mine.'

AV'RICE declar'd his love of gold;
His nation, or himself he sold;
He taught the sin of PRIDE betimes;
Was foster-father of all *crimes:*
He pawn'd his life; he stak'd his soul,
And found employment for the whole:
Acknowledg'd that he gain'd his wealth,
By FRAUD, by MURDER and by STEALTH:
On one so useful in her cause,
VICE well might lavish due applause.

The hagger'd host bow low the head,
The *Monster* rose, and thus she said:
'Ye *ministers* of VICE, draw near,
'For fame no longer persevere;
'No more your various parts disclose,
'Men *see, and hate you all as foes.*
'One yet remains among your crew,
'Then rise, SEDUCTION! claim your due.
'Your baleful presence quickly parts
'The tie that holds the happiest hearts;
'You *rob*—what *wealth* can ne'er repay;
'Like *Judas* with a kiss *betray:*
'Hence come the starving, trembling train,
'Who prostitute themselves for gain,
'Whose languid visages impart
'A smile, while anguish knaws the heart;
'Whose steps decoy unwary youth,
'From honour, honesty, and truth,
'Which follow'd 'till too late to mend,
'In ruin, and the gallows end—
'Be thine the post. Besides, who knows
'Where all thy consequences close?
'With thee, SEDUCTION! are ally'd
'HORROUR, DESPAIR and SUICIDE.
'YOU wound—but the *devoted* heart
'Feels not alone—the poignant smart:

'YOU wound—th' electrick pain extends
'To fathers, mothers, sisters, friends.
'MURDER may yet delight in blood,
'And deluge round the crimson flood;
'But sure his merits rank above,
'Who murders in the mask of love.'

LETTER XXVI.

MYRA *to Mrs.* HOLMES.

BOSTON.

IN one of my former letters I acquainted you that I suspected my brother to be in love, and now, Madam, I am enabled to tell you with whom—the amiable *Harriot.*

HARRIOT attended Mrs. *Francis* in her journey to *Rhodeisland,* and our young hero has, in her absence, been dreaming of his mistress; and, in a letter to her has written a description of his visionary interview. *Harriot,* with whom I maintain a constant correspondence, and who keeps no secret from me, inclosed the verses in her last, when lo! the hand writing of Master *Harrington.*

I WAS a little mortified that the young man had kept me in ignorance of his amour all this time, and this morning determined upon a little innocent revenge—"*Tommy,*" said I, as he entered the room, "here is a piece of poetry, written by an acquaintance of mine—I want your judgment on it"—"Poetry or rhyme," answered he, advancing towards me, and casting his eye on it—He took the letter and began to read——"Why do you blush, young man?" said I, "*Harriot* is a fine girl."——

THIS produced an *eclaircissement,* and as the matter must remain secret, for a certain weighty reason, I am to be the *confidante.*

I MUST acknowledge to you, Mrs. *Holmes,* there is a certain *je ne sçais quoi* in my amiable friend, that has always interested me in her favour—I have an affection for her which comes from the heart—an affection which I do not pretend to account for—Her dependance on Mrs. *Francis* hurts me—I do not think this lady is the gentle, complaisant being, that she appears to be in company—To behold so fine a girl

in so disagreeable a situation, might at first attract my commiseration and esteem, and a more intimate knowledge of her virtues might have ripened them into love. Certain it is, however, that whom I admire as a friend, I could love as a SISTER. In the feelings of the heart there can be no dissimulation.

PLEASE to tell Mr. *Worthy,* he may continue to write, and that I will condescend to read his letters.

FAREWEL!

LETTER XXVII.

WORTHY *to* MYRA.

BELLEVIEW.

I AM just returned from a melancholy excursion with *Eliza.* I will give you the history of it—We generally walk out together, but we this time went further than usual—The morning was calm and serene—all Nature was flourishing, and its universal harmony conspired to deceive us in the length of the way.

WHILE we were pursuing our walk, our ears were struck with a plaintive, musical voice, singing a melancholy tune.—"This," said Mrs. *Holmes,* "must be *Fidelia*—the poor distracted girl was carried off by a ruffian a few days before her intended marriage, and her lover, in despair, threw himself into the river"—*Eliza* could say no more—for *Fidelia* resumed her melancholy strain in the following words:——

> TALL rose the lily's slender frame,
> It shed a glad perfume;
> But ah! the cruel spoiler came,
> And nipt its opening bloom.

> Curse on the cruel spoiler's hand
> That stole thy bloom and fled—
> Curse on his hand—for thy true love
> Is number'd with the dead.

> Poor maiden! like the lily frail,
> 'Twas all in vain you strove;
> You heard the stranger's tender tale—
> But where was thy true love?
>
> Thou wast unkind and false to him,
> But he did constant prove;
> He plunged headlong in the stream—
> Farewel, farewel, my love!
>
> 'Twas where the river rolls along,
> The youth all trembling stood,
> Opprest with grief—he cast himself *suicide*
> Amidst the cruel flood.
>
> White o'er his head the billows foam,
> And circling eddies move;
> Ah! there he finds a watery tomb—
> Farewel, farewel, my love!

WE advanced towards the place from whence the sound issued, and *Fidelia,* who heard our approach, immediately rose from the ground; "I was tired," said she, "and sat down here to rest myself."

SHE was dressed in a long white robe, tied about the waist with a pink ribband; her fine brown hair flowed loosely round her shoulders —In her hand she held a number of wild flowers and weeds, which she had been gathering. "These," she cried, "are to make a nosegay for my love." "He hath no occasion for it," said *Eliza.* "Yes! where he lives," cried *Fidelia,* "there are plenty—and flowers that never fade too—I will throw them into the river, and they will swim to him—they will go straight to him"—"And what will he do with them?" I asked. "O!" said the poor girl as she looked wistfully on them, and sorted them in her hand, "he loves every thing that comes from me—he told me so"—"He will be happy to receive them," cried *Eliza*—"Where he is," said *Fidelia,* "is happiness—and happy are the flowers that bloom there—and happy shall I be, when I go to him—alas! I am very ill now"—"He will love you again," said *Eliza,* "when you find him out"—"O he was very kind," cried she, tenderly, "he delighted to walk with me over all these fields—but now, I am obliged to walk alone." *Fidelia* drew her hand across her cheek, and we wept with her.—"I must

go," she said, "I must go," and turned abruptly from us, and left us with great precipitation.

<div align="right">FAREWEL!</div>

LETTER XXVIII.

WORTHY *to* MYRA.

<div align="right">BELLEVIEW.</div>

My melancholy meditations led me yesterday to the same place where I had seen the distracted *Fidelia,* and walking down the hill I again beheld her by the side of a beautiful spring—Before I could come up to the place, she was gone—she went hastily over the field—I followed her—after a few minutes walk, I overtook her, and we both went on together towards a small, neat, farm house. An old man was sitting at the door—he gave a sigh as she passed by him to go in—I asked him if she was his daughter—"Alas!" said he, "my poor child—she has been in this state of affliction for near a twelve month." I inquired what cause produced the loss of her senses—He looked down sorrowfully—the question awakened the gloomy sensations of past evils, the recollection of which was painful, and opened wounds afresh that were not yet healed. "She has lost her lover," cried the old man—"the youth was the son of one of our neighbours—their infancy was marked by a peculiar attachment to each other. When the young people danced together, *Fidelia* was always the partner of *Henry*—as they grew up their mutual tenderness ripened into passionate affection. They were engaged to each other, and *Henry* saved all his little stock of money to begin the world by himself. All the town beheld them with pleasure—they wished them success and happiness—and from their knowledge of both their characters, were led to hope they would one day become good members of society—but these hopes are blasted, and they now bestow the bitterest curses on the wretch who hath crushed their expectations —who hath deprived *Fidelia* of her senses, and caused the death of her lover.

"THE gay *Williams* comes among us, and participates in our domestick pastimes—he singles out *Fidelia,* and is assiduous in his attentions

to her—her little heart is lifted up—but her prudence rises superiour to her vanity. *Henry* observes the operations of *Williams* and thinks he sees in him a powerful rival—the unhappy youth becomes melancholy —he sickens with jealousy—the pleasures of our country are forgotten by him—his thoughts are continually employed on his *Fidelia*.—To complete the measure of his promised happiness he wishes to call her his own—he declares the desire of his soul—*Fidelia* pledges her faith. He now sees the accomplishment of all his wishes in reversion—his heart leaps for joy—but—as the little paraphernalia is preparing, the ruffian hand of the Seducer dashes the cup of joy from their lips— *Fidelia* suddenly disappears—*Williams*—the ungrateful *Williams*—be- trays her to a carriage he had prepared, and she is hurried off. *Henry* stands astonished—wild with grief and dismay, he appears senseless and confounded.

"WHEN the heart is elevated by strong expectation—disappointment and misfortune come with redoubled force—To receive pain, when we look for pleasure, penetrates the very soul with accumulated anguish."

THE old man paused——He endeavoured to hide a tear that was stealing down his cheek—and to check the violence of his passion.

I ASKED him how long his daughter was missing—"Not long," he answered—"the young men, enraged at the insult, arm themselves and pursue the robber—they overtake him—*Williams* is wounded in the scuffle, and is carried away bleeding, by his servant—My daughter is regained—we thank Heaven for her restoration. She enquires for her *Henry*—alas! *Henry* is no more! The object of his love had flown from him, and with her, all the light of his soul—Darkness and grief had encompassed him—he had no resource, no consolation, no hope—she whom his soul loved was stolen—was wrested from his embrace. Who was there to administer relief?—Who was there to supply her loss?— Not one.—The light of his reason now became clouded—he is seized by despair, and urged forward by the torments of disappointed love, he plunges into the river—to close his sorrows with his life.

"THE loss of *Fidelia*'s senses followed this tragical event.

"SHE hears the fate of her lover and becomes petrified—the idea of her sorrows—her own agitation and care for her person, are lost in the reflection of her lover's death.—A while she raved—but is now some- what restored, and, as you see, the poor maniack strays about the fields harmless and inoffensive."

THE old man proceeded to inform me of the death of his wife—the idea of one misfortune aroused in him that of another—or rather there

was a gradual progression in them, and consequently a connexion—He told me she did not long survive the death of *Henry*. "O *Charlotte!*" he cried, "thou wast kind and cheerful—very pleasant hast thou been unto me. I will not cease to regret thy loss, till I meet thee in a better world."

"OUR hearts," continued the old man, addressing me, "are loosened from their attachment to this world by repeated strokes of misfortune. Wisely is it ordered thus. Every calamity severs a string from the heart —until one scene of sorrow on the back of another, matures us for eternity—Thus are our affections estranged from this scene of misery. The cord that detains the bird is severed in two—and it flies away.

"FORMERLY as I sat in this place—in the mild shade of the evening —when I had returned from my labour and took *Fidelia* on my knee, how often have I rendered thanks to Heaven for the happiness I enjoyed, and implored his power to make my child such another as *Charlotte*— This sweet remembrance yet swells and agitates my heart, and in the midst of the distress which surrounds me, I feel a consolation in tracing to you a feeble sketch of the happy times that are passed."

THE old man was sensibly affected—he delighted to dwell on what his child had been—he thought of those times—and he sighed when he contrasted them with the present.

"IN her disordered state," continued he, "she knows me not as a father—I spread my morsel before her, and she flies from it—she forgets the sound of my voice—she is no longer unto me as a daughter. She who hath so often said, she would support me with her arm, and lead me about, when I should be old and decriped—to her I call, but she returns me no answer. Is not the cause of my woe, a melancholy instance of the baleful art of the SEDUCER?—She is deprived of her reason, and knows not the weight of her misery; and I am doubly burdened with her affliction, and the accumulated misfortune of immature decripitude."

"SEDUCTION is a crime," I observed, "that nothing can be said to palliate or excuse."

"AND WO to him," added the old man, "who shall endeavour to extenuate it——*They have taken away my staff*"—continued he, raising a look of imploring mercy to Heaven, while a trembling tear rolled from his swollen eye, *"They have taken away my staff in my old age."*

FREELY did my heart share in the sorrows of the good old man— when I left him, I prayed Heaven to compassionate his distress—and as

I bent my pensive step towards *Belleview,* I had leisure to animadvert on the fatal tendency of SEDUCTION.

ADIEU!

LETTER XXIX.

Mrs. HOLMES *to* MYRA.

BELLEVIEW.

I AM sometimes mortified to find the books which I recommend to your perusal, are not always applicable to the situation of an *American* lady. The general observations of some *English* books are the most useful things contained in them; the principal parts being chiefly filled with local descriptions, which a young woman here is frequently at a loss to understand.

I SEND you a little work, entitled *"A Lady of Quality's Advice to her Children"* which, though not altogether free from this exception, is highly worthy of your attention. A parent who is represented struggling with the distress of a lingering illness, bequeaths a system of education to her offspring. I do not recommend it to you as a Novel, but as a work that speaks the language of the heart and that inculcates the duty we owe to ourselves, to society and the Deity.

DIDACTICK essays are not always capable of engaging the attention of young ladies. We fly from the laboured precepts of the essayist, to the sprightly narrative of the novelist. Habituate your mind to remark the difference between truth and fiction. You will then always be enabled to judge of the propriety and justness of a thought; and never be misled to form wrong opinions, by the meretricious *dress* of a pleasing tale. You will then be capable of deducing the most profitable lessons of instruction, and the design of your *reading* will be fully accomplished.——

HENCE you will be provided with a key to the characters of men: To unlock these curious cabinets is a very useful, as well as entertaining employment. Of those insidious gentlemen, who plan their advances towards us on the *Chesterfieldian* system, let me advise you to beware.

A prudent commander would place a double watch, if he apprehended the enemy were more disposed to take the fort by secresy and under-mining, than by an open assault.

I CANNOT but smile sometimes, to observe the ridiculous figure of some of our young gentlemen, who affect to square their conduct by his Lordship's principles of politeness—they never tell a story unless it be very short—they talk of decorum and the *etiquette*—they detest every thing vulgar or common—they are on the rack if an old man should let fall a proverb—and a thousand more trifling affectations, the ridicule of which arises, not so much from their putting on this foreign dress, as from their ignorance or vanity in pretending to imitate those rules which were designed for an English nobleman—Unless, therefore, they have a prospect of being called by Congress to execute some foreign negociation, they ought certainly to be minding their business.

THIS affectation of fine breeding is destructive to morals. Dissimu-lation and insincerity are connected with its tenets; and are mutually inculcated with the art of pleasing.

A PERSON of this character grounds his motives for pleasing on the most selfish principle—He is polite, not for the honour of obliging you, as he endeavours to make you believe, but that he himself might be obliged. Suspect him, therefore, of insincerity and treachery, who sac-rifices truth to complaisance, and advises you to the pursuit of an object, which would tend to his advantage.

ALWAYS distinguish the man of sense from the coxcomb. Mr. *Worthy* is possessed of a good understanding, and an exact judgment. If you are united with him, let it be the study of your life to preserve his love and esteem. His amiable character is adorned with modesty and a dis-position to virtue and sobriety. I never anticipate your future happiness, but I contemplate this part of his character with pleasure. But remember the fidelity of a wife alone, will not always secure the esteem of a hus-band; when her personal attractions do not continue to delight his eye, she will flatter his judgment. I think you are enabled to perform this, because you are solicitous to supply your mind with those amiable qual-ities which are more durable than beauty. When you are no longer surrounded with a flattering circle of young men, and the world shall cease to call you beautiful, your company will be courted by men of sense, who know the value of your conversation.

I AM pleased with the conduct of some agreeable girls, and the return of civility and attention they often make to the conceited compliments

of a certain class of beaux. These ladies wisely consider them as the butterflies of a day, and therefore generally scorn *to break them on a wheel!*

WHEN you are in company, where the vain and thoughtless endeavour to shew their ingenuity by ridiculing particular orders of men, your prudence will dictate to you not to countenance their abuse—The book I have just mentioned, intimates, that "there are a great many things done and said in company which a woman of virtue will neither see nor hear."—To discountenance levity, is a sure way to guard against the encroachment of temptation; to participate in the mirth of a buffoon, is to render yourself equally ridiculous. We owe to ourselves a *detestation* of folly, and to the world, the appearance of it. I would have you avoid coquetry and affectation, and the observance of my maxims will never make you a prude—Pretend, therefore, should a vain youth throw out illiberal sarcasms against Mechanicks, Lawyers, Ministers, Virtue, Religion, or any serious subject, not to comprehend the point of his wit.

I HAVE seldom spoken to you on the importance of Religion, and the veneration due to the characters of the Clergy. I always supposed your good sense capable of suggesting their necessity and eligibility. The Ministers of no nation are more remarkable for learning and piety than those of this country. The fool may pretend to scorn, and the irreligious to contemn, but every person of sense and reflection must admire that sacred order, whose business is to inform the understanding, and regulate the passions of mankind. Surely, therefore, that class of men, will continue to merit our esteem and affection, while virtue remains upon earth.

I AM always pleased with the reasonable and amiable light in which the Clergy are placed by the author of the *Guardian*—"The light," says he, "in which these points should be exposed to the view of one who is prejudiced against the names, *Religion, Church, Priest,* or the like, is to consider the Clergy as so many Philosophers, the Churches as Schools, and their Sermons as Lectures for the improvement and information of the audience. How would the heart of *Tully* or *Socrates* have rejoiced, had they lived in a nation where the law had made provision for philosophers to read lectures of philosophy, every seventh day, in several thousands of schools, erected at the publick charge, throughout the whole country, at which lectures, all ranks and sexes, without distinction, were obliged to be present, for their general improvement?"

YOU may, perhaps, think this letter too serious, but remember that virtue and religion are the foundation of education.

<div align="right">ADIEU!</div>

LETTER XXX.

Mrs. HOLMES *to* MYRA.

<div align="right">BELLEVIEW.</div>

YOU will observe, my dear friend, that most of the letters I have written to you of late, on female education, are confined to the subject of study. I am sensible of the ridicule sometimes levelled at those who are called learned ladies. Either these ladies must be uncommonly pedantick, or those who ridicule them, uncommonly ignorant—Do not be apprehensive of acquiring that title, or sharing the ridicule, but remember that the knowledge which I wish you to acquire, is necessary to adorn your many virtues and amiable qualifications. This ridicule is evidently a *transatlantick* idea, and must have been imbibed from the source of some *English* Novel or Magazine—The *American* ladies of this class, who come within our knowledge, we know to be justly celebrated as ornaments to society, and an honour to the sex. When it is considered how many of our countrywomen are capable of the task, it is a matter of regret that *American* literature boasts so few productions from the pens of the ladies.

SELF complacency is a most necessary acquirement—for the value of a woman will always be commensurate to the opinion she entertains of herself. A celebrated *European* wit, in a letter to a lady, concenters much good advice in one short rule of conduct: "REVERENCE THYSELF."

I WAS this morning reading *Swift*'s letter to a very young lady, on her marriage. Although this famous writer is not celebrated for delicacy or respect towards us, yet I wish some of his observations contained less truth—If you are in company, says this writer, when the conversation turns on the manners and customs of remote nations, or on books in verse or prose, or on the nature and limits of virtue and vice, it is a shame for a lady not to relish such discourses, not to improve by them,

THE POWER OF SYMPATHY 57

and endeavour by reading and information, to have her share in those entertainments, rather than turn aside, as is the usual custom, and consult with the woman who sits next her, about a new cargo of fans.

HE then descends to particulars, and insists on the necessity of orthography. Is it not a little hard, continues he, that not one gentleman's daughter in a thousand should be brought to read or understand her own natural tongue, or be judge of the easiest books that are written in it; as any one may find, who can have the patience to hear them mangle a Play or a Novel?

IF there be any of your acquaintance to whom this passage is applicable, I hope you will recommend the study of Mr. *Webster*'s Grammatical Institute, as the best work in our language to facilitate the knowledge of Grammar. I cannot but think Mr. *Webster* intended his valuable book for the benefit of his countrywomen: For while he delivers his *rules* in a pure, precise, and elegant style, he *explains* his meaning by *examples* which are calculated to inspire the female mind with a thirst for emulation, and a desire of virtue.

NO subject has been more exhausted than that of education. Many *Utopian* schemes have been delineated, and much speculation employed. When I peruse these labours, and am persuaded the intention of their authors is to promote our welfare, I feel myself prompted to a prudent and amiable demeanour; and I suppose every woman of reason and reflection feels the same inclination to virtue, and the same sensations of gratitude, in reading the works of those writers, the characteristicks of whom, are sentiment, morality and benevolence.

WHAT books do you read, my dear? We are now finishing *Barlow*'s Vision of *Columbus,* and shall begin upon *Dwight*'s Conquest of *Canaan* in a few days. It is very agreeable to read with one, who points out the beauties of the author as we proceed. Such an one is *Worthy.* —Sometimes Mr. *Holmes* makes one of our party, and his notes and references to the ancient poets are very entertaining. *Worthy* is delighted with the ease and freedom with which we live here. We have little concerts, we walk, we ride, we read, we have good company—this is *Belleview* in all its glory!

ADIEU, my dear—I shall continue this subject no longer, though I flatter myself you would receive my hints with satisfaction, because you must be persuaded I love you, and so interest myself in your welfare— I need not add that I think your conduct worthy of you. You are such a good girl that I know not in what to direct you; for you leave me no

room for advice—continue to anticipate the desires of my heart, and to
secure the high opinion you have there obtained.

<div align="right">YOUR FRIEND FOREVER!</div>

LETTER XXXI.

Mrs. HOLMES *to* MYRA.

<div align="right">BELLEVIEW.</div>

IF the affair of your brother and *Harriot* be serious, and matrimony is
really on the tapis, do not fail to make me *previously* acquainted with
it——I very much doubt the evidence of the verses—they weigh little
in my mind—and he is easily excused for sending them to so fine a girl
as *Harriot.*

YOUR observations on her dependence on Mrs. *Francis* do honour to
your heart—virtue does not consist in affluence and independence—nor
can it be reflected on us by the glory of our connexions—those who
pride themselves on it, make but an indifferent figure; for in the esti-
mation of all sensible people—true merit is personal.

HOWEVER, my dear friend, as one who wishes for your welfare and
the happiness of your family, I advise you to discourage the proposed
connexion—and if you cannot undertake this disagreeable task with a
certainty of success, do not fail to acquaint me of it *speedily.*

<div align="right">ADIEU!</div>

LETTER XXXII.

HARRINGTON *to* WORTHY.

<div align="right">BOSTON.</div>

WHAT ails my heart? I feel a void here—and yet I verge towards my
happiness—for a few days makes *Harriot* mine—*Myra* says I had *better*

not marry her. What could prompt her to use such an expression? *Better not marry her*. She has repeated it several times—and with too much eagerness—I give no heed to it—and yet why should it affect me in this manner? Is it an artifice to fathom the depth of my love? Such schemes are my utter aversion—it disturbs me—I hate such artifice—You cannot imagine how it touches my heart.

ADIEU!

LETTER XXXIII.

Mrs. HOLMES *to* MYRA.

BELLEVIEW.

IT is the duty of friends to be interested in all the concerns of one another—to join in their joys and to avert the stroke of danger. It is the duty of a centinel to give the alarm at the approach of what he may think such—and if the result does not prove to be a real evil—he has but performed his duty, and the action is meritorious.

IF your exertions to countermine the connexion of your brother with *Harriot* should prove ineffectual (and do not fail to acquaint me with it either way) I HAVE A TALE TO UNFOLD which may possibly forbid the bans.

LETTER XXXIV.

HARRINGTON *to* WORTHY.

BOSTON.

I FIND my temper grow extremely irritable—my sensibility is wounded at the slightest neglect—I am very tenacious of every thing, and of every body.

A PARTY was made yesterday to go on the water; I was omitted, and the neglect hurt me. I inquired the cause, and what think you is the

answer? "I am no company—I am asked a question and return nothing
to the point—I am absent—I am strangely altered within a few days—
I am thinking of a different subject when I ought to be employed in
conversation—I am extravagant in my observations—I am no com-
pany."

THEY would persuade me that I am little better than a mad man—I
have no patience with their nonsensical replies—Such wiseacres do not
deserve my pity.

FAREWEL!

LETTER XXXV.

MYRA *to* Mrs. HOLMES.

BOSTON.

YOUR letter is filled with such ambiguous expressions, that I am utterly
at a loss to discover your meaning.

I HAVE, however, sounded him on the article of marriage, and the
result is—he loves *Harriot* most passionately—and on account of my
father's aversion to early marriages, will marry her privately in a few
days.

THE oftener I read your letter, the more I am perplexed and aston-
ished: "YOU HAVE A TALE TO UNFOLD"—For Heaven's sake then unfold
it, before it be too late—and as you dread the consequence of keeping
it secret, by disclosing it to me, you will prevent the mischief, you so
much deprecate——I am all impatience.

ADIEU!

LETTER XXXVI.

HARRINGTON *to* WORTHY.

BOSTON.

I HAVE just left *Harriot*—but how have I left her? In tears. I wish I had not gone. Mrs. *Francis* had intrusted *Harriot* with some trifling commission—It was not done—she had not had time to perform it. *Harriot* was reprimanded——Yes! by Heaven—this Mrs. *Francis* had the insolence to reprimand *Harriot* in my presence—I was mortified— I walked to the window—my heart was on fire—my blood boiled in my veins—it is impossible to form an idea of the disorder of my nerves—*Harriot*'s were equally agitated—Mrs. *Francis* saw our confusion and retired—she left me so completely out of temper that I was forced to follow her example. I kissed away the tear from the cheek of *Harriot* and withdrew to my chamber.

HERE let me forget what has passed—my irritability will not permit it—my feelings are too easily set in motion to enjoy long quietness— my nerves are delicately strung; they are now out of tune, and it is a hard matter to harmonize them.

I FEEL *that I have a soul*—and every man of sensibility feels it within himself. I will relate a circumstance I met with in my late travels through *Southcarolina*—I was always susceptible of *touches of nature*.

I HAD often remarked a female slave pass by my window to a spring to fetch water. She had something in her air superior to those of her situation—a fire that the damps of slavery had not extinguished.

AS I was one day walking behind her, the wind blew her tattered handkerchief from her neck and exposed it to my sight—I asked her the cause of the scar on her shoulder—She answered composedly, and with an earnestness that proved she was not ashamed to declare it—"It is the mark of the whip," said she, and went on with the history of it, without my desiring her to proceed—"my boy, of about ten years old, was unlucky enough to break a glass tumbler—this crime was immediately inquired into—I trembled for the fate of my child, and was thought to be guilty. I did not deny the charge, and was tied up. My former good character availed nothing. Under every affliction, we may receive consolation; and during the smart of the whip, I rejoiced—be-

cause I shielded with my body the lash from my child; and I rendered thanks to the best of beings that I was allowed to suffer for him."

"HEROICALLY spoken!" said I, "may he whom you call the best of beings continue you in the same sentiments—may thy soul be ever disposed to SYMPATHIZE with thy children, and with thy brethren and sisters in calamity—then shalt thou feel every circumstance of thy life afford thee satisfaction; and repining and melancholy shall fly from thy bosom—all thy labours will become easy—all thy burdens light, and the yoke of slavery will never gall thy neck."

I WAS sensibly relieved as I pronounced these words, and I felt my heart glow with feelings of exquisite delight, as I anticipated the happy time when the sighs of the slave shall no longer expire in the air of freedom. What delightful sensations are those in which the heart is interested! In which it stoops to enter into the little concerns of the most remote ramification of Nature! Let the vain, the giddy, and the proud pass on without deigning to notice them—let them cheat themselves of happiness—these are circumstances which are important only to a sentimental traveller.

HAIL *Sensibility!* Sweetener of the joys of life! Heaven has implanted thee in the breasts of his children—to soothe the sorrows of the afflicted—to mitigate the wounds of the stranger who falleth in our way. *Thou* regardest with an eye of pity, those whom *wealth* and *ambition* treat in terms of reproach. Away, ye seekers of power—ye boasters of wealth—ye are the *Levite* and the *Pharisee,* who restrain the hand of charity from the indigent, and turn with indignation from the way-worn son of misery:—But *Sensibility* is the good *Samaritan,* who taketh him by the hand, and consoleth him, and poureth wine and oil into his wounds. Thou art a pleasant companion—a grateful friend—and a *neighbour* to those who are destitute of shelter.——

FROM thee! Author of Nature! from thee, thou inexhaustible spring of love supreme, floweth this tide of affection and SYMPATHY—thou whose tender care extendeth to the least of thy creation—and whose eye is not inattentive even though a sparrow fall to the ground.

LETTER XXXVII.

Mrs. HOLMES to MYRA.

BELLEVIEW, *12 O'CLOCK AT NIGHT.*

I CANNOT rest——this affair lies so heavy on my mind, that sleep flies from my eye-lids. Your brother *must* discontinue his addresses to *Harriot*——with what should I not have to upbraid myself, if, through my remissness—your brother marries his sister!

GREAT God! of what materials hast thou compounded the hearts of thy creatures! admire, O my friend! the operation of NATURE—and the power of SYMPATHY!——

HARRIOT IS YOUR SISTER! I dispatch the bearer at this late hour to confide in your bosom the important secret.

ADIEU!

LETTER XXXVIII.

MYRA to Mrs. HOLMES.

BOSTON.

ACCEPT my warmest acknowledgment, my good friend, for your kindness—Your letter sufficiently explains your former anxiety—it has removed all ambiguities.

YOUR servant entered hastily with the letter—and gave it me with evident tokens of its containing a matter of importance.—My father was present—I broke it open, not without agitation—I read it—but the shock was too severe—it fell from my hands, and I sunk into the chair.

MY fainting was not of any duration. I opened my eyes and found my father supporting me—but the idea of *Harriot* was still engraven deeply in my heart—I inquired for my sister—the tear rolled down his cheek—it was a sufficient answer to my inquiry—He said nothing— there was no necessity of his saying a word.

COULD I ask him to explain your letter? No—my heart anticipated

his feelings—the impropriety struck me at once. *"You have a tale to unfold."* Do not delay to unfold it.

<div align="right">ADIEU!</div>

<div align="center">

LETTER XXXIX.

Mrs. HOLMES *to* MYRA.

</div>

<div align="right">BELLEVIEW.</div>

I READILY undertake to give you a sketch of the history of *Harriot*. Her mother's name was *Maria Fawcet;* her person I yet recollect, and forgive me if I drop a tear of pity at the recital of her misfortunes.

MY mother and Mrs. *Holmes* were remarkable friends, and the intimacy, you know, was maintained between the two families. I was on a visit with my mother when the destiny of *Maria* led her to *Belleview*. I was frequently there during her illness—and was with her in her last moments.

IT was the custom of Mrs. *Holmes* to walk in the garden towards the close of the day. She was once indulging her usual walk, when she was alarmed by the complaints of a woman which came from the road. Pity and humanity were ever peculiar characteristicks of my amiable parent—She hastened to the place from whence the sound issued, and beheld a young woman, bathed in tears, sitting upon the ground. She inquired the cause of her distress, with that eager solicitude to relieve, which a sight so uncommon would naturally occasion. It was sometime before the distressed woman could return an intelligible answer, and then she with difficulty proceeded: "Your goodness, Madam, is un-merited—you behold a stranger, without home—without friends—and whose misery bears her down to an untimely grave—Life, truly is a blessing—but my life is become burthensome, and were the Almighty this moment to command me to the world of spirits, methinks I could gladly obey the summons, and rejoice in the stroke which bade me depart from sorrow and the world." "Moderate your grief, my dear woman, repine not at the will of Providence, nor suffer yourself to despair, however severe your misfortunes."

THE unfortunate woman was at length prevailed on to accompany

Mrs. *Holmes* into the house, she partook of some refreshment and retired to sleep. In a few days she appeared to be better; but it was a temporary recovery; she then told her story, with frequent interruptions, in substance as follows:——

History of Maria.

"I DATE the rise of my misfortunes," said *Maria*, "at the beginning of my acquaintance with the Honourable Mr. *Harrington*.—But for his solicitations I might still have lived in peace—a sister would not have had occasion to blush at the sound of my name—nor had a mother's pillow been steeped in tears, too fondly prone to remember a graceless but repenting child—We lived happily together in the days of my father, but when it pleased Providence to remove him, we no longer asserted our pretentions to that rank of life which our straitened finances were unable to continue—A young woman in no eligible circumstances, has much to apprehend from the solicitations of a man of affluence. I am now better persuaded of this truth, than I ever was before—for this was my unhappy situation—I always entertained a predilection for Mr. *Harrington*—he urged his passion with protestations of sincerity and affection—he found my heart too slightly guarded—he strove—he triumphed.

"——MUST I proceed!——

"A SMILING female was the offspring of our illicit connexion——Ah! my little *Harriot!*" continued *Maria*, as she wiped away a tear from her eye, "mayest thou enjoy that happiness which is denied to thy mother.

"OUR amour was not fated to last long—I discovered his gay temper to be materially altered—he was oftentimes thoughtful and melancholy, and his visits became suddenly shorter, and less frequent.

"I AFTERWARDS thought this change of conduct owing to jealousy—for he once asked me if a gentleman had called upon me—I persisted in avowing my abhorrence of his ungenerous suspicion—He left me abruptly, and I saw nothing of him after.

"A STROKE so unexpected fell heavy on my heart—it awakened me to the state of misery into which my imprudence had hurried me.—What recompense could I expect from my Seducer?—He had been married two years—From the inflexibility of his temper I had little to hope, and I formed a determination of leaving town, for I had now indubitable testimony of his affection being estranged from me—half frantick, I immediately set out—but whither I knew not—I walked with precipi-

tation until Providence directed me to your hospitable door: To your goodness, Madam, I am indebted for prolonging my existence a *few days:* For amidst the kindness and civilities of those around me, I feel myself rapidly verging towards the grave. I prepare myself for my approaching fate—and daily wait the stroke of death with trembling expectation."

SHE wrote to Mr. *Harrington* about a week before her decease—I transcribe the Letter:——

"The Hon. Mr. HARRINGTON.

"TO the man for whom my bleeding heart yet retains its wonted affection, though the author of my guilt and misery, do I address my feeble complaint—O! *Harrington,* I am verging to a long eternity—and it is with difficulty I support myself while my trembling hand traces the dictates of my heart. Indisposed as I am—and unable as I feel to prosecute this task—I however collect all my powers to bid you a long—a final farewel.

"OH! *Harrington,* I am about to depart—for why should I tarry here? In bitter tears of sorrow do I weep away the night, and the returning day but augments the anguish of my heart, by recalling to view the sad sight of my misfortunes. And have I not cause for this severe anguish, at once the sorrow and disgrace of my family?—Alas! my poor mother!—Death shall expiate the crime of thy daughter, nor longer raise the blush of indignation on thy glowing cheek.—Ought I not, therefore, to welcome the hand of death?

"BUT what will become of my poor helpless infant, when its mother lies forgotten in the grave? Wilt thou direct its feet in the path of virtue and rectitude?—Wilt thou shelter it from the rude blasts of penury and want?—Open your heart to the solicitude of a mother—of a mother agonizing for the future welfare of her child. Let me intreat you to perform this request—by the love which you professed for thy *Maria* —by her life which you have sacrificed.

"AND wilt thou not drop a tear of pity in the grave of thy *Maria?*— I know thy soul is a soul of sensibility; but my departure shall not grieve thee—no, my *Harrington,* it shall not wrest a sigh from thy bosom— rather let me live, and defy the malice and misery of the world—But can tenderness—can love atone for the sacrifices I have made?—Will it

blot out my errours from the book of memory? Will love be an excuse for my crime, or hide me from the eye of the malignant—No, my *Harrington*, it will not. The passion is unwarrantable. Be it thine, gentle *Amelia*—be it thine to check the obtruding sigh, and wipe away the tear from his face—for thou art his wife, and thy soul is the seat of compassion—But—for me——

"Farewel—farewel forever!

MARIA."

SHE survived but a short time—and frequently expressed a concern for her child—but Mrs. *Holmes* quieted her fears by promising to protect it. She accordingly made inquiry after it—and it is the same *Harriot* who was educated by her order, and whom she afterwards placed in the family of Mrs. *Francis*.

THE assurances of my mother were like balm to the broken hearted *Maria*—"I shall now," said she, "die in peace."

THE following is a copy of a letter written by the Rev. Mr. *Holmes* to the Hon. Mr. *Harrington:*——

"BELLEVIEW.

"SIR,

"WE have a scene of distress at our house peculiarly pathetick and affecting, and of which you, perhaps, are the sole author—You have had a criminal connexion with Miss *Fawcet*—you have turned her upon the world inhumanly—but chance—rather let me say Providence, hath directed her footsteps to my dwelling, where she is kindly entertained, and will be so, as long as she remains in this wilderness world, which is to be, I fear, but a short time—And shall she not, though she hath been decoyed from the road that leadeth to peace, long life and happiness—shall she not, if she return with tears of repentance and contrition, be entitled to our love and charity? Yes—this is my doctrine—If I behold any child of human nature distressed and forlorn, and in real want of the necessities of life, must I restrain or withhold the hand of charity—must I cease to recal the departing spirit of them that are ready to perish, until I make diligent inquiry into their circumstances and character? Surely, my friend, it is a duty incumbent on us by the ties of humanity and fellow feeling, and by the duty imposed on

us by our holy religion, equally to extend the hand of relief to *all the necessitous*—however they may be circumstanced in the great family of mankind.

"THE crime of *Maria* is not the blackest in the annals of human turpitude; but however guilty she might have been, the tears of penitence do certainly make atonement therefor.

"THUS much have I thought proper to say in vindication of my conduct—in sheltering under my roof a poor wanderer—who hath strayed, but not wantonly, and who hath now happily returned.

"ONE would imagine, there was little necessity of making such a vindication to you; but my sentiments always flow from the abundance of my heart, and I am willing the whole world should judge of those which influence my conduct——Now, though some men, whose charity is contracted, and who may be denominated *prudes in virtue,* might deem wrongfully of my attention to the calamity of this frail woman— yet let me appeal to the hearts and understandings of all men, and these in particular, if I have erred, whether it be not an errour on the side of humanity. Would to God such amiable errours were more frequent!— In as much, my friend, as there is joy in heaven over one sinner that repenteth, I may say with assurance that I have felt an emanation of this heavenly joy animate my heart, in beholding this woman delighting to steer her course heavenward.

"FROM the unhappy condition of *Maria,* I have been led to reflect on the mischievous tendency of SEDUCTION. Methinks I view the distressing picture in all its horrid colours.——

"BEHOLD the youthful virgin arrayed in all the delightful charms of vivacity, modesty and sprightliness—Behold even while she is rising in beauty and dignity, like a lily of the valley, in the full blossom of her graces, she is cut off suddenly by the rude hand of the Seducer. Unacquainted with his baseness and treachery, and too ready to repose confidence in him—she is deluded by the promises and flattery of the man who professes the greatest love and tenderness for her welfare:—But did she understand the secret villainy of his intentions—would she appear thus elate and joyous? Would she assent to her ruin? Would she subscribe her name to the catalogue of infamy? Would she kiss the hand of the atrocious dastard, already raised to give the final wound to her reputation and peace?

"O! WHY is there not an adequate punishment for this crime, when that of a common traitor is marked with its deserved iniquity and abhorrence!

"IS it necessary to depicture the state of this deluded young creature after her fall from virtue? Stung with remorse, and frantick with despair, does she not fly from the face of day, and secrete her conscious head in the bosom of eternal forgetfulness? Melancholy and guilt transfix her heart, and she sighs out her miserable existence—the prey of poverty, ignominy and reproach! Lost to the world, to her friends, and to herself, she blesses the approach of death in whatever shape he may appear, that terminates a life, no longer a blessing to its possessour, or a joy to those around her.

"BEHOLD her stretched upon the mournful bier!—Behold her silently descend to the grave!—Soon the wild weeds spring afresh round the *little hillock,* as if to shelter the remains of betrayed innocence—and the friends of her youth shun even the spot which conceals her relicks.

"SUCH is the consequence of SEDUCTION, but it is not the only consequence. Peace and happiness fly the nuptial couch which is unattended by love and fidelity. The mind no longer enjoys its quiet, while it ceases to cherish sentiments of truth and gratitude. The sacred *ties* of connubial duty are not to be violated with impunity; for though a violation of those *ties* may be overlooked by the eye of justice, the heart shall supply a *monitor,* who will not fail to correct those, who are hardy enough to burst them asunder.——I am, &c.

"W. HOLMES."

TO this Letter, Mr. *Harrington* returned the following Answer.

Hon. Mr. HARRINGTON *to the Rev. Mr.* HOLMES.

"PERMIT me, my ever honoured friend, to return you thanks for your late favours—need I add—an acknowledgment for your liberality? No —your heart supplies a source of pleasure which is contantly nourished by your goodness and universal charity.——

"THE picture you have exhibited of a ruined female is undoubtedly just, but that the *rude spoiler* has his share of remorse is equally so— The conclusion of your letter is a real picture of the situation of my heart.

"PERHAPS you was always ignorant of the real motives that influenced me, and gave a particular bias to my conduct—At an early period of my life, I adopted a maxim, that *the most necessary learning was a knowledge of the world,* the pursuit of which, quadrating with a vola-

tility of disposition, presented a variety of scenes to my heated imagination. The *eclat* of my companions gratifying my vanity and increasing the gale of passion, I became insensibly hurried down the stream of dissipation. Here I saw mankind in every point of view—from the acme of the most consummate refinement, to the most abject stage of degradation. I soon became a ready proficient in the great school of the world—but an alteration of conduct was soon after necessary—I was compelled to it, not so much from the world's abhorrence of a dissolute course of life, as the dictates of my own heart—It was, indeed, my policy to flatter the world, and exhibit a fair outside—for I was in love with *Amelia*—My licentious amour with *Maria* was secret—she was affectionate and tender—her manners were pleasing, but still I was unhappy.——

"MY career of dissipation, however alluring it struck my vitiated fancy, left little satisfaction on the mind—Reflection had its turn—and the happiness I had promised myself in a connexion with the amiable *Amelia*, I fully enjoyed in our marriage. A course of uninterrupted tranquillity ensued, but it was of short duration. The volatility of my temper, and the solicitude of my old associates, induced me at subsequent periods to fall again into my old vagaries. The taverns frequently found me engaged in meannesses derogatory to the character of a gentleman. These things I perceived affected the soul of *Amelia*—she was all meekness, gentleness and compassion, and she never once upbraided me with my illiberal conduct;

> But let concealment, like a worm in the bud,
> Feed on her damask cheek.

"BLESSED be that power who has implanted within us that consciousness of reproach, which springs from gentleness and love!—Hail sensibility! Ye eloquent *tears* of *beauty!* that add dignity to human nature by correcting its foibles—it was *these* that corrected my faults when recrimination would have failed of success—it was *these* that opened every avenue of contrition in my heart, when *words* would have dammed up every sluice of repentance.

"IT was now I appeared fully sensible that my conduct had hitherto been a course of disorder, and that systems of reformation, however well planned, had been overturned by the breath of adulation, before they had been thoroughly carried into execution—that I had been drifting upon a sea of inconsistency, without exercising my judgment; like

a ship without a rudder, buffetted on the bosom of the ocean, the sport of winds and waves.

"THE criminality of my connexion with *Maria* appeared with the most aggravated circumstances; it stung me with remorse—and I instantly determined, however severe the conflict, to tear her from my bosom—to see her no more.—But how was I to inform her of it?—In what manner was I to bring about such a task?—*Maria* must be sacrificed to the happiness of *Amelia*. This was all I had to perform—it was a short lesson, but it was a hard one for me to execute.

"WITH this determination, however, I entered the apartment of *Maria*—Duty to *Amelia* and gratitude to *Maria* interchangeably agitated me—the contention was dubious—but duty prevailed, and I adhered to my former resolution—yet how was I to tell her *this would be the last visit?*—Conscious she had ever acted in conformity to my wishes—how could I accuse her, without accusing myself?—I threw out a few inconsiderate, and ungrateful hints of jealousy, and left the room abruptly. The feelings of *Maria* must have been injured—but however her sensibility was affected, mine was doubly so; I felt for her—I felt for our infant, and these feelings were added to the afflictions which had already burst upon my devoted head. A few days consideration, however, convinced me of the impropriety and ingratitude of my behaviour to *Maria*—I hastened to tell her of it—to place her in a situation that should screen her from penury and malice—and to make provision for the child—but, she was not to be found. I was informed that she had suddenly disappeared, and that a countryman had, by her order, called and taken away the child but a few hours before. This information burst upon my head like the voice of sudden thunder—I stood motionless, but my agitation was too violent to be of any long duration.——

A natural tear I shed, but wip'd it soon.

"IT was your goodness, and the humanity of your family, that sheltered the wretched *Maria,* and provided for the helpless *Harriot*—Your feelings are your reward.

"FROM all the variegated scenes of my past life, I daily learn some new lesson of humanity. Experience hath been my tutor—I now take a retrospect of my past conduct with deliberation, but not without some serious reflection: Like a sailor, escaped from shipwreck, who sits safely on the shore and views the horrours of the tempest; but as the gale

subsides, and the waves hide their heads in the bosom of the deep, he beholds with greater concern the mischief of the storm, and the dangers he hath escaped. From what innate principle does this arise, but from the *God within the mind!*—I assert it for the honour of human nature, that no man, however dissolute, but comes back to the hour of reflection and solemn thoughtfulness—when the actions that are passed return upon the mind, and this *internal monitor* sits in judgment upon them, and gives her verdict of approbation or dislike.

"HE who listens to its call, views his character in its proper light—I have attended to its cry, and I see my deformity—I recal my mispent time, but in vain—I reflect on the misery of *Maria,* and I curse my temerity—I reflect on the state into which I have plunged a once happy female, and am eager to apply a speedy remedy, but this is vain also: Can I restore her that virtue—that innocence—that peace, of which I have unmanfully robbed her?——Let us leave the melancholy subject.——

"I WILL not so far supersede the fruit of your benevolence, as to presume to offer you any other recompense, than my sincere prayers for your happiness.

"I have the honour to be,
 "With respect,
 "Your &c.

 "J. HARRINGTON."

THE disorder of *Maria* was fatal and rapid—but I hasten to the last scene of her life—it has, though I was young, made an impression on my mind that time cannot efface. I went to her, as she was seated on the bed—virtue and harmony were blended in her aspect—she was serene and composed—and her mien, while it expressed a consciousness of superiour worth and dignity, exhibited in one view, a striking picture of the grandeur of the human soul—patient, though afflicted—of a spirit broken, and borne down by severe distress, yet striving to surmount all, and aspire to heaven. In what words shall I paint to you, my dear *Myra,* her heroism and greatness of mind? "Weep not for me," said she, perceiving my emotion—"Death has nothing shocking to me —I have familiarized myself to his terrours—I feel the gradual decay of mortality; and waiting with confidence in the father of mercy, I am prepared to resign this mortal breath—I resign it in firm assurance of the soul's blessed immortality—Death I view as freeing me from a world

which has lost its relish—as opening new scenes of happiness——But a few moments," continued she, clasping my hand, "and the scene of life is closed forever—Heaven opens on my soul—I go where all tears shall be wiped away—I welcome death as the angel of peace."——She uttered these words with a placid smile of resignation—her head sunk down on the pillow—and the next minute she was an angel.

"SOUL of the universe!" exclaimed my father-in-law—"there flew the gentlest spirit that ever animated human dust—Great were thy temptations—sincere thy repentance. If some human infirmity fell to thy lot, thy tears, dear shade, have washed out thy guilt forever!"

LETTER XL.

Mrs. HOLMES to MYRA.

BELLEVIEW.

HAVING presented you with several observations on Seduction, I think it will not be *mal apropos* to consider the question in another point of view, and discover how a woman may be accessary to her own ruin— It is hardly worth while to contend about the difference between the meaning of the terms *accessary* and *principal*. The difference, in fact, is small; but when a woman, by her imprudence, exposes herself, she is *accessary;* for though her heart may be pure, her conduct is a tacit invitation to the Seducer.

EDUCATED in the school of luxury and pride, the female heart grows gradually torpid to the fine feelings of sensibility—the blush of modesty wears off—the charms of elegant simplicity fade by degrees—and the continual hurry of dissipation, supersedes the improvement of serious reflection. Reflection is a kind of relaxation from frolicking—it encourages the progress of virtue, and upholds the heart from sinking to depravity.

WE may lay it down as a principle, that *that conduct which will bear the test of reflection, and which creates a pleasure in the mind from a consciousness of acting right, is virtuous: And she whose conduct will not bear this test, is necessarily degenerating, and she is assenting to her destruction.*

LET a lady be liberal or even magnificent, according to her circum-

stances or situation in life; but let the heart remain uncorrupt, let her not be contaminated by wealth, ambition or splendour. She may then take a happy retrospect of her conduct—her heart cannot upbraid her —and the suffrage of her own mind is a convincing proof that she has not strayed from the path of virtue.

HAPPY they who can thus reflect—who can recal to view the scenes that are passed, and behold their actions with reiterated satisfaction— they become ambitious of excelling in every thing virtuous, because they are certain of securing a continual reward: For as a mighty river fertilizes the country through which it passes and encreases in magnitude and force until it empty itself into the ocean: So virtue fertilizes or improves the heart, and gathers strength and vigour by continual progression, until it centre in the consummation of its desires.

DAZZLED by the glitter of splendour, and unmindful of the real charms of economy and simplicity, the female heart sighs for the enjoyment of fashion, and flutters to join the motley train of pleasure. But how is it deluded by empty deceptions! Like the fruit which sprang up in the infernal regions, beautiful to the eye, but which left upon the taste bitter ashes, and was followed by repentance—A great quantity of this kind of fruit presents itself to my rashly judging sex; and it frequently happens that their hearts have as little inclination to resist the temptation, as our general parent to refuse the fatal apple.

WE do not rouse to our aid fortitude to enable us to surmount the temptation, but yield ourselves to a kind of voluntary slavery. Hence it is observable, that a woman is often unhappy in the midst of pleasures—and petulent without cause—that she is trifling in matters of the highest importance; and the most momentous concern is considered futile, as whim and caprice may chance to dictate.

THE progress of female luxury, however slow it may appear, unless timely checked, works with infallible and destructive advances. The rule we at first adopted might perhaps answer this check; for by the examination there recommended, we behold the dangers of a continuation of such conduct—Ruin and contempt, the invariable concommitants of vice and immorality, proclaim their denunciations on a prosecution of it.

LET us examine the gradual steps, and the consequence of female luxury.—A desire to be admired is the first. Behold a woman surrounded by her worshippers, receiving the sacrifice of adulation—what was given her at first as compliment, she now demands as her due. She finds herself disappointed, and is mortified. The first desire still predom-

inating, she attaches herself to the votaries of pride, who direct their
feet in the paths of extravagance and irreligion. Thus sunk into effem-
inacy and meanness, *she forfeits her virtue rather than her pride.* Thus
terminates the career of a woman, whose mind is debilitated, and whose
life is expended in the pursuit of vanity.

IT is said of some species of *American* serpents, that they have the
power of charming birds and small animals, which they destine for their
prey. The serpent is stretched underneath a tree—it looks stedfastly on
the bird—their eyes meet to separate no more—the charm begins to
operate—the fascinated bird flutters and hops from limb to limb, till
unable any longer to extend its wings, it falls into the voracious jaws
of its enemy: This is no ill emblem of the fascinating power of pleasure.
Surrounded with temptation, and embarrassed in her circumstances, a
woman of dissipation becomes less tenacious of her honour—and falls
an easy prey to the fascinating power of the SEDUCER.

HAVING traced to you, my dear *Myra,* the rise, advancement and
termination of pleasure and pride in the female heart, it appears almost
unnecessary to remark that this conduct cannot bear the test of reflec-
tion and serious examination. We may, however, observe on the con-
trary, that a woman who advances a few steps, often hurries on still
further to prevent thought. This bars the way to a return to that conduct
which *can* give pleasure on recollection. She behaves to herself as the
populace did formerly to women suspected of witchcraft—they were
tied neck and heels and thrown into the river; if they swam they were
hung for witches—if they sank they were acquitted of the crime, but
drowned in the experiment: So when we only suspect our hearts of an
errour, we plunge still deeper into the sea of dissipation, to prevent the
trial of that conduct which impartial reason and judgment would
approve.

NOTWITHSTANDING I give this instance as an encouragement for vir-
tue; yet in all those I have mentioned is a woman *accessary* to her ruin.

DO not imagine, my dear *Myra,* that I mean to argue against all
pleasure—Many of us set out on a principle of false delicacy and de-
structive rivalship; we cannot behold a fine woman without wishing to
appear finer. A laudable emulation in the conduct of all women is ex-
tremely praiseworthy—it stimulates them in the line of their duty—
increases vivacity and good humour; and ambition, thus directed and
pursued, I beg leave to designate a female virtue, because it is productive
of the most happy consequences.

BUT it sometimes happens that particular virtues loose themselves in

their neighbouring vices, and this laudable emulation degenerates into destructive rivalship.

A GENTEEL, handsome woman, deservedly shares the esteem and admiration of all men; but why should this esteem and admiration, justly paid to merit, give us disquiet? the answer is ready. That desire to be admired, so predominant in all females, by degrees works itself into the ruling passion, and precludes from the mind the particular virtue of emulation; for why a woman who merits the love of the world, should draw on her the disapprobation of many of her own sex, can be accounted for, by no other principle, than the mean, pitiful passion of envy.

THIS may possibly give rise to defamation. It is astonishing how this practice prevails among a *few* persons—because it is known by experience, to prove subversive of its very intention.—The arrows of envy recoil upon herself.

HOW foolish must that woman appear who depreciates the merit of another, that she may appear unrivalled! She raises up the dykes of ill nature, and inundates the land with a flood of scandal, but unhappily drowns herself in the event.

I LEAVE it to the result of your observation, my dear *Myra,* whether the woman who is first to develope her stores of defamation, and through false emulation, the first to traduce a woman of real merit and virtue, is not also the first who becomes a scandal to herself, and consequently the first that is contemned.

HOW opposite are the pursuits and rewards of her who participates in every rational enjoyment of life, without mixing in those scenes of indiscretion which give pain on recollection!—Whose chymical genius leads her to extract the poison from the most luxuriant flowers, and to draw honey even from the weeds of society. She mixes with the world seemingly indiscriminately—and because she would secure to herself that satisfaction which arises from a consciousness of acting right, she views her conduct with an eye of scrutiny. Though her temper is free and unrestrained, her heart is previously secured by the precepts of prudence—for prudence is but another name for virtue. Her manners are unruffled, and her disposition calm, temperate and dispassionate, however she may be surrounded by the temptations of the world.

ADIEU!

LETTER XLI.

HARRINGTON *to* WORTHY.

BOSTON.

Pray that the sun of Thursday may rise propitious—that it may gild the face of nature with joy. It is the day that beholds thy friend united in the indissoluble bands of *Hymen.*

> Let this auspicious day be ever sacred,
> No mourning, no misfortune happen on it;
> Let it be marked for triumphs and rejoicings,
> Let happy lovers ever keep it holy,
> Choose it to bless their hopes and crown their wishes.

It is the day that gives me *Harriot* forever.

ADIEU!

LETTER XLII.

The Hon. Mr. HARRINGTON
to the Rev. Mr. HOLMES.

BOSTON.

You very well know of my amour with *Maria,* and that a daughter was the offspring of that illicit connexion—That sixteen years have elapsed since, by your goodness, she has lived with Mrs. *Francis,* and let me add, daily improving in beauty and every amiable accomplishment—But how shall we be able—how shall we pretend to investigate the great springs by which we are actuated, or account for the operation of SYMPATHY—my son, who has been at home about eight weeks, has accidentally seen her, and to complete THE TRIUMPH OF NATURE—has loved her. He is now even upon the point of marrying—

shall I proceed!—*of marrying his Sister!*—A circumstance seemingly
fortuitous has discovered this important affair—I fly to prevent incest
—Do not upbraid me with being the author of my own misfortunes.—
"This comes of your libertinism," you will say, "this comes of your
adultery!"——Spare your reflections, my friend—my heart is monitor
enough—I am strangely agitated!

ADIEU!

LETTER XLIII.

The Hon. Mr. HARRINGTON
to the Rev. Mr. HOLMES.

BOSTON.

MY heart failed me! twenty times have I attempted to break the matter
to my son—and twenty times have I returned from the task—I have
engaged a friend to acquaint him how nearly connected he already is
with the object of his love. This is a new, and to me a sorrowful instance
of the force of SYMPATHY—My grief is insupportable—my affliction is
greater than I can bear—it will bring down my grey hairs with sorrow
to the grave.

FAREWEL!

LETTER XLIV.

HARRINGTON *to* WORTHY.

BOSTON.

ALL my airy schemes of love and happiness are vanished like a dream.
Read this, and pity your unfortunate friend.

To Mr. T. HARRINGTON.

"SIR,

"YOU are about to marry a young lady of great beauty and ac-complishments—I beg you to bestow a few serious thoughts on this important business—Let me claim your attention, while I disclose an affair, which materially concerns you—*Harriot* must not be your wife—You know your father is averse to your early connecting yourself in marriage with any woman—The duty we owe a parent is sacred, but this is not the only barrier to your marriage—the ties of consanguinity prevent it—She is your SISTER——Your father, or Miss *Harrington,* will inform you more particularly—It is sufficient for me to have hinted it in time.——I am, with the most perfect esteem, and sincere wishes for your happiness, your

"UNKNOWN FRIEND, &c."

(*IN CONTINUATION.*)

THE gloom of melancholy in the faces of the family but too well cor-roborated this intelligence—so I asked no questions—they read in my countenance that I had received the letter, and my sister put into my hand *The History of Maria*—I concealed my emotion while I read the account—"It is a pitiful tale," said I, as I returned it—and walked out of the room to give vent to the agitation of my heart.

I HAVE not yet seen *Harriot*—*Myra* has run to greet her with the new title of *sister*. Adieu! my friend—little happiness is left for me in this world.

LETTER XLV.

MYRA *to* Mrs. HOLMES.

BOSTON.

IN what words shall I describe to you, my dear friend, the misery that has suddenly overwhelmed us! It is impossible to communicate the dis-tressed situation of *Harriot*—Expression is inadequate to give you an

idea of our meeting—I called her my friend—my sister—She always loved me—but joy and affection gave way to passion—Her speech refused its office—

> Sorrow in all its pomp was there,
> Mute and magnificent without a tear.

SHE had gained a sister—she had lost a lover—a burst of joy would suddenly break from her, but it was of short duration—and was succeeded by pangs of exquisite distress—nature was unable to support it, and she fainted under the weight of the severe conflict. Her constitution at best is feeble; her present illness is therefore attended with more danger—Unless a speedy alteration should take place, the physician has little hopes of her recovery.——Heaven preserve us!

FAREWEL!

LETTER XLVI.

HARRINGTON *to* WORTHY.

BOSTON.

I HAVE seen her—I prest her to my heart—I called her my Love—my *Sister*. Tenderness and sorrow were in her eyes—How am I guilty, my friend—How is this transport a crime? My love is the most pure, the most holy—*Harriot* beheld me with tears of the most tender affection—"Why," said she, "why, my friend, my dear *Harrington*, have I loved! but in what manner have I been culpable? HOW WAS I TO KNOW YOU WERE MY BROTHER?—Yes! I might have known it—how else could you have been so kind—so tender—so affectionate!"—Here was all the horrour of conflicting passions, expressed by gloomy silence—by stifled cries—by convulsions—by sudden floods of tears—The scene was too much for my heart to bear—I bade her adieu—my heart was breaking—I tore myself from her and retired.

WHAT is human happiness? The prize for which all strive, and so few obtain; the more eagerly we pursue it, the farther we stray from the object: Wherefore I have determined within myself that we increase in

misery as we increase in age—and if there are any happy they are those of thoughtless childhood.

I THEN viewed the world at a distance in perspective. I thought mankind appeared happy in the midst of pleasures that flowed round them. I now find it a deception, and am tempted sometimes to wish myself a child again. Happy are the dreams of infancy, and happy their harmless pursuits! I saw the *ignis fatuus,* and have been running after it, but now I return from the search. I return and bring back disappointment. As I reflect on these scenes of infantine ignorance, I feel my heart interested, and become sensibly affected—and however futile these feelings may appear as I communicate them to you—they are feelings I venture to assert which every one must have experienced who is possessed of a heart of sensibility.

ADIEU!

LETTER XLVII.

HARRINGTON *to* WORTHY.

BOSTON.

I NO longer receive satisfaction from the enjoyments of the world—society is distasteful to me—my favourite authors I have entirely relinquished—In vain I try to forget myself, or seek for consolation—my repose is interrupted by distressing visions of the night—my thoughts are broken—I cannot even think regularly.

HARRIOT is very weak—there is no hope of her life.

ADIEU!

LETTER XLVIII.

HARRINGTON *to* WORTHY.

BOSTON.

My dear friend, I have a great desire to see you—I wish you could come home speedily—I must be short—I have some serious business to do.

FAREWEL!

P.S. THEY say life is a blessing and it is our duty to improve and enjoy it; but when life becomes insupportable and we find no blessing in it—have we not a right to resign it?

FAREWEL!

LETTER XLIX.

The Hon. Mr. HARRINGTON
to the Rev. Mr. HOLMES.

BOSTON.

ACCUMULATED sorrows continue to break over my devoted head. *Harriot* is at times deprived of her reason, and we have no expectation of her recovery—my son is deeply affected—he seems strangely disordered.

REVOLVING in my mind all these things, and the unhappy affair that led to them, the whole train of my past life returned fresh upon my mind. Pained with the disagreeable picture, and oppressed with the weight of my affliction, I sunk down to sleep: These circumstances had so strongly impressed my imagination that they produced the following Dream—My blood is chilled with horrour as I write.

METHOUGHT I suddenly found myself in a large, open field, waste

and uncultivated—here I wandered in a solitary manner for some time—grief seized my heart at the awful appearance of the place, and I cried aloud—"How long shall I travel here, alone and friendless—a dusky mist swims before my sight, and the obscure horizon seems only to inclose this dismal wild!" Having advanced a few steps, I thought a light at a distance appeared to my doubtful view. Faint with fatigue, I approached it, and had the satisfaction to behold a person of the most benign aspect—a quiet serenity was painted on his brow, and happiness ineffable beamed from his divine countenance—Joy leaped in my bosom, and in the ecstacy of passion I endeavoured to clasp the blessed spirit to my heart; but it vanished in my embrace.

"TEACH me, blessed shade," said I, with a trembling voice—"teach me to find the habitations of men—What do I here?—Why am I doomed to explore the barren bosom of this baleful desert?" "*This,*" returned the spirit, in a voice, which, while it commanded veneration and love, struck awe and terrour into my soul—"*This* is not the habitation of the sons of mortality—it is the place appointed to receive the souls of all men, after they have resigned the bodies they animated on earth. Those who have violated the laws of reason, humanity, religion, and have dishonoured their God, here meet the punishment due to their crimes.

"ATTEND me, therefore, and view the condition of those thoughtless souls, who, a few days ago, were upon earth immersed in pleasure, luxury and vice—Regardless of futurity, and unprepared for their eternal summons to another world—and who persisted in the delight of their own eyes in opposition to the divine law, and deaf to the voice of reclaiming virtue. These, the sons of folly and riot, are smitten by the angel of death, while they are yet drinking of the bowl of vice—while the words of blasphemy yet dwell upon their tongues. And when their unhappy spirits sink to these infernal regions, their surviving companions rehearse their funeral panegyricks—the praise of one is, that he could drink the longest—the merit of another, that he could sing a good song—a third secures his fame by being excellent in mimickry and buffoonery—How unhappy must he be, who leaves no other testimony of his usefulness behind him!

"HOW different is the fate of the good man: While upon earth his life is employed in the cause of virtue—The happiness he bestows on those around him is reflected back with tenfold reward; and when he takes rank in that happy place, where there is fulness of joy, and leaves the world of mankind, what numbers are joined in the general concern for

his loss—The aged, while they prepare for the same journey, delight to dwell on his good actions—the virgin strews flowers on his grave, and the poet consumes the midnight oil to celebrate his virtues."

THERE was so much benignity in every word and action of my attendant, that I found myself imperceptibly attached to him. My attention to his discourse had prevented me from observing the progress we had made—for we had arrived at a place encircled with high walls—a great gate, at the command of my guide, instantly flew open—"Follow me," said he—I tremblingly obeyed.——

MY ears were instantaneously filled with the faint cries of those here doomed to receive the rewards of their demerits. Looking earnestly forward, I beheld a group of unhappy wretches—I observed a person who was continually tormenting them—he held in one hand a whip, the lashes of which were composed of adders, and the stings of scorpions; and in the other a large mirrour, which, when he held up to the faces of the tormented, exhibited their crimes in the most flagrant colours, and forced them to acknowledge the justness of their punishment. "These," said my guide, "who are scourged with a whip of scorpions, and who start with horrour at the reflection of their deeds upon earth, are the souls of the Gambler—the Prodigal—the Duelist, and the Ingrate.

"THOSE whom you see yonder," continued he, "those wasted, emaciated spirits, are the souls of the Envious—they are doomed to view the most beautiful fruit, which they can never taste, and behold pleasures which they can never enjoy. This punishment is adjudged them because most of those vile passions, by which men suffer themselves to be ruled, bring real evil, for promised good.

"FOR this reason the allwise Judge hath ordered the same passions still to inflame those ghosts, with which they were possessed on earth —Observe yon despicable crew!—behold the sin of Avarice!—those sordid ghosts are the souls of Misers—Lo! they eye their delightful bags with horrid pleasure; and with a ghastly smile, brood over their imaginary riches. Unable to carry their wealth about with them, they are confined to one spot, and in one position. This infernal joy is the source of their tortures, for behold them start at every sound, and tremble at the flitting of a shade. Thus are they doomed to be their own tormentors—to pore over their gold with immortal fear, apprehension, and jealousy, and to guard their ideal wealth with the tears of care, and the eyes of eternal watchfulness.

"BEHOLD here," continued my guide, "the miserable division of

Suicides!"—"Unhappy they!" added I, "who, repining at the ills of life, raised the sacrilegious steel against their own bosoms! How vain the reiterated wish to again animate the breathless clay—to breathe the vital air—and to behold the cheering luminary of Heaven!"—"Upbraid me not—O my father!" cried a voice—I looked up, and thought my son appeared among them—but immediately turning from so shocking a spectacle, I suddenly beheld my once loved *Maria*—"O delight of my youth! do I behold thee once more!—Let me hide my sorrows in thy friendly bosom." I advanced towards her—but she flew from me with scorn and indignation—"O speak! *Maria!* speak to me!" She pointed with her finger to a group of spirits, and was out of sight in a moment.

"LET me," said my conductor, "prepare you for a more dreadful sight." The increasing melancholy, and affecting gloom of the situation, forboded something terrifying to my soul—I looked toward the place where *Maria* had pointed, and saw a number of souls remote from any division of the unhappy. In their countenances were depicted more anguish, sorrow and despair—I turned my head immediately from this dreadful sight, without distinguishing the nature of their torments. Quivering with horrour, I inquired who they were—"These," answered my guide, with a sigh, "are the miserable race of SEDUCERS.—Repentance and shame drive them far from the rest of the accursed. Even the damned look on them with horrour, and thank fate their crimes are not of so deep a die."

HE had hardly finished, when a demon took hold of me, and furiously hurried me in the midst of this unhappy group—I was so terrified that it immediately roused me from my sleep.

EVEN now, while I write to you, my good friend, my hand trembles with fear at the painful remembrance—Yet

———'Twas but a dream, but then
So terrible, it shakes my very soul.——

FAREWEL!

LETTER L.

HARRIOT *to* HARRINGTON.

BOSTON.

MUST I then forget the endearments of the lover, and call you by the name of brother? But does our friendship remain upon this foundation? Is this all that unites us? And has there subsisted nothing more tender —a sentiment more voluntary in our hearts? My feelings affirm that there has. At the hour of our first interview I felt the passion kindle in my breast: Insensible of my own weakness, I indulged its increasing violence and delighted in the flame that fired my reason and my senses. Do you remember our walks, our conversations, our diversions?—The remembrance of these things fill my mind with inconceivable torture— they seem to reproach me with unmerited criminality—I deprecate, I detest all these scenes of gaity and frivolity—yet I have preserved my innocence and my virtue—what then have I to deprecate, what have I to detest?

ALAS! how have we been forming schemes of happiness, and mocking our hearts with unsubstantial joys. Farewel! farewel! ye gilded scenes of imagination. How have we been deluded by visionary prospects, and idly dwelt upon that happiness which was never to arrive. How fleeting have been the days that were thus employed!—when anticipation threw open the gates of happiness, and we vainly contemplated the approach of bliss;—when we beheld in reversion, the pleasures of life, and fondly promised ourselves, one day to participate in them;—when we beheld in the magick mirrour of futurity, the lively group of loves that sport in the train of joy. We observed in transports of delight the dear delusion, and saw them, as it were, in bodily form pass in review before us; as the fabled hero views the region of præexistant spirits, and beholds a race of men yet to be born.

SUCH was our hope, but even this fairy anticipation was not irrational. We were happy in idea, nor was the reality far behind. And why is the vision vanished? O! I sink, I die, when I reflect—when I find in my *Harrington* a brother—I am penetrated with inexpressible grief—I experience uncommon sensations—I start with horrour at the idea of incest—of ruin—of perdition.

HOW do I lament this fatal discovery, that includes the termination

of a faithful love! I think of him to whom I have resolved to be eternally constant—and ah! how often have I resolved it in my heart. I indulge, in idea, the recollection of his caresses—of his protestations, and of his truth and sincerity—I become lost in a wilderness, and still I travel on, and find myself no nearer an escape. I cherish the dear idea of a lover —I see the danger and do not wish to shun it, because, to avoid it, is to forget it—And can I, at one stroke, erase from my mind the remembrance of all in which my heart used to delight? Ah! I have not the fortitude—I have not the virtue, to "forget myself to marble." On the contrary, I strive no longer to remember our present connexion. I endeavour to forget—I curse the idea of a brother—my hand refuses to trace the word, and yet

————The name appears
Already written; blot it out my tears!

AH, whence this sorrow that invests my soul! This gloom that darkens—this fire of impassioned grief, that involves all my thoughts! why do I rave, and why do I again abandon myself to despair! Come, O *Harrington!* be a friend, a protector, a brother—be him, on whom I could never yet call by the tender, the endearing title of *parent.* I will reverence him in whom all the charities of life are united—I will be dutiful and affectionate to you, and you shall be unto me as a father— I will bend on the knee of respect and love, and will receive your blessing.

WHY did you go away so soon? Why leave me when I was incapable of bidding you adieu? When you pressed my cheek with the kiss of love, of fraternal affection, what meant its conscious glow? What meant the ebullition of my veins, the disorder of my nerves, the intoxication of my brain, the blood that mantled in my heart? My hand trembled, and every object seemed to swim before my doubtful view—Amidst the struggle of passion, how could I pronounce the word—how could I call you by the title of brother. True—I attempted to articulate the sound, but it died upon my tongue, and I sank motionless into your arms.

——ALLIED by birth, and in mind, and similar in age—and in thought still more intimately connected, the sympathy which bound our souls together, at first sight, is less extraordinary. Shall we any longer wonder at its irresistible impulse?—Shall we strive to oppose the *link of nature* that draws us to each other? When I reflect on this, I relapse into weakness and tenderness, and become a prey to warring passions.

I view you in two distinct characters: If I indulge the idea of one, the other becomes annihilated, and I vainly imagine I have my choice of a brother or———

I AM for a while calm—but alas! how momentary is that calmness; I dwell with rapture on what fancy has represented; but is the choice regulated by virtue? Is it prompted by reason? I recollect myself, and endeavour to rouse my prudence and fortitude; I abhor my conduct, and wish for obscurity and forgetfulness. Who can bear the torment of fluctuating passion? How deplorable is the contest? The head and the heart are at variance, but when Nature pleads, how feeble is the voice of Reason? Yet, when Reason is heard in her turn, how criminal appears every wish of my heart? What remorse do I experience? What horrours surround me? Will my feeble frame, already wasted by a lingering decline, support these evils? Will the shattered, frail bark outride the tempest, and will the waves of affliction beat in vain? Virtue, whose precepts I have not forgotten, will assist me—if not to *surmount,* at least to *suffer* with fortitude and patience.

OH! I fear, I fear my decaying health—If I must depart, let me beseech you to forget me—I know the strength of your passion, and I dread the fatal consequences my departure may occasion you.

ONCE more let me intreat you, my dear friend, to arm yourself with every virtue which is capable of sustaining the heaviest calamity. Let the impetuosity of the lover's passion be forgotten in the undisturbed quietness of the brother's affection, and may all the blessings that life can supply be yours—Seek for content, and you will find it, even though we should never meet again in this world.

ADIEU!

LETTER LI.

MYRA *to* Mrs. HOLMES.

BOSTON.

THE curtain is dropped, and the scene of life is forever closed—THE LOVELY HARRIOT IS NO MORE.

SHE is fit to appear in Heaven, for her life was a scene of purity and

innocence—If there is any consolation to be felt by a survivor, it is in the reflection of the amiable qualities of the deceased. My heart shall not cease to cherish her idea, for she was beautiful without artifice, and virtuous without affectation.

> See! there all pale and dead she lies;
> Forever flow my streaming eyes——
> There dwelt the fairest—lovliest mind,
> Faith, sweetness, wit together join'd.
> Dwelt faith and wit and sweetness there?
> O! view the change, and drop a tear.

MY brother is exceedingly agitated—He will never support this disastrous stroke—Nothing can attract his attention—nothing allay his grief—but it is the affliction of reason and not of weakness——God grant that it prove not fatal to him.

ADIEU!—ADIEU!—

LETTER LII.

HARRINGTON *to* WORTHY.

BOSTON.

SHE is gone—she is dead—she who was the most charming, the most gentle, is gone—You may come—you may desire to behold all that was lovely—but your eyes will not see her.

YES! I raved—I was distracted—but now I am calm and dispassionate—I am smooth as the surface of a lake—I shall see her again.

WHEN our spirits are disencumbered of this load of mortality, and they wing their flight to the celestial regions, shall we not then know those who were dear to us in this world? Shall we not delight in their society, as we have done in this state of existence? Yes—certainly we shall—we shall find them out in Heaven—there alone is happiness—there shall I meet her—there our love will not be a crime—Let me indulge this thought—it gives a momentary joy to my heart—it removes the dark mist that swims before my eyes—it restores tranquillity; but

the more I reflect on this thought—the more I long to be there—the
more I detest this world and all it contains. I sigh to fly away from it.

LETTER LIII.

HARRINGTON *to* WORTHY.

<div align="right">BOSTON.</div>

INGRATITUDE is a predominant principle in the conduct of man. The
perfidious——, who owes to me his reputation and fortune, and with
whom I intrusted a great part of my property, has deceived me. This
affair will materially retard my business.

TO be unfortunate in trade is not worth a sigh—to receive inattention
and incivility does not merit a frown; but *Ingratitude*—it is this that
cuts to the quick. Yet I freely give him my pity; for what man, who
considered for a moment the inconsistency of the human heart, would
hurl the thunderbolt of indignation at the head of an ingrate? What an
important little thing is man! he contrives to overreach his neighbour,
and mount to the enjoyment of riches, ambition and splendour; but
remembers not the period of enjoyment—that his life is a day, and his
space a point!

NATURALISTS inform us of insects whose term of existence is confined
to a few hours—What is the business and importance of such a life?

WOULD not a being, whose *circle of living* is immensity of ages, in-
quire with equal propriety, "What is the importance of *man*—What
actions can he perform—What happiness can he enjoy, whose insignif-
icant life is circumscribed to seventy years?"——In this point of view I
behold the tinsel, the vanity and noise of the world, and the little plots
and cunning artifices of mankind to cheat and ruin one another.

INGRATITUDE, then, is constitutional, and inseparable from human
nature, but it ought not to fill us with surprize, because it is no new
discovery—It has ever been invariably the characteristick of man. Is not
the page of antiquity distained with the blood of those who ought to
have received honour and adoration? Behold the brilliant race of the
world's benefactors: Consider their benevolent actions, and regard their
ungrateful return—these benefactors, who have been sent from heaven
to inform and entertain mankind, to defend the world from the arm of

tyranny, and to open the gates of salvation, have been despised, and banished, and poisoned and crucified.

BEHOLD the support of the *Roman* power, the invincible *Belisarius!* who protected his country from the ravage of the *Huns,* and displayed the *Roman* eagle in every quarter of the globe! Behold him fall a sacrifice to malice, to faction and ingratitude! Behold him cast out by the country he had defended, and for which he had wasted his life to protect and honour, and left alone to deplore his unfortunate condition, when he was old, and blind, and naked and miserable!

UNFORTUNATE is the man who trusts his happiness to the precarious friendship of the world—I every day become more of a misanthrope, and see nothing to increase my desire of living, but your esteem and affection. I want advice, but am too proud to let the world know I am weak enough to be under obligation to any one else.

THAT you may never want friends or advice, is the sincere prayer of

YOUR &c.

LETTER LIV.

HARRINGTON *to* WORTHY.

BOSTON.

ALL the scenes of my past life return fresh upon my memory. I examine every circumstance as they pass in review before me—I see nothing to cause any disagreeable or unwelcome sensations—no terrour upbraids me—no reproaching conscience stings my bosom as I reflect on the actions that are past. With her I expected happiness—I have expected a vain thing—for there is none—She is gone—gone to a far country— she is preparing a place for me—a place of unutterable bliss—But ah! an immeasurable gulph lies between us—Who can tell the distance that separates us? What labour—what toil—what pain must be endured in traversing the thorny paths that lead to her blessed abode?—And will she not receive me into those happy regions with as much joy—with as sincere a welcome—if I cut short my journey?—And will not the Eternal Dispenser of Good, pardon the awful deed that frees me from this world of misery—the deed by which I obtrude myself into his divine presence?

WHY must I wait the lingering hand of the grisly messenger to summon me to the world above?

LETTER LV.

HARRINGTON *to* WORTHY.

<div align="right">BOSTON.</div>

AM I a child that I should weep?—I have been meditating on the cause of my calamities—Why did my father love *Maria*—or rather, why did I love their *Harriot*? Curse on this tyrant custom that dooms such helpless children to oblivion or infamy! Had I known her to have been my sister, my love would have been regular—I should have loved her as a sister—I should have marked her beauty—I should have delighted in protecting it. I should have observed her growing virtues—I should have been happy in cherishing their growth. But alas! She is gone——and I cannot stay—I stand on the threshold of a vast eternity.

LETTER LVI.

HARRINGTON *to* WORTHY.

<div align="right">BOSTON.</div>

I AM determined to quit this life. I feel much easier since my determination. The step must not be taken with rashness. I must be steady—calm—collected—I will endeavour to be so.——

HER eager solicitation—the anxiety she always expressed for me————When I think she is no more, it wrings my heart with grief, and fills my eyes with tears——

——I MUST go——

THE idea chills me—I am frozen with horrour—cold damps hang on my trembling body—My soul is filled with a thousand troubled sensations——I must depart—it must be so—My love for thee, O

Harriot! is dearer than life—Thou hast first sat out—and I am to follow.——

WERE it possible that I *could live* with her, should I be happy? Would her presence restore peace and tranquillity to my disordered mind? Ah no! it never would *here*—it *never* would. I will fly to the place where she is gone—our love will there be refined—it will be freed from all criminality—I will lay my sorrows before her—and she shall wipe away all tears from my eyes.

WHEN the disembodied spirit flies above—when it leaves behind the senseless clay, and wings its flight—it matters not with me what they do with his remains.

Cover his head with a clod or a stone,
It is all one—it is all one!——

LETTER LVII.

HARRINGTON *to* WORTHY.

BOSTON.

THE longer I live, and the more I see of the misery of life—the more my desire of living is extinguished. What I formerly esteemed trifles, and would not deign to term misfortunes, now appear with a formidable aspect—though I once thought them harmless, and innoxious to my peace, they assume new terrours every day.—But is not this observation general? It is—It is thus every son of human nature, gradually wishes for death, and neglects to seek for, and improve those comforts, which by diligent search there is a possibility of attaining.

AM I to reason from analogy? I know what has been—the afflictions I have felt; but what is the prospect before me? The path is darkened by mists—

Puzzled in mazes, and perplex'd with errours—

Who is there hardy enough to try its difficulties? Is not the view horrible! My pains and anxieties have been severe—those, which, if I live, I shall suffer, may be yet more so—This idea sinks me to despair.

AS a thing becomes irksome to us, our detestation is always en-creased—Whatever object is disagreeable, we pine and sicken until it is moved out of sight. Life growing upon one in this manner—increasing in horrour—with continual apprehension of death—a certainty of sur-viving every enjoyment, and no prospect of being delivered from suspense—it is intolerable—he will assuredly be tempted to terminate the business with his own hand.

<p style="text-align:center">LETTER LVIII.</p>

WORTHY *to* HARRINGTON.

<p style="text-align:right">BELLEVIEW.</p>

You argue as if your reason were perverted—Let your mind be em-ployed, and time will wear out these gloomy ideas; for it is certainly a truth, that *the love of life increases with age*—Your letters, therefore, are predicated on the most erroneous principles.

REMEMBER the story of the old man, who had been buried in a dun-geon the greater part of his life, and who was liberated at an advanced age. He viewed, once more, the light of the sun, and the habitations of men—he had come into a new order of beings, but found their manners distasteful—In the midst of the sunshine of the world, he remembered the prison, where he had wasted his life, and he sighed to be again immured within its walls.

SUCH is our passion for life; we love it because we know it; and our attachment becomes the more riveted, the longer we are acquainted with it—Our prison grows familiar—we contemplate its horrours—but how-ever gloomy the walls that surround us, there is not one but sets a full value on his dreary existence—there is not one but finds his partiality for his dungeon increase, in proportion to the time he hath occupied it—for among the race of human beings confined to this narrow spot —how few are they who are hardy enough to break their prison?

LET us watch over all we do with an eye of scrutiny—the world will not examine the causes that give birth to our actions—they do not weigh the motives of them—they do not consider those things which influence our conduct—but as that conduct is more or less advantageous

to society, they deem it madness or wisdom, or folly or prudence—
Remember this——

<div align="right">ADIEU!</div>

LETTER LIX.

HARRINGTON *to* WORTHY.

<div align="right">BOSTON.</div>

You are egregiously mistaken, argue as you will.—My perceptions are
as clear as any one's—The burden that is at first heavy and inconve-
nient, galls us as we proceed—it soon becomes intolerable, we sink
under its weight, and lie gasping in the publick way long before night.

AS to the world—who strives to please it, will be deservedly
rewarded—he will reap his labour for his pains—Let it judge of my
conduct. I despise its opinion—*Independency of spirit* is my motto—I
think for myself.

LETTER LX.

HARRINGTON *to* WORTHY.

<div align="right">BOSTON.</div>

How vain is the wish that sighs for the enjoyment of worldly happi-
ness. Our imagination dresses up a phantom to impose on our reason:
As *Pygmalion* loved the work of his own hand—so do we fall in love
with the offspring of our brain. But our work illudes our embrace—we
find no substance in it—and then fall a weeping and complain of dis-
appointment. Miserable reasoners are we all.

WHY should I mourn the loss of *Harriot* any longer? Such is my
situation—in the midst of anxiety and distress, I complain of what can-
not be remedied.—I lament the loss of that which is irretrievable: So on

the sea-beat shore, the hopeless maid, unmindful of the storm, bewails her drowned lover.

LETTER LXI.

WORTHY *to* HARRINGTON.

BELLEVIEW.

I THANK you for your letters, but I wish you had something better for the subject of them—the sad repetition of your feelings and sorrows, pains me exceedingly—I promise to be with you soon—perhaps before you can receive this letter.

WHATEVER concerns my friend, most sensibly affects me—You, *Harrington,* are the friend of my heart, and nothing has so much grieved me as the story of your misfortunes.

IT is a maxim well received, and seems to be admitted an article in the moral creed of mankind, "that the enjoyments of life do not compensate the miseries." Since, then, we are born to suffer, and pain must attend us in all the stages of our journey, let us philosophically welcome our companion. The most eligible plan we can adopt, is to be contented in the condition that Providence hath assigned us. Let us trust that our burden will not be heavier than we can bear—When we adopt this plan, and are sensible we have this trust, our lesson is complete—we have learned all—we are arrived to the perfection of sublunary happiness.

DO not think I am preaching to you a mere sermon of morality—let me impress your mind with the folly of repining, and the blessing of a contented mind.

LET me intreat you not to puzzle your brain with vain speculations —if you are disposed to argue, do not put foolish cases that never existed—take the light of facts, and reason from them.

WHEN we are surrounded with the miseries of life—the baseness of false friends—the malice of enemies—when we are inveloped in those anxious fears, the result of too much sensibility, human nature feels a degree of oppression, which, without a manly exertion of reason and this practical philosophy, would be intolerable. I have heard you mention *St. Evremond,* as a philosopher of this kind. Arm yourself with his

prudence and fortitude—he, though in exile—though reduced almost
to penury, and labouring under the disadvantages of a bad constitution,
lived to be a very old man; he established a course of rational plea-
sures—for when the mind is employed, we regret the loss of time—we
become avaricious of life.

WHEN misfortunes come upon us without these consolations, it is
hard, I acknowledge, to buffet the storm—it is then human frailty is
most apparent—there is nothing left to hope—Reason is taken from
the helm of life—and Nature—helpless, debilitated Nature—lost to her-
self, and every social duty, splits upon the rocks of despair and suicide.
We have seen several examples of this—By exploring, and therefore
shunning the causes, let us avoid the catastrophe.

THE pensive and melancholy will muse over the ordinary accidents
of life, and swell them, by the power of imagination, to the heaviest
calamities. Hence we find a treacherous friend will sensibly affect some
men, and a capricious mistress will destroy a real lover: Hence people
in misfortune frequently construe the slightest inattention into neglect
and insult, and deem their best friends false and ungrateful. The sting
of ingratitude deeply pierces the heart of sensibility.

THE passions and affections which govern mankind are very incon-
sistent. Men, confined to the humble walks of life, sigh for the enjoy-
ment of wealth and power, which, when obtained, become loathsome
—The mind unaccustomed to such an easy situation, is discontented,
and longs to be employed in those things in which it was formerly
exercised.

THE greatest rulers and potentates become unhappy—they wish for
the charms of solitude and retirement, which, when attained, become
more irksome than their former condition—*Charles* the Fifth, of *Spain,*
resolved to taste the pleasures of a recluse life, by abdicating the
throne—he soon found his imagination had deceived him, and repented
of the step he had taken. This lazy life, when compared to the business
and grandeur of a court, became tasteless and insipid.—"The day," says
a historian, "he resigned his crown to his son, was the very day in which
he repented making him such a present."

IT is a great art to learn to be happy in the state in which we are
placed—I advise you to mingle in the concerns of your acquaintances
—be cheerful and undisturbed, nor give yourself up to those gloomy
ideas, which tend only to make you more wretched—If such obtrude
themselves, avoid being alone—I had rather be a dupe to my imagina-

tion than sacrifice an hour's easiness to my sensibility or understanding. Determine to be happy, and you will be so——

<div align="right">GOD BE WITH YOU!</div>

LETTER LXII.

HARRINGTON *to* WORTHY.

<div align="right">BOSTON.</div>

WHEN we seek for diversion in any place, and there is nothing to be found that we wish, it is certainly time to depart.

TOMORROW I go—There is nothing here that can calm the tumult of my soul—I fly from the sight of the human countenance—I fly from the face of day—I fly from books—Books that could always cheer me in a melancholy moment, are now terrifying—They recal scenes to my recollection that are past—pleasant scenes that I am never more to enjoy. They present pictures of futurity—of gloomy futurity—I just opened a book, and these are the words that I read:—"The time of my fading is near, and the blast that shall scatter my leaves. Tomorrow shall the traveller come, he that saw me in my beauty shall come; his eyes will search the field, but they will not find me."

THESE words pierce me to the quick—they are a dismal prospect of my approaching fate.

TOMORROW I shall go—But ah! whither?——

O! MY friend, when we find nothing we desire in this world, it is time to depart. To live is a disgrace—to die is a duty.

<div align="right">FAREWEL!</div>

LETTER LXIII.

WORTHY *to Mrs.* HOLMES.

BOSTON.

I ARRIVED in town last evening—you desired me to write you a statement of affairs as I should find them here—and of my marriage with the amiable *Myra*—I promised to obey—but how little do we know of the termination or consequence of the most probable event!

I SAW my beloved—her eyes were yet heavy and smarting with weeping for the death of *Harriot*—and *this,* once the house of joy and cheerfulness, is turned into the house of mourning. My unfortunate friend had just then fallen into a calm sleep, and it was impossible to see him—it was what I very much desired—but it was the wish of the family that I should desist for the present—he had not slept the evening before—he had been heard walking across his chamber all the night, with little intermission, oftentimes talking to himself in a passionate tone of voice.

THIS melancholy account deeply affected me—and I parted from my beloved, praying Heaven to give her consolation, and to be the support of my disordered friend.

IT is with difficulty I bring myself to the serious and painful employment of being the informer of unwelcome tidings—my heart feels the wound—vainly it tells me my friend is no more—my hand reluctantly traces—my friend—my *Harrington* is no more.

EARLY this morning I was surprised with a visit from a gentleman, whom I had formerly seen at *Myra*'s—it was the same neighbour who informed *Harrington* of his affinity to *Harriot*—he found a difficulty in his utterance—he told me, with trembling lips, my young friend *Harrington* was dead—"He has killed himself," said I—he asked me if I had heard the news—I told him my heart presaged it.

WHEN any uncommon event happens to us, we often have a presentiment of it—The circumstances of his death are these:—At midnight the gentleman heard the report of the pistol, and went into the house —he found the unhappy youth weltering in his blood—few signs of life remained—the ball had entered his brain—the surgeon came, but in a few hours he was cold. A few friends were requested to attend—and this gentleman had called upon me, by desire of *Myra*.

IT is not possible to describe the distress of the family and connexions—I shall leave it to your imagination.

A LETTER that he had written for me, laid unsealed upon the table, and *The Sorrows of Werter* was found lying by its side. I send you the letter—it appears to have been written at intervals, and expresses the disorder and agitation of his mind.

ADIEU!

LETTER LXIV.

HARRINGTON *to* WORTHY.

HARRIOT is dead—and the world to me is a dreary desert—I prepare to leave it—the fatal pistol is charged—it lies on the table by me, ready to perform its duty—but that duty is delayed till I take my last farewel of the best of friends.

YOUR letter is written with the impetuosity of an honest heart; it expresses great sincerity and tenderness.

I THANK you for all your good advice—it comes too late——O *Worthy!* she is dead—she is gone—never to return, never again to cheer my heart with her smiles and her amiable manners—her image is always before me—and can I forget her?—No!—She is continually haunting my mind, impressing the imagination with ideas of excellence—but she is dead—all that delighted me is become torpid—is descended into the cold grave.

- - - - With thee
Certain my resolution is to die;
How can I live without thee—how forego
Thy converse sweet, and love so dearly join'd,
To live again in these wild woods forlorn?
- -
- - - - loss of thee
Will never from my heart—no! no!—I feel
The link of nature draw me.
- - - - From thy state
Mine never shall be parted, bliss or woe.

THOU hast sat out on a long journey—but you shall not go alone—
I hasten to overtake thee. My resolution is not to be diverted—is not
to be shaken—I will not be afraid—I am inexorable——

——I HAVE just seen my father—he is dejected—sullen grief is fixed
on his brow—he tells me I am very ill—I looked at *Myra*—she wiped
her face with her handkerchief—perhaps they did not imagine this was
the last time they were to behold me.

SHE mentioned the name of *Worthy,* but my thoughts were differ-
ently engaged. She repeated your name, but I took no heed of it.——
Take her, my *Worthy*—*Myra* is a good girl—take her—comfort her.
Let not my departure interrupt your happiness—perhaps it may for a
short time. When the grass is grown over my grave, lead her to it, in
your pensive walks—point to the spot where my ashes are deposited—
drop one tear on the remembrance of a friend, of a brother—but I
cannot allow you to be grieved—grieve for me! Wretch that I am—
why do I delay——

——I WISH I could be buried by the side of her, then should the
passenger who knows the history of our unfortunate loves, say—"Here
lies *Harrington* and his *Harriot*—in their lives they loved, but were
unhappy—in death they sleep undivided."—Guardian spirits will pro-
tect the tomb which conceals her body—the body where every virtue
delighted to inhabit.——

DO not judge too rashly of my conduct—let me pray you to be
candid—I have taken advantage of a quiet moment, and written an
Epitaph—If my body were laid by her's, the inscription would be per-
tinent. Let no one concerned be offended at the moral I have chosen to
draw from our unfortunate story.

——MY heart sinks within me—the instrument of death is before
me—farewel! farewel!—My soul sighs to be freed from its confine-
ment—Eternal Father! accept my spirit——Let the tears of sorrow blot
out my guilt from the book of thy wrath.

LETTER LXV.

WORTHY *to Mrs.* HOLMES.

BOSTON.

WE have surmounted the performance of the last scene of our tragedy, with less difficulty and distress than I imagined. Great numbers crouded to see the body of poor *Harrington;* they were impressed with various emotions, for their sympathizing sorrow could not be concealed—Indeed a man without sensibility exhibits no sign of a soul. I was struck with admiration at the observations of the populace, and the justness of the character they drew of the deceased. "Alas!" said one—"poor youth, thou art gone. Thou wast of a promising genius, of violent passions, thou wast possessed of a too nice sensibility, and a dread of shame. It is only such an one who would take the trouble to kill himself. Ah! poor well natured, warm hearted, hot headed youth—how my heart bleeds for you! We consider thee as the dupe of Nature, and the sacrifice of Seduction."—The old father hears this, and becomes overwhelmed with shame and sorrow.

THE jury which sat upon the body of our friend, after mature consideration, brought in their verdict SUICIDE. The rigour of the law was not executed—the body was privately taken away, and I saw it deposited by the side of his faithful *Harriot.*

I SEND you inclosed a copy of the Monumental Inscription, as written by *Harrington.* I found it with many loose papers. It contains the story of our unfortunate friends, and a profitable moral is deduced from it.

THOUGH a few weeks begin to spread a calm over our passions, yet the recollection of our misfortunes will sometimes cause a momentary agitation, as the ocean retains its swell, after the storm subsides.

ADIEU!

Monumental Inscription.

THOU who shalt wander o'er these humble plains,
Where one kind grave their hapless dust contains,
O pass not on—if merit claim a tear,
Or dying virtue cause a sigh sincere.
Here rest their heads, consign'd to parent earth,

Who to one common father ow'd their birth;
Unknown this union—Nature still presides,
And Sympathy unites, whom Fate divides.
They see—they love—but heav'n their passion
 tries,
Their *love* sustains it, but their *mortal* dies.
Stranger! contemplate well before you part,
And take this serious counsel to thy heart:
Does some fair female of unspotted fame,
Salute thee, smiling, with a father's name,
Bid her detest the fell Seducer's wiles,
Who smiles to win—and murders as he smiles.
If ever wandering near this dark recess,
Where guardian spirits round the ether press;
Where, on their urn, celestial care descends,
Two lovers come, whom fair success attends,
"O'er the pale marble shall they join their heads,
"And drink the falling tears each other sheds,
"Then sadly say, with mutual pity mov'd,
"*O! may we never love as these have lov'd.*"

The END.

THE

COQUETTE;

OR, THE HISTORY OF ELIZA WHARTON;

A

NOVEL;

FOUNDED ON FACT.

By a Lady of Massachusetts.

THE

COQUETTE;

OR, THE

HISTORY OF ELIZA WHARTON;

A

NOVEL;

FOUNDED ON FACT.

By a LADY of MASSACHUSETTS.

[Hannah Foster]

Boston:

PRINTED BY SAMUEL ETHERIDGE,
FOR E. LARKIN,
No. 47, CORNHILL.

1797.

[TITLE PAGE OF THE FIRST EDITION OF 1797]

to Miss LUCY FREEMAN.

<div align="right">NEW-HAVEN.</div>

AN unusual sensation possesses my breast; a sensation, which I once thought could never pervade it on any occasion whatever. It is *pleasure*; pleasure, my dear Lucy, on leaving my paternal roof! Could you have believed that the darling child of an indulgent and dearly beloved mother would feel a gleam of joy at leaving her? but so it is. The melancholy, the gloom, the condolence, which surrounded me for a month after the death of Mr. Haly, had depressed my spirits, and palled every enjoyment of life. Mr. Haly was a man of worth; a man of real and substantial merit. He is therefore deeply, and justly regreted by *his* friends; he was chosen to be a future guardian, and companion for me, and was, therefore, beloved by *mine*. As their choice; as a good man, and a faithful friend, I esteemed him. But no one acquainted with the disparity of our tempers and dispositions, our views and designs, can suppose my heart much engaged in the alliance. Both nature and education had instilled into my mind an implicit obedience to the will and desires of my parents. To them, of course, I sacrificed my fancy in this affair; determined that my reason should concur with theirs; and on that to risk my future happiness. I was the more encouraged, as I saw, from our first acquaintance, his declining health; and expected, that the event would prove as it has. Think not, however, that I rejoice in his death. No; far be it from me; for though I believe that I never felt the passion of love for Mr. Haly; yet a habit of conversing with him, of hearing daily the most virtuous, tender, and affectionate sentiments from his lips, inspired emotions of the sincerest friendship, and esteem.

He is gone. His fate is unalterably, and I trust, happily fixed. He lived the life, and died the death of the righteous. O that my last end may be like his! This event will, I hope, make a suitable and abiding impression upon my mind; teach me the fading nature of all sublunary enjoyments, and the little dependence which is to be placed on earthly felicity. Whose situation was more agreeable; whose prospects more flattering, than Mr. Haly's? Social, domestic, and connubial joys were

fondly anticipated, and friends, and fortune seemed ready to crown every wish! Yet animated by still brighter hopes, he cheerfully bid them all adieu. In conversation with me, but a few days before his exit; "There is" said he, "but one link in the chain of life, undissevered; that, my dear Eliza, is my attachment to you. But God is wise and good in all his ways; and in this, as in all other respects, I would cheerfully say, His will be done."

You, my friend, were witness to the concluding scene; and therefore, I need not describe it.

I shall only add, on the subject, that if I have wisdom and prudence to follow his advice and example; if his prayers for my temporal and eternal welfare be heard and answered, I shall be happy indeed.

The disposition of mind, which I now feel, I wish to cultivate. Calm, placid, and serene; thoughtful of my duty, and benevolent to all around me, I wish for no other connection than that of friendship,

This Letter is all egotism, I have even neglected to mention the respectable, and happy friends, with whom I reside; but will do it in my next. Write soon, and often; and believe me sincerely yours,

ELIZA WHARTON.

LETTER II.

to the same

NEW-HAVEN.

TIME, which effaces every occasional impression, I find gradually dispelling the pleasing pensiveness, which the melancholy event, the subject of my last, had diffused over my mind. Naturally cheerful, volatile, and unreflecting, the opposite disposition, I have found to contain sources of enjoyment, which I was before unconscious of possessing.

My friends, here, are the picture of conjugal felicity. The situation is delightful. The visiting parties perfectly agreeable. Every thing tends to facilitate the return of my accustomed vivacity. I have written to my mother, and received an answer. She praises my fortitude, and admires the philosophy which I have exerted, under, what she calls, my heavy bereavement. Poor woman! She little thinks that my heart was un-

touched; and when that is unaffected, other sentiments and passions make but a transient impression. I have been, for a month or two, excluded from the gay world; and, indeed, fancied myself soaring above it. It is now that I begin to descend, and find my natural propensity for mixing in the busy scenes and active pleasures of life returning. I have received your letter; your moral lecture rather; and be assured, my dear, your monitorial lessons and advice shall be attended to. I believe I shall never again resume those airs, which you term *coquettish*, but which I think deserve a softer appellation; as they proceed from an innocent heart, and are the effusions of a youthful, and cheerful mind. We are all envited to spend the day, to morrow, at Col. Farington's, who has an elegant seat in this neighbourhood. Both he and his Lady are strangers to me; but the friends, by whom I am introduced, will procure me a welcome reception. Adieu. *optimism*

ELIZA WHARTON.

LETTER III.

to the same.

NEW-HAVEN.

Is it time for me to talk again of conquests? or must I only enjoy them in silence? I must write to you the impulses of my mind; or I must not write at all. You are not so morose, as to wish me to become a nun, would our country, and religion allow it. I ventured yesterday to throw aside the habiliments of mourning, and to array myself in those more adapted to my taste. We arrived at Col. Farington's about one o'clock. The Col. handed me out of the carriage, and introduced me to a large company assembled in the Hall. My name was pronounced with an *emphasis;* and I was received with the most flattering tokens of respect. *brag* When we were summoned to dinner, a young gentleman in a clerical dress offered me his hand, and led me to a table furnished with an elegant, and sumptuous repast, with more gallantry, and address than commonly fall to the share of students. He sat opposite me at table; and whenever I raised my eye, it caught his. The ease, and politeness of his manners, with his particular attention to me, raised my curiosity, and

induced me to ask Mrs. Laiton who he was? She told me that his name was Boyer; that he was descended from a worthy family; had passed with honor and applause through the university where he was educated; had since studied divinity with success; and now had a call to settle as a minister in one of the first parishes in a neighbouring state.

The gates of a spacious garden were thrown open, at this instant; and I accepted with avidity an invitation to walk in it. Mirth, and hilarity prevailed, and the moments fled on downy wings; while we traced the beauties of art and nature, so liberally displayed, and so happily blended in this delightful retreat. An enthusiastic admirer of scenes like these, I had rambled some way from the company, when I was followed by Mrs. Laiton to offer her condolence on the supposed loss, which I had sustained, in the death of Mr. Haly. My heart rose against the woman, so ignorant of human nature, as to think such conversation acceptable at such a time. I made her little reply, and waved the subject, though I could not immediately dispel the gloom which it excited.

The absurdity of a custom, authorising people at a first interview to revive the idea of griefs, which time has lulled, perhaps obliterated, is intolerable. To have our enjoyments arrested by the empty compliments of unthinking persons, for no other reason, than a compliance with fashion is to be treated in a manner, which the laws of humanity forbid.

We were soon joined by the gentlemen, who each selected his partner, and the walk was prolonged.

Mr. Boyer offered me his arm, which I gladly accepted; happy to be relieved from the impertinence of my female companion. We returned to tea, after which the ladies sung, and played by turns on the Piano Forte; while some of the gentlemen accompanied with the flute, the clarinet, and the violin, forming in the whole a very decent concert. An elegant supper, and half an hour's conversation after it, closed the evening; when we returned home, delighted with our entertainment and pleased with ourselves and each other. My imagination is so impressed with the festive scenes of the day, that Morpheus waves his ebon-wand in vain. The evening is fine beyond the power of description! all nature is serene and harmonious; in perfect unison with my present disposition of mind. I have been taking a retrospect of my past life; and a few juvenile follies excepted, which I trust the recording angel has blotted out with the tear of charity, find an approving conscience, and a heart at ease. Fortune, indeed, has not been very liberal of her gifts to me; but I presume on a large stock in the bank of friendship, which, united

with health and innocence, give me some pleasing anticipations of future felicity.

Whatever my fate may be, I shall always continue your

ELIZA WHARTON.

LETTER IV.

to Mr. SELBY.

NEW-HAVEN.

You ask me, my friend, whether I am in pursuit of truth, or a lady? I answer, both. I hope and trust they are united; and really expect to find truth and the virtues and graces besides in a fair form. If you mean by the first part of your question, whether I am searching into the sublimer doctrines of religion? To these I would by no means be inattentive; but to be honest, my studies of that kind have been very much interrupted of late. The respectable circle of acquaintances with which I am honored here, has rendered my visits very frequent and numerous. In one of these I was introduced to Miss Eliza Wharton; a young lady whose elegant person, accomplished mind, and polished manners have been much celebrated. Her fame has often reached me; but, as the queen of Sheba said to Solomon, the half was not told me. You will think, that I talk in the style of a lover. I confess it, nor am I ashamed to rank myself among the professed admirers of this lovely fair one. I am in no danger, however, of becoming an enthusiastic devotee. No, I mean to act upon just and rational principles. Expecting soon to settle in an eligible situation, if such a companion as I am persuaded she will make me, may fall to my lot, I shall deem myself as happy as this state of imperfection will admit. She is now resident at Gen. Richman's. The general and his lady are her particular friends. They are warm in her praises. They tell me, however, that she is naturally of a gay disposition. No matter for that; it is an agreeable quality, where there is discretion sufficient for its regulation. A cheerful friend, much more a cheerful wife is peculiarly necessary to a person of a studious and sedentary life. They dispel the gloom of retirement, and exhilerate the spirits depressed by intense ap-

plication. She was formerly addressed by the late Mr. Haly of Boston. He was not, it seems, the man of her choice; but her parents were extremely partial to him, and wished the connection to take place. She, like a dutiful child, sacrificed her own inclination to their pleasure, so far as to acquiesce in his visits. This she more easily accomplished, as his health, which declined from their first acquaintance, led her to suppose, as the event has proved, that he would not live to enter into any lasting engagements. Her father, who died some months before him, invited him to reside at his house, for the benefit of a change of air, agreeably to the advice of his physicians. She attended him during his last illness, with all the care and assiduity of a nurse; and with all the sympathising tenderness of a sister.

I have had several opportunities of conversing with her. She discovers an elevated mind, a ready apprehension, and an accurate knowledge of the various subjects which have been brought into view. I have not yet introduced the favorite subject of my heart. Indeed she seems studiously to avoid noticing any expression which leads towards it. But she must hear it soon. I am sure of the favor and interest of the friends with whom she resides. They have promised to speak previously in my behalf. I am to call as if accidentally this afternoon, just as they are to ride abroad. They are to refer me to Miss Wharton for entertainment, till their return. What a delightful opportunity for my purpose! I am counting the hours, nay, the very moments. Adieu. You shall soon hear again from your most obedient,

J. BOYER.

LETTER V.

to Miss LUCY FREEMAN.

NEW-HAVEN.

THESE bewitching charms of mine have a tendency to keep my mind in a state of perturbation. I am so pestered with these admirers; not that I am so very handsome neither; but I don't know how it is, I am certainly very much the taste of the other sex. Followed, flattered, and caressed; I have cards and compliments in profusion. But I must try to

be serious; for I have, alas! one serious lover. As I promised you to be particular in my writing, I suppose I must proceed methodically. Yesterday we had a party to dine. Mr. Boyer was of the number. His attention was immediately engrossed; and I soon perceived that every word, every action, and every look was studied to gain my approbation. As he sat next me at dinner, his assiduity and politeness were pleasing; and as we walked together afterwards, his conversation was improving. Mine was sentimental and sedate; perfectly adapted to the taste of my gallant. Nothing, however, was said particularly expressive of his apparent wishes. I studiously avoided every kind of discourse which might lead to this topic. I wish not for a declaration from any one, especially from one whom I could not repulse and do not intend to encourage at present. His conversation, so similar to what I had often heard from a similar character, brought a deceased friend to mind, and rendered me somewhat pensive. I retired directly after supper. Mr. Boyer had just taken leave.

Mrs. Richman came into my chamber as she was passing to her own. Excuse my intrusion, Eliza, said she; I thought I would just step in and ask you if you have passed a pleasant day?

Perfectly so, madam; and I have now retired to protract the enjoyment by recollection. What, my dear, is your opinion of our favorite Mr. Boyer? Declaring him your favorite, madam, is sufficient to render me partial to him. But to be frank, independent of that, I think him an agreeable man. Your heart, I presume, is now free? Yes, and I hope it will long remain so. Your friends, my dear, solicitous for your welfare, wish to see you suitably and agreeably connected. I hope my friends will never again interpose in my concerns of that nature. You, madam, who have ever known my heart, are sensible, that had the Almighty spared life, in a certain instance, I must have sacrificed my own happiness, or incurred their censure. I am young, gay, volatile. A melancholy event has lately extricated me from those shackles, which parental authority had imposed on my mind. Let me then enjoy that freedom which I so highly prize. Let me have opportunity, unbiassed by opinion, to gratify my natural disposition in a participation of those pleasures which youth and innocence afford. Of such pleasures, no one, my dear, would wish to deprive you. But beware, Eliza!—Though strowed with flowers, when contemplated by your lively imagination, it is, after all, a slippery, thorny path. The round of fashionable dissipation is dangerous. A phantom is often pursued, which leaves its deluded votary the real form of wretchedness. She spoke with an emphasis, and taking up

her candle, wished me a good night. I had not power to return the compliment. Something seemingly prophetic in her looks and expressions, cast a momentary gloom upon my mind! But I despise those contracted ideas which confine virtue to a cell. I have no notion of becoming a recluse. Mrs. Richman has ever been a beloved friend of mine; yet I always thought her rather prudish. Adieu,

ELIZA WHARTON.

LETTER VI.

to the same.

NEW-HAVEN.

I HAD scarcely seated myself at the breakfast table this morning, when a servant entered with a card of invitation from Major Sanford, requesting the happiness of my hand this evening, at a ball, given by Mr. Atkins, about three miles from this. I shewed the billet to Mrs. Richman, saying, I have not much acquaintance with this gentleman, madam; but I suppose his character sufficiently respectable to warrant an affirmative answer. He is a gay man, my dear, to say no more, and such are the companions we wish, when we join a party avowedly formed for pleasure. I then stepped into my apartment, wrote an answer, and dispatched the servant. When I returned to the parlour, something disapprobating appeared in the countenances of both my friends. I endeavoured without seeming to observe, to dissipate it by chit chat; but they were better pleased with each other than with me; and soon rising, walked into the garden, and left me to amuse myself alone. My eyes followed them through the window. Happy pair, said I. Should it ever be my fate to wear the hymenial chain, may I be thus united! The purest and most ardent affection, the greatest consonance of taste and disposition, and the most congenial virtue and wishes distinguish this lovely couple. Health and wealth, with every attendant blessing preside over their favored dwelling, and shed their benign influence without alloy. The consciousness of exciting their displeasure gave me pain; but I consoled myself with the idea that it was ill founded.

They should consider, said I, that they have no satisfaction to look for beyond each other.

There every enjoyment is centered; but I am a poor solitary being, who need some amusement beyond what I can supply myself. The mind, after being confined at home for a while, sends the imagination abroad in quest of new treasures, and the body may as well accompany it, for ought I can see.

General Richman and lady have ever appeared solicitous to promote my happiness since I have resided with them. They have urged my acceptance of invitations to join parties, though they have not been much themselves, of late; as Mrs. Richman's present circumstances render her fond of retirement. What reason can be assigned for their apparent reluctance to this evening's entertainment is to me incomprehensible; but I shall apply the chymical powers of friendship and extract the secret from Mrs. Richman to morrow, if not before. Adieu. I am now summoned to dinner, and after that shall be engaged in preparation till the wished for hour of hilarity and mirth engrosses every faculty of your

ELIZA WHARTON.

LETTER VII.

to Mr. SELBY.

NEW-HAVEN.

DIVINES need not declaim, nor philosophers expatiate on the disappointments of human life! Are they not legibly written on every page of our existence? Are they not predominantly prevalent over every period of our lives?

When I closed my last letter to you, my heart exulted in the pleasing anticipation of promised bliss; my wishes danced on the light breezes of hope, and my imagination dared to arrest the attention, and even claim a return of affection from the lovely Eliza Wharton! But imagination only, it has proved; and that dashed with the bitter ranklings of jealousy and suspicion.

But to resume my narrative. I reached the mansion of my friend about four. I was disagreeably struck with the appearance of a carriage

at the door, as it raised an idea of company which might frustrate my plan; but still more disagreeable were my sensations, when, on entering the parlour, I found Major Sanford evidently in a waiting posture. I was very politely received; and when Eliza entered the room with a brilliance of appearance and gaiety of manner, which I had never before connected with her character, I rose, as did Major Sanford who offered his hand, and led her to a chair. I forgot to sit down again, but stood transfixed by the pangs of disappointment. Miss Wharton appeared somewhat confused; but soon resuming her vivacity, desired me to be seated; inquired after my health, and made some common place remarks on the weather. Then apologizing for leaving me, gave her hand again to Major Sanford, who had previously risen, and reminded her that the time and their engagements made it necessary to leave the good company; which, indeed, they both appeared very willing to do. General Richman and lady took every method in their power to remove my chagrin, and atone for the absence of my fair one, but ill did they succeed. They told me that Miss Wharton had not the most distant idea of my visiting there, this afternoon; much less of the design of my visit; that for some months together, she had been lately confined by the sickness of Mr. Haly, whom she attended during the whole of his last illness; which confinement had eventually increased her desire of indulging her natural disposition for gaiety. She had, however, they said, an excellent heart and reflecting mind, a great share of sensibility, and a temper peculiarly formed for the enjoyments of social life. But this gentleman, madam, who is her gallant this evening—is his character unexceptionable? Will a lady of delicacy associate with an immoral, not to say profligate man? The rank and fortune of Major Sanford, said Mrs. Richman, procure him respect.

His specious manners render him acceptable in public company; but I must own that he is not the person with whom I wish my cousin to be connected, even for a moment. She never consulted me so little on any subject as on that of his card this morning. Before I had time to object, she dismissed the servant; and I forbore to destroy her expected happiness, by acquainting her with my disapprobation of her partner. Her omission was not design; it was juvenile indiscretion. We must, my dear sir, continued she, look with a candid eye on such excentricities. Faults, not foibles, require the severity of censure. Far, madam, be it from me to censure any conduct, which as yet I have observed in Miss Wharton; she has too great an interest in my heart to admit of that.

We now went into more general conversation. Tea was served; and

I soon after took leave. General Richman, however, insisted on my din-
ing with him on Thursday, which I promised. And here I am again over
head and ears in the hypo. A disease, you will say, peculiar to students.
I believe it peculiar to lovers; and with that class I must now rank
myself, though I did not know, until this evening, that I was so much
engaged as I find I really am. I knew, indeed, that I was extremely
pleased with this amiable girl; that I was interested in her favor; that I
was happier in her company than any where else, with innumerable
other circumstances, which would have told me the truth, had I ex-
amined them. But be that as it may; I hope, and trust that I am, and
ever shall be a reasonable creature; and not suffer my judgment to be
misled by the operations of a blind passion.

I shall now lay aside this subject, endeavor to divest even my imag-
ination of the charmer, and return until Thursday, to the contemplation
of those truths and duties, which have a happy tendency to calm the
jarring elements which compose our mortal frame. Adieu.

<div align="right">J. BOYER.</div>

LETTER VIII.

to Mr. CHARLES DEIGHTON.

<div align="right">NEW-HAVEN.</div>

WE had an elegant ball, last night, Charles; and what is still more to
the taste of your old friend, I had an elegant partner; one exactly cal-
culated to please my fancy; gay, volatile, apparently thoughtless of every
thing but present enjoyment. It was Miss Eliza Wharton, a young lady,
whose agreeable person, polished manners, and refined talents, have
rendered her the toast of the country around for these two years; though
for half that time she has had a clerical lover imposed on her by her
friends; for I am told it was not agreeable to her inclination. By this
same clerical lover of hers, she was for several months confined as a
nurse. But his death has happily relieved her, and she now returns to
the world with redoubled lustre. At present she is a visitor to Mrs.
Richman, who is a relation. I first saw her on a party of pleasure at Mr.
Frazier's where we walked, talked, sung, and danced together. I thought

her cousin watched her with a jealous eye; for she is, you must know, a prude; and immaculate, more so than you or I must be the man who claims admission to her society. But I fancy this young lady is a coquette; and if so, I shall avenge my sex, by retaliating the mischiefs, she meditates against us. Not that I have any ill designs; but only to play off her own artillery, by using a little unmeaning gallantry. And let her beware of the consequences. A young clergyman came in at Gen. Richman's yesterday, while I was waiting for Eliza, who was much more cordially received by the general and his lady, than was your humble servant: but I lay that up.

When she entered the room, an air of mutual embarrassment was evident. The lady recovered her assurance much more easily than the gentleman. I am just going to ride, and shall make it in my way to call and inquire after the health of my dulcinea. Therefore, adieu for the present.

PETER SANFORD.

LETTER IX.

to Miss LUCY FREEMAN.

NEW-HAVEN.

I AM not so happy to day in the recollection of last evening's entertainment, as I was in the enjoyment.

The explanation which I promised you from Mrs. Richman yesterday, I could not obtain. When I went down to dinner, some friends of General Richman's had accidentally dropped in, which precluded all particular conversation. I retired soon to dress, and saw Mrs. Richman no more, till I was informed that Major Sanford waited for me. But I was surprised on going into the parlour to find Mr. Boyer there. I blushed and stammered; but I know not why; for certain I am, that I neither love nor fear the good man yet, whatever I may do some future day. I would not be understood that I do not respect and esteem him; for I do both. But these are calm passions, which sooth rather than agitate the mind. It was not the consciousness of any impropriety of conduct; for I was far from feeling any. The entertainment for which I

was prepared was such as virtue would not disapprove, and my gallant was a man of fortune, fashion, and for ought I knew, of unblemished character.

But Mr. Boyer was much more disconcerted than myself. Indeed he did not recover his philosophy while I staid. I believe, by some hints I have received since, that he had some particular views, in which he was disappointed.

Our ball had every charm which could render a ball delightful. My partner was all ease, politeness, and attention; and your friend was as much flattered and caressed as variety itself could wish. We returned to General Richman's about two. Major Sanford asked leave to call and inquire after my health, this morning, and I am now expecting him. I rose to breakfast. The late hour of retiring to rest had not depressed, but rather exhilerated my spirits. My friends were waiting for me in the parlor. They received me sociably, inquired after my health, my last evening's entertainment, the company, &c. When, after a little pause, Mrs. Richman said, and how do you like Major Sanford, Eliza? Very well indeed, madam: I think him a finished gentleman. Will you, who are a connoisieur, allow him that title? No, my dear: in my opinion, he falls far below it; since he is deficient in one of the great essentials of the character, and that is, *virtue*. I am surprised, said I: but how has he incurred so severe a censure? By being a professed libertine; by having but too successfully practised the arts of seduction; by triumphing in the destruction of innocence and the peace of families!

O, why was I not informed of this before? But, perhaps, these are old affairs; the effects of juvenile folly; crimes of which he may have repented, and which charity ought to obliterate. No, my dear, they are recent facts; facts which he dares not deny; facts for which he ought to be banished from all virtuous society. I should have intimated this to you before, but your precipitate acceptance of his invitation deprived me of an opportunity, until it was too late to prevent your going with him; and we thought it best to protract your enjoyment as long as possible, not doubting but your virtue and delicacy would, in future, guard you against the like deception.

Must I then become an avowed prude at once; and refuse him admission, if he call, in compliance with the customary forms? By no means. I am sensible, that even the false maxims of the world must be complied with in a degree. But a man of Major Sanford's art can easily distinguish between a forbidding, and an encouraging reception. The former may, in this case, be given without any breach of the rules of

politeness. Astonished, and mortified, I knew not what further to say. I
had been so pleased with the man, that I wished to plead in his favor;
but virtue and prudence forbade. I therefore rose and retired. He is this
moment, I am told, below stairs. So that I must bid you adieu, until the
next post.

ELIZA WHARTON.

LETTER X.

to the same.

NEW-HAVEN.

UPON closing my last, I walked down, and found Major Sanford alone.
He met me at the door of the parlor; and taking my hand with an air
of affectionate tenderness, led me to a seat, and took one beside me. I
believe the gloom of suspicion had not entirely forsaken my brow. He
appeared, however, not to notice it; but after the compliments of the
day had passed, entered into an easy and agreeable conversation on the
pleasures of society: a conversation perfectly adapted to my taste, and
calculated to dissipate my chagrin, and pass the time imperceptibly. He
inquired the place of my native abode; and having informed him, he
said he had thoughts of purchasing the seat of Capt. Pribble, in that
neighborhood, for his residence; and could he be assured of my society
and friendship, his resolution would be fixed. I answered his compliment
only by a slight bow. He took leave, and I retired to dress for the day,
being engaged to accompany my cousin to dine at Mr. Laurence's, a
gentleman of fortune and fashion, in this vicinity. Mr. Laurence has but
one daughter, heiress to a large estate, with an agreeable form, but a
countenance, which to me, indicates not much soul. I was surprised in
the afternoon to see Major Sanford alight at the gate. He entered with
the familiarity of an old acquaintance; and, after accosting each of the
company, told me, with a low bow, that he did not expect the happiness
of seeing me again so soon. I received his compliment with a conscious
awkwardness. Mrs. Richman's morning lecture still rung in my head;
and her watchful eye now traced every turn of mine, and every action
of the major's. Indeed, his assiduity was painful to me; yet I found it

impossible to disengage myself a moment from him, till the close of the day brought our carriage to the door; when he handed me in, and pressing my hand to his lips, retired.

What shall I say about this extraordinary man? Shall I own to you, my friend, that he is pleasing to me? His person, his manners, his situation, all combine to charm my fancy; and to my lively imagination, strew the path of life with flowers. What a pity, my dear Lucy, that the graces and virtues are not oftner united! They must, however, meet in the man of my choice; and till I find such a one, I shall continue to subscribe my name

ELIZA WHARTON.

LETTER XI.

to Mr. CHARLES DEIGHTON.

NEW-HAVEN.

WELL, Charles, I have been manœuvring to day, a little revengefully. That, you will say, is out of character. So baleful a passion does not easily find admission among those softer ones, which you well know I cherish. However, I am a mere Proteus, and can assume any shape that will best answer my purpose.

I called this forenoon, as I told you I intended, at Gen. Richman's. I waited some time in the parlor alone, before Eliza appeared; and when she did appear, the distant reserve of her manners and the pensiveness of her countenance convinced me that she had been vexed, and I doubted not but Peter Sanford was the occasion. Her wise cousin, I could have sworn, had been giving her a detail of the vices of her gallant; and warning her against the danger of associating with him in future. Notwithstanding, I took no notice of any alteration in her behavior; but entered with the utmost facetiousness into a conversation which I thought most to her taste. By degrees, she assumed her usual vivacity; cheerfulness and good humor again animated her countenance. I tarried as long as decency would admit. She having intimated that they were to dine at my friend Lawrence's, I caught at this information; and de-

termined to follow them, and teaze the jealous Mrs. Richman, by playing off all the gallantry I was master of in her presence.

I went, and succeeded to the utmost of my wishes, as I read in the vexation, visible in the one; and the ease and attention displayed by the other. I believe too, that I have charmed the eye at least, of the amiable Eliza. Indeed, Charles, she is a fine girl. I think it would hurt my conscience to wound her mind or reputation. Were I disposed to marry, I am persuaded she would make an excellent wife; but that you know is no part of my plan, so long as I can keep out of the noose. Whenever I do submit to be shackled, it must be from a necessity of mending my fortune. This girl would be far from doing that. However, I am pleased with her acquaintance, and mean not to abuse her credulity and good nature, if I can help it.

PETER SANFORD.

LETTER XII.

to Miss LUCY FREEMAN.

NEW-HAVEN.

THE heart of your friend is again besieged. Whether it will surrender to the assailants or not, I am unable at present to determine. Sometimes I think of becoming a predestinarian, and submitting implicitly to fate, without any exercise of free will; but, as mine seems to be a wayward one, I would counteract the operations of it, if possible.

Mrs. Richman told me this morning, that she hoped I should be as agreeably entertained this afternoon, as I had been the preceding; that she expected Mr. Boyer to dine, and take tea; and doubted not but he would be as attentive and sincere to me, if not as gay and polite as the gentleman who obtruded his civilities yesterday. I replied that I had no reason to doubt the sincerity of the one, or the other, having never put them to the test, nor did I imagine I ever should. Your friends, Eliza, said she, would be very happy to see you united to a man of Mr. Boyer's worth; and so agreeably settled, as he has a prospect of being. I hope, said I, that my friends are not so weary of my company, as to wish to dispose of me. I am too happy in my present connections to quit them

for new ones. Marriage is the tomb of friendship. It appears to me a
very selfish state. Why do people, in general, as soon as they are married,
centre all their cares, their concerns, and pleasures in their own families?
former acquaintances are neglected or forgotten. The tenderest ties be-
tween friends are weakened, or dissolved; and benevolence itself moves
in a very limited sphere. It is the glory of the marriage state, she rejoined,
to refine, by circumscribing our enjoyments. Here we can repose in
safety.

> "The friendships of the world are oft
> Confed'racies in vice, or leagues in pleasure:
> Our's has the purest virtue for its basis;
> And such a friendship ends not but with life."

True, we cannot always pay that attention to former associates,
which we may wish; but the little community which we superintend is
quite as important an object; and certainly renders us more beneficial
to the public. True benevolence, though it may change its objects, is not
limited by time or place. Its effects are the same, and aided by a second
self, are rendered more diffusive and salutary.

Some pleasantry passed, and we retired to dress. When summoned
to dinner, I found Mr. Boyer below. If what is sometimes said be true,
that love is diffident, reserved, and unassuming, this man must be tinc-
tured with it. These symptoms were visible in his deportment when I
entered the room. However, he soon recovered himself, and the con-
versation took a general turn. The festive board was crowned with so-
ciability, and we found in reality, "The feast of reason, and the flow of
soul." After we rose from table, a walk in the garden was proposed, an
amusement we are all peculiarly fond of. Mr. Boyer offered me his arm.
When at a sufficient distance from our company, he begged leave to
congratulate himself on having an opportunity which he had ardently
desired for some time, of declaring to me his attachment; and of solic-
iting an interest in my favor; or, if he might be allowed the term, affec-
tion. I replied, that, Sir, is indeed laying claim to an important interest.
I believe you must substitute some more indifferent epithet for the pres-
ent. Well then, said he, if it must be so, let it be esteem, or friendship.
Indeed, Sir, said I, you are intitled to them both. Merit has always a
share in that bank; and I know of none, who has a larger claim on that
score, than Mr. Boyer. I suppose my manner was hardly serious enough
for what he considered a weighty cause. He was a little disconcerted;

but soon regaining his presence of mind, entreated me, with an air of earnestness, to encourage his suit, to admit his addresses, and, if possible, to reward his love. I told him, that this was rather a sudden affair to me; and that I could not answer him without consideration. Well then, said he, take what time you think proper, only relieve my suspense as soon as may be. Shall I visit you again to morrow? O, not so soon, said I. Next Monday, I believe will be early enough. I will endeavor to be at home. He thanked me even for that favor, recommended himself once more to my kindness; and we walked towards the company, returned with them to the house, and he soon took leave. I immediately retired to write this letter, which I shall close, without a single observation on the subject, until I know your opinion.

ELIZA WHARTON.

LETTER XIII.

to Miss ELIZA WHARTON.

HARTFORD.

And so you wish to have my opinion before you know the result of your own. This is playing a little too much with my patience. But, however, I will gratify you this once, in hopes that my epistle may have a good effect. You will ask, perhaps, whether I would influence your judgment? I answer, no; provided you will exercise it yourself: but I am a little apprehensive that your fancy will mislead you. Methinks I can gather from your letters, a predilection for this Major Sanford. But he is a rake, my dear friend; and can a lady of your delicacy and refinement, think of forming a connection with a man of that character? I hope not. Nay, I am confident you do not. You mean only to exhibit a few more girlish airs, before you turn matron. But I am persuaded, if you wish to lead down the dance of life with regularity, you will not find a more excellent partner than Mr. Boyer. Whatever you can reasonably expect in a lover, husband, or friend, you may perceive to be united in this worthy man. His taste is undebauched, his manners not vitiated, his morals uncorrupted. His situation in life is, perhaps, as elevated as you have a right to claim. Forgive my plainness, Eliza. It is the task of friend-

ship, sometimes to tell disagreeable truths. I know your ambition is to make a distinguished figure in the first class of polished society; to shine in the gay circle of fashionable amusements, and to bear off the palm amidst the votaries of pleasure. But these are fading honors, unsatisfactory enjoyments; incapable of gratifying those immortal principles of reason and religion, which have been implanted in your mind by nature; assiduously cultivated by the best of parents, and exerted, I trust, by yourself. Let me advise you then, in conducting this affair; an affair, big, perhaps, with your future fate, to lay aside those coquettish airs which you sometimes put on; and remember that you are not dealing with a fop, who will take advantage of every concession; but with a man of sense and honor, who will properly estimate your condescension, and frankness. Act then with that modest freedom, that dignified unreserve which bespeaks conscious rectitude and sincerity of heart.

I shall be extremely anxious to hear the process and progress of this business. Relieve my impatience, as soon as possible, and believe me yours, with undissembled affection.

LUCY FREEMAN.

LETTER XIV.

to Miss LUCY FREEMAN.

NEW-HAVEN.

I HAVE received, and read again and again, your friendly epistle. My reason and judgment entirely coincide with your opinion; but my fancy claims some share in the decision: and I cannot yet tell which will preponderate. This was the day fixed for deciding Mr. Boyer's cause. My friends here gave me a long dissertation on his merits. Your letter, likewise, had its weight, and I was candidly summing up the *pros* and *cons* in the garden, whither I had walked (Gen. Richman and lady having rode out) when I was informed that he was waiting in the parlor. I went immediately in (a good symptom, you will say) and received him very graciously. After the first compliments were over, he seemed eager to improve the opportunity to enter directly on the subject of his present visit. It is needless for me to recite to you, who have long been ac-

quainted with the whole process of courtship, the declarations, propositions, protestations, intreaties, looks, words and actions of a lover. They are, I believe, much the same, in the whole sex, allowing for their different dispositions, educations, and characters. But you are impatient I know for the conclusion. You have hastily perused the preceding lines, and are straining your eye forward to my part of the farce; for such it may prove after all. Well then, not to play too long with the curiosity, which I know to be excited, and actuated by real friendship, I will relieve it. I think you would have been pleased to have seen my gravity, on this important occasion. With all the candor and frankness which I was capable of assuming, I thus answered his long harangue, to which I had listened, without interrupting him. Self-knowledge, sir, that most important of all sciences, I have yet to learn. Such have been my situations in life, and the natural volatility of my temper, that I have looked but little into my own heart, in regard to its future wishes and views. From a scene of constraint and confinement, ill suited to my years and inclination, I have just launched into society. My heart beats high in expectation of its fancied joys. My sanguine imagination paints, in alluring colors, the charms of youth and freedom, regulated by virtue and innocence. Of these, I wish to partake. While I own myself under obligations for the esteem which you are pleased to profess for me, and in return, acknowledge, that neither your person nor manners are disagreeable to me, I recoil at the thought of immediately forming a connection, which must confine me to the duties of domestic life, and make me dependent for happiness, perhaps too, for subsistence, upon a class of people, who will claim the right of scrutinising every part of my conduct; and by censuring those foibles, which I am conscious of not having prudence to avoid, may render me completely miserable. While, therefore, I receive your visits, and cultivate towards you sentiments of friendship and esteem, I would not have you consider me as confined to your society, or obligated to a future connection. Our short acquaintance renders it impossible for me to decide what the operations of my mind may hereafter be. You must either quit the subject, or leave me to the exercise of my free will, which perhaps may coincide with your present wishes. Madam, said he, far is the wish from me to restrain your person or mind. In your breast I will repose my cause. It shall be my study to merit a return of affection; and I doubt not, but generosity and honor will influence your conduct towards me. I expect soon to settle among a generous and enlightened people, where I flatter myself I shall be exempt from those difficulties, and embarrassments, to which

too many of my brethren are subject. The local situation is agreeable, the society refined and polished; and if, in addition, I may obtain that felicity which you are formed to bestow, in a family connection, I shall be happy indeed.

He spoke with emphasis. The tear of sensibility sparkled in his eye. I involuntarily gave him my hand, which he pressed with ardor to his lips. Then rising, he walked to the window to conceal his emotion. I rang the bell and ordered tea; during, and after which, we shared that social converse, which is the true zest of life, and which, I am persuaded, none but virtuous minds can participate. General Richman and lady returned with the shades of the evening. The penetrating eye of my cousin traced in *our* countenances the progress of the cause, and the smile of approbation animated *hers*. Mr. Boyer asked the favor of my company to ride to morrow morning, which was granted. He tarried to supper, and took his leave. I retired immediately to my chamber, to which I was followed by Mrs. Richman. I related to her the conversation, and the encouragement which I had given to Mr. Boyer. She was pleased; but insisted that I should own myself somewhat engaged to him. This, I told her I should never do to any man, before the indissoluble knot was tied. That, said I, will be time enough to resign my freedom. She replied that I had wrong ideas of freedom, and matrimony; but she hoped that Mr. Boyer would happily rectify them.

I have now, my dear friend, given you an account of my present situation, and leave you to judge for yourself concerning it. Write me your opinion, and believe me ever yours.

ELIZA WHARTON.

LETTER XV.

to Miss ELIZA WHARTON.

HARTFORD.

I CONGRATULATE you, my dear Eliza, on the stability of your conduct towards Mr. Boyer. Pursue the system which you have adopted, and I dare say, that happiness will crown your future days. You are indeed very tenacious of your freedom, as you call it; but that is a play about

words. A man of Mr. Boyer's honor and good sense will never abridge any privileges which virtue can claim.

When do you return to embellish our society, here? I am impatient to see you, and likewise this amiable man. I am much interested in his favor. By the way, I am told that Major Sanford has been to look at the seat of Captain Pribble, which is upon sale. It is reported that he will probably purchase it. Many of our gentry are pleased with the prospect of such a neighbor. As an accomplished gentleman, say they, he will be an agreeable addition to our social parties; and as a man of property, and public spirit, he will be an advantage to the town; but, from what I have heard of him, I am far from supposing him a desirable acquisition in either of these respects. A man of a vicious character cannot be a good member of society. In order to that, his principles and practice must be uncorrupted: in his morals, at least, he must be a man of probity, and honor. Of these qualifications, if I mistake not, this gallant of yours cannot boast. But I shall not set up for a censor. I hope neither you nor I shall have much connection with him. My swain interests himself very much in your affairs. You will possibly think him impertinent; but I give his curiosity a softer name. Should I own to you that I place great confidence in his integrity and honor, you would, perhaps, laugh at my weakness; but, my dear, I have pride enough to keep me above coquettry, or prudery; and discretion enough, I hope, to secure me from the errors of both. With him I have determined to walk the future round of life. What folly then would it be to affect reserve and distance, relative to an affair in which I have so much interest? Not that I am going to betray your secrets. These I have no right to divulge; but I must be the judge what may, and what may not be communicated. I am very much pressed for an early day of consummation; but I shall not listen to a request of that kind, till your return. Such is my regard for you, that a union of love would be imperfect, if friendship attended not the rites. Adieu.

LUCY FREEMAN.

LETTER XVI.

to Miss LUCY FREEMAN.

WE go on charmingly here; almost as soft and smooth as your lady-ship. It seems to me that love must stagnate, if it have not a light breeze of discord once in a while to keep it in motion. We have not tried any yet, however. We had a lovely tour this forenoon; were out three long hours, and returned to dinner in perfect harmony.

Mr. Boyer informed me that he should set out to morrow morning, for his future residence, and soon put on the sacred bands. He solicited an epistolary correspondence, at the same time, as an alleviation of the care which that weighty charge would bring on his mind. I consented; telling him, that he must not expect any thing more than general subjects from me.

We were somewhat interrupted in our confidential intercourse, in the afternoon, by the arrival of Major Sanford. I cannot say that I was not agreeably relieved. So sweet a repast, for several hours together, was rather sickening to my taste. My enamorato looked a little mortified at the cheerful reception which I gave the intruder, and joined not so plac-idly in the social conversation, as I could have wished.

When Mr. Boyer, after the Major took leave, pressed me to give him some assurance of my constancy, I only reminded him of the terms of our engagement. Seeing me decided, he was silent on the subject, and soon bid me an affectionate adieu; not expecting, as he told me, the pleasure of a personal interview again, for two or three months.

Thus far we have proceeded in this sober business. A good beginning, you will say. Perhaps it is. I do not, however, feel myself greatly inter-ested in the progress of the negociation. Time may consolidate my af-fections, and enable me to fix them on some particular object. At present the most lively emotions of my heart are those of friendship; that friend-ship which I hope you will soon participate with your faithful

ELIZA WHARTON.

Letter XVII.

to Mr. Selby.

<div align="right">NEW-HAVEN.</div>

I HAVE succeeded in my addresses to the lovely Eliza Wharton; as far at least as I had any reason to expect from our short acquaintance. I find the graces of her person and mind rise in my esteem; and have already enjoyed, in her society, some of the happiest hours of my life. She is kind, affable, and condescending; yet I must own that I have not been able to infuse into her bosom, the ardor which I feel in my own. I know that the native modesty of the sex would restrain the discovery; but there is an animation of countenance, which betrays the sensations of the heart, that I find wanting in hers on this occasion.

I have just taken leave of my fair, and propose returning to morrow morning; to take upon me the solemn charge, which lies with such weight upon my mind, that I need every support, both human and divine. Eliza has promised to correspond with me. From this I anticipate a source of pleasure, which alone can atone for her absence. I am, &c.

<div align="right">J. BOYER.</div>

Letter XVIII.

to Mr. Charles Deighton.

<div align="right">NEW-HAVEN.</div>

Do you know, Charles, that I have commenced lover? I was always a general one; but now I am somewhat particular. I shall be the more interested, as I am likely to meet with difficulties; and it is the glory of a rake, as well as a Christian to combat obstacles. This same Eliza, of whom I have told you, has really made more impression on my heart, than I was aware of; or than the sex, take them as they rise, are wont to do. But she is besieged by a priest (a likely lad though.) I know not how it is, but they are commonly successful with the girls, even the

gayest of them. This one, too, has the interest of all her friends, as I am
told. I called yesterday, at General Richman's, and found this pair to-
gether, apparently too happy in each other's society for my wishes. I
must own, that I felt a glow of jealousy, which I never experienced
before; and vowed revenge for the pain it gave me, though but momen-
tary. Yet Eliza's reception of me was visibly cordial; nay, I fancied my
company as pleasing to her as that which she had before. I tarried not
long, but left him to the enjoyment of that pleasure which I flatter myself
will be short-lived. O, I have another plan in my head; a plan of neces-
sity, which, you know, is the mother of invention. It is this: I am very
much courted and caressed by the family of Mr. Lawrence, a man of
large property in this neighborhood. He has only one child; a daughter,
with whom I imagine the old folks intend to shackle me in the bonds
of matrimony. The girl looks very well. She has no soul though, that I
can discover. She is heiress, nevertheless, to a great fortune; and that is
all the soul I wish for in a wife. In truth, Charles, I know of no other
way to mend my circumstances. But lisp not a word of my embarrass-
ments for your life. Show and equipage are my hobby-horse; and if any
female wish to share them with me, and will furnish me with the means
of supporting them, I have no objection. Could I conform to the sober
rules of wedded life, and renounce those dear enjoyments of dissipation,
in which I have so long indulged, I know not the lady in the world with
whom I would sooner form a connection of this sort than with Eliza
Wharton. But it will never do. If my fortune, or hers were better, I
would risk a union; but as they are, no idea of the kind can be admitted.
I shall endeavor, notwithstanding, to enjoy her company as long as
possible. Though I cannot possess her wholly myself, I will not tamely
see her the property of another.

I am now going to call at General Richman's, in hopes of an oppor-
tunity to profess my devotion to her. I know I am not a welcome visitor
to the family; but I am independent of their censure or esteem, and mean
to act accordingly.

PETER SANFORD.

LETTER XIX.

to Miss LUCY FREEMAN.

I FIND the ideas of sobriety, and domestic solitude, I have been culti-
vating for three days past, somewhat deranged by the interruption of a
visitor, with whom, I know, you will not be pleased. It is no other than
Major Sanford. I was walking alone in the garden yesterday, when he
suddenly appeared to my view. How happy am I, said he, seizing my
hand, in this opportunity of finding you alone; an opportunity, Miss
Wharton, which I must improve in expatiating on a theme, that fills my
heart, and solely animates my frame.

I was startled at his impetuosity, and displeased with his freedom.
Withdrawing my hand, I told him, that my retirement was sacred. He
bowed submissively; begged pardon for his intrusion, alledged, that he
found no body but the servants in the house; that they informed him, I
was alone in the garden, which intelligence was too pleasing for him to
consult any forms of ceremony for the regulation of his conduct. He
then went on rhapsodically to declare his passion, his suspicions, that I
was forming a connection with Mr. Boyer, which would effectually de-
stroy all his hopes of future happiness. He painted the restraint, the
confinement, the embarrassments to which a woman, connected with a
man of Mr. Boyer's profession, must be subjected; however agreeable
his person might be. He asked if my generous mind could submit to
cares and perplexities like these; whether I could not find greater sources
of enjoyment in a more elevated sphere of life, or share pleasures better
suited to my genius and disposition, even in a single state? I listened to
him involuntarily. My heart did not approve his sentiments, but my ear
was charmed with his rhetoric, and my fancy captivated by his address.

He invited my confidence, by the most ardent professions of friend-
ship, and labored to remove my suspicions by vows of sincerity. I was
induced by his importunity, gradually to disclose the state of affairs
between Mr. Boyer and myself. He listened eagerly; wished not, he said,
to influence me unduly; but if I were not otherwise engaged, might he
presume to solicit a place in my friendship and esteem; be admitted to
enjoy my society, to visit me as an acquaintance, and to attend my

excursions and amusements, as a brother, if no more? I replied, that I
was a pensioner of friendship, at present; that my friends were extremely
refined in their notions of propriety, and that I had no right to receive
visitants independent of them. I understand you, madam, said he. You
intimate that my company is not agreeable to them: but I know not
why. Surely my rank in life is as elevated; and my knowledge of, and
acceptance in the world, are as extensive as General Richman's. I hope,
said I, since we are engaged in the conversation, that you will excuse
my frankness, if I tell you, that the understanding and virtue of this
worthy couple, induce them, without any regard to rank, to bestow their
esteem wherever it is merited. I cannot say that you are not a sharer.
Your own heart can best determine, whether upon their principles, you
are, or not! He appeared mortified, and chagrined; and we had walked
some distance without exchanging a word, or a look. At last, he re-
joined, I plead guilty to the charge, madam, which they have undoubt-
edly brought against me, of imprudence and folly in many particulars;
yet of malignancy and vice I am innocent. Brought up in affluence;
innured from my infancy to the gratification of every passion; the in-
dulgence of every wish, it is not strange, that a life of dissipation and
gaiety should prove alluring to a youthful mind, which had no care but
to procure what it deemed enjoyment. In this pursuit I have perhaps
deviated from the rigid rules of discretion, and the harsher laws of
morality.

But let the veil of charity be drawn over my faults; let the eye of
candor impartially examine my present behavior; let the kind and le-
nient hand of friendship assist in directing my future steps; and, perhaps,
I may not prove unworthy of associating with the respectable inhabi-
tants of this happy mansion; for such I am sure it must be, while hon-
ored with Miss Wharton's presence. But, circumstanced as you and I
are, at present, I will not sue for your attention, as a lover; but rest
contented, if possible, with that share of kindness, and regard, which
your benevolence may afford me as a friend. I bowed in approbation
of his resolution. He pressed my hand with ardor to his lips; and at that
instant General Richman entered the garden. He approached us cheer-
fully, offered Major Sanford his hand with apparent cordiality, and told
us pleasantly, that he hoped he should not be considered as an intruder.
By no means, sir, said Major Sanford. It is I who have incurred that
imputation. I called this afternoon to pay you my respects; when being
informed that you and your lady were abroad, and that Miss Wharton

was in the garden, I took the liberty to invade her retirement. She has graciously forgiven my crime, and I was just affixing the seal to my pardon as you entered.

We then returned into the house. Mrs. Richman received us politely. During tea, the conversation turned on literary subjects, in which I cannot say that the Major bore a very distinguished part. After he was gone, Mrs. Richman said, I hope you have been agreeably entertained, Miss Wharton? I did not chuse my company, madam, said I. Nor, said she, did you refuse it, I presume. Would you not have me respect the rights of hospitality towards your guests, when you are absent, madam? If you had acted from that motive, I own my obligations to you, my dear; but even that consideration can hardly reconcile me to the sacrifice of time, which you have made to the amusement of a seducer. I hope, madam, you do not think me an object of seduction! I do not think you seducible; nor was Richardson's Clarissa, till she made herself the victim, by her own indiscretion. Pardon me, Eliza, this is a second Lovelace. I am alarmed by his artful intrusions. His insinuating attention to you are characteristic of the man. Come, I presume you are not interested to keep his secrets, if you know them. Will you give me a little sketch of his conversation? Most willingly, said I; and, accordingly, related the whole. When I had concluded, she shook her head, and replied, beware, my friend, of his arts. Your own heart is too sincere to suspect treachery and dissimulation in another; but suffer not your ear to be charmed by the syren voice of flattery; nor your eye to be caught by the phantom of gaiety and pleasure. Remember your engagements to Mr. Boyer. Let sincerity and virtue be your guides, and they will lead you to happiness and peace. She waited not for an answer, but immediately rising, begged leave to retire, alledging that she was fatigued. Gen. Richman accompanied her, and I hastened to my apartment, where I have written thus far, and shall send it on for your comments. I begin to think of returning soon to your circle. One inducement is, that I may be free from the intrusions of this man. Adieu.

ELIZA WHARTON.

LETTER XX.

to Mrs. M. WHARTON.

NEW-HAVEN.

FROM the conversation of the polite, the sedate, the engaging and the gay; from corresponding with the learned, the sentimental and the refined, my heart and my pen turn with ardor and alacrity to a tender and affectionate parent, the faithful guardian and guide of my youth; the unchanging friend of my riper years. The different dispositions of various associates, sometimes perplex the mind, which seeks direction; but in the disinterested affection of the maternal breast, we fear no dissonance of passion, no jarring interests, no disunion of love. In this seat of felicity is every enjoyment which fancy can form, or friendship, with affluence, bestow; but still my mind frequently returns to the happy shades of my nativity. I wish there to impart my pleasures, and share the counsels of my best, my long tried and experienced friend. At this time, my dear mamma, I am peculiarly solicitous for your advice. I am again inportuned to listen to the voice of love; again called upon to accept the addresses of a gentleman of merit and respectability. You will know the character of the man, when I tell you, it is Mr. Boyer. But his situation in life! I dare not enter it. My disposition is not calculated for that sphere. There are duties arising from the station, which I fear I should not be able to fulfil; cares and restraints to which I could not submit. *This* man is not disagreeable to me; but if I must enter the connubial state, are there not *others*, who may be equally pleasing in their persons, and whose profession may be more conformable to my taste? You, madam, have passed through this scene of trial, with honor and applause. But alas! can your volatile daughter ever acquire your wisdom; ever possess your resolution, dignity and prudence?

I hope soon to converse with you personally upon the subject, and to profit by your precepts and example. I anticipate the hour of my return to your bosom, with impatience. My daily thoughts and nightly dreams restore me to the society of my beloved mamma; and, till I enjoy it in reality, I subscribe myself your dutiful daughter,

ELIZA WHARTON.

LETTER XXI.

to Miss ELIZA WHARTON.

HARTFORD.

How welcome to me, my dear Eliza, are the tidings of your return?
My widowed heart has mourned your absence, and languished for the
company of its now, dearest connection. When stript of one dependence,
the mind naturally collects, and rests itself in another. Your father's
death deprived me, for a while, of every enjoyment. But a reviving sense
of the duties which I owed to a rising family, roused me from the leth-
argy of grief. In my cares I found an alleviation of my sorrows. The
expanding virtues of my children soothed and exhilerated my drooping
spirits; and my attention to their education, and interest, was amply
rewarded by their proficiency and duty. In them, every hope, every
pleasure now centres. They are the axis on which revolves the temporal
felicity of their mother. Judge then, my dear, how anxiously I must
watch, how solicitously I must regard every circumstance which relates
to their welfare and prosperity! Exquisitely alive to these sensations,
your letter awakens my hopes and my fears. As you are young and
charming, a thousand dangers lurk unseen around you. I wish you to
find a friend and protector, worthy of being rewarded by your love and
your society. Such a one, I think, Mr. Boyer will prove. I am, therefore,
sorry, since there can be no other, that his profession should be an
objection in your mind. You say, that I have experienced the scenes of
trial, connected with that station. I have, indeed; and I will tell you the
result of this experience. It is, that I have found it replete with happiness.
No class of society has domestic enjoyment more at command, than
clergymen. Their circumstances are generally a decent competency. They
are removed alike from the perplexing cares of want, and from the
distracting parade of wealth. They are respected by all ranks, and par-
takers of the best company. With regard to its being a dependent situ-
ation, what one is not so? Are we not all links in the great chain of
society, some more, some less important; but each upheld by others,
throughout the confederated whole? In whatever situation we are
placed, our greater or less degree of happiness must be derived from
ourselves. Happiness is in a great measure the result of our own dis-
positions and actions. Let us conduct uprightly and justly; with propri-

ety and steadiness; not servilely cringing for favor, nor arrogantly claiming more attention and respect than our due; let us bear with fortitude the providential, and unavoidable evils of life, and we shall spend our days with respectability and contentment, at least.

I will not expatiate on the topic of your letter, till we have a personal interview, for which I am, indeed, impatient. Return, my daughter, as soon as politeness will allow, to your expecting friends; more especially, to the fond embraces of your affectionate mother,

M. WHARTON.

LETTER XXII.

to Miss ELIZA WHARTON.

HAMPSHIRE.

Can time, can distance, can absence allay, or extinguish the sentiments of refined affection, the ardor of true love? No, my dear Eliza. If I may judge by my own heart, I shall say they cannot. Amidst the parade which has attended me, the interesting scenes in which I have been engaged, and the weighty cares, which have occupied my attention, your idea has been the solace of my retired moments; the soother of every anxious thought. I recal, with pleasure, the conversation which we have shared. I dwell with rapture on the marks of favor which I have received from you. My first wish is the continuance and increase of these favors; my highest ambition, to deserve them. I look forward and anticipate with impatience, the future enjoyment of your society; and hope we shall one day experience the reality of those beautiful lines of Thompson:

> ——"An elegant sufficiency,
> Content, retirement, rural quiet, friendship;
> Books, ease and alternate labor, useful life;
> Progressive virtue, and approving heaven;
> These are the matchless joys of virtuous love."

Mr. Selby, my particular friend, will have the honor of delivering this letter. He will be able to give you any information, relative to our public

transactions, which you may wish. May I solicit the favor of a line, through him, in return? It will relieve, in some measure, the tediousness of this separation. I intend to pay my respects to you personally, in about a fortnight; till when, I subscribe myself your sincere and affectionate friend,

J. BOYER.

LETTER XXIII.

to the Rev. J. BOYER.

NEW-HAVEN.

I HAVE executed your commission, and been amply rewarded for my trouble, by the pleasure I enjoyed in the society of the agreeable family to which I was introduced; especially of the amiable and accomplished lady, who is the object of your particular regard. I think she fully justifies your partiality to her. She appears to possess both the virtues and the graces. Her form is fine, and her countenance interests us at once in her favor. There is a mixture of dignity and ease, which commands respect, and conciliates affection. After these encomiums, will you permit me to say, there is an air of gaiety in her appearance and deportment, which favors a little of coquetry. I am persuaded, however, that she has too much good sense to practice its arts. She received your letter very graciously, asked leave to retire a few moments; and returned with a smile of complacency on her brow, which I construe favorably to you.

There was a Mr. Laurence, with his lady and daughter, and a certain Major Sanford, at the house. The latter, I believe, in the modern sense of the phrase, *is much of a gentleman*, that is, a man of show and fashion.

Miss Wharton asked me, when I should leave town, and when I should return, or have an opportunity of conveyance to Hampshire? I told her I should write by the next post, and if she had any commands, would be happy to execute them. She would send a line to her friend, she said, if I would take the trouble to inclose it in my letter. I readily consented; and told her, that I would call and receive her favor to morrow morning. This chit-chat was a little aside, but I could not but ob-

serve, that the foresaid Major Sanford had dropped his part in the conversation of the rest of the company, and was attending to us, though he endeavored to conceal his attention, by looking carelessly over a play, which lay on the window by him. Yet he evidently watched every word and action of Miss Wharton, as if he were really interested in her movements.

It is said she has many admirers, and I conceive it very possible that this may be one of them; though, truly, I do not think that she would esteem such a conquest any great honor. I now joined in the general topic of conversation, which was politics. Mrs. Richman and Miss Wharton judiciously, yet modestly bore a part; while the other ladies amused themselves with Major Sanford, who was making his sage remarks on the play, which he still kept in his hand. General Richman at length observed, that we had formed into parties. Major Sanford, upon this, laid aside his book. Miss Laurence simpered; and looked as if she was well pleased with being in a party with so fine a man; while her mother replied, that she never meddled with politics; she thought they did not belong to ladies. Miss Wharton and I, said Mrs. Richman, must beg leave to differ from you, madam. We think ourselves interested in the welfare and prosperity of our country; and, consequently, claim the right of inquiring into those affairs, which may conduce to, or interfere with the common weal. We shall not be called to the senate or the field to assert its privileges, and defend its rights, but we shall feel for the honor and safety of our friends and connections, who are thus employed. If the community flourish and enjoy health and freedom, shall we not share in the happy effects? if it be oppressed and disturbed, shall we not endure our proportion of the evil? Why then should the love of our country be a masculine passion only? Why should government, which involves the peace and order of the society, of which we are a part, be wholly excluded from our observation? Mrs. Laurence made some slight reply and waved the subject. The gentlemen applauded Mrs. Richman's sentiments as truly Roman; and what was more, they said, truly republican.

I rose to take leave, observing to Miss Wharton, that I should call to morrow as agreed. Upon this, Gen. Richman politely requested the favor of my company at dinner. I accepted his invitation, and bid them good night. I shall do the same to you for the present; as I intend, to morrow to scribble the cover, which is to inclose your Eliza's letter.

T. SELBY.

LETTER XXIV.

to the Rev. J. BOYER.

I RESUME my pen, having just returned from Gen. Richman's; not with an expectation, however, of your reading this, till you have perused, and reperused the inclosed. I can bear such neglect, in this case, as I have been alike interested myself.

I went to Gen. Richman's at twelve o'clock. About a mile from thence, upon turning a corner, I observed a gentleman and lady on horseback, some way before me, riding a very moderate pace, and seemingly in close conversation. I kept at the same distance from them, till I saw them stop at the General's gate. I then put on, and coming up with them, just as they alighted, and was surprised to find them no other than Major Sanford and Miss Wharton. They were both a little disconcerted at my salutation; I know not why. Miss Wharton invited him in; but he declined, being engaged to dine. Gen. Richman received us at the door. As I handed Miss Wharton in, he observed jocosely, that she had changed company. Yes sir, she replied, more than once, since I went out, as you doubtless observed. I was not aware, said Mrs. Richman, that Major Sanford was to be of your party to day. It was quite accidental, madam, said Miss Wharton. Miss Laurence and I had agreed last evening, to take a little airing, this forenoon. A young gentleman, a relation of her's, who is making them a visit, was to attend us. We had not rode more than two miles, when we were overtaken by Major Sanford, who very politely asked leave to join our party. Miss Laurence very readily consented; and we had a very sociable ride. The fineness of the day induced me to protract the enjoyment of it abroad; but Miss Laurence declined riding so far as I proposed, as she had engaged company to dine. We therefore parted till evening, when we are to meet again. What, another engagement! said Mrs. Richman. Only to the assembly, madam. May I inquire after your gallant, my dear? But I have no right, perhaps, to be inquisitive, said Mrs. Richman. Miss Wharton made no reply; and the conversation took a general turn. Miss Wharton sustained her part with great propriety. Indeed, she discovers a fund of useful knowledge, and extensive reading, which render her peculiarly entertaining; while the brilliancy of her wit, the fluency of her language,

the vivacity and ease of her manners, are inexpressibly engaging. I am going myself to the assembly this evening, though I did not mention it to General Richman; I therefore took my leave soon after dinner.

I have heard so much in praise of Miss Wharton's penmanship, in addition to her other endowments, that I am almost tempted to break the seal of her letter to you; but I forbear. Wishing you much happiness in the perusal of it, and more in the possession of its writer, I subscribe myself, yours, &c.

T. SELBY.

LETTER XXV.

to the Rev. J. BOYER.

NEW-HAVEN.

Sir,

YOUR favor of the 4th inst. came to hand yesterday. I received it with pleasure, and embrace this early opportunity of contributing my part to a correspondence, tending to promote a friendly and social intercourse. An epistolary communication between the sexes has been with some, a subject of satire and censure; but unjustly, in my opinion. With persons of refinement and information, it may be a source of entertainment and utility. The knowledge and masculine virtues of your sex may be softened, and rendered more diffusive by the inquisitiveness, vivacity, and docility of ours; drawn forth and exercised by each other.

In regard to the *particular* subject of your's I shall be silent. Ideas of that kind are better conveyed, on my part, by words, than by the pen.

I congratulate you on your agreeable settlement, and hope it will be productive of real and lasting happiness. I am convinced that felicity is not confined to any particular station, or condition in life; yet methinks some are better calculated to afford it to me, than others.

Your extract from a favorite poet is charmingly descriptive; but is it not difficult to ascertain what we can pronounce "an elegant sufficiency?" Perhaps you will answer as some others have done, We can attain it by circumscribing our wishes within the compass of our abili-

ties. I am not very avaricious; yet I must own that I should like to enjoy it without so much trouble as that would cost me.

Excuse my seeming levity. You have flattered my cheerfulness by commending it; and must, therefore, indulge me in the exercise of it. I cannot conveniently be at the pains of restraining its sallies, when I write in confidence.

Is a sprightly disposition, in your view, indicative of a giddy mind, or an innocent heart? Of the latter, I presume; for I know you are not a misanthrope.

We expect the pleasure of Mr. Selby's company to dinner. You are, certainly, under obligations to his friendship for the liberal encomiums he bestowed on you, and your prospects yesterday. Mrs. Richman rallied me after he was gone, on my listening ear. The General and she unite in requesting me to present their respects. Wishing you health and happiness, I subscribe myself your friend,

ELIZA WHARTON.

LETTER XXVI.

to Miss LUCY FREEMAN.

NEW-HAVEN.

I AM perplexed and embarrassed, my friend, by the assiduous attentions of this Major Sanford. I shall write circumstantially, and frankly to you, that I may have the benefit of your advice. He came here, last Monday, in company with Mr. Laurence, his wife, and daughter, to make us a visit. While they were present, a Mr. Selby, a particular friend of Mr. Boyer, came in, and delivered me a letter from him. I was really happy in the reception of this proof of his affection. His friend gave a very flattering account of his situation and prospects.

The watchful eye of Major Sanford traced every word and action, respecting Mr. Boyer, with an attention, which seemed to border on anxiety. That, however, did not restrain, but rather accellerate my vivacity and inquisitiveness on the subject; for I wished to know whether it would produce any real effect upon him, or not.

After Mr. Selby's departure, he appeared pensive, and thoughtful,

the remainder of the evening; and evidently sought an opportunity of speaking to me aside; which I studiously avoided. Miss Laurence and I formed an engagement to take an airing in the morning on horseback; attended by a relation of hers, who is now with them. They called for me about ten, when we immediately set out upon our preconcerted excursion. We had not proceeded far, before we were met by Major Sanford. He was extremely polite, and finding our destination was not particular, begged leave to join our party. This was granted, and we had an agreeable tour for several miles; the time being passed in easy, and unstudied remarks upon obvious occurrences. Maj. Sanford could not, however, conceal his particular attention to me, which rather nettled Miss Laurence. She grew somewhat serious, and declined riding so far as we had intended; alledging that she expected company to dine.

Major Sanford understanding that she was going to the assembly in the evening with Mr. Gordon, solicited me to accept a ticket and form a party with them. The entertainment was alluring, and I consented. When we had parted with Miss Laurence, Major Sanford insisted on my riding a little farther; saying, he must converse with me on a particular subject; and if I refused him this opportunity, that he must visit me, at my residence, let it offend whom it would. I yielded to his importunity; and we rode on. He then told me that his mind was in a state of suspense and agitation, which was very painful to bear; and which I only could relieve; that my cheerful reception of Mr. Boyer's letter, yesterday, and deportment respecting him, had awakened in his breast all the pangs of jealousy, which the most ardent love could feel; that my treatment of Mr. Boyer's friend convinced him that I was more interested in his affairs than I was willing to own; that he foresaw himself to be condemned to an eternal separation; and the total loss of my favor and society, as soon as time and circumstances would allow.

His zeal, his pathos, alarmed me. I begged him to be calm. To you, said I, as a friend, I have intrusted my situation in relation to Mr. Boyer. You know that I am under no special obligation to him; and I do not intend to form any immediate connection. Mr. Boyer must have different ideas, madam; and he has reason for them, if I may judge by appearances. When do you expect another visit from him? In about a fortnight. And is my fate to be then decided; and so decided, as I fear it will be, through the influence of your friends, if not by your own inclination? My friends, sir, will not control; they will only advise to what they think most for my interest; and I hope, that my conduct will not be unworthy of their approbation. Pardon me, my dear Eliza, said

he, if I am impertinent; it is my regard for you which impels me to the presumption. Do you intend to give your hand to Mr. Boyer? I do not intend to give my hand to any man at present. I have but lately entered society; and wish, for a while, to enjoy my freedom, in the participation of pleasures, suited to my age and sex. These, said he, you are aware, I suppose, when you form a connection with that man, you must renounce; and content yourself with a confinement to the tedious round of domestic duties, the pedantic conversation of scholars, and the invidious criticisms of a whole town. I have been accustomed, said I, and am therefore attached to men of letters; and as to the praise or censure of the populace, I hope always to enjoy that approbation of conscience, which will render me superior to both. But you forget your promise, not to talk in this style; and have deviated far from the character of a friend and brother, with which you consented to rest satisfied. Yes, but I find myself unequal to the task. I am not stoic enough, tamely to make so great a sacrifice. I must plead for an interest in your favor, till you banish me from your presence, and tell me plainly that you hate me. We had by this time reached the gate; and as we dismounted, were unexpectedly accosted by Mr. Selby, who had come agreeably to his promise, to dine with us, and receive my letter to Mr. Boyer.

Major Sanford took his leave as General Richman appeared at the door. The General and his lady rallied me on my change of company; but very prudently concealed their sentiments of Major Sanford, while Mr. Selby was present. Nothing material occurred before, and during dinner; soon after which, Mr. Selby went away. I retired to dress for the assembly; and had nearly completed the labor of the toilet, when Mrs. Richman entered. My friendship for you, my dear Eliza, said she, interests me so much in your affairs, that I cannot repress my curiosity to know who has the honor of your hand, this evening. If it be any honor, said I, it will be confered on Major Sanford. I think it far too great to be thus bestowed, returned she. It is perfectly astonishing to me, that the virtuous part of my sex will countenance, caress, and encourage those men, whose profession it is to blast their reputation, destroy their peace, and triumph in their infamy! Is this, madam, the avowed design of Major Sanford? I know not what he avows; but his practice too plainly bespeaks his principles and views. Does he now practice the arts you mention; or do you refer to past follies? I cannot answer for his present conduct; his past has established his character. You, madam, are an advocate for charity; that, perhaps, if exercised in

this instance might lead you to think it possible for him to reform; to become a valuable member of society; and, when connected with a lady of virtue and refinement, to be capable of making a good husband. I cannot conceive that such a lady would be willing to risk her all upon the slender prospect of his reformation. I hope the one with whom I am conversing, has no inclination to so hazardous, an experiment. Why, not much. Not much! If you have any, why do you continue to encourage Mr. Boyer's addresses? I am not sufficiently acquainted with either yet, to determine which to take. At present, I shall not confine myself in any way. In regard to these men, my fancy and my judgment are in scales. Sometimes one preponderates, sometimes the other. Which will finally outweigh, time alone can reveal. O my cousin, beware of the delusions of fancy! Reason must be our guide, if we would expect durable happiness. At this instant a servant opened the door, and told me that Major Sanford waited in the parlor. Being ready, I wished Mrs. Richman a good evening, and went down. Neither General Richman nor his lady appeared. He therefore handed me immediately into his phaeton, and we were soon in the assembly room.

I was surprised, on my entrance, to find Mr. Selby there, as he did not mention, at dinner, his intention of going. He attached himself to our party; and, in the intervals of dancing, took every opportunity of conversing with me. These, however, were not many; for Major Sanford assiduously precluded the possibility of my being much engaged by any one else. We passed the evening very agreeably; but the Major's importunity was rather troublesome, as we returned home. He insisted upon my declaring whether Mr. Boyer really possessed my affections; and whether I intended to confer myself on him or not. If, said he, you answer me in the affirmative, I must despair; but if you have not absolutely decided against me, I will still hope, that my persevering assiduity, my faithful love, may at last be rewarded. I told him that I was under no obligation to give him any account of my disposition towards another; and that he must remember the terms of our present association, to which he had subscribed. I therefore begged him to wave the subject now, if not forever. He asked my pardon, if he had been impertinent; but desired leave to renew his request, that I would receive his visits, his friendly visits. I replied, that I could not grant this; and that he must blame himself, not me, if he was an unwelcome guest at General Richman's. He lamented the prejudices which my friends had imbibed against him; but flattered himself that I was more liberal than

to be influenced by them, without any positive proof of demerit; as it was impossible that his conduct towards me should ever deviate from the strictest rules of honor and love.

What shall I say now, my friend? This man, to an agreeable person has superadded, graceful manners, an amiable temper, and a fortune sufficient to ensure the enjoyments of all the pleasing varieties of social life. Perhaps a gay disposition, and a lax education may have betrayed him into some scenes of dissipation. But is it not an adage generally received, that "*a reformed rake makes the best husband?*" My fancy leads me for happiness to the festive haunts of fashionable life. I am at present, and know not but I ever shall be, too volatile for a confinement to domestic avocations, and sedentary pleasures. I dare not, therefore, place myself in a situation where these must be indispensable. Mr. Boyer's person, and character are agreeable. I really esteem the man. My reason and judgment, as I have observed before, declare for a connection with him, as a state of tranquillity and rational happiness. But the idea of relinquishing those delightful amusements and flattering attentions, which wealth and equipage bestow, is painful. Why were not the virtues of the one, and the graces and affluence of the other combined? I should then have been happy indeed! But, as the case now stands, I am loath to give up either; being doubtful which will conduce most to my felicity.

Pray write me impartially; let me know your real sentiments, for I rely greatly upon your opinion. I am, &c.

ELIZA WHARTON.

LETTER XXVII.

to the Rev. Mr. BOYER.

NEW-HAVEN.

I AM quite a convert to Pope's assertion, that "Every woman is, at heart, a rake." How else can we account for the pleasure which they evidently receive from the society, the flattery, the caresses of men of that character? Even the most virtuous of them seem naturally prone to gaiety, to pleasure, and, I had almost said, to dissipation! How else shall we

account for the existence of this disposition, in your favorite fair? It cannot be the result of her education. Such a one as she has received, is calculated to give her a very different turn of mind. You must forgive me, my friend, for I am a little vexed, and alarmed on your account. I went last evening to the assembly, as I told you in my last that I intended. I was purposely without a partner, that I might have the liberty to exercise my gallantry, as circumstances should invite. Indeed, I must own, that my particular design was, to observe Miss Wharton's movements, being rather inclined to jealousy in your behalf. She was handed into the assembly room by Major Sanford. The brilliance of their appearance, the levity of their manners, and the contrast of their characters I found to be a general subject of speculation. I endeavored to associate with Miss Wharton, but found it impossible to detach her a moment from the coxcomb who attended her. If she has any idea of a connection with you, why does she continue to associate with another, especially with one of so opposite a description? I am seriously afraid, that there is more intimacy between them, than there ought to be, considering the encouragement she has given you.

I hope you will not be offended by my freedom in this matter. It originates in a concern for your honor and future happiness. I am anxious, lest you should be made the dupe of a coquette, and your peace of mind fall a sacrifice to an artful debauchee. Yet I must believe, that Miss Wharton has, in reality, all that virtue and good sense of which she enjoys the reputation; but her present conduct is mysterious.

I have said enough (more than I ought, perhaps) to awaken your attention to circumstances, which *may* lead to important events. If they appear of little, or no consequence to you, you will at least ascribe the mention of them to motives of sincere regard, in your friend and humble servant,

T. SELBY.

LETTER XXVIII.

to Mr. CHARLES DEIGHTON.

NEW-HAVEN.

I GO on finely with my amour. I have every encouragement that I could wish. Indeed my fair one does not verbally declare in my favor; but then, according to the vulgar proverb, *that actions speak louder than words,* I have no reason to complain; since she evidently approves my gallantry, is pleased with my company, and listens to my flattery. Her sagatious friends have undoubtedly given her a detail of my vices. If, therefore, my past conduct has been repugnant to her notions of propriety, why does she not act consistently, and refuse at once to associate with a man whose character she cannot esteem? But no; that, Charles, is no part of the female plan: our entrapping a few of their sex, only discovers the gaiety of our dispositions, the insinuating graces of our manners, and the irresistible charms of our persons and address. These qualifications are very alluring to the sprightly fancy of the fair. They think to enjoy the pleasures which result from this source; while their vanity and ignorance prompt each one to imagine herself superior to delusion; and to anticipate the honor of reclaiming the libertine, and reforming the rake! I dont know, however, but this girl will really have that merit with me; for I am so much attached to her, that I begin to suspect I should sooner become a convert to sobriety than lose her. I cannot find that I have made much impression on her heart as yet. Want of success in this point mortifies me extremely, as it is the first time I ever failed. Besides, I am apprehensive that she is prepossessed in favor of the other swain, the clerical lover, whom I have mentioned to you before. The chord, therefore, upon which I play the most, is the dissimilarity of their dispositions and pleasures. I endeavor to detach her from him, and disaffect her towards him; knowing, that if I can separate them entirely, I shall be more likely to succeed in my plan. Not that I have any thoughts of marrying her myself; that will not do at present. But I love her too well to see her connected with another for life. I must own myself a little revengeful too in this affair. I wish to punish her friends, as she calls them, for their malice towards me; for their cold and negligent treatment of me whenever I go to the house. I know that to frustrate their designs of a connection between Mr. Boyer and Eliza

would be a grievous disappointment. I have not yet determined to se-
duce her, though, with all her pretensions to virtue, I do not think it
impossible. And if I should, she can blame none but herself, since she
knows my character, and has no reason to wonder if I act consistently
with it. If she will play with a lion, let her beware of his paw, I say. At
present, I wish innocently to enjoy her society; it is a luxury which I
never tasted before. She is the very soul of pleasure. The gayest circle is
irradiated by her presence, and the highest entertainment receives its
greatest charm from her smiles. Besides, I have purchased the seat of
Capt. Pribble, about a mile from her mother's; and can I think of suf-
fering her to leave the neighborhood, just as I enter it? I shall exert
every nerve to prevent that, and hope to meet with the usual success of

PETER SANFORD.

LETTER XXIX.

to Miss ELIZA WHARTON.

HARTFORD.

You desire me to write to you, my friend; but if you had not, I should
by no means have refrained. I tremble at the precipice on which you
stand; and must echo, and re-echo the seasonable admonition of the
excellent Mrs. Richman, "Beware of the delusions of fancy!" You are
strangely infatuated by them! Let not the magic arts of that worthless
Sanford lead you, like an *ignis fatuus* from the path of rectitude and
virtue!

I do not find, in all your conversations with him, that one word about
marriage drops from his lips. This is mysterious? No, it is characteristic
of the man. Suppose, however, that his views are honorable; yet what
can you expect, what can you promise yourself from such a connection?
"A reformed rake," you say, "makes the best husband;" a trite, but a
very erroneous maxim, as the fatal experience of thousands of our sex
can testify. In the first place, I believe that rakes very seldom *do* reform,
while their fortunes and constitutions enable them to pursue their licen-
tious pleasures. But even allowing this to happen, can a woman of re-
finement and delicacy enjoy the society of a man, whose mind has been

corrupted, whose taste has been vitiated, and who has contracted a
depravity both of sentiment and manners, which no degree of repen-
tance can wholly efface? Besides, of true love they are absolutely inca-
pable. Their passions have been too much hackneyed to admit so pure
a flame. You cannot anticipate sincere and lasting respect from them.
They have been so long accustomed to the company of those of our
sex, who observe no esteem; that the greatest dignity and purity of
character can never excite it in their breasts. They are naturally prone
to jealousy. Habituated to an intercourse with the baser part of the sex,
they level the whole, and seldom believe any to be incorruptible. They
are always hard hearted and cruel. How else could they triumph in the
miseries which they frequently occasion? Their specious manners may
render them agreeable companions abroad; but at home the evil pro-
pensities of their minds will invariably predominate. They are steeled
against the tender affections, which render domestic life delightful;
strangers to the kind, the endearing sympathies of husband, father, and
friend! The thousand nameless attentions which soften the rugged path
of life, are neglected; and deemed unworthy of notice by persons who
have been innured to scenes of dissipation and debauchery! and is a
man of this description to be the partner, the companion, the bosom
friend of my Eliza? Forbid it heaven! Let not the noble qualities, so
lavishly bestowed upon her, be thus unworthily sacrificed!

You seem to be particularly charmed with the fortune of Major San-
ford; with the gaiety of his appearance; with the splendor of his equi-
page; with the politeness of his manners; with what you call the graces
of his person! These, alas! are superficial, ensnaring endowments. As to
fortune, prudence, economy, and regularity are necessary to preserve it,
when possessed. Of these Major Sanford is certainly destitute; unless
common fame (which more frequently tells truth than some are willing
to allow) does him great injustice. As to external parade, it will not
satisfy the rational mind, when it aspires to those substantial pleasures
for which yours is formed. And as to the graces of person and manners,
they are but a wretched substitute for those virtues which adorn and
dignify human life. Can you, who have always been used to serenity
and order in a family, to rational, refined and improving conversation,
relinquish them, and launch into the whirlpool of frivolity, where the
correct taste and the delicate sensibility which you possess must con-
stantly be wounded by the frothy and illiberal sallies of licentious wit?

This, my dear, is but a faint picture of the situation to which you
seem inclined! Reverse the scene, and you will perceive the alternative,

which is submitted to your option, in a virtuous connection with Mr. Boyer. Remember that you are acting for life; and that your happiness in this world, perhaps in the next, depends on your present choice!

I called, last evening, to see your mamma. She is fondly anticipating your return, and rejoicing in the prospect of your agreeable and speedy settlement. I could not find it in my heart to distress her by intimating that you had other views. I wish her benevolent bosom never more to feel the pangs of disappointed hope.

I am busily engaged in preparing for my nuptials. The solemn words "as long as ye both shall live," render me thoughtful and serious. I hope for your enlivening presence soon; which will prove a seasonable cordial to the spirits of your

<div align="right">LUCY FREEMAN.</div>

LETTER XXX.

to Miss LUCY FREEMAN.

<div align="right">NEW-HAVEN.</div>

I BELIEVE your spirits need a cordial indeed, my dear Lucy; after drawing so dreadful a portrait of my swain. But I call him mine no longer. I renounce him entirely. My friends shall be gratified. And if their predictions are verified, I shall be happy in a union with the man of their choice. General Richman and lady have labored abundantly to prove that my ruin was inevitable if I did not immediately break all intercourse with Major Sanford. I promised a compliance with their wishes; and have accomplished the task, though a hard one I found it. Last Thursday he was here, and desired leave to spend an hour with me. I readily consented, assuring my friends it should be the last hour, which I would ever spend in his company.

He told me that he was obliged to leave town for a few days; and, as I should probably see Mr. Boyer, before his return, he could not depart in peace without once more endeavoring to interest me in his favor; to obtain some token of esteem, some glimpse of hope, that I would not utterly reject him, to support him in his absence. I thanked him for the polite attention he had paid me, since our acquaintance;

told him that I should ever retain a grateful sense of his partiality to me; that he would ever share my best wishes; but that all connection of the kind, to which he alluded, must from that time, for ever cease.

He exerted all his eloquence to obtain a retraction of that sentence, and ran, with the greatest volubility, through all the protestations, prayers, entreaties, professions and assurances which love could feel or art contrive. I had resolution, however, to resist them, and to command my own emotions on the occasion, better than my natural sensibility gave me reason to expect.

Finding every effort vain, he rose precipitately, and bade me adieu. I urged his tarrying to tea; but he declined, saying, that he must retire to his chamber, being, in his present state of mind, unfit for any society, as he was banished from mine. I offered him my hand, which he pressed with ardor to his lips, and bowing in silence, left the room.

Thus terminated this affair; an affair, which, perhaps, was only the effect of mere gallantry on his part, and of unmeaning pleasantry on mine; and which, I am sorry to say, has given my friends so much anxiety and concern. I am under obligations to them for their kind solicitude, however causeless it may have been.

As an agreeable companion, as a polite and finished gallant, Major Sanford is all that the most lively fancy could wish. And as you have always affirmed that I was a little inclined to coquetry, can you wonder at my exercising it upon so happy a subject? Besides, when I thought more seriously, his liberal fortune was extremely alluring to me, who, you know, have been hitherto confined to the rigid rules of prudence and economy, not to say, necessity in my finances.

Miss Laurence called on me yesterday, as she was taking the air, and asked me whether Major Sanford took leave of me when he left town? He was here last week, said I, but I did not know that he was gone away. O yes, she replied, he is gone to take possession of his seat, which he has lately purchased of Captain Pribble. I am told it is superb; and it ought to be, if it have the honor of his residence. Then you have a great opinion of Major Sanford, said I. Certainly; and has not every body else? said she. I am sure he is a very fine gentleman. Mrs. Richman smiled rather contemptuously, and I changed the subject.

I believe that the innocent heart of this simple girl is a little taken in.

I have just received a letter from Mr. Boyer, in the usual style. He expects the superlative happiness of kissing my hand next week. O dear! I believe I must begin to fix my phiz. Let me run to the glass and try if I can make up one that will look *madamish*. Yes, I succeed very well.

I congratulate you on your new neighbor; but I advise friend George to have the guardian knot tied immediately, lest you should be ensnared by his bewitching 'squire.

I have been trying to seduce General Richman to accompany me to the assembly, this evening, but cannot prevail. Were Mrs. Richman able to go with us, he would be very happy to wait on us together; but to tell the truth, he had rather enjoy her company at home, than any which is to be found abroad. I rallied him on his old fashioned taste; but my heart approved and applauded his attachment. I despise the married man or woman, who harbors an inclination to partake of separate pleasures.

I am told, that a servant man inquires for me below; the messenger of some enamoured swain, I suppose. I will step down and learn what message he brings——

Nothing extraordinary; it is only a card of compliments from a Mr. Emmons, a respectable merchant of this city, requesting the honor to wait on me to the assembly this evening. A welcome request, which I made no hesitation to grant. If I must resign these favorite amusements, let me enjoy as large a share as possible, till the time arrive. Adieu. I must repair to the toilet and adorn for a new conquest, the person of

ELIZA WHARTON.

LETTER XXXI.

to Miss ELIZA WHARTON.

HARTFORD.

I AM very happy to find you are in so good spirits, Eliza, after parting with your favorite swain. For I perceive that he is really the favorite of your fancy, though your heart cannot esteem him; and, independent of that, no sensations can be durable.

I can tell you some news of this strange man. He has arrived, and taken possession of his seat. Having given general invitations, he has been called upon and welcomed by most of the neighboring gentry. Yesterday he made an elegant entertainment. Friend George (as you call him) and I were of the number, who had cards. Twenty one couple

went, I am told. We did not go. I consider my time too valuable to be
spent in cultivating acquaintance with a person from whom neither
pleasure nor improvement are to be expected. His profuseness may bribe
the unthinking multitude to show him respect; but he must know, that
though

> "Places and honors have been bought for gold,
> Esteem and love were never to be sold."

I look upon the vicious habits, and abandoned character of Major
Sanford, to have more pernicious effects on society, than the perpetra-
tions of the robber and the assassin. These, when detected, are rigidly
punished by the laws of the land. If their lives be spared, they are
shunned by society, and treated with every mark of disapprobation and
contempt. But to the disgrace of humanity and virtue, the assassin of
honor; the wretch, who breaks the peace of families, who robs virgin
innocence of its charms, who triumphs over the ill placed confidence of
the inexperienced, unsuspecting, and too credulous fair, is received, and
caressed, not only by his own sex, to which he is a reproach, but even
by ours, who have every conceivable reason to despise and avoid him.
Influenced by these principles, I am neither ashamed nor afraid openly
to avow my sentiments of this man, and my reasons for treating him
with the most pointed neglect.

I write warmly on the subject; for it is a subject in which I think the
honor and happiness of my sex concerned. I wish they would more
generally espouse their own cause. It would conduce to the public weal,
and to their personal respectability. I rejoice, heartily, that you have had
resolution to resist his allurements, to detect and repel his artifices. Res-
olution, in such a case, is absolutely necessary; for,

> "In spite of all the virtue we can boast,
> The woman that deliberates is lost."

As I was riding out, yesterday, I met your mamma. She wondered
that I was not one of the party at our new neighbor's. The reason,
madam, said I, is that I do not like the character of the man. I know
nothing of him, said she; he is quite a stranger to me, only as he called
at my house, last week, to pay me his respects, as he said, for the sake
of my late husband, whose memory he revered; and because I was the
mother of Miss Eliza Wharton, with whom he had the honor of some

little acquaintance. His manners are engaging, and I am sorry to hear that his morals are corrupt.

This, my dear, is a very extraordinary visit. I fear that he has not yet laid aside his arts. Be still on your guard, is the advice of your sincere and faithful friend,

LUCY FREEMAN.

LETTER XXXII.

to Mr. CHARLES DEIGHTON.

HARTFORD.

I AM really banished and rejected; desired never more to think of the girl I love, with a view of indulging that love, or of rendering it acceptable to its object! You will perhaps, dispute the propriety of the term, and tell me it is not love, it is only gallantry, and a desire to exercise it with her, as favorite nymph. I neither know, nor care by what appellation you distinguish it, but it truly gives me pain. I have not felt one sensation of genuine pleasure since I heard my sentence; yet I acquiesced in it, and submissively took my leave; though I doubt not but I shall retaliate the indignity one time or other.

I have taken possession of my new purchase, an elegant and delightful residence. It is rendered more so by being in the vicinity of my charmer's native abode. This circumstance will conduce much to my enjoyment, if I can succeed in my plan of separating her from Mr. Boyer. I know that my situation and mode of life are far more pleasing to her than his, and shall therefore trust to my appearance and address for a reestablishment in her favor. I intend, if possible, to ingratiate myself with her particular friends. For this purpose, I called last week at her mother's, to pay my respects to her (so I told the good woman) as an object of my particular regard; and as the parent of a young lady, whom I had the honor to know and admire. She received me very civilly, thanked me for my attention, and invited me to call whenever I had opportunity; which was the very thing I wanted. I intend likewise, to court popularity. I don't know but I must accept, by and by, some lucrative office in the civil department. Yet I cannot bear the idea of

confinement to business. It appears to me quite inconsistent with the character of a gentleman; I am sure it is, with that of a man of pleasure. But something I must do; for I tell you, in confidence, that I was obliged to mortgage this place, because I had not wherewithal to pay for it. But I shall manage matters very well, I have no doubt, and keep up the appearance of affluence, till I find some lady in a strait for a husband, whose fortune will enable me to extricate myself from these embarrassments. Do come and see me, Charles; for, notwithstanding all my gaiety and parade, I have some turns of the hypo, some qualms of conscience, you will call them; but I meddle not with such obsolete words. And so good bye to you, says

PETER SANFORD.

LETTER XXXIII.

to Miss LUCY FREEMAN

NEW-HAVEN.

My Dear Friend,
I BELIEVE I must begin to assume airs of gravity; and they will not be quite so foreign to my feelings now, as at some other times. You shall know the reason. I have been associated for three days, with sentiment and sobriety, in the person of Mr. Boyer. I don't know but this man will seduce me into matrimony. He is very eloquent upon the subject; and his manners are so solemn, that I am strongly tempted, yet I dare not to laugh. Really, Lucy, there is something extremely engaging and soothing too, in virtuous and refined conversation. It is a source of enjoyment which cannot be realised by the dissolute and unreflecting. But then, this particular theme of his, is not a favorite one to me; I mean, as connected with its consequences, care and confinement. However, I have compounded the matter with him, and conditioned that he shall expatiate on the subject, and call it by what name he pleases, *platonic* or *conjugal,* provided he will let me take my own time for the consummation. I have consented that he shall escort me, next week, to see my mamma and my Lucy. O, how the idea of returning to that revered mansion, to those beloved friends, exhilerates my spirits!

General Richman's politeness to me has induced him to invite a large party of those gentlemen and ladies who have been particularly attentive to me, during my residence here, to dine and take tea, to morrow. After that, I expect to be engaged in making farewell visits, till I leave the place. I shall, therefore, forego the pleasure of telling you any occurrences, subsequent to this date, until you see and converse with your sincere friend,

ELIZA WHARTON.

LETTER XXXIV.

to Mrs. RICHMAN.

HARTFORD.

Dear Madam,

THE day after I left your hospitable dwelling, brought me safe to that of my honored mamma; to the seat of maternal and filial affection; of social ease and domestic peace; of every species of happiness which can result from religion and virtue; from refinement in morals, and manners.

I found my brother and his wife, with Lucy Freeman and Mr. Sumner, waiting to receive and bid me welcome. I flew with extacy to the bosom of my mamma, who received me with her accustomed affection, testified by the expressive tears of tenderness which stole silently down her widowed cheek. She was unable to speak. I was equally so. We therefore indulged, a moment, the pleasing emotions of sympathising sensibility. When disengaged from her fond embrace, I was saluted by the others in turn; and having recovered myself, I presented Mr. Boyer to each of the company, and each of the company to him. He was cordially received by all, but more especially by my mamma.

The next day I was called upon and welcomed by several of my neighboring acquaintance; among whom I was not a little surprised to see Major Sanford. He came in company with Mr. Stoddard and Lady, whom he overtook, as he told me, near by; and, as they informed him that the design of their visit was to welcome me home, he readily accepted their invitation to partake of the pleasure which every one must receive on my return. I bowed slightly at his compliment, taking no

visible notice of any peculiarity of expression either in his words or looks.

His politeness to Mr. Boyer, appeared to be the result of habit. Mr. Boyer's to him, to be forced by respect to the company to which he had gained admission. I dare say, that each felt a conscious superiority; the one on the score of merit; the other on that of fortune. Which ought to outweigh, the judicious mind will easily decide. The scale, as I once observed to you, will turn as fancy or reason preponderates. I believe the esteem which I now have for Mr. Boyer, will keep me steady; except, perhaps, some little excentricities, now and then, just by way of variety. I am going to morrow morning to spend a few days with Lucy Freeman; to assist in the preparation for, and the solemnization of her nuptials. Mr. Boyer, in the mean time, will tarry among his friends in town. My mamma is excessively partial to him; though I am not yet jealous that she means to rival me. I am not certain, however, but it might be happy for him if she should. For I suspect, notwithstanding the disparity of her age, that she is better calculated to make him a good wife than I am or ever shall be.

But to be sober. Please, madam, to make my compliments acceptable to those of your neighbors, whose politeness and attention to me, while at your house, have laid me under particular obligations of gratitude and respect. My best regards attend General Richman. Pray tell him, that though I never expect to be so good a wife as he is blessed with; yet I intend, after a while (when I have sowed all my wild oats) to make a tolerable one.

I am anxious to hear of a wished for event and of your safety. All who know you, feel interested in your health and happiness; but none more warmly than your obliged and affectionate

ELIZA WHARTON.

LETTER XXXV.

to Miss ELIZA WHARTON.

<div align="right">NEW-HAVEN.</div>

I WRITE a line, at Mrs. Richman's request, just to inform you, Eliza, that yesterday, that lovely and beloved woman presented me with a daughter. This event awakens new sensations in my mind; and calls into exercise a kind of affection which had before lain dormant. I feel already the tenderness of a parent; while imagination fondly traces the mother's likeness in the infant form. Mrs. Richman expects to receive your congratulations, in a letter by the next post. She bids me tell you, moreover, that she hopes soon to receive an invitation, and be able to attend to the consummation you talk of. Give Mrs. Richman's and my particular regards to your excellent mother; and to the worthy Mr. Boyer. With sentiments of esteem and friendship, I am, &c.

<div align="right">S. RICHMAN.</div>

LETTER XXXVI.

to Mrs. RICHMAN.

<div align="right">HARTFORD.</div>

FROM the scenes of festive mirth, from the conviviality of rejoicing friends, and from the dissipating amusements of the gay world, I retire with alacrity, to hail my beloved friend on the important charge which she has received; on the accession to her family, and, may I not say, on the addition to her care; since that care will be more than counterbalanced by the pleasure it confers. Hail happy babe! Ushered into the world by the best of mothers; entitled by birth-right to virtue and honor; defended by parental love, from the weakness of infancy and childhood, by guardian wisdom from the perils of youth, and by affluent independence from the griping hand of poverty, in more advanced life! May

these animating prospects be realised by your little daughter; and may you long enjoy the rich reward of seeing her all that you wish!

Yesterday, my dear friend, Lucy Freeman gave her hand to the amiable and accomplished Mr. George Sumner. A large circle of congratulating friends were present. Her dress was such as wealth and elegance required. Her deportment was every thing that modesty and propriety could suggest. They are, indeed, a charming couple. The consonance of their dispositions, the similarity of their tastes, and the equality of their ages are a sure pledge of happiness. Every eye beamed with pleasure on the occasion, and every tongue echoed the wishes of benevolence. Mine only was silent. Though not less interested in the felicity of my friend than the rest, yet the idea of a separation; perhaps, of an alienation of affection, by means of her entire devotion to another, cast an involuntary gloom over my mind. Mr. Boyer took my hand, after the ceremony was past. Permit me, Miss Wharton, said he, to lead you to your lovely friend; her happiness must be heightened by your participation of it. Oh no; said I, I am too selfish for that. She has conferred upon another that affection which I wished to engross. My love was too fervent to admit a rival. Retaliate then, said he, this fancied wrong, by doing likewise. I observed that this was not a proper time to discuss that subject; and, resuming my seat, endeavored to put on the appearance of my accustomed vivacity. I need not relate the remaining particulars of the evening's entertainment. Mr. Boyer returned with my mamma, and I remained at Mrs. Freeman's.

We are to have a ball here, this evening. Mr. Boyer has been with us, and tried to monopolize my company; but in vain. I am too much engaged by the exhilerating scenes around, for attending to a subject which affords no variety. I shall not close this till to morrow.

——I am rather fatigued with the amusements of last night, which were protracted to a late hour. Mr. Boyer was present; and I was pleased to see him not averse to the entertainment, though his profession prevented his taking an active part. As all the neighboring gentry were invited, Mr. Freeman would, by no means, omit Major Sanford, which his daughter earnestly solicited. It happened (unfortunately, shall I say?) that I drew him for a partner. Yet I must own, that I felt very little reluctance to my lot. He is an excellent dancer, and well calculated for a companion in the hours of mirth and gaiety. I regretted Mr. Boyer's being present, however; because my enjoyment seemed to give him pain. I hope he is not inclined to the passion of jealousy. If he is, I fear it will be somewhat exercised.

Lucy Freeman, now Mrs. Sumner, removes, next week, to Boston. I have agreed to accompany her, and spend a month or two in her family. This will give variety to the journey of life. Be so kind as to direct your next letter to me there.

Kiss the dear little babe for me. Give love, compliments, &c. as respectively due; and believe me, with every sentiment of respect, your affectionate

ELIZA WHARTON.

LETTER XXXVII.

to Mr. CHARLES DEIGHTON.

HARTFORD.

Dear Charles,

My hopes begin to revive. I am again permitted to associate with my Eliza; invited to the same entertainment! She does not refuse to join with me in the mazy dance, and partake the scenes of festive mirth. Nay, more; she allows me to press her hand to my lips; and listens to the sighing accents of love. Love her, I certainly do. Would to heaven I could marry her! Would to heaven I had preserved my fortune; or she had one to supply its place! I am distracted at the idea of losing her forever. I am sometimes tempted to solicit her hand in serious earnest; but if I should, poverty and want must be the consequence. Her disappointment in the expectation of affluence and splendor, which I believe her ruling passion, would afford a perpetual source of discontent and mutual wretchedness.

She is going to Boston with her friend, Mrs. Sumner. I must follow her. I must break the connection, which is rapidly forming, between her and Mr. Boyer; and enjoy her society a while longer, if no more.

I have had a little intimation from New-Haven, that Miss Laurence is partial to me, and might easily be obtained, with a handsome property into the bargain. I am neither pleased with, nor averse to the girl. But she has money, and that may supply the place of love, by enabling me to pursue independent pleasures. This she must expect, if she marries a man of my cast. She doubtless knows my character; and if she is so vain

of her charms or influence, as to think of reforming or confining me, she must bear the consequences.

However, I can keep my head up, at present, without recourse to the noose of matrimony; and shall, therefore, defer any particular attention to her, till necessity requires it.

I am, &c.

PETER SANFORD.

LETTER XXXVIII.

to Mrs. M. WHARTON

BOSTON.

You commanded me, my dear mamma, to write you. That command, I cheerfully obey, in testimony of my ready submission and respect. No other avocation could arrest my time, which is now completely occupied in scenes of amusement.

Mrs. Sumner is agreeably settled and situated. She appears to be possessed of every blessing which can render life desirable. Almost every day, since our arrival, has been engrossed by visitants. Our evenings, we have devoted to company abroad; and that more generally than we should otherwise have done, as my stay is limited to so short a period. The museum, the theatres, the circus and the assemblies have been frequented.

Mrs. Sumner has made me several presents, notwithstanding which, the articles requisite to a fashionable appearance, have involved me in considerable expense. I fear that you will think me extravagant when you are told how much.

Mr. Boyer tarried in town about a week, having business. He appeared a little concerned at my taste for dissipation, as he once termed it. He even took the liberty to converse seriously on the subject.

I was displeased with his freedom; and reminded him that I had the disposal of my own time, as yet; and that while I escaped the censure of my own heart, I hoped that no one else would presume to arraign it. He apologised, and gave up his argument.

I was much surprised, the first time I went to the play, to see Major

Sanford in the very next box. He immediately joined our party; and wherever I have been since, I have been almost sure to meet him.

Mr. Boyer has taken his departure; and I do not expect to see him again, till I return home.

O mamma! I am embarrassed about this man. His worth I acknowledge; nay, I esteem him very highly. But can there be happiness with such a disparity of dispositions?

I shall soon return to the bosom of domestic tranquillity, to the arms of maternal tenderness, where I can deliberate and advise at leisure, about this important matter. Till when,

I am, &c.

ELIZA WHARTON.

LETTER XXXIX.

to Mr. T. SELBY.

HAMPSHIRE.

Dear Sir,

I BELIEVE that I owe you an apology for my long silence. But my time has been much engrossed of late; and my mind much more so. When it will be otherwise, I cannot foresee. I fear, my friend, that there is some foundation for your suspicions respecting my beloved Eliza. What pity it is, that so fair a form, so accomplished a mind, should be tarnished, in the smallest degree, by the follies of coquetry! If this be the fact, which I am loth to believe, all my regard for her shall never make me the dupe of it.

When I arrived at her residence, at New-Haven, where, I told you in my last, I was soon to go, she gave me a most cordial reception. Her whole behavior to me was correspondent with those sentiments of esteem and affection which she modestly avowed. She permitted me to accompany her to Hartford, to restore her to her mother, and to declare my wish to receive her again from her hand. Thus far, all was harmony and happiness. As all my wishes were consistent with virtue and honor, she readily indulged them. She took apparent pleasure in my company,

encouraged my hopes of a future union, and listened to the tender accents of love.

But the scenes of gaiety, which invited her attention, reversed her conduct. The delightful hours of mutual confidence, of sentimental converse, and of the interchange of refined affection, were no more! Instead of these, parties were formed, unpleasing to my taste; and every opportunity was embraced to join in diversions, in which she knew I could not consistently take a share. I, however, acquiesced in her pleasure, though I sometimes thought myself neglected, and even hinted it to her mother. The old lady apologised for her daughter, by alledging that she had been absent for a long time; that her acquaintances were rejoiced at her return, and welcomed her by striving to promote her amusement.

One of her most intimate friends was married during my stay; and she appeared deeply interested in the event. She spent several days in assisting her, previous to the celebration. I resided, in the mean time, at her mamma's, visiting her at her friend's, where Major Sanford, among others, was received as a guest. Mrs. Sumner acquainted me that she had prevailed on Miss Wharton to go and spend a few weeks with her at Boston, whither she was removing; and urged my accompanying them. I endeavored to excuse myself, as I had been absent from my people a considerable time, and my return was now expected. But their importunity was so great, and Eliza's declaration that it would be very agreeable to her, so tempting, that I consented. Here I took lodgings and spent about a week, taking every opportunity to converse with Eliza, striving to discover her real disposition towards me. I mentioned the inconvenience of visiting her so often as I wished, and suggested my desire to enter, as soon as might be, into a family relation. I painted in the most alluring colours the pleasures resulting from domestic tranquillity, mutual confidence, and conjugal affection; and insisted on her declaring frankly whether she designed to share this happiness with me, and when it should commence. She owned that she intended to give me her hand; but when she should be ready, she could not yet determine. She pretended a promise from me to wait her time; to consent that she should share the pleasures of the fashionable world, as long as she chose, &c.

I then attempted to convince her of her mistaken ideas of pleasure; that the scenes of dissipation, of which she was so passionately fond, afforded no true enjoyment; that the adulation of the coxcomb could not give durability to her charms, or secure the approbation of the wise

and good; nor could the fashionable amusements of brilliant assemblies, and crouded theatres furnish the mind with

> "That which nothing earthly gives, or can destroy,
> The soul's calm sunshine, and the heart felt joy."

These friendly suggestions, I found were considered as the theme of a priest; and my desire to detach her from such empty pursuits, as the selfishness of a lover. She was even offended at my freedom; and warmly affirmed, that no one had a right to arraign her conduct. I mentioned Major Sanford who was then in town, and who (though she went to places of public resort with Mr. and Mrs. Sumner) always met and gallanted her home. She rallied me upon my jealousy, as she termed it; wished that I would attend her myself, and then she should need no other gallant. I answered that I had rather resign that honor to another; but wished, for her sake, that he might be a gentleman whose character would not disgrace the company with which he associated. She appeared mortified and chagrined in the extreme. However, she studiously suppressed her emotions; and even soothed me with the blandishments of female softness. We parted amicably. She promised to return soon, and prepare for a compliance with my wishes. I cannot refuse to believe her! I cannot cease to love her! My heart is in her possession. She has a perfect command of my passions. Persuasion dwells on her tongue. With all the boasted fortitude and resolution of our sex, we are but mere machines. Let love once pervade our breasts; and its object may mould us into any form that pleases her fancy, or even caprice.

I have just received a letter from Eliza, informing me of her return to Hartford. To morrow I shall set out on a visit to the dear girl; for, my friend, notwithstanding all her foibles, she is very dear to me. Before you hear from me again, I expect that the happy day will be fixed; the day which shall unite, in the most sacred bands, this lovely maid, and your faithful friend,

J. BOYER.

LETTER XL.

to Mr. T. SELBY.

<div align="right">HAMPSHIRE.</div>

I HAVE returned; and the day, indeed, is fixed; but Oh! how different from my fond expectations! It is not the day of union, but the day of final separation; the day which divides me from my charmer; the day which breaks asunder the bands of love; the day on which my reason assumes its empire, and triumphs over the arts of a finished coquette! Congratulate me, my friend, that I have thus overcome my feelings, and repelled the infatuating wiles of a deceitful girl. I would not be understood to impeach Miss Wharton's virtue; I mean her chastity. Virtue in the common acceptation of the term, as applied to the sex, is confined to that particular, you know. But in my view, this is of little importance, where all other virtues are wanting!

When I arrived at Mrs. Wharton's, and inquired for Eliza, I was told that she had rode out; but was soon expected home. An hour after, a phaeton stopped at the door, from which my fair one alighted, and was handed into the house by Major Sanford, who immediately took leave. I met her and offered my hand, which she received with apparent tenderness.

When the family had retired after supper, and left us to talk on our particular affairs, I found the same indecision, the same loathness to bring our courtship to a period, as formerly. Her previous excuses were renewed, and her wishes to have a union still longer delayed, were zealously urged. She could not bear the idea of confinement to the cares of a married life at present; and begged me to defer all solicitation on that subject to some future day. I found my temper rise, and told her plainly, that I was not thus to be trifled with; that if her regard for me was sincere; if she really intended to form a connection with me, she could not thus protract the time, try my patience, and prefer every other pleasure to the rational interchange of affection, to the calm delights of domestic life. But in vain did I argue against her false notions of happiness; in vain did I represent the dangerous system of conduct, which she now pursued, and urge her to accept, before it was too late, the hand and heart which were devoted to her service. That, she said, she purposed, ere long to do; and hoped amply to reward my faithful love;

but she could not fix the time this evening. She must consider a little further; and likewise consult her mother. Is it not Major Sanford whom you wish to consult, madam? said I. She blushed, and gave me no answer. Tell me, Eliza, I continued, tell me frankly, if he has not supplanted me in your affections; if he be not the cause of my being thus evasively, thus cruelly treated? Major Sanford, sir, replied she, has done you no harm. He is a particular friend of mine; a polite gentleman, and an agreeable neighbor; and therefore I treat him with civility; but he is not so much interested in my concerns, as to alter my disposition towards any other person. Why, said I, do you talk of friendship with a man of his character? Between his society and mine, there is a great contrast. Such opposite pursuits and inclinations cannot be equally pleasing to the same taste. It is therefore necessary, that you renounce the one, to enjoy the other. I will give you time to decide which. I am going to a friend's house to spend the night; and will call on you to morrow, if agreeable, and converse with you further upon the matter. She bowed assent, and I retired.

The next afternoon I went as agreed; and found her mamma and her alone in the parlor. She was very pensive and appeared to have been in tears. The sight affected me. The idea of having treated her harshly, the evening before, disarmed me of my resolution to insist on her decision that day. I invited her to ride with me and visit a friend, to which she readily consented. We spent our time agreeably. I forebore to press her on the subject of our future union; but strove rather to soothe her mind, and inspire her with sentiments of tenderness towards me. I conducted her home, and returned early in the evening to my friend's, who met me at the door; and jocosely told me, that he expected I should now rob them of their agreeable neighbor. But, added he, we have been apprehensive that you would be rivalled, if you delayed your visit much longer. I did not suspect a rival, said I. Who can the happy man be? I can say nothing from personal observation, said he; but fame, of late, has talked loudly of Major Sanford and Miss Wharton. Be not alarmed, continued he, seeing me look grave. I presume no harm is intended. The Major is a man of gallantry, and Miss Wharton is a gay lady; but I dare say that your connection will be happy, *if it be formed*. I noticed a particular emphasis on the word *if*; and as we were alone, I followed him with questions, till the whole affair was developed. I informed him of my embarrassment; and he gave me to understand that Eliza's conduct had, for some time past, been a subject of speculation in the town; that formerly, her character was highly esteemed; but that her intimacy

with a man of Sanford's known libertinism; more especially as she was supposed to be engaged to another, had rendered her very censurable; that they were often together; that wherever she went, he was sure to follow, as if by appointment; that they walked, talked, sung and danced together in all companies; that some supposed he would marry her; others, that he only meditated adding her name to the black catalogue of deluded wretches, whom he had already ruined!

I rose, and walked the room in great agitation. He apologized for his freedom; was sorry if he had wounded my feelings; but friendship alone had induced him frankly to declare the truth, that I might guard against duplicity and deceit.

I thanked him for his kind intensions; and assured him that I should not quit the town till I had terminated this affair, in one way or another.

I retired to bed, but sleep was a stranger to my eyes. With the dawn I rose; and after breakfast walked to Mrs. Wharton's, who informed me, that Eliza was in her chamber, writing to a friend, but would be down in a few minutes. I entered into conversation with the old lady on the subject of her daughter's conduct; hinted my suspicions of the cause, and declared my resolution of knowing my destiny immediately. She endeavored to extenuate, and excuse her as much as possible; but frankly owned that her behavior was mysterious; that no pains had been wanting, on her part, to alter and rectify it; that she had remonstrated, expostulated, advised and entreated, as often as occasion required. She hoped that my resolution would have a good effect, as she knew that her daughter esteemed me very highly.

In this manner we conversed till the clock struck twelve; and Eliza, not appearing, I desired her mamma to send up word that I waited to see her. The maid returned with an answer that she was indisposed, and had lain down. Mrs. Wharton observed, that she had not slept for several nights, and complained of the head ache in the morning. The girl added, that she would wait on Mr. Boyer in the evening. Upon this information I rose and abruptly took my leave. I went to dine with a friend, to whom I had engaged myself the day before; but my mind was too much agitated to enjoy either the company or the dinner. I excused myself from tarrying to tea, and returned to Mrs. Wharton's. On inquiry, I was told that Eliza had gone to walk in the garden; but desired that no person might intrude on her retirement. The singularity of the request awakened my curiosity, and determined me to follow her. I sought her in vain, in different parts of the garden, till, going towards an arbor, almost concealed from sight, by surrounding shrubbery, I dis-

covered her, sitting in close conversation with Major Sanford! My blood chilled in my veins, and I stood petrified with astonishment, at the disclosure of such baseness and deceit. They both rose in visible confusion. I dared not trust myself to accost them. My passions were raised, and I feared that I might say or do something unbecoming my character. I therefore gave them a look of indignation and contempt, and retreated to the house. I traversed the parlor hastily, overwhelmed with chagrin and resentment! Mrs. Wharton inquired the cause. I attempted to tell her, but my tongue refused utterance! While in this situation, Eliza entered the room. She was not less discomposed than myself. She sat down at the window and wept. Her mamma wept likewise. At length she recovered herself, in a degree, and desired me to sit down. I answered no; and continued walking. Will you, said she, permit me to vindicate my conduct and explain my motives? Your conduct, said I, cannot be vindicated; your motives need no explanation; they are too apparent! How, Miss Wharton, have I merited this treatment from you? But I can bear it no longer. Your indifference to me proceeds from an attachment to another; and forgive me, if I add, to one, who is the disgrace of his own sex, and the destroyer of yours. I have been too long the dupe of your dissimulation and coquetry. Too long has my peace of mind been sacrificed to the arts of a woman, whose conduct has proved her unworthy of my regard; insensible to love, gratitude and honor!

To you, madam, said I, turning to her mother, I acknowledge my obligations for your friendship, politeness and attention. I once hoped for the privilege of rocking for you the cradle of declining age. I am deprived of that privilege; but I pray that you may never want a child, whose love and duty shall prove a source of consolation and comfort!

Farewell! If we never meet again in this life, I hope and trust we shall in a better; where the parent's eye shall cease to weep for the disobedience of a child; and the lover's heart to bleed for the infidelity of his mistress!

I turned to Eliza, and attempted to speak; but her extreme emotion softened me, and I could not command my voice. I took her hand, and bowing, in token of an adieu, went precipitately out of the house. The residence of my friend, with whom I lodged, was at no great distance, and thither I repaired. As I met him in the entry, I rushed by him, and betook myself to my chamber.

The fever of resentment, and the tumult of passion began now to give place to the softer emotions of the soul. I found myself perfectly unmanned. I gave free scope to the sensibility of my heart; and

the effeminate relief of tears materially lightened the load which oppressed me.

After this arduous struggle I went to bed; and slept more calmly than for several nights before. The next morning I wrote a farewell letter to Eliza (a copy of which I shall inclose to you) and ordering my horse to be brought, left town immediately.

My resentment of her behavior has much assisted me in erasing her image from my breast. In this exertion I have succeeded beyond my most sanguine expectations. The more I reflect on her temper and disposition, the more my gratitude is enlivened towards the wise Disposer of all events for enabling me to break asunder the snares of the deluder. I am convinced, that the gaiety and extravagance of her taste, the frivolous levity of her manners disqualify her for the station in which I wished to have placed her. These considerations, together with that resignation to an overruling Providence which the religion I profess, and teach, requires me to cultivate, induce me cheerfully to adopt the following lines of an ingenious poet:

"Since all the downward tracts of time,
 God's watchful eye surveys,
Oh, who so wise to choose our lot,
 Or regulate our ways?

Since none can doubt his equal love,
 Unmeasurably kind,
To his unerring gracious will,
 Be every wish resign'd.

Good, when he gives, supremely good,
 Not less when he denies;
E'en crosses from his sovereign hand,
 Are blessings in disguise."

I am, &c.

J. BOYER.

to Miss ELIZA WHARTON.

ENCLOSED IN THE FOREGOING.

HARTFORD.

Madam,

FEARING, that my resolution may not be proof against the eloquence of those charms, which have so long commanded me, I take this method of bidding you a final adieu. I write not as a lover. That connection between us is for ever dissolved; but I address you as a friend; a friend to your happiness, to your reputation, to your temporal and eternal welfare. I will not rehearse the innumerable instances of your imprudence and misconduct, which have fallen under my observation. Your own heart must be your monitor! Suffice it for me to warn you against the dangerous tendency of so dissipated a life; and to tell you that I have traced (I believe aright) the cause of your dissimulation and indifference to me. They are an aversion to the sober, rational, frugal mode of living, to which my profession leads; a fondness for the parade, the gaiety, not to say, the licentiousness of a station calculated to gratify such a disposition; and a prepossession for Major Sanford, infused into your giddy mind by the frippery, flattery and artifice of that worthless and abandoned man. Hence you preferred a connection with him, if it could be accomplished; but a doubt, whether it could, together with the advice of your friends, who have kindly espoused my cause, have restrained you from the avowal of your real sentiments, and led you to continue your civilities to me. What the result of your coquetry would have been, had I waited for it, I cannot say, nor have I now any desire or interest to know. I tear from my breast the idea which I have long cherished of future union and happiness with you in the conjugal state. I bid a last farewell to these fond hopes, and leave you for ever!

For your own sake, however, let me conjure you to review your conduct, and before you have advanced beyond the possibility of returning to rectitude and honor, to restrain your steps from the dangerous path in which you now tread!

Fly Major Sanford. That man is a deceiver. Trust not his professions. They are certainly insincere; or he would not affect concealment; he would not induce you to a clandestine intercourse! Many have been the victims of his treachery! O Eliza! add not to the number! Banish him from your society, if you wish to preserve your virtue unsullied, your

character unsuspicious! It already begins to depreciate. Snatch it from the envenomed tongue of slander, before it receive an incurable wound!

Many faults have been visible to me; over which my affection once drew a veil. That veil is now removed. And, acting the part of a disinterested friend, I shall mention some few of them with freedom. There is a levity in your manners, which is inconsistent with the solidity and decorum becoming a lady who has arrived to years of discretion. There is also an unwarrantable extravagance betrayed in your dress. Prudence and economy are such necessary, at least, such decent virtues, that they claim the attention of every female, whatever be her station or her property. To these virtues you are apparently inattentive. Too large a portion of your time is devoted to the adorning of your person.

Think not that I write thus plainly from resentment. No; it is from benevolence. I mention your foibles, not to reproach you with them, but that you may consider their nature and effects, and renounce them.

I wish you to regard this letter as the legacy of a friend; and to improve it accordingly. I shall leave town before you receive it. O, how different are my sensations at going, from what they were when I came! but I forbear description.

Think not, Eliza, that I leave you with indifference! The conflict is great; the trial is more than I can calmly support! Yet the consciousness of duty, affords consolation. A duty I conceive it to be, which I owe to myself; and to the people of my charge, who are interested in my future connection.

I wish not for an answer; my resolution is unalterably fixed. But should you hereafter be convinced of the justice of my conduct; and become a convert to my advice, I shall be happy to hear it.

That you may have wisdom to keep you from falling, and conduct you safely through this state of trial to the regions of immortal bliss, is the fervent prayer of your sincere friend, and humble servant,

J. BOYER.

LETTER XLI.

to Mrs. LUCY SUMNER.

HARTFORD.

THE retirement of my native home is not so gloomy, since my return from Boston, as I expected, from the contrast between them.

Indeed, the customs and amusements of this place are materially altered, since the residence of Major Sanford among us. The dull, old fashioned sobriety which formerly prevailed, is nearly banished; and cheerfulness, vivacity, and enjoyment are substituted in its stead. Pleasure is now diffused through all ranks of the people, especially the rich; and surely it ought to be cultivated, since the wisest of men informs us, that "a merry heart doth good like a medicine." As human life has many diseases, which require medicines, are we not right in selecting the most agreeable and palatable? Major Sanford's example has had great influence upon our society in general; and though some of our old dons think him rather licentious; yet, for ought I can see, he is as strict an observer of decorum, as the best of them. True, he seldom goes to church; but what of that? The Deity is not confined to temples made with hands. He may worship him as devoutly elsewhere, if he chuses; and who has a right to say he does not?

His return from Boston was but a day or two after mine. He paid me an early visit; and, indeed, has been very attentive ever since. My mamma is somewhat precise in her notions of propriety; and of course, blames me for associating so freely with him. She says, that my engagements to Mr. Boyer ought to render me more sedate; and more indifferent to the gallantry of mere *pleasure-hunters*, to use her phrase. But I think otherwise. If I am to become a recluse, let me, at least, enjoy those amusements, which are suited to my taste, a short time first. Why should I refuse the polite attentions of this gentleman? They smoothe the rugged path of life, and wonderfully accelerate the lagging wheels of time.

Indeed, Lucy, he has an admirable talent for contributing to vary, and increase amusement. We have few hours unimproved. Some new plan of pleasure, and sociability is constantly courting our adoption. He lives in all the magnificence of a prince; and why should I, who can doubtless share that magnificence if I please, forego the advantages and

indulgences it offers, merely to gratify those friends who pretend to be better judges of my happiness than I am myself.

I have not yet told my mamma that he entertains me with the lover's theme; or, at least, that I listen to it. Yet I must own to you, from whom I have never concealed an action or idea, that his situation in life charms my imagination; that the apparent fervor and sincerity of his passion affect my heart. Yet there is something extremely problematical in his conduct. He is very urgent with me to dissolve my connection with Mr. Boyer, and engage not to marry him without his consent; or knowledge, to say no more. He warmly applauds my wish, still longer to enjoy the freedom and independence of a single state; and professedly adopts it for his own. While he would disconnect me from another, he mysteriously conceals his own intentions and views. In conversation with him yesterday, I plainly told him that his conduct was unaccountable; that if his professions and designs were honorable he could not neglect to mention them to my mamma; that I should no longer consent to carry on a clandestine intercourse with him; that I hourly expected Mr. Boyer, whom I esteemed, and who was the favorite of my friends; and that unless he acted openly in this affair before his arrival, I should give my hand to him.

He appeared thunderstruck at this declaration. All his words and actions were indicative of the most violent emotions of mind. He entreated me to recall the sentence; for I knew not, he said, his motives for secrecy; yet he solemnly swore that they were honorable. I replied in the words of the poet,

"Trust not a man, they are by nature cruel,
False, deceitful, treacherous, and inconstant.
When a man talks of love, with caution hear him;
But if he swear, he'll certainly deceive you."

He begged that he might know by what means he had provoked my suspicions; by what means he had forfeited my confidence? His importunity vanquished my fortitude; and before we parted, I again promised to make him acquainted, from time to time, with the progress of my connection with Mr. Boyer.

Now, my dear friend, I want your advice more than ever. I am inadvertently embarrassed by this man; and how to extricate myself, I know not. I am sensible that the power is in my hands; but the disposition (shall I confess it) is wanting!

"I know the right, and I approve it too;
I know the wrong, and yet the wrong pursue!"

I have just received a card from Major Sanford, inviting me to ride
this afternoon. At first I thought of returning a negative answer; but
recollecting that Mr. Boyer must soon be here, I concluded it best to
embrace this opportunity, of talking further with him. I must now pre-
pare to go; but shall not close this letter, for I intend writing in contin-
uation, as events occur, till this important business is decided.

Tuesday evening. The little tour which I mentioned to you this af-
ternoon, was not productive of a final determination. The same plea
was repeated over, and over again, without closing the cause. On my
return I found Mr. Boyer waiting to receive me. My heart beat an in-
voluntary welcome. I received him very cordially, though with a kind
of pleasure mixed with apprehension. I must own that his conversation
and manners are much better calculated to bear the scrutinising eye of
a refined understanding and taste, than Major Sanford's. But whether
the fancy ought not to be consulted about our settlement for life, is with
me a question.

When we parted last, I had promised Mr. Boyer, to inform him pos-
itively, at this visit, when my hand should be given. He therefore came,
as he told me in the course of our conversation, with the resolution of
claiming the fulfilment of this promise.

I begged absolution; told him, that I could not possibly satisfy his
claim; and sought still to evade, and put off the important decision. He
grew warm; and affirmed that I treated him ungenerously, and made
needless delays. He even accused me of indifference towards him; and
of partiality to another. Major Sanford he believed, was the man who
robbed him of the affection which he had supposed his due. He warned
me against any intercourse with him, and insisted that I must renounce
the society of the one or the other immediately. He would leave me, he
said, this evening and call to morrow to know the result of my deter-
mination. It was late before he bade me good night; since which I have
written these particulars. It is now time to lay aside my pen, and delib-
erate what course to take.

Wednesday Evening. Last night I closed not my eyes. I rose this
morning with the sun, and went into the garden till breakfast. My
mamma doubtless saw the disorder of my mind, but kindly avoided any
inquiry about it. She was affectionately attentive to me, but said nothing
of my particular concerns. I mentioned not my embarrassment to her.

She had declared herself in favor of Mr. Boyer; therefore I had no ex-
pectation, that she would advise impartially. I retired to my chamber,
and remained in a kind of reverie, for more than an hour; when I was
roused by the rattling of a carriage at the door. I hastened to the win-
dow, and saw Major Sanford just driving away. The idea of his having
been to converse with my mamma, gave me new sensations. A thousand
perplexities occurred to my mind relative to the part most proper for
me to act in this critical situation. All these might have been avoided,
had I gone down and inquired into the matter; but this I delayed till
dinner. My mamma then informed me, that Major Sanford had been
with her, and inquired for me; but that she thought it unnecessary to
call me, as she presumed I had no particular business with him. I knew
the motives by which she was actuated, and was vexed at her evasions.
I told her plainly, that she would never carry her point in this way; that
I thought myself capable of conducting my own affairs; and wished her
not to interfere, except by her advice, which I should always listen to,
and comply with when I could possibly make it consistent with my
inclination and interest. She wept at my undutiful anger (of which I
have severely repented since) and affectionately replied, that my hap-
piness was the object of her wishes and prayers; conformably to which
she felt constrained, freely to speak her mind, though it incurred my
displeasure. She then went through again with all the comparative cir-
cumstances and merits of the two candidates for my favor, which have
perpetually rung in my ears for months. I shed tears at the idea of my
embarrassment; and in this condition Mr. Boyer found us. He appeared
to be affected by my visible disorder; and without inquiring the cause,
endeavored to dissipate it. This was kindly done. He conversed upon
indifferent subjects; and invited me to ride, and take tea with your
mamma, to which I readily consented. We found her at home; and
passed the time agreeably, excepting the alloy of your absence. Mr.
Boyer touched lightly on the subject of our last evening's debate; but
expatiated largely on the pleasing power of love; and hoped that we
should one day both realize and exemplify it in perfection. When we
returned, he observed that it was late, and took his leave; telling me
that he should call to morrow; and begged that I would then relieve his
suspense. As I was retiring to bed, the maid gave me a hint that Major
Sanford's servant had been here and left a letter. I turned instantly back
to my mamma, and telling her my information, demanded the letter.
She hesitated, but I insisted on having it; and seeing me resolute, she
reluctantly gave it into my hand. It contained the following words:

"Am I forsaken? Am I abandoned? Oh my adorable Eliza, have you sacrificed me to my rival? Have you condemned me to perpetual banishment, without a hearing?

I came this day, to plead my cause at your feet; but was cruelly denied the privilege of seeing you! My mind is all anarchy and confusion! My soul is harrowed up with jealousy! I will be revenged on those who separate us, if that distracting event take place! But it is from your lips only that I can hear my sentence! You must witness its effects! To what lengths my despair may carry me, I know not! You are the arbitress of my fate!

Let me conjure you to meet me in your garden to morrow at any hour you shall appoint. My servant will call for an answer in the morning. Deny me not an interview; but have pity on your faithful

Sanford."

I wrote for answer, that I would meet him to morrow, at five o'clock in the afternoon.

I have now before me another night for consideration; and shall pass it in that employment. I purpose not to see Mr. Boyer, till I have conversed with Major Sanford.

Thursday Morning. The morning dawns, and ushers in the day; a day, perhaps big with the fate of your friend! What that fate may be is wrapped in the womb of futurity; that futurity which a kind Providence has wisely concealed from the penetration of mortals!

After mature consideration; after revolving and re-revolving every circumstance on both sides of the question, I have nearly determined, in compliance with the advice of my friends, and the dictates of my own judgment, to give Mr. Boyer the preference, and with him to tread the future round of life.

As to the despair of Major Sanford, it does not much alarm me. Such violent passions are seldom so deeply rooted, as to produce lasting effects. I must, however, keep my word, and meet him according to promise.

Mr. Boyer is below. My mamma has just sent me word that he wished to see me. My reply was that I had lain down, which was a fact.

One o'Clock. My mamma, alarmed by my indisposition, has visited my apartment. I soon convinced her that it was but trifling, owing principally to the want of sleep; and that an airing in the garden, which I intended towards night, would restore me.

Ten o'clock, at night. The day is past! and such a day it has been, as I hope never more to see!

At the hour appointed, I went tolerably composed and resolute into the garden. I had taken several turns, and retired into the little arbor, where you and I have spent so many happy hours, before Major Sanford entered. When he appeared, a consciousness of the impropriety of this clandestine intercourse suffused my cheek, and gave a coldness to my manners. He immediately penetrated the cause, and observed that my very countenance told him he was no longer a welcome guest to me. I asked him if he ought so to be; since his motives for seeking admission, were unworthy of being communicated to my friends? That he said was not the case, but that prudence in the present instance required a temporary concealment.

He then undertook to exculpate himself from blame, assuring me that as soon as I should discountenance the expectations of Mr. Boyer, and discontinue the reception of his address, his intentions should be made known. He was enlarging upon this topic, when we heard a footstep approaching us; and looking up saw Mr. Boyer within a few paces of the arbor.—Confusion seized us both! We rose involuntarily from our seats, but were mute as statues! He spoke not a word, but casting a look of indignant accusation at me, a glance which penetrated my very soul, turned on his heel, and walked hastily back to the house.

I stood a few moments, considering what course to take, though shame and regret had almost taken from me the power of thought.

Major Sanford took my hand. I withdrew it from him. I *must* leave you, said I. Where will you go? said he. I will go and try to retrieve my character. It has suffered greatly by this fatal interview.

He threw himself at my feet and exclaimed, leave me not, Eliza, I conjure you not to leave me. Let me go now, I rejoined, or I bid you farewell for ever. I flew precipitately by him, and went into the parlor, where I found Mr. Boyer and my mamma, the one traversing the room in the greatest agitation; the other in a flood of tears! Their appearance affected me; and I wept like an infant! when I had a little recovered myself, I begged him to sit down; He answered no. I then told him, that however unjustifiable my conduct might appear, perhaps I might explain it to his satisfaction, if he would hear me; that my motives were innocent, though they doubtless wore the aspect of criminality, in his view. He sternly replied, that no palliation could avail; that my motives were sufficiently notorious! He accused me of treating him ill, of rendering

him the dupe of coquetting artifice, of having an intrigue with Major Sanford, and declared his determination to leave me for ever, as unworthy of his regard, and incapable of love, gratitude, or honor!—There was too much reason in support of his accusations for me to gainsay them, had his impetuosity suffered me to attempt it.

But in truth I had no inclination to self defence. My natural vivacity had forsaken me; and I listened without interrupting him to the fluency of reproachful language, which his resentment inspired. He took a very solemn and affectionate leave of my mamma; thanking her for her politeness, and wishing her much future felicity. He attempted to address me, I suppose somewhat in the same way, but his sensibility overcame him; and he only took my hand, and bowing in silence, departed.

The want of rest for two long nights together, the exercise of mind, and conflict of passions, which now tortured my breast, were too much for me to support!

When I saw that he was gone; that he had actually forsaken me, I fainted. My mamma, with the assistance of the maid, soon restored me.

When I opened my eyes, and beheld this amiable and tender parent, watching and attending me with the most anxious concern; without one reproachful word, without one accusing look, my reflections upon the part I had acted, in defeating her benevolent wishes, were exquisitely afflictive! But we mutually forbore to mention the occasion of my illness; and I complied with her advice to take some refreshment, and retire to my chamber. I am so much fatigued by the exertions of the day, that rest is absolutely necessary; and I lay aside my pen to seek it.

Friday Morning. When I shall again receive the balmy influence of sleep, I know not. It has absolutely forsaken me at present. I have had a most restless night. Every awakening idea presented itself to my imagination; whether I had sustained a real loss in Mr. Boyer's departure; reflections on my own misconduct, with the censure of my friends, and the ill-natured remarks of my enemies, excited the most painful anxiety in my mind!

I am going down, but how shall I see my mamma? To her will I confess my faults, in her maternal breast repose my cares, and by her friendly advice regulate my conduct. Had I done this before, I might have escaped this trouble, and saved both her and myself many distressing emotions!

Friday Evening. I have had a long conversation with my mamma,

which has greatly relieved my mind. She has soothed me with the most endearing tenderness.

Mr. Atkins, with whom Mr. Boyer lodged, while in town, called here this afternoon. I did not see him, but he told my mamma that Mr. Boyer had returned home, and left a letter for me, which he had promised to convey with his own hand. By this letter I am convinced that the dye is absolutely cast, with respect to him, and that no attempts on my part to bring about a reconciliation would be either prudent or successful. He has penetrated the cause of my proceedings; and such is his resentment, that I am inclined not much to regret his avoiding another interview.

My excuses would be deemed utterly insufficient, and truth would not befriend and justify me.

As I know you are impatient to hear from me, I will now dispatch this long letter without any other addition, than that I am your sincere friend,

ELIZA WHARTON.

LETTER XLII.

TO MR. CHARLES DEIGHTON

HARTFORD.

WELL, Charles, the show is over, as we yankees say; and the girl is my own. That is, if I will have her. I shall take my own time for that, however. I have carried my point, and am amply revenged on the whole posse of those dear friends of hers. She was entangled by a promise (not to marry this priest without my knowledge,) which her conscience would not let her break. Thank God, I have no conscience. If I had, I believe it would make wretched work with me! I suppose she intended to have one, or the other of us; but preferred me. I have escaped the noose, this time, and I'll be fairly hanged, if I ever get so near it again. For indeed Charles, I was seriously alarmed. I watched all their motions; and the appearances of harmony between them awakened all my activity and zeal. So great was my infatuation, that I verily believe I should have asked her in marriage, and risked the consequences, rather than to have lost her!

I went to the house, while Mr. Boyer was in town, but her mamma refused to call her, or to acquaint her that I was there. I then wrote a despairing letter, and obtained a conference with her in the garden. This was a fortunate event for me. True, Eliza was very haughty, and resolutely insisted on immediate declaration or rejection. And I cannot say what would have been the result, if Mr. Boyer had not surprized us together. He gave us a pretty harsh look and retired without speaking a word.

I endeavored to detain Eliza, but in vain. She left me on my knees, which are always ready to bend on such occasions.

This finished the matter, it seems. I rose, and went into a near neighbor's to observe what happened; and in about half an hour saw Mr. Boyer come out, and go to his lodgings.

This, said I to myself, is a good omen. I went home, and was informed next day, that he had mounted his horse and departed.

I heard nothing more of her till yesterday, when I determined to know how she stood affected towards me. I therefore paid her a visit, her mamma being luckily abroad.

She received me very placidly, and told me, on inquiry, that Mr. Boyer's resentment at her meeting me in the garden was so great, that he had bid her a final adieu. I congratulated myself on having no rival; hoped that her favor would now be unbiassed, and that in due time I should reap the reward of my fidelity. She begged me not to mention the subject; said she had been perplexed by our competition, and wished not to hear any thing further about it at present. I bowed in obedience to her commands and changed the discourse.

I informed her, that I was about taking a tour to the southward; that I should be absent several months, and trusted that on my return her embarrassments would be over.

I left her with regret. After all, Charles, she is the *summum bonum* of my life. I must have her in some way or other. No body else shall, I am resolved.

I am making preparations for my journey; which between you and me, is occasioned by the prospect of making a speculation, by which I hope to mend my affairs. The voyage will at least lessen my expenses, and screen me from the importunity of creditors till I can look about me.

PETER SANFORD.

LETTER XLIII.

to Miss ELIZA WHARTON

NEW-HAVEN.

My Dear Eliza,

THROUGH the medium of my friends at Hartford I have been informed of the progress of your affairs, as they have transpired. The detail which my sister gave me of your separation from Mr. Boyer was painful; as I had long contemplated a happy union between you. But still more disagreeable sensations possessed my breast, when told that you had suffered your lively spirits to be depressed, and resigned yourself to solitude and dejection!

Why, my dear friend, should you allow this event thus to affect you? Heaven, I doubt not, has happiness still in store for you—perhaps greater than you could have enjoyed in that connection. If the conviction of any misconduct on your part, give you pain, dissipate it by the reflection, that unerring rectitude is not the lot of mortals, that few are to be found who have not deviated in a greater or less degree from the maxims of prudence. Our greatest mistakes may teach lessons which will be useful through life.

But I will not moralize. Come and see us; and we will talk over the matter once, and then dismiss it for ever. Do prevail on your mamma to part with you a month or two at least. I wish you to witness how well I manage my nursery business. You will be charmed with little Harriot. I am already enough of the mother to think her a miniature of beauty and perfection.

How natural, and how easy the transition from one stage of life to another! Not long since I was a gay, volatile girl; seeking satisfaction in fashionable circles and amusements; but now I am thoroughly domesticated. All my happiness is centered within the limits of my own walls; and I grudge every moment that calls me from the pleasing scenes of domestic life. Not that I am so selfish as to exclude my friends from my affection or society. I feel interested in their concerns, and enjoy their company. I must own, however, that conjugal and parental love are the main springs of my life. The conduct of some mothers in depriving their helpless offspring of the care and kindness which none but a mother can feel, is to me unaccountable. There are many nameless

attentions which nothing short of maternal tenderness, and solicitude can pay; and for which the endearing smiles, and progressive improvements of the lovely babe are an ample reward.

How delightful to trace from day to day the expansion of reason and the dawnings of intelligence! Oh, how I anticipate the time, when these faculties shall be displayed by the organs of speech; when the lisping accent shall heighten our present pleasure, and the young idea be capable of direction "how to shoot"! General Richman is not less interested by these enjoyments than myself. All the father beams in his eye! All the husband reigns in his heart, and pervades his every action!

Miss Lawrence is soon to be married to Mr. Laiton. I believe he is a mere fortune-hunter. Indeed she has little to recommend her to any other. Nature has not been very bountiful, either to her body, or mind. Her parents have been shamefully deficient in her education; but have secured to her what they think the chief good; not considering that happiness is by no means the invariable attendant of wealth.

I hope this incoherent scroll will amuse, while it induces you speedily to favor us with another visit.

My best wishes attend your honored mamma, while I subscribe myself, &c.

A. RICHMAN.

LETTER XLIV.

to Mrs. LUCY SUMNER.

HARTFORD.

I AM extremely depressed, my dear Lucy! The agitating scenes, through which I have lately passed, have broken my spirits, and rendered me unfit for society.

Major Sanford has visited me, and taken his leave. He is gone to the southward on a tour of two or three months. I declined any further conversation with him, on the subject of love. At present, I wish not to hear it mentioned by any one.

I have received a very friendly and consolatory letter from Mrs. Richman. She invites me to spend a few months with her; which with my

optimism

mamma's consent I shall do. I hope the change of situation and company will dissipate the gloom which hangs over my mind.

It is a common observation, that we know not the value of a blessing but by deprivation.

This is strictly verified in my case. I was insensible of my regard for Mr. Boyer, till this fatal separation took place. His merit and worth now appear in the brightest colors. I am convinced of that excellence which I once slighted; and the shade of departed happiness haunts me perpetually! I am sometimes tempted to write him, and confess my faults; to tell him the situation of my mind, and to offer him my hand. But he has precluded all hopes of success, by the severity of his letter to me. At any rate, I shall do nothing of the kind, till my return from New Haven.

I am the more willing to leave home, as my affairs are made a town talk. My mamma persuades me to disregard it. But how can I rise superior to "The world's dread laugh, which scarce the firm philosopher can scorn?"

Pray remember me to Mr. Sumner. You are happy, my friend, in the love and esteem of a worthy man; but more happy still, in deserving them. Adieu.

ELIZA WHARTON.

LETTER XLV.

to the same.

HARTFORD.

I HAVE returned to the once smiling seat of maternal affection; but I find not repose and happiness, even there!

In the society of my amiable friends at New-Haven, I enjoyed every thing that friendship could bestow; but rest to a disturbed mind was not in their power.

I was on various parties of pleasure, and passed through different scenes of amusement; but with me they have lost their charms. I relished them not as formerly.

Mrs. Richman advises me to write to Mr. Boyer, and I have con-

cluded to act accordingly. If it answer no other purpose, it will be a relief to my mind. If he ever felt for me the tenderness and regard which he professed, methinks they cannot be entirely obliterated. If they still remain, perhaps I may rekindle the gentle flame, and we may both be happy. I may at least recal his esteem, and that will be a satisfaction to my conscious mind.

I wonder what has become of Major Sanford! Has he too forsaken me? Is it possible for him wilfully to neglect me? I will not entertain so injurious a suspicion.

Yet, if it were the case, it would not affect me like Mr. Boyer's disaffection; for I frankly own, that my fancy, and a taste for gaity of life, induced me to cherish the idea of a connection with Major Sanford; while Mr. Boyer's real merit has imprinted those sentiments of esteem and love in my heart, which time can never efface.

Instead of two, or three, more than twelve months have elapsed, and I have not received a line from Major Sanford in all that time, which I fully expected, though he made no mention of writing; nor have I heard a syllable about him, except a report circulated by his servants, that he is on the point of marrying, which I do not believe. No, it is impossible! I am persuaded that his passion for me, was sincere, however deceitful he may have been with others. But I will not bestow an anxious thought upon him. My design relative to Mr. Boyer, demands my whole attention.

My hopes and fears alternately prevail, and my resolution is extremely fluctuating. How it finally terminates you shall hear in my next. Pray write to me soon. I stand in need of the consoling power of friendship. Nothing can beguile my pensive hours, and exhilerate my drooping spirits, like your letters.

Let me know how you are to be entertained this winter at the theatre. That, you know, is a favorite amusement of mine. You see I can step out of myself a little. Afford an assisting hand, and perhaps I may again be fit for society.

ELIZA WHARTON.

LETTER XLVI.

to the Rev. J. BOYER.

<div align="right">HARTFORD.</div>

Sir,

IT is partly in compliance with your desire, in your last letter to me, in which you tell me, "that when I am convinced of the justice of your conduct, and become a convert to your advice, you shall be happy to hear it;" and partly from a wish to inform you, that such is in truth my present state of mind, that I now write to you.

I cannot but hope that this letter coming from the hand which you once sought, will not be unacceptable.

Pope very justly observes, "that every year is a critic on the last." The truth of this observation is fully exemplified in my years! How severely this condemns the follies of the preceding, my own heart alone can testify!

I shall not offer any palliation, or apology for my misconduct. You told me it admitted none. I frankly confess it; and if the most humble acknowledgement of my offences, with an assurance that they have cost me the deepest repentance, can in any degree atone for them, I now make that atonement. Casting off the veil of dissimulation, I shall write with frankness; believing you possessed of more honor than to make any ungenerous use of the confidence reposed in you.

To say that I ever esteemed you, may, perhaps, appear paradoxical, when compared with certain circumstances which occurred during our acquaintance; but to assert that I loved you, may be deemed still more so. Yet these are real facts, facts of which I was then sensible, and by which I am now more than ever affected.

I think you formerly remarked, that absence served but to heighten real love. This I find by experience. Need I blush to declare these sentiments, when occasion like this, calls for the avowal? I will go even further, and offer you that heart which once you prized; that hand which you once solicited. The sentiments of affection, which you then cultivated, though suppressed, I flatter myself are not wholly obliterated. Suffer me then to rekindle the latent flame; to revive that friendship and tenderness, which I have so foolishly neglected. The endeavor of my

future life shall be to reward your benevolence, and perhaps we may yet be happy together.

But let not this offer of myself constrain you. Let not pity influence your conduct. I would have you return, if that pleasing event take place, a voluntary act. Receive or consent not to confer happiness.

I thought it a duty which I owed to you, and to myself, to make this expiation; this sacrifice of female reserve, for the wrongs I have done you. As such I wish you to accept it; and if your affections are intirely alienated, or otherwise engaged; if you cannot again command the respect and love which I would recal, do not despise me for the concessions I have made. Think as favorably of my past faults, and of my present disposition, as charity will allow. Continue, if possible, to be my friend, though you cease to be my lover.

Should this letter find you in the full possession of happiness, let not the idea of your once loved Eliza, thus intruding itself again upon your thoughts, interrupt your enjoyments. May some distinguished female, as deserving, as fair, partake with you of that bliss which I have forfeited.

Whatever may be my destiny, my best wishes shall ever attend you, and a pleasing remembrance of your honorable attentions preside, till death, in the breast of,

ELIZA WHARTON.

LETTER XLVII.

to Miss ELIZA WHARTON.

HAMPSHIRE.

Madam,

As I was sitting last evening in my study, a letter was handed me by a servant; upon which I no sooner cast my eye, than I recognized, with surprise, the hand and seal of my once loved, but to me long lost Eliza! I opened it hastily, and with still greater surprise, read the contents!

You write with frankness. I shall answer in the same manner.

On reviewing our former intercourse, be assured, that I have not an

accusing thought in my heart. The regard which I felt for you was tender and animated, but it was not of that passionate kind which ends in death or despair. It was governed by reason, and had a nobler object in view, than mere sensual gratification. It was excited by the appearance of excellent qualities. Your conduct, at length, convinced me it was misplaced; that you possessed not, in reality, those charms which I had fondly ascribed to you. They were inconsistent, I conceived, with that artifice and dissimulation, of which you strove to render me the dupe. But thank heaven, the snare was broken. My eyes were opened to discover your folly; and my heart, engaged, as it was, exerted resolution and strength to burst asunder the chain by which you held me enslaved, and to assert the rights of an injured man.

The parting scene, you remember. I reluctantly bade you adieu. I tore myself from you, determined to eradicate your idea from my breast! Long and severe was the struggle. I at last vanquished, as I thought, every tender passion of my soul, (for they all centered in you) and resigned myself to my God, and my duty; devoting those affections to friendship, which had been disappointed in love. But they are again called into exercise. The virtuous, the amiable, the accomplished Maria Selby possesses my entire confidence and esteem; and I trust I am not deceived, when I think her highly deserving of both. With her I expect soon to be united in the most sacred and endearing of human relations; with her to pass my future days in serenity and peace.

Your letter, therefore, came too late; were there no other obstacle to the renewal of our connection. I hope at the close of life, when we take a retrospect of the past, that neither of us shall have reason to regret our separation.

Permit me to add, that for your own sake, and for the sake of your ever valued friends, I sincerely rejoice that your mind has regained its native strength and beauty; that you have emerged from the shade of fanciful vanity. For although to adopt your own phrase, I cease to style myself your lover, among the number of your friends, I am happy to be reckoned. As such, let me conjure you, by all that is dear and desirable, both in this life, and another, to adhere, with undeviating exactness, to the path of rectitude and innocence; and to improve the noble talents, which heaven has liberally bestowed upon you, in rendering yourself amiable, and useful to your friends. Thus will you secure your own, while you promote the happiness of all around you.

I shall ever cherish sentiments of kindness towards you, and with gratitude remember your condescension, in the testimony of regard, which you have given me in your last letter.

I hope soon to hear that your heart and hand are bestowed on some worthy man, who deserves the happiness you are formed to communicate. Whatever we may have called errors, will, on my part, be for ever buried in oblivion; and for your own peace of mind, I entreat you to forget that any idea of a connection between us ever existed.

I shall always rejoice at the news of your welfare, and my ardent prayers will daily arise for your temporal and eternal felicity.

I am, &c.

J. BOYER.

LETTER XLVIII.

to Mrs. LUCY SUMNER.

HARTFORD.

HEALTH, placid serenity, and every domestic pleasure, are the lot of my friend; while I, who once possessed the means of each, and the capacity of tasting them, have been tossed upon the waves of folly, till I am shipwrecked on the shoals of despair!

Oh my friend, I am undone! I am slighted, rejected by the man who once sought my hand, by the man who still retains my heart! and what adds an insupportable poignancy to the reflection, is self-condemnation! From this inward torture, where shall I flee? Where shall I seek that happiness which I have madly trifled away?

The inclosed letters,* will show you whence this tumult of soul arises. But I blame not Mr. Boyer. He has acted nobly. I approve his conduct, though it operates my ruin!

He is worthy of his intended bride, and she is what I am not, worthy of him. Peace and joy be their portion, both here and hereafter! But what are now my prospects? what are to be the future enjoyments of my life?

Oh that I had not written to Mr. Boyer! by confessing my faults, and by avowing my partiality to him, I have given him the power of triumphing in my distress; of returning to my tortured heart all the pangs

* See the two preceding Letters. [Foster's note.]

of slighted love! and what have I now to console me? my bloom is decreasing; my health is sensibly impaired. Those talents, with the possession of which I have been flattered, will be of little avail when unsupported by respectability of character!

My mamma, who knows too well the distraction of my mind, endeavors to sooth and compose me, on Christian principles; but they have not their desired effect. I dare not converse freely with her on the subject of my present uneasiness, lest I should distress her. I am therefore, obliged to conceal my disquietude, and appear as cheerful as possible in her company, though my heart is ready to burst with grief!

Oh that you were near me, as formerly, to share and alleviate my cares! to have some friend in whom I could repose confidence, and with whom I could freely converse, and advise, on this occasion, would be an unspeakable comfort!

Such a one, next to yourself, I think Julia Granby to be. With your leave and consent I should esteem it a special favor if she would come and spend a few months with me. My mamma joins in this request. I would write to her on the subject, but cannot compose myself at present. Will you prefer my petition for me?

If I have not forfeited your friendship, my dear Mrs. Sumner, write to me, and pour its healing balm into the wounded mind of your

<div align="right">Eliza Wharton.</div>

Letter xlix.

to Miss Eliza Wharton.

<div align="right">BOSTON.</div>

Your truly romantic letter came safe to hand. Indeed, my dear, it would make a very pretty figure in a novel. A bleeding heart, slighted love, and all the *et ceteras* of romance, enter into the composition!

Excuse this raillery; and I will now write more seriously. You refer yourself to my friendship for consolation. It shall be exerted for the purpose. But I must act the part of a skilful surgeon, and probe the wound, which I undertake to heal.

she's changed 191

Where, O Eliza Wharton! Where is that fund of sense, and sentiment which once animated your engaging form? Where that strength of mind, that independence of soul, that alacrity and sprightliness of deportment, which formerly raised you superior to every adverse occurrence? Why have you resigned these valuable endowments, and suffered yourself to become the sport of contending passions?

You have now emerged from that mist of fanciful folly, which, in a measure obscured the brilliance of your youthful days.

True, you figured among the first rate coquettes; while your friends, who knew your accomplishments, lamented the misapplication of them; but now they rejoice at the returning empire of reason.

True, you have erred; mislead by the gaiety of your disposition, and that volatility, and inconsideration, which were incident to your years; but you have seen, and nobly confessed your errors. Why do you talk of slighted love? True, Mr. Boyer, supposing you disregarded him, transferred his affections to another object; but have you not your admirers still among men of real merit? Are you not esteemed, and caressed by numbers, who know you capable of shining in a distinguished sphere of life? Turn then, my friend, from the gloomy prospect, which your disturbed imagination has brought into view. Let reason and religion erect their throne in your breast; obey their dictates and be happy. Past experience will point out the quicksands which you are to avoid in your future course.

Date then, from this, a new era of life; and may every moment be attended with felicity. Follow Mr. Boyer's advice, and forget all former connections.

Julia accepts your invitation. Nothing short of your request could induce me to part with her. She is a good girl; and her society will amuse and instruct you.

I am, &c.
LUCY SUMNER.

<p style="text-align:center">LETTER L.</p>

<h1 style="text-align:center">to Mrs. LUCY SUMNER.</h1>

MY Julia Granby has arrived. She is all that I once was; easy, sprightly, debonair. Already has she done much towards relieving my mind. She endeavors to divert, and lead my thoughts into a different channel from that to which they are now prone. Yesterday, we had each an invitation to a ball. She labored hard to prevail on me to go; but I obstinately refused. I cannot yet mix with gay and cheerful circles. I therefore alledged that I was indisposed, and persuaded her to go without me.

The events of my life have always been unaccountably wayward. In many instances I have been ready to suppose that some evil genius presided over my actions, which has directed them contrary to the sober dictates of my own judgment.

I am sometimes tempted to adopt the sentiment expressed in the following lines of the poet,

> "To you, great gods, I make my last appeal;
> O, clear my conscience, or my crimes reveal!
> If wand'ring through the paths of life I've run;
> And backward trod the steps, I sought to shun,
> Impute my errors to your own decree;
> My feet were guilty, but my heart was free."

I suppose you will tell me, that the fate I accuse, through the poet, is only the result of my own imprudence. Well, be it what it may; either the impulse of my own passions, or some higher efficiency; sure I am, that I pay dear for its operation.

I have heard it remarked, that experience is the preceptor of fools; but that the wise need not its instruction. I believe I must be content to rank accordingly, and endeavor to reap advantage from its tuition.

Julia urges me to revisit the scenes of amusements and pleasure; in which she tells me, she is actuated by selfish motives. She wishes it for her own sake. She likes neither to be secluded from them, nor to go alone. I am sometimes half inclined to seek, in festive mirth, a refuge from thought and reflection. I would escape, if possible, from the idea

of Mr. Boyer. This I have never been able to accomplish, since he dropped a tear upon my hand, and left me. I marked the spot with my eye; and twenty times in a day, do I view it, and fondly imagine it still there! How could I give him pain! I hope his happy Maria never will! I hope she will reward that merit, which I have slighted! but I forbear. This theme carries away my pen, if I but touch upon it. And no wonder; for it is the sole exercise of my thoughts! Yet I will endeavor to divert them. Send me some new books; not such, however, as will require much attention. Let them be plays or novels, or any thing else, that will amuse and extort a smile.

Julia and I have been rambling in the garden. She insisted upon my going with her into the arbor, where I was surprised with Major Sanford. What a croud of painful ideas rushed upon my imagination! I believe she repented her rashness. But no more of this. I must lay aside my pen; for I can write nothing else!

<div align="right">ELIZA WHARTON.</div>

LETTER LI.

to Mrs. LUCY SUMNER.

<div align="right">HARTFORD.</div>

Dear Madam,

You commanded me to write you respecting Miss Wharton; and I obey. But I cannot describe to you the surprising change, which she has undergone. Her vivacity has entirely forsaken her; and she has actually become, what she once dreaded above all things, a recluse! She flies from company, as eagerly as she formerly sought it! Her mamma is exceedingly distressed by the settled melancholy which appears in her darling child; but neither of us think it best to mention the subject to her. We endeavor to find means to amuse her; and we flatter ourselves that the prospect of success rather increases. It would add greatly to my happiness, to contribute, in any degree, to restore her to herself, to her friends, and to society.

We are all invited to dine abroad to morrow; and to oblige me, she has consented to go.

Pray madam, write to her often. Your letters may do much for her. She is still feelingly alive to the power of friendship; and none can exercise it upon her to greater acceptance, or with more advantage than yourself.

Major Sanford's house is undergoing a complete repair. The report is, that he is soon to be married. Miss Wharton has heard, but does not believe it. I hope, for her sake, it will prove true. For, at any rate, he is about returning; and from her mamma's account of his past conduct towards Eliza, were he to return unconnected, he would probably renew his attentions; and though they might end in marriage, her happiness would not be secured. She has too nice a sense of love and honor, to compound with his licentious principles. A man, who has been dissolute before marriage, will very seldom be faithful afterwards.

I went into Eliza's chamber the other day, and found her with a miniature picture in her hand. You pretend to be a physiognomist, Julia, said she. What can you trace in that countenance? I guessed whose it was; and looking wistfully at it, replied, I believe the original is an artful, designing man. He looks to me like a Chesterfieldian. Pray who is he? Major Sanford, said she; and I am afraid you have hit his character exactly. Sure I am, that the appearance of those traits in it has made my heart ache! She wept, as she spoke it.

Poor girl! I wish he may never give you greater cause to weep! She is strongly blind to the vices and imperfections of this man. Though naturally penetrating, he has some how or other, cast a deceptious mist over her imagination, with respect to himself. She professes neither to love, nor esteem him; and owns that his ungenerous artifice mislead her in her treatment of Mr. Boyer. Yet she has forgiven him, and thinks him a pleasing companion!

How prone to error is the human mind! How much lighter than the breath of zephyrs the operations of fancy! Strange then, it should ever preponderate over the weightier powers of the understanding!

But I will not moralize. My business here is to dissipate, not to collect ideas; and I must regulate myself accordingly.

I am endeavoring to prepare Eliza, by degrees, to accompany me to Boston, the ensuing winter; but think it doubtful whether I shall succeed. I shall, however, return myself; till when, I am, &c.

JULIA GRANBY.

Letter lii.

to Miss Eliza Wharton.

BOSTON.

My Dear Eliza,

I received yours of the 24th ult. and thank you for it; though it did not afford me those lively sensations of pleasure, which I usually feel at the perusal of your letters. It inspired me both with concern, and chagrin. With concern, lest your dejection of mind should affect your health; and with chagrin at your apparent indulgence of melancholy. Indeed, my friend, your own happiness and honor, require you to dissipate the cloud which hangs over your imagination.

Rise then above it; and prove yourself superior to the adverse occurrences which have befallen you. It is by surmounting difficulties, not by sinking under them, that we discover our fortitude. True courage consists not in flying from the storms of life; but in braving and steering through them with prudence. Avoid solitude. It is the bane of a disordered mind; though of great utility to a healthy one. Your once favorite amusements court your attention. Refuse not their solicitations. I have contributed my mite, by sending you a few books; such as you requested. They are of the lighter kind of reading; yet perfectly chaste; and if I mistake not, well adapted to your taste.

You wish to hear from our theatre. I believe it will be well supplied with performers this winter. Come and see whether they can afford you any entertainment. Last evening I attended a tragedy; but never will I attend another. I have not yet been able to erase the gloom which it impressed upon my mind. It was Romeo and Juliet. Distressing enough to sensibility this! Are there not real woes (if not in our own families, at least among our own friends, and neighbors) sufficient to exercise our sympathy and pity, without introducing fictitious ones into our very diversions? How can that be a diversion, which racks the soul with grief, even though that grief be imaginary. The introduction of a funeral solemnity, upon the stage, is shocking indeed!

Death is too serious a matter to be sported with! An opening grave cannot be a source of amusement to any considerate mind! The closing scene of life can be no pastime, when realized! it must therefore awaken painful sensations, in the representation!

The circus is a place of fashionable resort of late, but not agreeable to me. I think it inconsistent with the delicacy of a lady, even to witness the indecorums, which are practised there; especially, when the performers of equestrian feats are of our own sex. To see a woman depart so far from the female character, as to assume the masculine habit and attitudes; and appear entirely indifferent, even to the externals of modesty, is truly disgusting, and ought not to be countenanced by our attendance, much less by our approbation. But setting aside this circumstance, I cannot conceive it to be a pleasure to sit a whole evening, trembling with apprehension, lest the poor wight of a horseman, or juggler, or whatever he is to be called, should break his neck in contributing to our entertainment.

With Mr. Bowen's museum, I think you were much pleased. He has made a number of judicious additions to it, since you were here. It is a source of rational and refined amusement. Here the eye is gratified, the imagination charmed, and the understanding improved. It will bear frequent reviews without palling on the taste. It always affords something new; and for one, I am never a weary spectator.

Our other public, and private places of resort, are much as you left them.

I am happy in my present situation; but when the summer returns, I intend to visit my native home. Again, my Eliza, will we ramble together in those retired shades which friendship has rendered so delightful to us. Adieu, my friend, till then. Be cheerful, and you will yet be happy.

LUCY SUMNER.

LETTER LIII.

to Mrs. LUCY SUMNER.

raving

HARTFORD.

GRACIOUS Heaven! What have I heard? Major Sanford is married! Yes, the ungrateful, the deceitful wretch, is married! He has forsworn, he has perjured, and given himself to another! That, you will say, is nothing strange. It is characteristic of the man. It may be so; but I could not be convinced of his perfidy, till now!

Perhaps it is all for the best. Perhaps, had he remained unconnected, he might still have deceived me; but now I defy his arts!

They tell me, he has married a woman of fortune. I suppose he thinks, as I once did, that wealth can ensure happiness. I wish he may enjoy it.

This event would not affect me at all, were it not for the depression of spirits which I feel, in consequence of a previous disappointment; since which, every thing of the kind agitates and overcomes me. I will not see him. If I do, I shall betray my weakness, and flatter his vanity; as he will doubtless think he has the power of mortifying me by his connection with another.

Before this news discomposed me, I had attained to a good degree of cheerfulness. Your kind letter, seconded by Julia's exertions, had assisted me in regulating my sensibility. I have been frequently into company, and find my relish for it gradually returning.

I intend to accept the pleasure to which you invite me, of spending a little time with you, this winter. Julia and I will come together. Varying the scene may contribute effectually to dissipate the gloom of my imagination. I would fly to almost any resort, rather than my own mind. What a dreadful thing it is to be afraid of one's own reflections, which ought to be a constant source of enjoyment! But I will not moralize. I am sufficiently melancholy, without any additional cause to increase it!

ELIZA WHARTON.

LETTER LIV.

to Mr. CHARLES DEIGHTON.

HARTFORD.

Dear Deighton,

W HO do you think is writing to you? Why, it is your old friend, metamorphosed into *a married man*! You stare, and can hardly credit the assertion. I cannot realize it myself; yet, I assure you, Charles, it is absolutely true! Necessity, dire necessity, forced me into this dernier resort. I told you, some time ago, it would come to this.

I stood aloof, as long as possible; but in vain did I attempt to shun

the noose. I must either fly to this resource; or give up all my show, equipage, and pleasure, and degenerate into a downright plodding money-catcher, for a subsistance. I chose the first; and who would not? yet I feel some remorse at taking the girl to wife, from no better motives. She is really too good for such an imposition. But she must blame herself, if she suffer hereafter; for she was visibly captivated by my external appearance; and wanted but very little solicitation to confer herself, and fortune on so charming a fellow. Her parents opposed her inclination, for a while, because I was a stranger, and rather too gay for their taste. But she had not been used to contradiction, and could not bear it; and therefore they ventured not to cross her. So I bore off the prize; and a prize she really is. Five thousand pounds in possession, and more in reversion, if I do not forfeit it. This will compensate for some of my past mistakes, and set matters right for the present. I think it doing much better than to have taken the little Laurence girl, I told you of, with half the sum. Besides, my Nancy is a handsomer, and more agreeable person. But that is of little consequence to me, you know. "Beauty soon grows familiar to the lover." Were I a lover, it would be of no great avail. A lover I am; yet not of my wife. The dart which I received from Miss Wharton, sticks fast in my heart; and I assure you, I could hardly persuade myself even to appear unfaithful to her. O, Eliza, accuse me not of infidelity; for your image is my constant companion! A thousand times have I cursed the unpropitious stars, which withheld from her a fortune. That would have enabled me to marry her; and with her, even wedlock would have been supportable.

I am told, that she is still single. Her sober lover never returned. Had he loved as I did, and do, he could not have been so precipitate. But these stoic souls are good for nothing, that I know of, but

"Fix'd like a plant, to one peculiar spot,
To draw nutrition, propagate, and rot."

I want to see Eliza, and I must see her; yet I dread an interview. I shall frankly confess my motives for marrying; and the reasons of my conduct, before I went away. I shall own that my circumstances would not allow me to possess her; and yet that I could not resign her to another.

When I make up the matter with her, I shall solicit her friendship for my wife. By this mean I may enjoy her society, at least, which will alleviate the confinement of a married state. To my spouse I must be as

civil as possible. I really wish she had less merit, that I might have a plausible excuse for neglecting her.

To morrow I shall go to Mrs. Wharton's. I am very much taken up with complimental visits, at present. What deference is always paid to equipage! They may talk of this virtue, their learning, and what not; but without either of them, I shall bear off the palm of respect from those, who have them, unadorned with gold, and its shining appendages.

Every thing hereabouts recals Eliza to my mind. I impatiently anticipate the hour, which will convey me to her presence.

PETER SANFORD.

LETTER LV.

to Mrs. LUCY SUMNER.

HARTFORD.

A NEW scene has opened upon us to day, my dear Mrs. Sumner; a visit from Major Sanford. My mamma, Miss Granby, and myself, were sitting together in the chamber. Miss Granby was entertaining us by reading aloud in Millot's elements of history, when a servant rapped at the door, and handed in the following billet.

"Will Miss Wharton condescend to converse a few moments with her once favored Sanford? He is but too sensible that he has forfeited all claim to the privilege. He therefore presumes not to request it on the score of merit, or of former acquaintance; but solicits it from her benevolence, and pity."

I read and showed it to my mamma, and Julia. What, said I, shall I do? I wish not to see him. His artifice has destroyed my peace of mind; and his presence may open the wounds which time is closing. Act, said my mamma, agreeably to the dictates of your own judgment. I see no harm in conversing with him, said Julia. Perhaps it may remove some disagreeable thoughts, which now oppress and give you pain. And as he is no longer a candidate for your affections, added she, with a smile, it

will be less hazardous than formerly. He will not have the insolence to speak; nor you the folly to hear, the language of love.

He was accordingly invited in. When I rose to go down, I hesitated, and even trembled. I fear, said I, to myself, it will be too much for me; yet why should it? Conscious innocence will support me. This he has not. When I entered the room he stepped forward to meet me. Confusion and shame were visibly depicted in his countenance. He approached me hastily; and without uttering a word, took my hand. I withdrew it. O! Miss Wharton, said he, despise me not. I am convinced that I deserve your displeasure, and disdain; but my own heart has avenged your cause. To your own heart, then, said I, I will leave you! But why do you again seek an interview with one whom you have endeavored to mislead; with one whom you have treated with unmerited neglect? Justice to myself required my appearing before you; that by confessing my faults, and obtaining your forgiveness, I might soften the reproaches of my own mind. Will you be seated, sir? said I. Will you, rejoined he, condescend to sit with me, Eliza? I will, sir, answered I. The rights of hospitality I shall not infringe. In my own house, therefore, I shall treat you with civility. Indeed, said he, you are very severe; but I have provoked all the coldness and reserve which you can inflict!

I am a married man, Eliza. So I understand, said I; and I hope you will never treat your wife with the dissimulation and falsehood, which you have exercised towards me. Would to heaven, exclaimed he, that you were my wife! I should not then fail in my love or duty as a husband! Yet she is an amiable girl; and, had I a heart to give her, I might still be happy! but that, alas! I can never recal. Why, then, said I, did you marry her? You were doubtless master of your own actions. No, said he, I was not. The embarrassed state of my affairs precluded the possibility of acting as I wished. Loving you most ardently, I was anxious to prevent your union with another, till I could so far improve my circumstances, as to secure you from poverty and want in a connection with me. My regard was too sincere to permit me to deceive you, by a marriage which might have proved unhappy for us both. My pride forbad my telling you the motives of my delay; and I left you to see if I could place myself in a situation worthy of your acceptance. This I could not effect; and therefore have run the risk of my future happiness, by marrying a lady of affluence. This secures to me the externals of enjoyment; but my heart, I fear, will never participate it. Yet it affords me some degree of satisfaction that I have not involved you in distress. The

only alleviation of which my banishment from you is capable, is your forgiveness. In compassion, then, refuse it not! It cannot injure you! To me it will be worth millions! He wept! Yes, Lucy, this libertine; this man of pleasure and gallantry wept! I really pitied him from my heart. I forgive you, said I, and wish you happy; yet, on this condition only, that you never again pollute my ears with the recital of your infamous passion. Yes, infamous, I call it, for what softer appellation can be given to such professions from a married man? Harbor not an idea of me, in future, inconsistent with the love and fidelity which you owe your wife; much less, presume to mention it, if you wish not to be detested by me; and for ever banished from my presence. He expressed gratitude for his absolution even upon these terms; and hoped his future conduct would entitle him to my friendship and esteem. That, I replied, time only can determine.

One favor more he begged leave to solicit; which was, that I would be a neighbor to his wife. She was a stranger, he said, and would deem my society a particular privilege. This, I told him, I could not grant, at present, whatever I might do hereafter. He did not urge it any further, but inquired after my mamma, and expressed a wish to see her. I rung the bell, and ordered her and Miss Granby to be called. When they came, he was very polite to them both; and, after usual compliments, told my mamma that he was happy in having obtained my forgiveness, to which he was anxious to have her seal affixed. My daughter, said she, is the injured party; and if she be satisfied, I shall not complain. He thanked her for her condescention; informed her that he was married, and requested her to visit his wife. We then conversed upon different subjects for a short time, and he took his leave. A sigh escaped him as he departed; and a gloom was visible in his countenance, which I never observed before.

I must acknowledge that this interview has given me satisfaction. I have often told you that if I married Major Sanford, it would be from a predilecton for his situation in life. How wretched must have been my lot, had I discovered, too late, that he was by no means possessed of the independence, which I fondly anticipated. I knew not my own heart, when I contemplated a connection with him. Little did I think that my regard for Mr. Boyer was so deeply rooted, as I now find it. I foolishly imagined that I could turn my affections into what channel I pleased. What then must have been my feelings, when I found myself deprived both of inward peace, and outward enjoyment! I begin now to emerge

from the darkness, in which I have been long benighted! I hope the tragic comedy, in which I have acted so conspicuous a part, will come to a happy end.

Julia and I talk, now and then, of a journey to Boston. As yet I have not resolution to act with much decision upon the subject. But, wherever I am, and whatever may be my fate, I shall always be your's in truth,

ELIZA WHARTON.

LETTER LVI.

to Mrs. LUCY SUMNER.

HARTFORD.

I BEGIN to hope we shall come to rights here, by and by. Major Sanford has returned; has made us a visit; and a treaty of peace, and amity (but not of commerce,) is ratified.

Eliza appears to be rapidly returning to her former cheerfulness, if not gaity. I hope she will not diverge too far from her present sedateness and solidity; yet I am not without apprehensions of danger, on that score. One extreme commonly succeeds another. She tells me, that she assiduously cultivates her natural vivacity; that she finds her taste for company and amusements increasing; that she dreads being alone, because past scenes arise to view which vex and discompose her.

These are indications of a mind not perfectly right. I flatter myself, however, that the time is not far distant, when her passions will vibrate with regularity.

I need not repeat to you any thing relative to Major Sanford's conciliatory visit. Eliza has given you a particular, and I believe, a faithful detail. I was called down to see this wonderful man; and disliked him exceedingly. I am astonished that Eliza's penetrating eye, has not long since read his vices in his very countenance. I am told by a friend, who has visited them, that he has an agreeable wife; and I wish she may find him a husband of the same description; but I very much doubt the accomplishment of my wish. For I have no charity for these reformed rakes.

We were walking abroad the other afternoon, and met Major San-

ford and lady. Eliza did not see them till they were very near us. She started, turned pale, and then colored like crimson. I cannot but think, a little envy rankled in her heart. Major Sanford very politely accosted us; and congratulated Mrs. Sanford on this opportunity of introducing her to a particular friend; presenting Eliza. She received her with an easy dignity, and bid her welcome to this part of the country. Mrs. Sanford answered her modestly; hoped for the pleasure of a further acquaintance; and urged us, as we were not far from their house, to return with them to tea. We declined; and, wishing each other a good evening, parted. Major Sanford's eyes were rivetted on Eliza, the whole time we were together; and he seemed loath to remove them, when we separated. I suspect there is some truth in his tale of love. I shall therefore discourage Eliza from associating with him under any pretext whatever. She appeared more pensive and thoughtful than common, as we returned home; and said little the rest of the evening; but next morning was as chatty as ever.

She is warm in the praises of Mrs. Sanford, thinks her an accomplished woman, and wonders that the major could suggest an idea of marrying her for her money. She intends, she says, to visit her soon; and wishes me to accompany her. This, for her own sake, I shall defer, as long as possible.

I am, &c.

JULIA GRANBY.

LETTER LVII.

to Mrs. LUCY SUMNER.

HARTFORD.

By Julia's advice, we have neglected the repeated invitations of Major Sanford, to visit and commence neighborhood with them, till yesterday; when we received a polite billet, requesting the honor of our company to dine. My mamma declined going; but said she had no objection to our compliance with the message, if we thought proper. Julia and I accordingly went. We found a large company assembled in a spacious hall, splendidly furnished and decorated. They were all very polite and

attentive to me; but none more so than Major Sanford and his lady, who jointly strove to dissipate the pensiveness of my mind, which I found it impossible to conceal. When we were summoned to dinner, the major being near me, offered his hand, and leading me into the dining room, seated me at a table furnished with all the variety which could please the eye, or regale the taste of the most luxurious epicure. The conversation turned on various subjects, literary, political, and miscellaneous. In the evening we had a ball. Major Sanford gave the hand of his wife to a Mr. Grey, alledging that he was a stranger, and therefore, entitled to particular attention; and then solicited mine for himself. I was on the point of refusing him, but recollecting that it might have the appearance of continued resentment, contrary to my declaration of forgiving what was past, I complied. He was all kindness, and assiduity; the more so, I imagine, with a view to make amends for his former ingratitude and neglect. Tenderness is now peculiarly soothing to my wounded heart. He took an opportunity of conversing with his wife and me together; hoped she would be honored with my friendship, and acquaintance; and begged, for her sake, that I would not be a stranger at his house. His Nancy, he said, was far removed from her maternal friends; but I could supply their place, if I would generously undertake the task. She joined in expressing the same sentiments and wishes. Alas! Sir, said I, Eliza Wharton is not now what she once was! I labor under a depression of spirits, which must render my company rather painful than pleasing to my friends. The idea of what I had been, contrasted with what I then was, touched my sensibility; and I could not restrain the too officious tear from stealing down my cheek. He took me by the hand, and said, you distress me, Miss Wharton, indeed, you distress me! Happiness must, and shall attend you! Cursed be the wretch, who could wound a heart like your's!

Julia Granby now joined us. An inquisitive concern was visible in her countenance.

I related this conversation to her, after we returned home; but she approved it not.

She thought Major Sanford too particularly attentive to me, considering what had previously happened. She said it would be noticed by others, and the world would make unfavorable remarks upon any appearance of intimacy between us. I care not for that, said I. It is an ill-natured, misjudging world; and I am not obliged to sacrifice my friends to its opinion. Were Major Sanford a single man I should avoid his society; but since he is married; since his wife is young, beautiful and

lovely, he can have no temptation to injure me. I therefore see no evil, which can arise from the cultivation of friendship with *her,* at least. I relish company so little, that I may surely be indulged in selecting that which is most agreeable to my taste, to prevent my becoming quite a misanthrope.

I thank you, my dear Mrs. Sumner, for your kind letter. It was a reasonable cordial to my mind; and I will endeavor to profit by your advice.

Your remarks on the public entertainments are amusing, and as far as I am a judge, perfectly just.

I think it a pity they have not female managers for the theatre. I believe it would be under much better regulations, than at present.

With cordial respects to Mr. Sumner, I subscribe myself, yours in sincerity,

ELIZA WHARTON.

LETTER LVIII.

to Mr. CHARLES DEIGHTON.

HARTFORD.

REJOICE with me, my friend, that I have made my peace with the mistress of my heart. No devotee could have been more sincere in his penitence, than I was in mine. Indeed, Charles, I never knew I had so much sensibility before! Why, I was as much a woman as the very weakest of the sex!

But I dealt very plainly and sincerely with her, to be sure; and this atones for all past offences, and procures absolution for many others yet to be committed.

The dear girl was not inexorable; she was as placable and condescending as I could expect, considering the nature of the crime, which was apparently slighting her person and charms, by marrying another. This you know is one of the nicest points with the ladies. Attack their honor, that is their chastity, and they construe it to be the effect of excessive love, which hurries you a little beyond the bounds of prudence. But touch their vanity, by preferring another, and they will seldom par-

don you. You will say I am very severe upon the sex. And have I not reason to be so, since I have found so many frail ones among them. This, however, is departing from my subject.

Eliza is extremely altered! Her pale dejected countenance, with the sedateness of her manners, so different from the lively glow of health, cheerfulness and activity which formerly animated her appearance and deportment, struck me very disagreeably.

With all my gallantry, and fluency in love matters, I was unable to acquit myself tolerably; or to address her with any degree of ease and confidence. She was very calm; and spoke with great indifference about my marriage, &c. which mortified me exceedingly. Yet I cannot consent to believe that her present depression of spirits arises solely from Mr. Boyer's infidelity. I flatter myself that I am of sufficient consequence to her, to have contributed in a degree.

When I inquired after her health, she told me she had been indisposed; but was now much better. This indisposition, I am informed, was purely mental; and I am happy to observe her recovering from it. I frequently visit her, sometimes with, and sometimes without my wife; of whom, through my mediation, she has become a favorite. I have married, and according to the general opinion, reformed. Yet I suspect my reformation, like most others of the kind, will prove instable as "the baseless fabric of a vision;" unless I banish myself entirely from her society. But that I can never do; for she is still lovely in my eyes, and I cannot control my passions. When absent from her, I am lost to every thing but her idea. My wife begins to rally me on my fondness for Miss Wharton. She asked me the other day if she had a fortune? No, said I, if she had I should have married her. This wounded her sensibility. I repented of my sincerity, and made my peace for that time. Yet, I find myself growing extremely irritable, and she must take heed how she provokes me; for I do not love her; and I think the name of wife becomes more and more distasteful to me every day.

In my mind Eliza has no competitor. But I must keep up appearances, though I endeavor to regain her love. I imagine that the enjoyment of her society, as a neighbor and friend may content me for the present, and render my condition supportable.

Farewell, Charles. I hope you will never be embarrassed with a wife, nor lack some favorite nymph to supply the place of one.

PETER SANFORD.

LETTER LIX.

to Mrs. LUCY SUMNER.

HARTFORD.

Dear Lucy,

I INTENDED, this week, to have journeyed to Boston with Julia Granby; but my resolution fails me. I find it painful even to think of mixing again with the gay multitude. I believe the melancholy reflections, by which I am oppressed, will be more effectually, if not more easily surmounted, by tarrying where they are rendered familiar, than by going from them awhile, and then returning.

Julia will therefore go without me. I envy her no enjoyment there, except your company.

The substitution of friendship in the place of love for Major Sanford, I find productive of agreeable sensations. With him, he assures me, it is a far more calm, and rational pleasure. *He* treats me with the affection and tenderness of a brother; and his *wife*, who exceeds him in professions of regard, with all the consoling softness, and attention of a sister. Indeed, their politeness has greatly contributed to revive the cheerfulness of my natural disposition.

I believe the major's former partiality to me, as a lover, is intirely obliterated; and for my part, I feel as little restraint in his company, and his lady's, as in that of any other in the neighborhood.

I very much regret the departure of Julia; and hope you will permit her to return to me again, as soon as possible. She is a valuable friend. Her mind is well cultivated; and she has treasured up a fund of knowledge and information, which renders her company both agreeable and useful in every situation of life. We lately spent the afternoon and evening at Mr. Smith's. They had a considerable number of visitants; and among the rest, Major Sanford. His wife was expected, but did not come, being indisposed.

I believe, my friend, you must excuse me if my letters are shorter than formerly. Writing is not so agreeable to me as it used to be. I love my friends as well as ever; but I think they must be weary of the gloom and dulness which pervades my present correspondence. When my pen

shall have regained its original fluency and alertness, I will resume and prolong the pleasing task.

I am, my dear Lucy, yours most affectionately,

<div align="right">ELIZA WHARTON.</div>

LETTER LX.

to the same.

<div align="right">HARTFORD.</div>

Dear Madam,

AGREEABLY to your desire, every art has been tried, every allurement held out, every argument used, and every plan adopted which Mrs. Wharton and I could devise to induce Eliza to accompany me to Boston; but all in vain. Sometimes she has been almost persuaded to a compliance with our united request; but soon has resolutely determined against it. I have observed her sentiments to be suddenly changed after being in company with Major Sanford. This alarms us exceedingly. Indeed the major seems to have insinuated himself into her good opinion more than ever. She is flattered into the belief that his attention to her is purely the result of friendship and benevolence.

I have not so favorable an opinion of the man, as to suppose him capable of either. He has become very familiar here. He calls in almost every day. Sometimes he but just inquires after our health; and sometimes makes long visits. The latter is his invariable practice, when he finds Eliza alone. Mrs. Wharton always avoids seeing him if she can. She dreads, she says, his approaching the house.

I entered the parlor the other day, somewhat suddenly, and found him sitting very near Eliza, in a low conversation. They both rose in apparent confusion, and he soon retired.

When he was gone; I suspect, said I, that the major was whispering a tale of love, Eliza? Do you imagine, said she, that I would listen to such a theme from a married man? I hope not, said I; but his conduct towards you indicates a revival of his former sentiments, at least. I was not aware of that, said she. As yet I have observed nothing in his behavior to me, inconsistent with the purest friendship.

We drank tea not long since at Mr. Smith's. Late in the afternoon, Major Sanford made his appearance to apologize, as he said, for Mrs. Sanford, who was indisposed, and could not enjoy the pleasure of the visit she had contemplated. He was very gay, the whole evening; and when the company separated, he was the first to present his arm to Eliza, who accepted it without hesitation. A Mr. Newhall attended me, and we endeavored to keep them company; but they evidently chose to walk by themselves. Mr. Newhall observed, that if Major Sanford were not married, he should suspect he still intended a union with Miss Wharton. I replied, that their former intercourse having terminated in friendship, rendered them more familiar with each other, than with the generality of their acquaintance.

When we reached the house, Mr. Newhall chose not to go in, and took his leave. I waited at the door for Eliza and Major Sanford. At some little distance I saw him press her hand to his lips. It vexed me exceedingly; and no sooner had they come up, than I sullenly bade him good night, and walked directly in. Eliza soon followed me. I sat down by the fire in a thoughtful posture. She did the same. In this situation we both remained for some time, without speaking a word. At length she said, you seem not to have enjoyed your walk, Miss Granby; did you not like your gallant? Yes, said I, very well; but I am mortified that you were not better provided for. I make no complaint, rejoined she; I was very well entertained. That is what displeases me, said I; I mean your visible fondness for the society of such a man. Were you averse to it, as you ought to be, there would be no danger. But he has an alluring tongue, and a treacherous heart. How can you be pleased and entertained by his conversation? to me it appears totally repugnant to that refinement and delicacy for which you have always been esteemed.

His assiduity, and obtrusion ought to alarm you. You well know what his character has been. Marriage has not changed his disposition. It is only a cloak which conceals it. Trust him not then, my dear Eliza! If you do, depend upon it, you will find his professions of friendship to be mere hypocricy, and deceit! I fear that he is acting over again the same unworthy arts, which formerly mislead you. Beware of his wiles! Your friends are anxious for you. They tremble at your professed regard, and apparent intimacy with that unprincipled man. My friends, said she, are very jealous of me, lately. I know not how I have forfeited their confidence, or incurred their suspicion. By encouraging that attention, I warmly replied, and receiving those caresses from a married man, which are due from him to none but his wife! He is a villain, if he

deceived her into marriage by insincere professions of love. If he had then an affection for her, and has already discarded it, he is equally guilty! Can *you* expect sincerity from the man, who withholds it from an amiable, and deserving wife? No, Eliza; it is not love, which induces him to entertain you with the subject! It is a baser passion; and if you disdain not his artifice; if you listen to his flattery, you will, I fear, fall a victim to his evil machinations! If he conducted like a man of honor, he would merit your esteem; but his behavior is quite the reverse! Yet vile as he is, he would not dare to lisp his insolent hopes of your regard, if you punished his presumption with the indignation it deserves; if you spurned from your presence the ungrateful wretch, who would requite your condescension by triumphing in your ruin!

She now burst into tears, and begged me to drop the subject. Her mind, she said, was racked by her own reflections. She could bear but little. Kindness deceived, and censure distressed her!

I assured her of my good intentions; that as I saw her danger, I thought it a duty of the friendship and affection I bore her, solemnly to warn her against it before we parted. We talked over the matter more calmly, till she professed herself resolved in future to avoid his company, and reject his insinuations.

The next day, as I walked out, I met Major Sanford. He accosted me very civilly. I barely bid him good morning, and passed on.

I made it in my way to call at his house, and bid Mrs. Sanford adieu; not expecting another opportunity equally favorable. When I entered the parlor, she was playing a melancholy air on the harpsicord. She rose, and gave me a polite and graceful reception. I told her, as I was soon to leave town, I called to take my leave of her; a compliment, which her attention to me required. Are you going to leave us then, Miss Granby? said she. I shall regret your departure exceedingly. I have so few friends in this part of the country, that it will give me sensible pain to part with one I so highly value.

I told her in the course of conversation, that I expected the pleasure of seeing her yesterday at Mr. Smith's; and was very sorry for the indisposition, which prevented her favoring us with her company. Indeed, said she, I did not know I was expected there! Were you there pray? Yes, said I; and Major Sanford excused your not coming, on the account I have mentioned. Well, said she, this is the first word I ever heard about it; he told me that business led him abroad! Did he gallant any lady? O, said I, he was with us all together. We had no particular gallants.

Seeing her curiosity excited, I heartily repented saying any thing of

the matter, and waved the subject. Little did I suspect him to have been guilty of so base an artifice! It was evidently contrived to facilitate an interview with Eliza.

When I returned I related this affair to Mrs. Wharton and her daughter. The old lady and I expatiated largely on the vileness of this conduct; and endeavored to expose it to Eliza's view in its true colors. She pretended not to justify it. Yet she looked as if she wished it in her power.

I am now preparing for my journey to Boston; which I must however defer another week, for the sake of a more agreeable passage in the stage. I regret leaving Eliza! I tremble at her danger! She has not the resolution to resist temptation, which she once possessed. Her mind is surprisingly weakened! She appears sensible of this; yet adds to it by yielding to her own imbecility. You will receive a letter from her with this; though I had much difficulty to persuade her to write. She has unfortunately become very averse to this, her once favorite amusement.

As I shall soon have the pleasure of conversing with you personally, I conclude without any other addition to this scroll, than the name of your obliged

JULIA GRANBY.

LETTER LXI.

to Miss ELIZA WHARTON.

BOSTON.

My Dear Friend,

I HAVE received your letters, and must own to you that the perusal of them gave me pain. Pardon my suspicions, Eliza: they are excited by real friendship. Julia, you say, approves not Major Sanford's particular attention to you. Neither do I. If you recollect, and examine his conversation in his conciliatory visit, you will find it replete with sentiments, for the avowal of which, he ought to be banished from all virtuous society.

Does he not insidiously declare that you are the only object of his affections; that his union with another was formed from interested

views; and though that other is acknowledged to be amiable and excellent, still he has not a heart to bestow, and expects not happiness with her? Does this discover even the appearance of amendment? Has he not, by false pretensions, mislead a virtuous woman, and induced her to form a connection with him? She was a stranger to his manner of life; and doubtless allured, as you have been, by flattery, deceit, and external appearance, to trust his honor; little thinking him wholly devoid of that sacred tie! What is the reward of her confidence? Insensibility to her charms, neglect of her person, and professed attachment to another!

Is he the man, my dear Eliza, whose friendship you wish to cultivate? Can that heavenly passion reside in a breast, which is the seat of treachery, duplicity, and ingratitude? You are too sensible of its purity and worth, to suppose it possible. The confessions of his own mouth condemn him. They convince me that he is still the abandoned libertine; and that marriage is but the cloak of his intrigues. His officious attentions to you are alarming to your friends. You own your mind weakened, and peculiarly susceptible of tender impressions. Beware how you receive them from him. Listen not a moment to his flattering professions. It is an insult upon your understanding for him to offer them. It is derogatory to virtue for you to hear them.

Slight not the opinion of the world. We are dependent beings; and while the smallest traces of virtuous sensibility remain, we must feel the force of that dependence, in a greater or less degree. No female, whose mind is uncorrupted, can be indifferent to reputation. It is an inestimable jewel, the loss of which can never be repaired. While retained, it affords conscious peace to our own minds, and ensures the esteem and respect of all around us.

Blessed with the company of so disinterested and faithful a friend, as Julia Granby, some deference is certainly due to her opinion and advice. To an enlarged understanding, a cultivated taste, and an extensive knowledge of the world, she unites the most liberal sentiments, with a benevolence, and candor of disposition, which render her equally deserving of your confidence and affection.

I cannot relinquish my claim to a visit from you this winter. Marriage has not alieniated, or weakened my regard for my friends. Come, then, to your faithful Lucy. Have you sorrows? I will sooth, and alleviate them. Have you cares? I will dispel them. Have you pleasures? I will heighten them. Come then, let me fold you to my expecting heart. My

happiness will be partly suspended till your society render it complete.
Adieu.

LUCY SUMNER.

LETTER LXII.

to Miss JULIA GRANBY.

HARTFORD.

Dear Julia,

I HOPE Mrs. Sumner and you will excuse my writing but one letter, in
answer to the number I have received from you both. Writing is an
employment, which suits me not at present. It was pleasing to me for-
merly, and therefore, by recalling the idea of circumstances and events
which frequently occupied my pen in happier days, it now gives me
pain. Yet I have just written a long consolatory letter to Mrs. Richman.
She has buried her babe; her little Harriot, of whom she was doatingly
fond.

It was a custom with some of the ancients, we are told, to weep at
the birth of their children.

Often should we be impelled to a compliance with this custom, could
we foresee the future incidents of their lives. I think, at least, that the
uncertainty of their conduct and condition in more advanced age, may
reconcile us to their removal to a happier state, before they are capable
of tasting the bitterness of woe.

> "Happy the babe, who, priviledg'd by fate,
> To shorter labors, and a lighter weight,
> Receiv'd but yesterday the gift of breath;
> Order'd to morrow, to return to death."

Our domestic affairs are much as when you left us. Nothing remark-
able has occurred in the neighborhood, worth communicating. The
company and amusements of the town are as usual, I suppose. I frequent
neither of them. Having incurred so much censure by the indulgence of

a gay disposition, I am now trying what a recluse and solitary mode of life will produce. You will call me splenetic. I own it. I am pleased with nobody; still less with myself. I look around for happiness, and find it not. The world is to me a desart! If I indulge myself in temporary enjoyment, the consciousness or apprehension of doing amiss, destroys my peace of mind. And, when I have recourse to books, if I read those of serious description, they remind me of an awful futurity, for which I am unprepared; if history, it discloses facts in which I have no interest; if novels, they exhibit scenes of pleasure which I have no prospect of realizing!

My mamma is solicitously attentive to my happiness; and though she fails of promoting it; yet I endeavor to save her the pangs of disappointment, by appearing what she wishes.

I anticipate, and yet I dread your return; a paradox this, which time alone can solve.

Continue writing to me, and intreat Mrs. Sumner, in my name, to do likewise. Your benevolence must be your reward.

ELIZA WHARTON.

LETTER LXIII.

to Miss ELIZA WHARTON.

BOSTON.

A PARADOX, indeed, is the greater part of your letter to us, my dear Eliza. We had fondly flattered ourselves that the melancholy of your mind was exterminated. I hope no new cause has revived it. Little did I intend, when I left you, to have been absent so long; but Mrs. Sumner's disappointment, in her plan of spending the summer at Hartford, induced me, in compliance with her request, to prolong my residence here.

But for your sake, she now consents to my leaving her, in hopes I may be so happy as to contribute to your amusement.

I am both pleased and instructed by the conduct of this amiable woman. As I always endeavored to imitate her discreet and modest behavior in a single state; so likewise shall I take her for a pattern, should I ever enter a married life. She is most happily united. Mr. Sum-

ner, to all the graces and accomplishments of the gentleman, adds the still more important and essential properties of virtue, integrity and honor. I was once present when a person was recommended to her for a husband. She objected that he was a rake. True, said the other, he has been, but he has reformed. That will never do for me, rejoined she; I wish my future companion to need no reformation: a sentiment worthy the attention of our whole sex; the general adoption of which, I am persuaded, would have a happy influence upon the manners of the other.

I hope neither you, nor I, Eliza, shall ever be tried by a man of debauched principles. Such characters I conceive to be totally unfit for the society of women, who have any claim to virtue and delicacy.

I intend to be with you, in about a month. If agreeable to you, we will visit, and spend a few weeks with the afflicted Mrs. Richman. I sincerely sympathize with her, under her bereavement. I know her fondness for you will render your company very consoling to her; and I flatter myself that I should not be an unwelcome guest.

Make my respects to your mamma; and believe me ever yours,

JULIA GRANBY.

LETTER LXIV.

to Mrs. LUCY SUMNER.

HARTFORD.

Dear Madam,

I HAVE arrived in safety, to the mansion of our once happy and social friends. But I cannot describe to you, how changed, how greatly changed this amiable family appears since I left it. Mrs. Wharton met me at the door; and tenderly embracing, bade me a cordial welcome. You are come, Julia, said she, I hope, to revive and comfort us. We have been very solitary during your absence. I am happy madam, said I, to return; and my endeavors to restore cheerfulness and content, shall not be wanting. But, where is Eliza? By this time we had reached the back parlor, whither Mrs. Wharton led me; and the door being open, I saw Eliza, reclined on a settee, in a very thoughtful posture. When I

advanced to meet her, she never moved; but sat "like patience on a monument, smiling at grief!"

I stopped involuntarily, and involuntarily raising my eyes to heaven, exclaimed, is that Eliza Wharton! She burst into tears; and attempted to rise, but sunk again into her seat. Seeing her thus affected, I sat down by her; and throwing my arm about her neck, why these tears? said I. Why this distress, my dear friend? Let not the return of your Julia give you pain! She comes to sooth you with the consolations of friendship! It is not pain, said she, clasping me to her breast; it is pleasure, too exquisite for my weak nerves to bear! See you not, Julia, how I am altered? Should you have known me for the sprightly girl, who was always welcome at the haunts of hilarity and mirth? Indeed, said I, you appear indisposed, but I will be your physician. Company, and change of air will, I doubt not, restore you. Will these cure disorders of the mind, Julia? They will have a powerful tendency to remove them, if rightly applied; and I profess considerable skill in that art. Come, continued I, we will try these medicines in the morning. Let us rise early, and step into the chaise; and after riding a few miles, call and breakfast with Mrs. Freeman. I have some commissions from her daughter. We shall be agreeably entertained there, you know.

Being summoned to supper, I took her by the hand, and we walked into another room, where we found her brother, and his wife, with her mamma waiting for us. We were all very chatty; even Eliza resumed, in a degree, her former sociability. A settled gloom, notwithstanding, brooded on her countenance; and a deep sigh often escaped her, in spite of her evident endeavors to suppress it. She went to bed before us; when her mamma informed me that her health had been declining for some months, that she never complained, but studiously concealed every symptom of indisposition. Whether it were any real disorder of body, or whether it arose from her depression of spirits, she could not tell; but supposed they operated together, and mutually heightened each other.

I inquired after Major Sanford; whether he and Eliza had associated together during my absence? Sometimes, she said, they seemed on good terms; and he frequently called to see her; at others, they had very little, if any correspondence at all. She told me that Eliza never went abroad, and was very loath to see company at home; that her chief amusement consisted in solitary walks; that the dreadful idea of her meeting Major Sanford in these walks, had now and then intruded upon her imagination; that she had not the least evidence of the fact, however; and indeed,

was afraid to make any inquiries into the matter, lest her own suspicions should be discovered; that the major's character was worse than ever; that he was much abroad, and frequently entertained large parties of worthless bacchanalians at his house; that common report said he treated his wife with indifference, neglect, and ill nature; with many other circumstances, which it is not material to relate.

Adieu, my dear friend, for the present. When occasion requires, you shall hear again from your affectionate

JULIA GRANBY.

LETTER LXV.

to Mr. CHARLES DEIGHTON.

HARTFORD.

GOOD news, Charles, good news! I have arrived to the utmost bounds of my wishes; the full possession of my adorable Eliza! I have heard a quotation from a certain book; but what book it was I have forgotten, if I ever knew. No matter for that; the quotation is, that "stolen waters are sweet, and bread eaten in secret is pleasant." If it has reference to the pleasures, which I have enjoyed with Eliza, I like it hugely, as Tristram Shandy's father said of Yorick's sermon; and I think it fully verified.

I had a long and tedious siege. Every method which love could suggest, or art invent, was adopted. I was sometimes ready to despair, under an idea that her resolution was unconquerable, her virtue impregnable. Indeed, I should have given over the pursuit long ago, but for the hopes of success I entertained from her parleying with me, and in reliance upon her own strength, endeavoring to combat, and counteract my designs. Whenever this has been the case, Charles, I have never yet been defeated in my plan. If a lady will consent to enter the lists against the antagonist of her honor, she may be sure of losing the prize. Besides, were her delicacy genuine, she would banish the man at once, who presumed to doubt, which he certainly does, who attempts to vanquish it!

But, far be it from me to criticise the pretensions of the sex. If I gain

the rich reward of my dissimulation and gallantry, that you know is all
I want.

To return then to the point. An unlucky, but not a miraculous ac-
cident, has taken place, which must soon expose our amour. What can
be done? At the first discovery, absolute distraction seized the soul of
Eliza, which has since terminated in a fixed melancholy. Her health too
is much impaired. She thinks herself rapidly declining; and I tremble
when I see her emaciated form!

My wife has been reduced very low, of late. She brought me a boy
a few weeks past, a dead one though.

These circumstances give me neither pain nor pleasure. I am too
much ingrossed by my divinity, to take an interest in any thing else.
True, I have lately suffered myself to be somewhat engaged here and
there by a few jovial lads, who assist me in dispelling the anxious
thoughts, which my perplexed situation excites. I must, however, seek
some means to relieve Eliza's distress. My finances are low; but the last
fraction shall be expended in her service, if she need it.

Julia Granby is expected at Mrs. Wharton's every hour. I fear that
her inquisitorial eye will soon detect our intrigue, and obstruct its con-
tinuation. Now there's a girl, Charles, I should never attempt to seduce;
yet she is a most alluring object, I assure you. But the dignity of her
manners forbid all assaults upon her virtue. Why, the very expression
of her eye, blasts in the bud, every thought, derogatory to her honor;
and tells you plainly, that the first insinuation of the kind, would be
punished with eternal banishment and displeasure! Of her there is no
danger! But I can write no more, except that I am, &c.

PETER SANFORD.

LETTER LXVI.

to Mrs. LUCY SUMNER.

HARTFORD.

OH, my friend! I have a tale to unfold; a tale which will rend every
nerve of sympathizing pity, which will rack the breast of sensibility, and

unspeakably distress your benevolent heart! Eliza—Oh the ruined, lost Eliza!

I want words to express the emotions of indignation, and grief which oppress me! But I will endeavor to compose myself; and relate the circumstances as they came to my knowledge.

After my last letter, Eliza remained much in the same gloomy situation as I found her. She refused to go, agreeably to her promise, to visit your mamma; and under one pretext or another, has constantly declined accompanying me any where else, since my arrival.

Till last Thursday night she slept in the same bed with me; when she excused herself, by saying she was restless, and should disturb my repose. I yielded to her humor of taking a different apartment, little suspecting the real cause! She frequently walked out; and though I sometimes followed, I very seldom found her. Two or three times, when I happened to be awake, I heard her go down stairs; and on inquiry in the morning, she told me that she was very thirsty, and went down for water. I observed a degree of hesitancy in her answers, for which I could not account. But last night, the dreadful mystery was developed! A little before day, I heard the front door opened with great caution. I sprang from my bed, and running to the window, saw by the light of the moon, a man going from the house. Soon after I perceived a footstep upon the stairs, which carefully approached and entered Eliza's chamber.

Judge of my astonishment, my surprise, my feelings, upon this occasion! I doubted not but Major Sanford was the person I had seen; and the discovery of Eliza's guilt, in this infamous intrigue, almost deprived me of thought and recollection! My blood thrilled with horror at this sacrifice of virtue! After a while I recovered myself, and put on my clothes. But what to do, I knew not; whether to go directly to her chamber, and let her know that she was detected; or to wait another opportunity.

I resolved on the first. The day had now dawned. I tapped at her door; and she bid me come in. She was sitting in an easy chair by the side of her bed. As I entered she withdrew her handkerchief from her face; and looking earnestly at me, said, what procures me the favor of a visit, at this early hour, Miss Granby? I was disturbed, said I, and wished not to return to my bed. But what breaks your rest; and calls you up so unseasonably, Eliza? Remorse, and despair, answered she, weeping. After what I have witnessed, this morning, rejoined I, I cannot wonder at it! Was it not Major Sanford whom I saw go from the house some time ago? She was silent, but tears flowed abundantly. It is too

late, continued I, to deny, or evade. Answer my question sincerely; for, believe me, Eliza, it is not malice, but concern for you, which prompts it. I will answer you, Julia, said she. You have discovered a secret, which harrows up my very soul! A secret, which I wished you to know, but could not exert resolution to reveal! Yes! It was Major Sanford; the man who has robbed me of my peace; who has triumphed in my destruction; and who will cause my sun to sit at noon!

I shudder, said I, at your confession! Wretched, deluded girl! Is this a return for your parent's love, and assiduous care; for your friends' solicitude, and premonitory advice? You are ruined, you say! You have sacrificed your virtue to an abandoned, despicable profligate! And you live to acknowledge and bear your infamy! I do, said she; but not long shall I support this burden! See you not, Julia, my decaying frame, my faded cheek, and tottering limbs? Soon shall I be insensible to censure and reproach! Soon shall I be sequestered in that mansion, "where the wicked cease from troubling, and where the weary are at rest!" Rest! said I, can you expect to find rest either in this world, or another, with such a weight of guilt on your head? She exclaimed, with great emotion, add not to the upbraidings of a wounded spirit! Have pity upon me, Oh! my friend, have pity upon me!

Could you know what I suffer, you would think me sufficiently punished! I wish you no other punishment, said I, than what may effect your repentance and reformation. But your mother, Eliza! She cannot long be ignorant of your fall; and I tremble to think of her distress! It will break her widowed heart! How has she loved; how has she doated upon you! Dreadful is the requital which you have made! My mother, rejoined she—Oh, name her not! The very sound is distraction to me! Oh! my Julia, if your heart be not shut against mercy and compassion towards me, aid me through this trying scene! Let my situation call forth your pity, and induce you, undeserving as I am, to exert it in my behalf!

During this time, I had walked the chamber. My spirits had been raised above their natural key, and were exhausted. I sat down, but thought I should have fainted, till a copious flood of tears gave me relief. Eliza was extremely affected. The appearance of calamity which she exhibited would have softened the most obdurate anger. Indeed, I feared some immediate and fatal effect. I therefore seated myself beside her; and assuming an air of kindness, compose yourself, Eliza, said I; I repeat what I told you before, it is the purest friendship, which thus interests me in your concerns. This, under the direction of charity, induces me again to offer you my hand. Yet you have erred against knowledge and

reason; against warning and counsel. You have forfeited the favor of your friends; and reluctant will be their forgiveness. I plead guilty, said she, to all your charges. From the general voice I expect no clemency. If I can make my peace with my mother, it is all I seek or wish on this side the grave.

In your benevolence I confide for this. In you, I hope to find an intercessor. By the remembrance of our former affection and happiness, I conjure you, refuse me not. At present, I entreat you to conceal from her this distressing tale. A short reprieve is all I ask. Why, said I, should you defer it? When the painful task is over, you may find relief in her lenient kindness. After she knows my condition, I cannot see her, resumed she, till I am assured of her forgiveness. I have not strength to support the appearance of her anger and grief. I will write to her what I cannot speak. You must bear the melancholy message, and plead for me, that her displeasure may not follow me to the grave; whither I am rapidly hastening. Be assured, replied I, that I will keep your secret as long as prudence requires. But I must leave you now: your mamma will wonder at our being thus closetted together. When opportunity presents, we will converse further on the subject. In the mean time, keep yourself as composed as possible, if you would avoid suspicion. She raised her clasped hands, and with a piteous look, threw her handkerchief over her face, and reclined in her chair, without speaking a word. I returned to my chamber, and endeavored to dissipate every idea which might tend to disorder my countenance, and break the silence I wished to observe, relative to what had happened.

When I went down, Mrs. Wharton desired me to step up, and inform Eliza that breakfast was ready. She told me she could not yet compose herself sufficiently to see her mamma; and begged me to excuse her absence as I thought proper. I accordingly returned for answer to Mrs. Wharton, that Eliza had rested but indifferently, and being somewhat indisposed, would not come down, but wished me to bring her a bowl of chocolate, when we had breakfasted. I was obliged studiously to suppress even my thoughts concerning her, lest the emotions they excited might be observed. Mrs. Wharton conversed much of her daughter, and expressed great concern about her health and state of mind. Her return to this state of dejection, after having recovered her spirits and cheerfulness, in a great degree, was owing, she feared, to some cause unknown to her; and she entreated me to extract the secret, if possible. I assured her of my best endeavors, and doubted not, I told her, but I should be able in a few days to effect what she wished.

Eliza came down and walked in the garden before dinner; at which she commanded herself much better than I expected. She said that a little ride might, she imagined, be of service to her; and asked me if I would accompany her a few miles in the afternoon. Her mamma was much pleased with the proposition; and the chaise was accordingly ordered.

I observed to Eliza, as we rode, that with her natural and acquired abilities, with her advantages of education, with her opportunities of knowing the world, and of tracing the virtues and vices of mankind to their origin, I was surprised at her becoming the prey of an insidious libertine, with whose character she was well acquainted, and whose principles she was fully apprised would prompt him to deceive and betray her. Your surprise is very natural, said she. The same will doubtless be felt and expressed by every one to whom my sad story is related. But the cause may be found in that unrestrained levity of disposition, that fondness for dissipation and coquetry which alienated the affections of Mr. Boyer from me. This event fatally depressed, and enfeebled my mind. I embraced with avidity the consoling power of friendship, ensnaringly offered by my seducer; vainly inferring from his marriage with a virtuous woman, that he had seen the error of his ways, and forsaken his licentious practices, as he affirmed, and I, fool that I was, believed it!

It is needless for me to rehearse the perfidious arts, by which he insinuated himself into my affections, and gained my confidence. Suffice it to say, he effected his purpose! But not long did I continue in the delusive dream of sensual gratification. I soon awoke to a most poignant sense of his baseness, and of my own crime and misery. I would have fled from him; I would have renounced him for ever; and by a life of sincere humility and repentance, endeavored to make my peace with heaven, and to obliterate, by the rectitude of my future conduct, the guilt I had incurred; but I found it too late! My circumstances called for attention; and I had no one to participate my cares, to witness my distress, and to alleviate my sorrows, but him. I could not therefore prevail on myself, wholly to renounce his society. At times I have admitted his visits; always meeting him in the garden, or grove adjoining; till of late, the weather, and my ill health induced me to comply with his solicitations, and receive him into the parlor.

Not long, however, shall I be subject to these embarrassments. Grief has undermined my constitution. My health has fallen a sacrifice to a disordered mind. But I regret not its departure! I have not a single wish

to live. Nothing which the world affords can restore my former serenity and happiness!

The little innocent I bear, will quickly disclose its mother's shame! God Almighty grant it may not live as a monument of my guilt, and a partaker of the infamy and sorrow, which is all I have to bequeath it! Should it be continued in life, it will never know the tenderness of a parent; and, perhaps, want and disgrace may be its wretched portion! The greatest consolation I can have, will be to carry it with me to a state of eternal rest; which, vile as I am, I hope to obtain, through the infinite mercy of heaven, as revealed in the gospel of Christ.

I must see Major Sanford again. It is necessary to converse further with him, in order to carry my plan of operation into execution. What is this plan of operation, Eliza? said I. I am on the rack of anxiety for your safety. Be patient, continued she, and you shall soon be informed. To morrow I shall write my dreadful story to my mother. She will be acquainted with my future intentions; and you shall know, at the same time, the destination of your lost friend. I hope, said I, that you have formed no resolution against your own life. God forbid, rejoined she. My breath is in his hands, let him do what seemeth good in his sight! Keep my secret one day longer, and I will never more impose so painful a silence upon you.

By this time we had reached home. She drank tea with composure, and soon retired to rest. Mrs. Wharton eagerly inquired whether I had found out the cause of Eliza's melancholy. I have urged her, said I, on the subject; but she alledges that she has particular reasons for present concealment. She has, notwithstanding, promised to let me know, the day after to morrow. Oh, said she, I shall not rest till the period arrives. Dear, good woman, said I to myself, I fear you will never rest afterwards!

This is our present situation. Think what a scene rises to the view of your Julia! She must share the distresses of others, though her own feelings, on this unhappy occasion, are too keen to admit a moment's serenity! My greatest relief is in writing to you; which I shall do again by the next post. In the mean time, I must beg leave to subscribe myself, sincerely yours,

JULIA GRANBY.

LETTER LXVII.

to the same.

ALL is now lost; lost, indeed! She is gone! Yes, my dear friend, our beloved Eliza, is gone! Never more shall we behold this once amiable companion, this once innocent and happy girl. She has forsaken, and, as she says, bid an everlasting adieu to her home, her afflicted parent and her friends! But I will take up my melancholy story where I left it in my last.

She went, as she told me she expected, into the garden, and met her detestable paramour. In about an hour she returned, and went directly to her chamber. At one o'clock I went up, and found her writing, and weeping. I begged her to compose herself, and go down to dinner. No; she said, she could not eat; and was not fit to appear before any body. I remonstrated against her immoderate grief; represented the injury she must sustain by the indulgence of it, and conjured her to suppress the violence of its emotions.

She entreated me to excuse her to her mamma; said she was writing to her, and found it a task too painful to be performed with any degree of composure; that she was almost ready to sink under the weight of her affliction; but hoped and prayed for support, both in this, and another trying scene, which awaited her. In compliance with her desire, I now left her; and told her mamma that she was very busy in writing; wished not to be interrupted at present; but would take some refreshment, an hour or two hence. I visited her again, about four o'clock; when she appeared more calm and tranquil.

It is finished, said she, as I entered her apartment, it is finished. What said I, is finished? No matter, replied she; you will know all to morrow, Julia. She complained of excessive fatigue, and expressed an inclination to lie down; in which I assisted her, and then retired. Some time after her mamma went up, and found her still on the bed. She rose, however, and accompanied her down stairs. I met her at the door of the parlor, and taking her by the hand, inquired how she did? Oh, Julia, miserably indeed, said she. How severely does my mother's kindness reproach me! How insupportably it increases my self-condemnation! She wept; she wrung her hands, and walked the room in the greatest agony! Mrs.

Wharton was exceedingly distressed by her appearance. Tell me, Eliza, said she, tell me the cause of your trouble! Oh, kill me not by your mysterious concealment! My dear child, let me, by sharing, alleviate your affliction! Ask me not, madam, said she; O my mother, I conjure you not to insist on my divulging to night, the fatal secret which engrosses and distracts my mind! To morrow I will hide nothing from you. I will press you no further, rejoined her mamma. Chuse your own time, my dear; but remember, I must participate your grief, though I know not the cause.

Supper was brought in; and we endeavored to prevail on Eliza to eat, but in vain. She sat down, in compliance with our united importunities; but neither of us tasted food. It was removed untouched. For a while, Mrs. Wharton and I gazed in silent anguish upon the spectacle of woe, before us! At length, Eliza rose to retire. Julia, said she, will you call at my chamber, as you pass to your own? I assented. She then approached her mamma, fell upon her knees before her, and clasping her hand, said, in broken accents, Oh madam! can you forgive a wretch, who has forfeited your love, your kindness, and your compassion? Surely, Eliza, said she, you are not that being! No, it is impossible! But however great your transgression, be assured of my forgiveness, my compassion, and my continued love! Saying this, she threw her arms about her daughter's neck, and affectionately kissed her. Eliza struggled from her embrace, and looking at her with wild despair, exclaimed, this is too much! Oh, this unmerited goodness is more than I can bear! She then rushed precipitately out of the room, and left us overwhelmed in sympathy and astonishment!

When Mrs. Wharton had recovered herself a little, she observed, that Eliza's brain was evidently disordered. Nothing else, continued she, could impel her to act in this extraordinary manner. At first she was resolved to follow her; but I dissuaded her from it, alledging, that as she had desired me to come into her chamber, I thought it better for me to go alone. She acquiesced; but said she should not think of going to bed; but would, however, retire to her chamber, and seek consolation there. I bade her good night; and went up to Eliza, who took me by the hand and led me to the toilet, upon which she laid the two inclosed letters, the one to her mamma, and the other to me. These, said she, contain what I had not resolution to express. Promise me, Julia, that they shall not be opened till to morrow morning. I will, said I. I have thought and wept, continued she, till I have almost exhausted my strength, and my reason. I would now obtain a little respite, that I may

226 HANNAH WEBSTER FOSTER

prepare my mind for the account I am one day to give at a higher tribunal than that of earthly friends. For this purpose, what I have written, and what I shall yet say to you, must close the account between you and me. I have certainly no balance against you, said I. In my breast you are fully acquitted. Your penitential tears have obliterated your guilt, and blotted out your errors with your Julia. Henceforth, be they all forgotten. Live, and be happy. Talk not, said she, of life. It would be a vain hope, though I cherished it myself.

> "That I must die, it is my only comfort;
> Death is the privilege of human nature;
> And life without it were not worth our taking.
> Thither the poor, the prisoner and the mourner
> Fly for relief, and lay their burdens down!"

You have forgiven me, Julia; my mother has assured me of her forgiveness, and what have I more to wish? My heart is much lightened by these kind assurances; they will be a great support to me in the dreadful hour which awaits me! What mean you, Eliza? said I. I fear some desperate purpose labors in your mind. Oh, no, she replied; you may be assured your fear is groundless. I know not what I say; my brain is on fire; I am all confusion! Leave me, Julia; when I have had a little rest, I shall be composed. These letters have almost distracted me; but they are written, and I am comparatively easy. I will not leave you, Eliza, said I, unless you will go directly to bed, and endeavor to rest. I will, said she, and the sooner the better. I tenderly embraced her, and retired, though not to bed. About an hour after, I returned to her chamber, and opening the door very softly, found her apparently asleep. I acquainted Mrs. Wharton with her situation, which was a great consolation to us both; and encouraged us to go to bed. Having suffered much in my mind, and being much fatigued, I soon fell asleep; but the rattling of a carriage, which appeared to stop at a little distance from the house, awoke me. I listened a moment, and heard the door turn slowly on its hinges. I sprang from my bed, and reached the window just in time to see a female handed into a chaise by a man who hastily followed her, and drove furiously away! I at once concluded they could be no other than Eliza and Major Sanford. Under this impression I made no delay, but ran immediately to her chamber. A candle was burning on the table; but Eliza was not there! I thought it best to acquaint her mamma with the melancholy discovery; and steping to her apartment

for the purpose, found her rising. She had heard me walk, and was anxious to know the cause. What is the matter, Julia, said she; what is the matter? Dear madam, said I, arm yourself with fortitude! What new occurrence demands it? rejoined she. Eliza has left us! Left us! what mean you? She is just gone! I saw her handed into a chaise, which instantly disappeared!

At this intelligence she gave a shriek, and fell back on her bed! I alarmed the family, and by their assistance soon recovered her. She desired me to inform her of every particular relative to her elopement, which I did; and then delivered her the letter which Eliza had left for her. I suspect, said she, as she took it; I have long suspected, what I dared not believe! The anguish of my mind has been known only to myself, and my God! I could not answer her, and therefore withdrew. When I had read Eliza's letter to me, and wept over the sad fall; and, as I fear, the total loss of this once amiable and accomplished girl, I returned to Mrs. Wharton. She was sitting in her easy chair; and still held the fatal letter in her hand. When I entered, she fixed her streaming eyes upon me, and exclaimed, O Julia, this is more than the bitterness of death! True, madam, said I, your affliction must be great; yet that all-gracious Being, who controls every event, is able, and I trust, disposed to support you! To Him, replied she, I desire humbly to resign myself; but I think I could have borne almost any other calamity with greater resignation and composure than this. With how much comparative ease could I have followed her to the grave, at any period since her birth! Oh, my child, my child! dear, very dear hast thou been to my fond heart! Little did I think it possible for you to prepare so dreadful a cup of sorrow for your widowed mother! But where, continued she, where can the poor fugitive have fled? Where can she find that protection and tenderness, which, notwithstanding her great apostasy, I should never have withheld? From whom can she receive those kind attentions, which her situation demands.

The agitation of her mind had exhausted her strength; and I prevailed on her to refresh, and endeavor to compose herself to rest; assuring her of my utmost exertions to find out Eliza's retreat, and restore her to a mother's arms.

I am obliged to suppress my own emotions; and to bend all my thoughts towards the alleviation of Mrs. Wharton's anxiety and grief.

Major Sanford is from home, as I expected; and I am determined, if he return, to see him myself, and extort from him the place of Eliza's concealment. Her flight, in her present state of health, is inexpressibly

distressing to her mother; and, unless we find her soon, I dread the effects!

I shall not close this, till I have seen or heard from the vile miscreant who has involved a worthy family in wretchedness!

Friday Morning—Two days have elapsed without affording us much relief. Last evening, I was told that Major Sanford was at home. I immediately wrote him a billet, entreating and conjuring him to let me know where the hapless Eliza had fled. He returned me the following answer.

"Miss Granby need be under no apprehensions, respecting the situation of our beloved Eliza. She is well provided for, conveniently accommodated, and has every thing to make her happy, which love or affluence can give.

Major Sanford has solemnly sworn not to discover her retreat. She wishes to avoid the accusations of her friends, till she is better able to bear them.

Her mother may rest assured of immediate information, should any danger threaten her amiable daughter; and also of having seasonable notice of her safety."

Although little dependence can be placed upon this man; yet these assurances have, in a great degree, calmed our minds. We are, however, contriving means to explore the refuge of the wanderer; and hope, by tracing his steps, to accomplish our purpose. This we have engaged a friend to do.

I know, my dear Mrs. Sumner, the kind interest you will take in this disastrous affair. I tremble to think what the event may be! To relieve your suspense, however, I shall write you every circumstance, as it occurs. But at present, I shall only enclose Eliza's letters to her mamma, and me, and, subscribe myself your sincere and obliged friend,

JULIA GRANBY.

LETTER LXVIII.

to Mrs. M. WHARTON.

<div align="right">TUESDAY.</div>

My Honored And Dear Mamma,

IN what words, in what language shall I address you? What shall I say on a subject which deprives me of the power of expression? Would to God I had been totally deprived of that power before so fatal a subject required its exertion! Repentance comes too late, when it cannot prevent the evil lamented. For your kindness, your more than maternal affection towards me, from my infancy to the present moment, a long life of filial duty and unerring rectitude could hardly compensate. How greatly deficient in gratitude must I appear then, while I confess, that precept and example, counsel and advice, instruction and admonition, have been all lost upon me!

Your kind endeavors to promote my happiness have been repaid by the inexcusable folly of sacrificing it. The various emotions of shame, and remorse, penitence and regret, which torture and distract my guilty breast, exceed description. Yes, madam, your Eliza has fallen; fallen, indeed! She has become the victim of her own indiscretion, and of the intrigue and artifice of a designing libertine, who is the husband of another! She is polluted, and no more worthy of her parentage! She flies from you, not to conceal her guilt, that she humbly and penitently owns; but to avoid what she has never experienced, and feels herself unable to support, a mother's frown; to escape the heart-rending sight of a parent's grief, occasioned by the crimes of her guilty child!

I have become a reproach and disgrace to my friends. The consciousness of having forfeited their favor, and incurred their disapprobation and resentment, induces me to conceal from them the place of my retirement; but, lest your benevolence should render you anxious for my comfort in my present situation, I take the liberty to assure you that I am amply provided for.

I have no claim even upon your pity; but from my long experience of your tenderness, I presume to hope it will be extended to me. Oh, my mother, if you knew what the state of my mind is, and has been, for months past, you would surely compassionate my case! Could tears efface the stain, which I have brought upon my family, it would, long since have been washed away! But, alas, tears are vain; and vain is my

bitter repentance! It cannot obliterate my crime, nor restore me to innocence and peace! In this life I have no ideas of happiness. These I have wholly resigned! The only hope which affords me any solace, is that of your forgiveness. If the deepest contrition can make an atonement; if the severest pains, both of body and mind, can restore me to your charity, you will not be inexorable! Oh, let my sufferings be deemed a sufficient punishment; and add not the insupportable weight of a parent's wrath! At present, I cannot see you. The effect of my crime is too obvious to be longer concealed, to elude the invidious eye of curiosity. This night, therefore, I leave your hospitable mansion! This night I become a wretched wanderer from thy paternal roof! Oh, that the grave were this night to be my lodging! Then should I lie down and be at rest! Trusting in the mercy of God, through the mediation of his son; I think I could meet my heavenly father with more composure and confidence, than my earthly parent!

Let not the faults and misfortunes of your daughter oppress your mind. Rather let the conviction of having faithfully discharged your duty to your lost child, support and console you in this trying scene.

Since I wrote the above, you have kindly granted me your forgiveness, though you knew not how great, how aggravated was my offence! You forgive me, you say: Oh, the harmonious, the transporting sound! It has revived my drooping spirits; and will enable me to encounter, with resolution, the trials before me!

Farewell, my dear mamma! pity and pray for your ruined child; and be assured, that affection and gratitude will be the last sentiments, which expire in the breast of your repenting daughter.

<div align="right">ELIZA WHARTON.</div>

<div align="center">LETTER LXIX.</div>

<div align="center">*to Miss* JULIA GRANBY.</div>

<div align="right">TUESDAY.</div>

My Dear Friend,

BY that endearing title you permit me still to address you, and such you have always proved yourself, by a participation of my distresses, as

well as by the consoling voice of pity and forgiveness. What destiny Providence designs for me, I know not; but I have my forebodings that this is the last time I shall ever accost you! Nor does this apprehension arise merely from a disturbed imagination. I have reason to think myself in a confirmed consumption, which commonly proves fatal to persons in my situation. I have carefully concealed every complaint of the kind from my mamma, for fear of distressing her; yet I have never been insensible of their probable issue, and have bidden a sincere welcome to them, as the harbingers of my speedy release from a life of guilt and woe!

I am going from you, Julia. This night separates us, perhaps, for ever! I have not resolution to encounter the tears of my friends; and therefore seek shelter among strangers; where none knows, or is interested in my melancholy story. The place of my seclusion I studiously conceal; yet I shall take measures that you may be apprized of my fate.

Should it please God to spare and restore me to health, I shall return, and endeavor, by a life of penitence and rectitude, to expiate my past offences. But should I be called from this scene of action; and leave behind me a helpless babe, the innocent sufferer of its mother's shame, Oh, Julia, let your friendship for me extend to the little stranger! Intercede with my mother to take it under her protection; and transfer to it all her affection for me; to train it up in the ways of piety and virtue, that it may compensate her for the afflictions which I have occasioned!

One thing more I have to request. Plead for me with my two best friends, Mrs. Richman and Mrs. Sumner. I ask you not to palliate my faults; that cannot be done; but to obtain, if possible, their forgiveness. I cannot write all my full mind suggests on this subject. You know the purport; and can better express it for me.

And now, my dear Julia, recommending myself again to your benevolence, to your charity and (may I add?) to your affection; and entreating that the fatal consequences of my folly, now fallen upon my devoted head, may suffice for my punishment; let me conjure you to bury my crimes in the grave with me, and to preserve the remembrance of my former virtues, which engaged your love and confidence; more especially of that ardent esteem for you, which will glow till the last expiring breath of your despairing

ELIZA WHARTON.

Letter lxx.

to Mr. Charles Deighton.

I HAVE, at last, accomplished the removal of my darling girl, from a place where she thought every eye accused, and every heart condemned her.

She has become quite romantic in her notions. She would not permit me to accompany her, lest it should be reported that we had eloped together. I provided amply for her future exigencies, and conveyed her by night to the distance of ten or twelve miles, where we met the stage, in which I had previously secured her a seat. The agony of her grief at being thus obliged to leave her mother's house, baffles all description.

It very sensibly affected me, I know. I was almost a penitent. I am sure I acted like one, whether I were sincere or not. She chose to go where she was totally unknown. She would leave the stage, she said, before it reached Boston, and take passage in a more private carriage to Salem, or its vicinity, where she would fix her abode; chalking the initials of my name over the door, as a signal to me of her residence.

She is exceedingly depressed; and says she neither expects nor wishes to survive her lying in. Insanity, for aught I know, must be my lot, if she should die. But I will not harbor the idea. I hope, one time or other, to have the power to make her amends, even by marriage. My wife may be provoked, I imagine, to sue for a divorce. If she should, she would find no difficulty in obtaining it; and then I would take Eliza in her stead. Though I confess that the idea of being thus connected with a woman whom I have been able to dishonor would be rather hard to surmount. It would hurt even my delicacy, little as you may think me to possess, to have a wife whom I know to be seducible. And, on this account, I cannot be positive that even Eliza would retain my love.

My Nancy and I have lived a pretty uncomfortable life, of late. She has been very suspicious of my amour with Eliza; and now and then expressed her jealous sentiments a little more warmly than my patience would bear. But the news of Eliza's circumstances and retirement, being publicly talked of, have reached her ears, and rendered her quite outrageous. She tells me she will no longer brook my indifference and infidelity; intends soon to return to her father's house, and extricate herself

from me intirely. My general reply to all this, is, that she knew my
character before we married, and could reasonably expect nothing less
than what has happened. I shall not oppose her leaving me, as it may
conduce to the execution of the plan I have hinted above.

To morrow I shall set out to visit my disconsolate fair one. From my
very soul I pity her; and wish I could have preserved her virtue consis-
tently with the indulgence of my passion. To her I lay not the principal
blame, as in like cases, I do to the sex in general. My finesse was too
well planned for detection, and my snares too deeply laid for any one
to escape who had the least warmth in her constitution, or affection in
her heart. I shall, therefore, be the less whimsical about a future con-
nection, and the more solicitous to make her reparation, should it ever
be in my power.

Her friends are all in arms about her. I dare say I have the impre-
cations of the whole fraternity. They may thank themselves in part; for
I always swore revenge for their dislike and coldness towards me. Had
they been politic, they would have conducted more like the aborigines
of the country, who are said to worship the devil out of fear.

I am afraid I shall be obliged to remove my quarters; for Eliza was
so great a favorite in town, that I am looked upon with an evil eye. I
plead with her before we parted last, to forgive my seducing her; al-
ledged my ardent love, and my inability to possess her in any other way.
How, said she, can that be love which destroys its object? But granting
what you say, you have frustrated your own purpose. You have de-
prived yourself of my society, which might have been innocently en-
joyed. You have cut me off from life in the midst of my days. You have
rendered me the reproach of my friends, the disgrace of my family, and
a dishonor to virtue and my sex! but I forgive you, added she. Yes,
Sanford, I forgive you; and sincerely pray for your repentance and ref-
ormation. I hope to be the last wretched female, sacrificed by you to
the arts of falsehood and seduction!

May my unhappy story serve as a beacon to warn the American fair
of the dangerous tendency and destructive consequences of associating
with men of your character, of destroying their time, and risking their
reputation by the practice of coquetry and its attendant follies! But for
these, I might have been honorably connected; and capable, at this mo-
ment, of diffusing and receiving happiness! But for your arts, I might
have remained a blessing to society, as well as the delight and comfort
of my friends!

Your being a married man unspeakably aggravates both your guilt

and mine. This circumstance annexes indelible shame to our crime! You have rent asunder the tenderest ties of nature! You have broken the bonds of conjugal love, which ought ever to be kept sacred and inviolate! You have filled with grief and discontent the heart of your amiable wife, whom gratitude, if no other principle, should have induced you to cherish with tenderness; and I, wretch that I am, have been your accomplice!

But I cease to reproach you. You have acted but too consistently with the character, which I was sufficiently apprised you sustained. The blame then may be retorted on myself, for disregarding the counsels, warnings and admonitions of my best friends. You have prided yourself in the character of a libertine. Glory no longer in your shame! You have accomplished your designs; your dreadful designs against me! Let this suffice. Add not to the number of those deluded creatures, who will one day rise up in judgment against you, and condemn you.

By this time we had nearly reached the inn, and were soon to part. I seized her hand and exclaimed, you must not leave me, Eliza, with that awful anathema on your lips! Oh, say that you will forget my past faults. That, said she, I shall soon do; for in the grave there is no remembrance! This to my mind, was a harsher sentence than the other; and almost threw me into despair. Never was I so wrought upon before! I knew not what to say or do! She saw my distress, and kindly softened her manner. If I am severe, said she, it is because I wish to impress your mind with such a sense of your offences against your Maker, your friends and society in general, as may effect your repentance and amendment. I wish not to be your accuser, but your reformer. On several accounts, I view my own crime in a more aggravated light than yours; but my conscience is awakened to a conviction of my guilt. Yours, I fear is not. Let me conjure you to return home, and endeavor by your future kindness and fidelity to your wife, to make her all the amends in your power. By a life of virtue and religion, you may yet become a valuable member of society, and secure happiness both here and hereafter.

I begged leave to visit her retirement next week, not in continuation of our amour, but as a friend, solicitous to know her situation and welfare. Unable to speak, she only bowed assent. The stage being now ready, I whispered some tender things in her ear, and kissing her cheek, which was all she would permit, suffered her to depart.

My body remains behind; but my soul, if I have any, went with her! This was a horrid lecture, Charles! She brought every charge against

me, which a fruitful and gloomy imagination could suggest! But I hope, when, she recovers, she will resume her former cheerfulness, and become as kind and agreeable as ever. My anxiety for her safety is very great. I trust, however, it will soon be removed; and peace and pleasure be restored to your humble servant,

PETER SANFORD.

LETTER LXXI.

to Mrs. LUCY SUMNER.

HARTFORD.

THE drama is now closed! A tragical one indeed it has proved!

How sincerely, my dear Mrs. Sumner, must the friends of our departed Eliza, sympathize with each other; and with her afflicted, bereaved parent!

You have doubtless seen the account, in the public papers, which gave us the melancholy intelligence. But I will give you a detail of circumstances.

A few days after my last was written, we heard that Major Sanford's property was attached, and he a prisoner in his own house. He was the last man, to whom we wished to apply for information respecting the forlorn wanderer; yet we had no other resource. And after waiting a fortnight in the most cruel suspense, we wrote a billet, entreating him, if possible, to give some intelligence concerning her. He replied, that he was unhappily deprived of all means of knowing himself; but hoped soon to relieve his own, and our anxiety about her.

In this situation we continued, till a neighbor (purposely, we since concluded) sent us a Boston paper. Mrs. Wharton took it, and inconscious of its contents, observed that the perusal might divert her, a few moments. She read for some time; when it suddenly dropped upon the floor. She clasped her hands together, and raising her streaming eyes to heaven, exclaimed, It is the Lord; let him do what he will! Be still, O my soul, and know that he is God!

What, madam, said I, can be the matter? She answered not; but with inexpressible anguish depicted in her countenance, pointed to the paper.

I took it up, and soon found the fatal paragraph. I shall not attempt to paint our heart felt grief and lamentation upon this occasion; for we had no doubt of Eliza's being the person described, as a stranger, who died at Danvers, last July. Her delivery of a child; her dejected state of mind; the marks upon her linen; indeed, every circumstance in the advertisement convinced us beyond dispute that it could be no other. Mrs. Wharton retired immediately to her chamber, where she continued overwhelmed with sorrow that night and the following day. Such, in fact, has been her habitual frame ever since; though the endeavors of her friends, who have sought to console her, have rendered her somewhat more conversable. My testimony of Eliza's penitence, before her departure, is a source of comfort to this disconsolate parent. She fondly cherished the idea, that having expiated her offence by sincere repentance and amendment, her deluded child finally made a happy exchange of worlds. But the desperate resolution, which she formed, and executed of becoming a fugitive; of deserting her mother's house and protection, and of wandering and dying among strangers, is a most distressing reflection to her friends; especially to her mother, in whose breast so many painful ideas arise, that she finds it extremely difficult to compose herself to that resignation, which she evidently strives to exemplify.

Eliza's brother has been to visit her last retreat; and to learn the particulars of her melancholy exit. He relates, that she was well accommodated, and had every attention and assistance, which her situation required. The people where she resided appear to have a lively sense of her merit and misfortunes. They testify her modest deportment, her fortitude under the sufferings to which she was called, and the serenity and composure, with which she bid a last adieu to the world. Mr. Wharton has brought back several scraps of her writing, containing miscellaneous reflections on her situation, the death of her babe, and the absence of her friends. Some of these were written before, some after her confinement. These valuable testimonies of the affecting sense, and calm expectation she entertained of her approaching dissolution, are calculated to sooth and comfort the minds of mourning connections. They greatly alleviate the regret occasioned by her absence, at this awful period.

Her elopement can be equalled only by the infatuation which caused her ruin.

> "But let no one reproach her memory.
> Her life has paid the forfeit of her folly.
> Let that suffice."

I am told that Major Sanford is quite frantic. Sure I am that he has reason to be. If the mischiefs he has brought upon others return upon his own head, dreadful indeed must be his portion! His wife has left him, and returned to her parents. His estate, which has been long mortgaged, is taken from him; and poverty and disgrace await him! Heaven seldom leaves injured innocence unavenged! Wretch, that he is, he ought for ever to be banished from human society! I shall continue with Mrs. Wharton, till the lenient hand of time has assuaged her sorrows; and then make my promised visit to you. I will bring Eliza's posthumous papers with me, when I come to Boston, as I have not time to copy them now.

I foresee, my dear Mrs. Sumner, that this disastrous affair will suspend your enjoyments, as it has mine. But what are our feelings, compared with the pangs which rend a parent's heart? This parent, I here behold, inhumanly stripped of the best solace of her declining years, by the ensnaring machinations of a profligate debauchee! Not only the life, but what was still dearer, the reputation and virtue of the unfortunate Eliza, have fallen victims at the shrine of *libertinism!* Detested be the epithet! Let it henceforth bear its true signature, and candor itself shall call it *lust* and *brutality!*

Execrable is the man, however arrayed in magnificence, crowned with wealth, or decorated with the external graces and accomplishments of fashionable life, who shall presume to display them, at the expense of virtue and innocence! Sacred names! attended with real blessings; blessings too useful and important to be trifled away! My resentment at the base arts, which must have been employed to complete the seduction of Eliza, I cannot suppress. I wish them to be exposed, and stamped with universal ignominy! Nor do I doubt but you will join with me in execrating the measures by which *we* have been robbed of so valuable a friend; and *society,* of so ornamental a member. I am, &c.

JULIA GRANBY.

LETTER LXXII.

to Mr. CHARLES DEIGHTON.

HARTFORD.

CONFUSION, horror and despair are the portion of your wretched, unhappy friend! Oh, Deighton, I am undone! Misery irremediable is my future lot! She is gone; yes, she is gone for ever! The darling of my soul, the centre of all my wishes and enjoyments is no more! Cruel fate has snatched her from me; and she is irretrievably lost! I rave, and then reflect: I reflect, and then rave! I have not patience to bear this calamity, nor power to remedy it! Where shall I fly from the upbraidings of my mind, which accuses me as the murderer of my Eliza? I would fly to death, and seek a refuge in the grave; but the forebodings of a retribution to come, I cannot away with! Oh, that I had seen her; that I had once more asked her forgiveness! But even that privilege, that consolation was denied me! The day on which I meant to visit her, most of my property was attached, and to secure the rest, I was obliged to shut my doors, and become a prisoner in my own house! High living, and old debts, incurred by extravagance, had reduced the fortune of my wife to very little, and I could not satisfy the clamorous demands of my creditors.

I would have given millions, had I possessed them, to have been at liberty to see, and to have had power to preserve Eliza from death! But in vain was my anxiety; it could not relieve; it could not liberate me! When I first heard the dreadful tidings of her exit, I believe I acted like a madman! Indeed, I am little else now!

I have compounded with my creditors, and resigned the whole of my property.

Thus, that splendor and equipage, to secure which, I have sacrificed a virtuous woman, is taken from me; that poverty, the dread of which prevented my forming an honorable connection with an amiable and accomplished girl, the only one I ever loved, has fallen, with redoubled vengeance, upon my guilty head; and I must become a vagabond in the earth!

I shall fly my country as soon as possible; I shall go from every object which reminds me of my departed Eliza! But never, never shall I eradicate from my bosom the idea of her excellence; or the painful remem-

brance of the injuries I have done her! Her shade will perpetually haunt me! The image of her, as she appeared when mounting the carriage which conveyed her for ever from my sight, she waved her hand in token of a last adieu, will always be present to my imagination! The solemn counsel she gave me before we parted, never more to meet, will not cease to resound in my ears!

While my being is prolonged, I must feel the disgraceful, and torturing effects of my guilt in seducing her! How madly have I deprived her of happiness, of reputation, of life! Her friends, could they know the pangs of contrition, and the horror of conscience which attend me, would be amply revenged!

It is said, she quitted the world with composure and peace. Well she might! She had not that insupportable weight of iniquity, which sinks me to despair! She found consolation in that religion, which I have ridiculed as priestcraft and hypocrisy! But whether it be true, or false, would to heaven I could now enjoy the comforts, which its votaries evidently feel!

My wife has left me. As we lived together without love, we parted without regret.

Now, Charles, I am to bid you a long, perhaps, a last farewell. Where I shall roam in future, I neither know nor care; I shall go where the name of Sanford is unknown; and his person and sorrows unnoticed.

In this happy clime I have nothing to induce my stay. I have not money to support me with my profligate companions; nor have I any relish, at present, for their society. By the virtuous part of the community, I am shunned as the pest and bane of social enjoyment. In short I am debarred from every kind of happiness. If I look back, I recoil with horror from the black catalogue of vices, which have stained my past life, and reduced me to indigence and contempt. If I look forward, I shudder at the prospects which my foreboding mind presents to view, both in this and a coming world! This is a deplorable, yet just picture of myself! How totally the reverse of what I once appeared!

Let it warn you, my friend, to shun the dangerous paths which I have trodden, that you may never be involved in the hopeless ignominy and wretchedness of

PETER SANFORD.

LETTER LXXIII.

to Miss JULIA GRANBY.

BOSTON.

A MELANCHOLY tale have you unfolded, my dear Julia; and tragic indeed is the concluding scene!

Is she then gone! gone in this most distressing manner! Have I lost my once loved friend; lost her in a way which I could never have conceived to be possible.

Our days of childhood were spent together in the same pursuits, in the same amusements. Our riper years encreased our mutual affection, and maturer judgment most firmly cemented our friendship. Can I then calmly resign her to so severe a fate! Can I bear the idea of her being lost to honor, to fame, and to life! No; she shall still live in the heart of her faithful Lucy; whose experience of her numerous virtues and engaging qualities, has imprinted her image too deeply on the memory to be obliterated. However she may have erred, her sincere repentance is sufficient to restore her to charity.

Your letter gave me the first information of this awful event. I had taken a short excursion into the country, where I had not seen the papers; or if I had, paid little or no attention to them. By your directions I found the distressing narrative of her exit. The poignancy of my grief, and the unavailing lamentations which the intelligence excited, need no delineation. To scenes of this nature, you have been habituated in the mansion of sorrow, where you reside.

How sincerely I sympathize with the bereaved parent of the dear, deceased Eliza, I can feel, but have not power to express. Let it be her consolation, that her child is at rest. The resolution which carried this deluded wanderer thus far from her friends, and supported her through her various trials, is astonishing! Happy would it have been, had she exerted an equal degree of fortitude in repelling the first attacks upon her virtue! But she is no more; and heaven forbid that I should accuse or reproach her!

Yet, in what language shall I express my abhorrence of the monster, whose detestable arts have blasted one of the fairest flowers in creation? I leave him to God, and his own conscience! Already is he exposed in his true colors! Vengeance already begins to overtake him! His sordid

mind must now suffer the deprivation of those sensual gratifications, beyond which he is incapable of enjoyment!

Upon your reflecting and steady mind, my dear Julia, I need not inculcate the lessons which may be drawn from this woe-fraught tale; but for the sake of my sex in general, I wish it engraved upon every heart, that virtue alone, independent of the trappings of wealth, the parade of equipage, and the adulation of gallantry, can secure lasting felicity. From the melancholy story of Eliza Wharton, let the American fair learn to reject with disdain every insinuation derogatory to their true dignity and honor. Let them despise, and for ever banish the man, who can glory in the seduction of innocence and the ruin of reputation. To associate, is to approve; to approve, is to be betrayed!

I am, &c.

LUCY SUMNER.

LETTER LXXIV.

to Mrs. M. WHARTON.

BOSTON.

Dear Madam,

WE have paid the last tribute of respect to your beloved daughter. The day after my arrival, Mrs. Sumner proposed that we should visit the sad spot which contains the remains of our once amiable friend. The grave of Eliza Wharton, said she, shall not be unbedewed by the tears of friendship.

Yesterday we went accordingly, and were much pleased with the apparent sincerity of the people, in their assurances that every thing in their power had been done to render her situation comfortable. The minutest circumstances were faithfully related; and from the state of her mind, in her last hours, I think much comfort may be derived to her afflicted friends.

We spent a mournful hour, in the place where she is interred, and then returned to the inn, while Mrs. Sumner gave orders for a decent stone to be erected over her grave, with the following inscription:

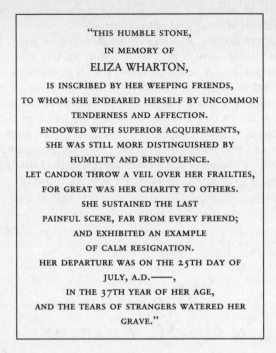

"THIS HUMBLE STONE,

IN MEMORY OF

ELIZA WHARTON,

IS INSCRIBED BY HER WEEPING FRIENDS,
TO WHOM SHE ENDEARED HERSELF BY UNCOMMON
TENDERNESS AND AFFECTION.
ENDOWED WITH SUPERIOR ACQUIREMENTS,
SHE WAS STILL MORE DISTINGUISHED BY
HUMILITY AND BENEVOLENCE.
LET CANDOR THROW A VEIL OVER HER FRAILTIES,
FOR GREAT WAS HER CHARITY TO OTHERS.
SHE SUSTAINED THE LAST
PAINFUL SCENE, FAR FROM EVERY FRIEND;
AND EXHIBITED AN EXAMPLE
OF CALM RESIGNATION.
HER DEPARTURE WAS ON THE 25TH DAY OF
JULY, A.D.——,
IN THE 37TH YEAR OF HER AGE,
AND THE TEARS OF STRANGERS WATERED HER
GRAVE."

I hope, madam, that you will derive satisfaction from these exertions of friendship, and that, united to the many other sources of consolation with which you are furnished, they may alleviate your grief; and while they leave the pleasing remembrance of her virtues, add the supporting persuasion, that your Eliza is happy.

I am, &c.

JULIA GRANBY.

F I N I S .

EXPLANATORY NOTES

Notes to THE POWER OF SYMPATHY: OR, THE TRIUMPH OF NATURE. FOUNDED IN TRUTH.

Title page: *FAIN would he strew life's thorny Way with Flowers . . . And win the Mind to Sentiment and Truth:* This epigraph seems to have been written by Brown himself.

LETTER I

Page 9 *the moralist and the amoroso—the sentiment and the sensibility:* The parallel construction suggests the uneasy cultural tension with the terms *sentiment* and *sensibility*. Here, moralists are equated with those who have sentiment, amorosos (here, those who are fond of being in love) with those who have sensibility. All these terms, with the multiplicity of meanings they signify, were contested during this era. As the Editor's Introduction suggests, a central issue in the novel relates to the development of a sensibility that has rational controls over it.

10 *God of Love:* Invocations to gods of love are common in eighteenth-century writings, especially in poetry. Here, the God of Love is probably Eros, the Greek god of sexual love (Amor, or Cupid, in Roman stories).

10 *Stygian:* Pertaining to the river Styx, gloomy, dark, infernal.

10 *Elysium:* In Greek myth, Elysium is the abode of the blessed after death; in general terms, any place or condition of ideal happiness.

LETTER III

Page 11 *why art thou not arrayed in canonicals:* That is, why are you not dressed like a clergyman. To dress in canonicals would be dressing according to prescribed ecclesiastic rules.

11 *the pike of Teneriffe:* Tenerife, or Teneriffe, was the largest and most important of the Canary Islands, situated west of Africa. It served as a directional marker for passing sailors.

11 *monitorial:* Cautioning, warning.

11 *not so much of a republican . . . to wed any person of this class*: That is, Harrington considers himself sufficiently above the station of Harriot that she cannot be deemed a worthy partner for him. Here, "republican" refers to someone who has little care about social station, someone, in fact, who considers all persons equal, regardless of social level. Thus, when Harrington goes on to mention the "democratick empire of virtue," he is mocking all those who consider virtue a truer measure of goodness and just station than wealth. Harrington is signaling the assumptions of many elite-class persons of his era, although the tone of the statements is joking. The irony of the situation suggests to a reader that Harrington is to be criticized for holding these attitudes.

11 *immured in a nunnery*: Confined, imprisoned in a place for nuns. The phrasing suggests anti-Catholic biases common during the era and more and more frequently found in fiction of the day.

LETTER IV

Page 12 *swain*: An affectionate and familiar poetic term for a man who is lovesick, drawn from the pastoral mode of Brown's day.

LETTER VII

Page 15 *"Was I in a desert," says Sterne, "I would find wherewith . . . I would rejoice along with them"*: A quotation from *A Sentimental Journey through France and Italy. By Mr. Yorick*, published in two volumes in 1768, written by Laurence Sterne (1713–68) and published the year he died. The chapters of *A Sentimental Journey* are unnumbered; the quotation occurs in "Remise, Calais," nearly midway through volume 1.

16 *Temple of Apollo*: In Greek mythology, Apollo is the sun god but also the god of poetry, music, medicine, and prophecy. The "temple" on the estate of the Holmeses represents a seat of the arts for the family.

16 *Rural Inscription*: This was Brown's own poem.

16 *Mars*: The Roman god of war.

16 *mazy ground*: As the setting seems to be a pastoral one, the mazy ground is probably a description of ground covered with maize, or corn, or else a general reference to maize-colored (that is, orange-yellow) ground. (Corn is associated with fertility in North American pastorals.) Alternatively, the reference could indicate a green area planted with bushes that form a garden maze.

16 *woodland sisters*: Perhaps a reference to nymphs of trees.

17 *votive wreath*: A wreath given as a pledge or offering.

17 *contemn*: Condemn.

17 *"where every breeze breathes health, and every sound is the echo of tranquillity"*: The original source for this line is uncertain. Two different poems might seem to have contributed to the figures used in these lines. The poem

"London" (1738) by Samuel Johnson (1709–84) includes the lines: "There ev'ry bush with nature's musick rings, / There ev'ry breeze bears health upon its wings" ("London," lines 220–21). And *An Essay on Criticism* (1711) by Alexander Pope (1688–1744) has the famous line, "The Sound must seem an Eccho to the Sense" (*Essay on Criticism,* line 365).

LETTER XI

Page 21 *corrupt or mortified members:* Of the body, in this instance, referring to dying, dead, or gangrenous members (arms, legs, hands, feet).

21 *"to smite them with an apoplexy . . . dying of a consumption":* The source for this quotation has not been located.

23 *desultory reading:* Reading that is haphazard, random, and unguided by a mentor who could instruct.

23 *Miss Whitman:* A reference to Eliza Whitman, whose story is told in Brown's own note to the text. Brown's note repeats the *Massachusetts Centinel,* September 20, 1788, comments upon Whitman's death, that "She was a great reader of novels and romances and having imbibed her ideas of *the characters of men,* from those fallacious sources, became vain and coquetish." Her story was fictionalized in Hannah Webster Foster's *The Coquette.* The Editor's Introduction provides background on Whitman's life.

23 *puerperal fever:* A fever connected with or following childbirth.

23 *"Must I die alone? . . .":* The letter survived among Whitman's papers at the Bell Tavern.

23 *like the dying Swan, sings her own Elegy:* Proverbially, the swan is said to sing most sweetly just before it dies.

24 *The description of her unfortunate passion will remind the critical reader of the famous ode of Sappho:* Sappho was a Greek lyric poet who flourished around 600 B.C. and who was credited even in her own day for her poetic excellencies. The famous story of Sappho's love is probably one that comes from an ode written to Phaeon. According to the story—but probably not the actual events that occurred—Phaeon was a boatman of Mitylene whom Sappho loved; when his ardor turned to disdain, Sappho threw herself into the sea.

24 *"Disappointment" [poem]:* The poem was Elizabeth Whitman's poem.

24 *Hesper:* Hesper, or Hesperus, is the planet Venus, as the evening star.

24 *Fidelio:* Fidelio is a common name for a lover in pastoral poems of this era.

24 *thy token:* Evidently, "Fidelio" gave "Eliza" a token of his love, which she treasured.

24 *fair Canäan:* In biblical terms, the ancient land between the Jordan and the Mediterranean gained by the Israelites, but perhaps an oblique reference to New Canaan, Connecticut.

25 *Eliza's early tomb:* Elizabeth Whitman was thirty-six years old when she died.

25 *"Lost in the magick of that sweet employ, / To build gay scenes and fashion future joy":* A line written by Elizabeth Whitman.

25 *spleen:* Here, melancholia, or ill temper. From the medieval times through the seventeenth century in Britain, a theory of physiology (adapted from the conceptions of cardinal humors of the ancients) commonly associated a person's general character and bodily health with certain characteristics located, it was thought, in one of what were considered the four fluids of the body: blood, phlegm, choler (yellow bile), and melancholy (black bile). This theory was extended to what were called the four "humours," or personality traits, so that the temperament of a person was said to derive from the relative balance (or imbalance) of the bodily fluids, which, according to some theorists of the day, gave off "vapors."

25 *Rochefoucault's maxims:* The reference is to François, Duc de la Rochefoucauld (1613–80), whose *Reflections, or Sentences and Moral Maxims* (1665) went through many editions during his lifetime and later. In the conversation that follows, Rev. Mr. Holmes is likely referring to Maxim 39: "Interest speaks all sorts of tongues, and plays all sorts of parts, even that of disinterestedness." The epigraph to the first edition (published anonymously), not repeated in later editions of the *Reflections,* reads: "Our virtues are most frequently but vices disguised."

26 *Swift, in speaking of those maxims . . . affirms, "They argue no corrupted mind / In him—the fault is in mankind":* Jonathan Swift (1667–1745), in "Verses on the Death of Dr. S[wift], D.S.P.D. Occasioned by Reading a Maxim in Rochefoucault" (1739): "As *Rochefoucault* his Maxims drew / From Nature, I believe 'em true: / They argue no corrupted Mind / In him; the Fault is in Mankind" (lines 1–4).

27 *as long as vice and folly continue to predominate . . . an auxiliary to the pulpit:* The reference is difficult to trace. Joseph Addison (1672–1719) wrote on manners and morals in a number of periodicals during the eighteenth century. He collaborated with Sir Richard Steele (1672–1729) in creating essays for *The Tatler* and *The Spectator,* both of them periodicals developed as essay serials; he tends to be the one who is associated with *The Guardian,* as well, although Steele started up that essay serial and although other writers contributed to that series. All three periodical series were immensely popular in the colonies and the new republic. In the opening number of *The Guardian,* actually written by Steele, the author comments that this series by the "Guardian" should assist in the development of morals and manners. The "Guardian" concludes: "My Design upon the whole is no less, than to make the Pulpit, the Bar, and the Stage, all act in Concert in the Care of Piety, Justice and Virtue" (no. 1, March 12, 1713).

LETTER XII

Page 27 *metaphysical nicety:* Too abstract a point.

27 *diverting herself with the cuts in Gay's Fables:* That is, she was looking at the woodcuts or prints accompanying an edition of *The Fables* (first published in 1727), a collection of highly didactic poetic fables, by John Gay (1685–1732).

28 *A Sentimental Journey through France and Italy, by Mr. Yorick:* See the note at 15 above.

28 *bettermost genii:* Here, socially "better" people.

28 *Sentiment out of date—alas! poor Yorick . . . Shandean tone:* These are allusions to Laurence Sterne's *Tristram Shandy* (1760–67). The novel produced a sensation, first in England, then in all Europe, from the publication of its first volumes. The character Yorick "dies" at the conclusion of volume 1, chapter 12, where Tristram "buries" him in a page of black, quoting Shakespeare's Hamlet's words to Yorick's skull (*Hamlet* 5.1.179–80), which also are said to appear as Yorick's "monumental inscription."

28 *these antis . . . gods of the Canaanites:* That is, those readers who are against sentiment have no more to do with "Yorick" than they do with the gods of those Israelites who captured Canaan. Worthy suggests here that readers who do not like sentiment are not only uncouth but perhaps immoral.

28 *inadvertantly:* Inadvertently, accidentally.

29 *the insignificant petit maitre:* A little or insignificant man; literally, an insignificant little master.

LETTER XIII

Page 31 *boquets:* That is, bouquets of real flowers, of which Myra's embroidery is an artful rendering.

31 *loadstone:* Lodestone, a magnetic mineral.

LETTER XIV

Page 31 *the philosopher's stone:* The philosophers' or philosopher's stone was a substance reputed to have the power of transforming any metal into gold.

32 *chymical:* That is, chemical.

LETTER XVII

Page 33 *"a mechanick's daughter":* The lines between the classes were more fluid in British North America than in Europe, but Anglo-Americans nonetheless retained certain prejudices against those who had to work for their living. To

have been the daughter of an artisan while in upper-class society would have required a good deal of training for a young woman, training that this fictional young woman had evidently received. Harrington is here showing a more "democratic" temper than he held when he wrote Letter III, perhaps because of the influence Harriot (who presumably has no property or "good" lineage) has had upon him.

34 *"I like a democratical better than any other kind of government"*: Harrington here is saying that he prefers government according to equality in degree rather than in property necessarily. His condemnation of the slaveholding society of the South suggests the growing tensions in Anglo-American society of this era over slaveowning and governance.

34 *Lycurgus:* A ninth-century lawmaker of Sparta, the traditional author of its laws and institutions.

Letter XIX

Page 35 *the ecstacy of Orpheus . . . Eurydice vanished to the shades:* Orpheus was a musician famous for his ability to charm all animate and inanimate objects by playing his lyre sweetly. In Greek legend, Orpheus descended living into Hades (Hell) to bring back his wife, Eurydice, from death. His music succeeded in charming even those in Hades, but Orpheus looked back to make sure Eurydice was following him and thus lost her forever. The tale of love between Orpheus and Eurydice—and Orpheus's loss of Eurydice—was a common reference in eighteenth-century neoclassical poetry.

35 *provident:* Frugal, sparing.

Letter XX

Page 36 *the Knight of La Mancha:* Don Quixote de la Mancha, "the Knight of the Woeful Countenance," a character created by Don Miguel de Cervantes Saavedra. *Don Quixote* was published first in Madrid (part 1, 1605; part 2, 1615) but achieved international acclaim quickly and was much imitated by eighteenth-century writers in England and America.

36 *no Musselman ever travelled barefooted to Mecca with more sincere devotion:* That is, no one could be more devout. "Mussulmans" are Muslims, followers of Mohammed; in the Mohammedan sense, Mussulmans are true believers. Brown here takes advantage of the cultural fascination of Europeans for what they considered "Oriental" culture.

37 *the Houri:* Probably a reference to one of the beautiful virgins of the paradise in the Koran, the sacred text of Islam. Alternatively, the Hours, or Horae, in classical mythology were goddesses who presided over changes in the seasons.

37 *Though sleep . . . TEAR behind [poem]:* This was Brown's own poem.

LETTER XXI

Page 38 *precipitate:* Lacking in deliberation, hasty, sudden.

39 *ignis fatuus:* Scientifically, a phosphorescent light that flits over swampy ground at night, perhaps a result of spontaneous combustion of gases; figuratively, an illusion, something that misleads.

39 *compunction:* In the original, "compuction"; the typographical error has been corrected.

LETTER XXIII

Page 42 *temerariously:* Rashly, recklessly.

42 *harrow up:* Inflict with distress, torment.

43 *the douceurs and the graces:* Behaviors indicating sweetness and complaisance.

43 *principle of mediocrity:* That is, principle of moderation.

LETTER XXIV

Page 43 *it:* That is, the poem Harrington sent to her included in Letter XX.

LETTER XXV

Page 44 *"The Court of Vice" [poem]:* In the context of the novel, this poem is said to have been written by Myra's brother, Harrington. In fact, this was Brown's own poem. In addition to being published in the novel, the poem was published in a Boston publication, *Herald of Freedom,* January 23, 1789.

44 *Apologue:* Moral fable.

45 *Tendry:* Offer, proposal, tender.

46 *hagger'd:* That is, haggard, worn.

46 *Judas:* After Judas Iscariot, the apostle who betrayed Christ, one who betrays under the appearance of friendship.

LETTER XXVI

Page 47 *an eclaircissement:* A moment of clarification or enlightenment.

47 *confidante:* A woman with whom secrets or private matters are shared.

47 *a certain je ne sçais quoi:* A certain *je ne sais quoi,* an unidentifiable quality; literally, a quality that is indescribable.

LETTER XXVII

Page 48 *"Tall rose the lily's slender frame" [poem]*: This was Brown's own poem.

LETTER XXVIII

Page 51 *the little paraphernalia is preparing*: That is, as preparations for the wedding were taking place. *Paraphernalia* is here being used in its original common-law sense, as a married woman's personal property exclusive of her dowry.

52 *decriped*: Evidently, decrepit, infirm from old age.

52 *to compassionate*: To pity.

53 *to animadvert*: To turn the mind toward, and criticize, censure, or moralize upon.

LETTER XXIX

Page 53 *A Lady of Quality's Advice to Her Children*: The volume, *Advice from a Lady of Quality to Her Children, in the Last Stage of a Lingering Illness*, sometimes subtitled in English "In a Series of Evening-Conferences on the Most Interesting Subjects," went through several editions in London and Boston beginning in 1778. For background on this volume, see the Introduction and Appendix I.

53 *Chesterfieldian system*: The reference here and in the following paragraph is to Philip Dormer Stanhope, fourth Earl of Chesterfield (1694–1773), known as Lord Chesterfield, whose *Letters to His Son* were published in two volumes the year following his death. The *Letters* are not very complimentary to women; indeed, women are said in one letter to "have one object, this is their beauty; upon which, scarce any flattery is too gross for them to swallow" (London, Oct. 16, O.S. 1747). The letters also suggest that dissimulation is a key to social success.

54 *conceited compliments*: Here, witty, fanciful, or exaggerated compliments.

55 *These ladies wisely consider them as the butterflies of a day, and . . . scorn to break them on a wheel*: That is, wise young women consider men who are merely witty to be flitting and inconstant; they don't consider such men to be worth the trouble of torturing with any sort of training in civility. The expression "to break upon the wheel" refers to a medieval torture used formerly in Europe in which criminals were severely tortured or put to death by being stretched on a cart wheel or cross and, thus extended, having their limbs broken with heavy bars usually made of iron. The figure used here bears a slight resemblance to one used by Alexander Pope (1688–1744) in the *Epistle to Dr. Arbuthnot* (1735), where Pope castigates John Hervey (1696–1743), Baron Hervey of Ickworth, called "Sporus" in the *Epistle*: "Let *Sporus* tremble—What, that Thing

251251

of silk, / *Sporus*, that mere white Curd of Ass's milk? / Satire or Sense alas! can *Sporus* feel? / Who breaks a Butterfly upon a Wheel?" (lines 305–308).

55 *"there are . . . hear.":* This is a loose rendering of a passage from "Conference X" of *Advice from a Lady of Quality to Her Children.* "Your sex," the passage begins, "requires the utmost circumspection; what among MEN is reputed a venial fault, is an absolute crime with us." The author continues: "There are a thousand things said and done in their company, which a woman ought neither to hear nor see. I would wish that a young woman should be silent and modest; and the world, dissipated as it is, expects the same. Its judgment of us is very severe; and it often fixes our character for life."

55 *To discountenance levity:* To disapprove of or dismiss silly or frivolous manners and conversation.

55 *I am always pleased . . . by the author of the Guardian:* The passage quoted is taken from *The Guardian,* no. 130, August 10, 1713. This particular number was written by Deane Bartlett, of Merton College, an acquaintance of Sir Richard Steele, the originator of the periodical essay series, *The Guardian.* The passage quoted is taken nearly verbatim from no. 130, with the key exception being that the names Tully and Socrates are reversed.

It is interesting to note that Mrs. Holmes's statement, "I am always pleased with the reasonable and amiable light in which the Clergy are placed by the author of the *Guardian,*" along with the passage next quoted, are copied from Sir Richard Steele's own writings. In his *Apology for Himself and His Writings* (1714), Steele quotes three paragraphs from this *Guardian* and comments: "This most reasonable and amiable Light in which the Clergy are here placed, comes from that modest and good Man the Rev. Mr. Bartlett."

See note to page 27 above.

55 *prejudiced:* The typographical error, "prejuced" in the original, has been corrected.

55 *Tully:* The commonly used name for Marcus Tullius Cicero (106–43 B.C.), famed orator, philosopher, and statesman.

55 *Socrates:* The famous Greek philosopher (470–399 B.C.) who was considered, above all else, a noble exponent of the ethical life.

LETTER XXX

Page 56 *transatlantick idea:* That is, the ridicule of learned women comes from Europe, not from British North America.

56 *A celebrated European wit, in a letter to a lady:* The exact reference is difficult to trace. This seems to have been a common attitude inculcated during the eighteenth century. In *The Spectator,* no. 15, March 17, 1711, Joseph Addison (1672–1719) commented: "True happiness is of a retired nature, and an enemy to pomp and noise; it arises, in the first place, from the enjoyment of one's self; and, in the next, from the friendship and conversation of a few select companions." Francis Bacon (1561–1626) had said in *New Atlantis* (1618) that "The

reverence of a man's self is, next to religion, the chiefest bridle of all vices." In the sixth of the *Night Thoughts* (1742–46), Edward Young (1681–1765) wrote: "Revere thyself,—and yet thyself despise."

56 *Swift's letter to a very young lady, on her marriage:* The comments that follow come more or less from the letter Jonathan Swift (1667–1745) wrote to a young woman, probably either Lady Betty Moore (married to George Rochfort) or to Mrs. John Rochfort; the letter was published as a tract under the title *A Letter to a Young Lady, on Her Marriage. Written in the Year 1723.* The letter, rather contemptuous of women and their abilities, comments: "If you are in Company with Men of Learning; although they happen to discourse of Arts and Sciences out of your Compass, yet you will gather more Advantage by listening to them, than from all the Nonsense and Frippery of your own Sex: But, if they be Men of Breeding as well as Learning, they will seldom engage in any Conversation where you ought not to be a Hearer, and in Time have your Part. If they talk of the Manners and Customs of the several Kingdoms of *Europe*; of Travels into remote Nations; of the State of their own Country; or of the great Men and Actions of *Greece* and *Rome:* If they give their Judgment upon the *English* and *French* Writers, either in Verse or Prose; or of the Nature and Limits of Virtue and Vice; it is a Shame for an *English* Lady not to relish such Discourses, not to improve by them, and endeavour by Reading and Information, to have her Share in those Entertainments; rather than turn aside, as it is the usual Custom, and consult with the Woman who sits next her, about a new Cargo of Fans."
 The next paragraph in Swift's letter is referenced as well: "It is a little hard, that not one Gentleman's Daughter in a Thousand, should be brought to read, or understand her own Natural Tongue, or be Judge of the easiest Books that are written in it; as any one may find, who can have the Patience to hear them, when they are disposed to mangle a Play or Novel, where the least Word out of the common Road, is sure to disconcert them; and it is no wonder, when they are not so much as taught to spell in their Childhood, nor can ever attain to it in their whole Lives."

57 *orthography:* Here, learning letters; learning how to read.

57 *Mr. Webster's Grammatical Institute:* Noah Webster (1758–1843) published *A Grammatical Institute of the English Language* (1783–85), comprised of a spelling book, grammar, and reader.

57 *a thirst for emulation:* Here, a wish to imitate or equally excel.

57 *Barlow's Vision of Columbus:* Joel Barlow (1754–1812) published *The Vision of Columbus* (1787), the poem considered to be the first major American poem in the epic genre.

57 *Dwight's Conquest of Canaan:* Timothy Dwight (1752–1817) published *The Conquest of Canaan* (1785), a well-known and highly regarded patriotic allegory on a biblical subject.

LETTER XXXI

Page 58 *on the tapis:* On the table, under consideration. This expression was popular with members of the elite class of this era. A *tapis* was the word used in Europe for a heavy tapestry used as a curtain, wall hanging, or carpet; such finery would have signaled a certain level of wealth. This perhaps explains the popular use of the term at this time in British North America.

LETTER XXXIII

Page 59 *centinel:* Guard, usually of a military fortification.

59 *countermine:* Frustrate, defeat, oppose.

59 *the bans:* The banns, public announcements, frequently taking place in a church, of an intended marriage.

LETTER XXXIV

Page 60 *wiseacres:* Those who are offensive and self-assured.

LETTER XXXVI

Page 62 *ye are the Levite and the Pharisee:* Levites, of the tribe of Levi, were assistants to the temple priests of the Jews. Pharisees were members of an ancient Jewish sect that emphasized strict following of the Mosaic law; figuratively, the term *pharisee* designates a hypocritically self-righteous person.

62 *the good Samaritan:* In the parable in the New Testament of the Bible, the Good Samaritan was the only man among a number of passers-by to help another man who had been beaten and robbed. Figuratively, the term identifies a compassionate person who helps others.

LETTER XXXIX

Page 65 *precipitation:* Here, haste.

68 *all the necessitous:* That is, all persons in need.

69 *to depicture:* To picture, to delineate.

69 *nuptial couch:* That is, the bed of those wed in matrimony.

69 *connubial duty:* Matrimonial responsibility.

69 *quadrating with a volatility of disposition:* That is, corresponding with a disposition or personality type that is changeable, flighty, even explosive.

70 *licentious amour:* Here, sexual entanglement outside of marriage.

70 *"But let concealment, like a worm in the bud, / Feed on her damask cheek":* In *Twelfth Night* (1602) by William Shakespeare (1564–1616), Viola describes

EXPLANATORY NOTES

Olivia to the duke: "[s]he never told her love, / But let concealment like a worm i' th' bud / Feed on her damask cheek . . ." (2.4.110–12).

71 *"A natural tear I shed, but wip'd it soon"*: This line is adapted from the concluding lines of *Paradise Lost* (1667) by John Milton (1608–74), where Eve and Adam are cast out of the Garden of Eden: "They looking back, all th' eastern side beheld / Of Paradise, so late their happy seat, / Wav'd over by that flaming brand, the Gate / With dreadful faces throng'd and fiery arms. / Some natural tears they dropped, but wip'd them soon; / The world was all before them, where to choose / Their place of rest, and Providence their guide: / They hand in hand with wandering steps and slow / Through Eden took their solitary way" (*Paradise Lost* 12.641–49).

LETTER XL

Page 73 *mal apropos*: Out of place, inappropriate.

74 *Like the fruit . . . which left upon the taste bitter ashes*: A reference to Sodom apples which grew, according to legend, on the spot where that accursed city once stood. Beautiful and tantalizing, the apples dissolved into ashes when plucked. John Milton (1608–74), a writer much admired in the British colonies, wrote of these apples in *Paradise Lost* (1667), at the point where the devils cast into Hell see apples: "There stood / a grove hard by, . . . to aggravate / Their penance, laden with fair fruit, like that / Which grew in Paradise. . . . Greedily they plucked / The fruitage fair to sight, like that which grew / near that bituminous lake where Sodom flamed; / This more delusive, not the touch, but taste / Deceived; they fondly thinking to allay / Their appetite with gust, instead of fruit / Chewed bitter ashes, which th' offended taste / With spattering noise rejected" (10.547–67).

LETTER XLI

Page 77 *Hymen*: That is, matrimony; Hymen is the Greek god of marriage.

77 *"Let this auspicious day be ever sacred . . . and crown their wishes"*: This was Brown's own poem.

LETTER XLIV

Page 79 *consanguinity*: Blood relationship.

LETTER XLV

Page 80 *"Sorrow in all its pomp was there, / Mute and magnificent without a tear"*: These relate to a poem written by John Dryden (1631–1700). The lovely, moving poem on the death of King Charles II, "Threnodia Augustalis: A Funeral-Pindarique Poem Sacred to the Happy Memory of King Charles II" (1685) includes these lines: "Horrour in all his Pomp was there, / Mute and magnificent without a Tear" ("Threnodia Augustalis" 2.51–52).

LETTER XLVI

Page 81 *ignis fatuus:* See the note to page 39 above.

LETTER XLIX

Page 83 *panegyricks:* Panegeric, usually a formal composition of praise, frequently spoken at a person's death.

85 *"—'Twas but a dream . . . soul":* The source of this quotation has not been located.

LETTER L

Page 86 *in reversion:* Here, in belief about the future.

87 *"forgot myself to marble":* This is a reference to *Il Penseroso* (1645) by John Milton (1608–1674). The speaker in the poem asks Melancholy to come out, draped in darkness: "Com, but keep thy wonted state, / With eev'n step, and musing gate, / And looks commercing with the skies, / Thy rapt soul sitting in thine eyes: / There held in holy passion still, / Forget thy self to Marble, till / With a sad Leaden downward cast, / Thou fix them on the earth as fast" (*Il Penseroso*, lines 37–44). Milton was much admired by eighteenth-century poets.

87 *"—The name appears / Already written; blot it out my tears!":* The lines are probably adapted from "Eloisa to Abelard" (1717) a poem by Alexander Pope (1688–1744), where Eloisa begins her story of woe over her lover, Abelard, whom she has been forbidden to see: "Dear fatal name! rest ever unreveal'd, / Nor pass these lips in holy silence seal'd: / Hide it, my heart, within that close disguise, / Where, mix'd with God's, his lov'd Idea lies. / Oh write it not, my hand—The name appears / Already written—wash it out, my tears!" (lines 9–16).

88 *rapture:* The typographical error "rupture" has here been corrected.

LETTER LI

Page 89 *"See! there all pale and dead she lies . . . drop a tear":* This was Brown's own poem.

LETTER LIII

Page 90 *distained:* That is, stained.

91 *the support of the Roman power, the invincible Belisarius, who protected his country from the ravage of the Huns:* Belisarius (505?–565) is considered the greatest general of the Byzantine empire.

91 *precarious:* Unstable; archaically, dependent upon the will or favor of another.

LETTER LVI

Page 93 *"Cover his head . . . it is all one"*: The source for this quotation has not been located.

LETTER LVII

Page 93 *innoxious*: Not noxious, not harmful or injurious.

93 *"Puzzled in mazes, and perplex'd with errours"*: This line comes from *Cato. A Tragedy* (1713) by Joseph Addison (1672–1719). The two noble brothers, Marcus and Portius, sons of Cato, are discussing the means by which they can defend themselves against the onslaughts of Caesar, who is about to give them battle: "Remember what our father oft has told us: / The ways of heaven are dark and intricate; / Puzzled in mazes, and perplext with errors, / Our understanding traces 'em in vain, / Lost and bewildered in the fruitless search; / Nor sees with how much art the windings run, / Nor where the regular confusion ends" (*Cato* 1.1.47–53).

LETTER LX

Page 95 *Pygmalion*: A sculptor and king of Cypress, Pygmalion was said to have fallen in love with an ivory statue he had made of a woman; at his request, the goddess Aphrodite gave the statue life.

95 *illudes*: That is, eludes, evades, moves away from.

LETTER LXI

Page 96 *a maxim well received . . . "that the enjoyments of life do not compensate the miseries"*: This is a common maxim, though it received a certain amount of publicity in the then well-known and much-admired poem, *Solomon on the Vanity of the World: A Poem in Three Books* (1718), by Matthew Prior (1664–1721). In the Preface to *Solomon*, Prior commented, "The Pleasures of Life do not compensate the Miseries: Age steals upon Us unawares; and Death, as the only Cure of our Ills, ought to be expected, but not feared. This Instruction is to be illustrated by the Action of some great Person. Who therefore more proper for the Business than Solomon himself?"

96 *sublunary happiness*: That is, happiness on earth; literally, happiness beneath the moon.

96 *inveloped*: Enveloped, enclosed.

96 *St. Evremond*: Charles de Marguetel de Saint-Denis, Seigneur de Saint-Evrêmond (1613–1703) was a French author admired for his ethics. He was favored by French governmental authorities until he published a letter approving the peace of the Pyrenees and expressing support for freethinkers in France. In 1660 he went to England, and he lived there in exile at the court of Charles II

until his death. His works include critiques and letters first published collectively in 1705.

97 *Charles the Fifth, of Spain, resolved to taste the pleasures of a recluse life*: Charles V of Spain (1500–58), Holy Roman Emperor, had numerous military and legal successes before abdicating the throne of the Netherlands (1555) and Spain (1556) in favor of his son, Philip II; he abdicated the throne of Germany (1556) in favor of his brother, Ferdinand I. During Charles V's reign, the Spanish conquered Mexico and Peru. He subsequently lived in the monastery of Yuste in Spain, where he died.

LETTER LXII

Page 98 *"The time of my fading is near . . . they will not find me"*: This is a passage from *Songs of Selma*, one of the shorter poems of the Ossian of James Macpherson (1736–96). Macpherson published the "poems" of Ossian—really his own verses in supposed translation—as if they had been written by the Gaelic bard of the third century. The songs of Selma are quoted at length in *The Sorrows of Young Werther*, by Johann Wolfgang von Goethe (1749–1832), a sentimental novel tremendously popular in its own day. *The Sorrows of Young Werther* is mentioned in the next letter as the book Harrington was reading at the time he died; the reference is probably to Werther's suicide. The quotation used here is a replica of the Macpherson-Ossian. It is unclear whether Brown was using Macpherson's Ossian directly or using their representations in the Goethe novel in book 2, the last chapter, at December 20. Goethe's novel, *Die Leiden des jungen Werthers* was first published in German in 1774. Translated into many languages almost immediately, the novel was published in English as *The Sorrows of Werter* beginning in 1779; it went through eight publications in Britain by 1789, and it was published in Philadelphia in 1784 and in Connecticut in 1789. Despite the disdain held toward the book by moral critics, it achieved a high degree of popularity in the early Republic.

LETTER LXIII

Page 100 *The Sorrows of Werter:* See the note at 98.

LETTER LXIV

Page 100 *"—With thee / Certain my resolution is to die . . . bliss or woe"*: This was Brown's own poem.

101 *Guardian:* Printed as "Gaurdian" in the original.

LETTER LXV

Page 102 *Monumental Inscription:* This was Brown's own poem.

103 *guardian:* Printed as "gaurdian" in the original.

Notes to *The Coquette; Or, The History of Eliza Wharton; A Novel; Founded on Fact.*

LETTER I

Page 108 *undissevered:* Unbroken.

LETTER II

Page 109 *monitorial:* Cautionary; supervisory.

109 *envited:* That is, invited.

LETTER III

Page 109 *habiliments:* Clothes, dress.

110 *Piano Forte:* Piano.

110 *Morpheus waves his ebon-wand in vain:* That is, Eliza is not sleepy. In classical mythology, Morpheus is the god of sleep and of dreaming; here, he wields a black wand.

LETTER IV

Page 111 *as the queen of Sheba said to Solomon, the half was not told me:* The reference bears the language of the story of the Queen of Sheba as told in the Bible. The Queen of Sheba, a ruler over the lands of the Sabaeans (in classical and biblical stories, the most important people of South Arabia), was said to have heard reports of the wisdom of King Solomon. The biblical story of their meeting—to which she brought many gifts—appears in 1 Kings 10. After she put to Solomon the many questions she devised in order to test his wisdom, she said, according to the Bible, "It was a true report that I heard in mine own land of thy acts and of thy wisdom. Howbeit I believed not the words, until I came, and mine eyes had not seen it: and, behold, the half was not told me: thy wisdom and prosperity exceedeth thy fame which I heard" (1 Kings 10.6–7).

LETTER V

Page 113 *strowed:* Strewn.

LETTER VI

Page 114 *billet:* Little letter, note.

114 *disapprobating:* Disapproving.

114 *to wear the hymenial chain:* That is, to be married. Hymen, in classical mythology, is the god of marriage.

LETTER VII

Page 117 *in the hypo:* Feeling melancholy, depressed.

LETTER VIII

Page 118 *dulcinea:* Here, lady-love. Dulcinea is the name Don Quixote gives to the woman he loves in the romance *Don Quixote* (part 1, 1605; part 2, 1615) by Miguel de Cervantes Saavedra (1547–1616).

LETTER XI

Page 121 *Proteus:* A classical sea deity who could change his shape at will.

LETTER XII

Page 122 *predestinarian:* Here, one who believes that life is determined in advance, thus making null the effects of individual choice and effort.

123 *"The friendships of the world . . . friendship ends not but with life":* The source of the quotation has not been located.

123 *diffusive:* Here, profuse.

123 *"The feast of reason, and the flow of soul":* A line in an imitation of the Roman poet Horace (65–8 B.C.), written by Alexander Pope (1688–1744). In *The First Satire of the Second Book of Horace* (1733), Pope wrote of those he would welcome to his grotto, a meditative cavern in his famous garden: "There St. John [i.e., Henry St. John, Viscount Bolingbroke] mingles with my friendly Bowl, / The Feast of Reason, and the Flow of Soul" (lines 127–28).

LETTER XIII

Page 124 *undebauched:* Uncorrupted, virtuous.

125 *condescension:* Here, the gracious manner in which one accepts another's attention.

LETTER XIV

Page 125 *preponderate:* Exceed another in weight, force, or power.

127 *indissoluble knot:* Here, the marriage tie.

LETTER XV

Page 128 *vicious:* Here, morally dislikable.

128 *swain:* An affectionate and familiar poetic term for a man who is lovesick, drawn from the pastoral mode of the day.

128 *consummation:* Conclusion, fulfillment, in this case of the marriage agreement made between the two.

LETTER XVI

Page 129 *put on the sacred bands:* That is, be robed as a minister for the congregation to which he has been called.

129 *enamorato:* The one enamored, in love.

LETTER XVII

Page 130 *my fair:* A formal, poetic way for a man to describe his lover.

LETTER XVIII

Page 131 *equipage:* Ornament, furnishings.

LETTER XIX

Page 132 *deranged:* Here, put out of order.

134 *chuse:* That is, choose.

134 *Richardson's Clarissa . . . a second Lovelace:* When Samuel Richardson (1689–1761) published *Clarissa Harlowe, or the History of a Young Lady* (first four volumes, 1747; last four volumes, 1748), there were few fictional accounts of seduction; after the novel was published, the popularity of the seduction novel was secured. In the novel, Clarissa, a model of feminine virtue, is taken off by the rake Lovelace, who torments and seduces her with the assistance of accomplices of questionable morals. With this open allusion to Clarissa, the course of *The Coquette* seems well announced, with the difference between the two novels residing in the differences between the central women characters.

LETTER XX

Page 135 *inportuned:* Importuned, requested.

LETTER XXI

Page 136 *a decent competency:* That is, sufficient means (in terms of wealth) for a comfortable existence.

LETTER XXII

Page 137 *your idea has been the solace of my retired moments:* That is, thoughts of you have provided me solace, or comfort.

137 *those beautiful lines of Thompson: / —"An elegant sufficiency . . . are the matchless joys of virtuous love":* James Thomson (1700–48), who was ex-

tremely popular among late-eighteenth-century writers, published a four-part sequence collectively known as *The Seasons* in 1730. The original version of the poem (without the lines quoted) was first published in 1728. The lines quoted here are from the version of "Spring" published in 1744 and then again in 1746: "An elegant Sufficiency, Content, / Retirement, rural Quiet, Friendship, Books, / Ease and alternate Labour, useful Life, / Progressive Virtue, and approving Heaven. / These are the matchless Joys of virtuous Love" (lines 1158–62).

LETTER XXIII

Page 139 *conduce to, or interfere with the common weal:* Contribute to the success or detriment of the commonwealth.

139 *The gentlemen applauded Mrs. Richman's sentiments as truly Roman; and what was more, they said, truly republican:* The men considered Mrs. Richman to have expressed herself in ways that would assist the new confederation of states. In the Federal era, analogies were often made between the Federal government, often called the New Republic, and the democratic (here, "republican") form of the government of ancient Rome, which gave representation to all citizens.

LETTER XXV

Page 141 *inst.:* Instant, that is, of the current month.

LETTER XXVI

Page 145 *phaeton:* A light, open, four-wheeled carriage usually drawn by two horses.

146 *an adage generally received, that "a reformed rake makes the best husband":* This (misleading) assertion was commonly used during the eighteenth century.

LETTER XXVII

Page 146 *Pope's assertion, that "Every woman is, at heart, a rake":* Alexander Pope (1688–1744) wrote in "Of the Characters of Women" (1735), the second of his *Moral Essays* addressed to his friend Martha Blount: "Men, some to Business, some to Pleasure take, / But every Woman is, at heart, a Rake: / Men, some to Quiet, some to publick Strife, / But every Lady would be Queen for life" (lines 215–18).

147 *coxcomb:* Conceited dandy, fop. This would have been a very insulting term when used with regard to someone of the upper-middle or upper classes who called himself a gentleman.

147 *debauchee:* Someone who lacks any virtue whatsoever; a libertine.

LETTER XXVIII

Page 148 *the vulgar proverb, that actions speak louder than words:* This is a common (i.e., "vulgar") expression.

148 *sagatious:* Sagacious, that is to say wise, prudent.

149 *irradiated:* Here, lit with radiant or glowing light; made brilliant.

LETTER XXIX

Page 149 *ignis fatuus:* Scientifically, a phosphorescent light that flits over swampy ground at night, perhaps a result of spontaneous combustion of gases; figuratively, an illusion, something that misleads.

LETTER XXX

Page 152 *phiz:* Facial expression ("phiz" refers to "face").

153 *guardian knot:* The matrimonial bond. The word *guardian* here might be a play on the sound of the term *Gordian knot,* the intricate knot made by King Gordius of Phrygia and cut by Alexander the Great who had heard from an oracle that whoever broke the knot would eventually become king of Asia.

LETTER XXXI

Page 154 *"Places and honors have been bought for gold, / Esteem and love were never to be sold":* Similar lines occur in *An Essay on Man* (1733–34) by Alexander Pope (1688–1744): "To whom can Riches give Repute, or Trust, / Content, or Pleasure, but the Good and Just? / Judges and Senates have been bought for gold, / Esteem and Love were never to be sold" (*Essay on Man* 4.185–88).

154 *"In spite of all the virtues we can boast, / The woman that deliberates is lost":* These are the words of Marcia, the central female character in *Cato. A Tragedy* (1713) by Joseph Addison (1672–1719). Marcia is the virtuous and dutiful daughter of the noble and stoic Cato. The lines read: "When love once pleads admission to our hearts / In spite of all the virtue we can boast / The woman that deliberates is lost" (4.1.29–31).

LETTER XXXII

Page 155 *nymph:* Here, a young girl, especially a beautiful one.

156 *hypo:* Melancholy, gloom.

LETTER XXXIII

Page 156 *compounded the matter with him:* That is, come to an agreement or settlement about the matter.

LETTER XXXIX

Page 165 *"That which nothing earthly gives, or can destroy, / The soul's calm sunshine, and the heart felt joy"*: These lines occur in *An Essay on Man* (1733–34) by Alexander Pope (1688–1744): "What nothing Earthly gives, or can destroy, / The Soul's calm sunshine, and the heart-felt joy, / Is Virtue's Prize: A better would you fix?" (*Essay on Man*, 4.167–69). The reader might be interested in knowing that the lines are quoted in *Meditations and Contemplations* (2 parts, 1746–47) by James Hervey (1714–58), a devotional writer popular in the colonies (especially in the South), who is elsewhere quoted in the novel.

LETTER XL

Page 170 *lines of an ingenious poet: "Since all the downward tracts of time, / God's watchful eye surveys . . . E'en crosses from his sovereign hand, / Are blessings in disguise"*: With only the slightest variation (in punctuation, and in the substitution of "And" for "Or" in the fourth line quoted), these lines appear in "Reflections on a Flower Garden," in *Meditations and Contemplations*, by James Hervey (1714–58), a devotional writer popular in the colonies, especially in the southern colonies. The lines are used in a section of the "Reflections" related to the conception of resignation to God's will: "What a striking argument is here for *resignation*," Hervey wrote, "unfeigned resignation, to all the disposals of *Providence!* . . . Be still, then, thou uneasy mortal; know that God is unerringly wise; and be assured, that, amidst the greatest multiplicity of beings, he does not overlook thee."

LETTER XLI

Page 173 *the wisest of men informs us, that "a merry heart doth good like a medicine"*: A quotation from the book of Proverbs in the Old Testament, "A merry heart doeth good like a medicine" (Proverbs 17.22).

173 *old dons:* Here, old men.

174 *the words of the poet, / "Trust not a man, they are by nature cruel . . . But if he swear, he'll certainly deceive you"*: The original source for these lines is unclear. The play *The Orphan* (1680), by Thomas Otway (1652–85), includes the following lines that are close to but not the same as the lines Foster uses here: "Trust not a man. We are by nature false, / Dissembling, subtle, cruel, and unconstant. / When a man talks of love, with caution trust him; But if he swears, he'll certainly deceive thee" (*The Orphan*, Act 2, lines 286–89). Otway's *The Orphan* was being performed with increasing regularity during the eighteenth century, especially in the southern colonies.

175 *"I know the right, and I approve it too; / I know the wrong, and yet the wrong pursue"*: The lines are similar but not exactly the same as those in two texts Foster might have known. Ovid (43 B.C.–A.D. 18) wrote in *Metamorphoses*

7.17: "I see the right, and I approve it, too, / Condemn the wrong and yet the wrong pursue." The lines are the same as those printed in a translation edited by Sir Samuel Garth (1661–1719).

176 *excepting the alloy of your absence:* Except that your absence made it less enjoyable than it might have been.

LETTER XLII

Page 180 *posse:* Here, a group summoned for protection.

181 *summum bonum:* The greatest or supreme good (Latin).

181 *speculation:* Here, an engagement in risky business in an effort to gain quick or considerable profit. Sanford is hinting that he is going back to find a wealthy woman.

LETTER XLIII

Page 183 *how I anticipate the time . . . "how to shoot":* These words echo some lines on child rearing from the 1728 and later versions of "Spring" in *The Seasons* (1730) by James Thomson (1700–48): "Then infant Reason grows apace, and calls / For the kind Hand of an assiduous Care: / Delightful task! to rear the tender Thought, / To teach the young Idea how to shoot" ("Spring," 1728 version, lines 1062–65).

LETTER XLIV

Page 184 *"The world's dread laugh, which scarce the firm philosopher can scorn":* An echo of some lines from the 1730 and later versions of "Autumn" in *The Seasons* (first published as a collection, 1730) by James Thomson (1700–48). In this section of "Autumn," the poet describes Palemon's recognition of his love for Lavinia: "He saw her charming, but he saw not half / The charms her downward modesty conceal'd. / That very moment love and chaste desire / Sprung in his bosom, to himself unknown; / For still the world prevail'd, and its dread laugh, / Which scarce the firm philosopher can scorn, / Should his heart own a gleaner in the field: / And thus in secret to his soul he sigh'd" ("Autumn," 1730 version, lines 226–33).

LETTER XLVI

Page 186 *Pope very justly observes, "that every year is a critic on the last":* This statement is adapted from *An Essay on Criticism* (1711) by Alexander Pope (1688–1744): "But you, with Pleasure own your Errors past, / And make each Day a Critique on the last" (*An Essay on Criticism*, lines 570–71).

LETTER L

Page 192 *alledged:* That is, alleged, declared or affirmed.

192 *lines of the poet, "To you, great gods, I make my last appeal; . . . My feet were guilty, but my heart was free":* The source of this quotation is *Oedipus, a Tragedy* (1679), a much-admired version of the Oedipus-Jocasta story written by John Dryden (1631–1700). After learning that Jocasta, the woman he has married, is his mother, Oedipus exclaims: "To you, good Gods, I make my last appeal; / Or clear my Vertues or my Crime reveal: / If wandring in the maze of Fate I run, / And backward trod the paths I sought to shun, / Impute my Errours to your own Decree; / My hands are guilty, but my heart is free" (3.1.588–93).

LETTER LI

Page 194 *He looks to me like a Chesterfieldian:* That is, he is one who, lacking any moral restraint, does not value women and thus treats them in an immoral fashion, without compunction. The reference is to Philip Dormer Stanhope, fourth Earl of Chesterfield (1694–1773), known as Lord Chesterfield, whose *Letters to His Son* were published in two volumes the year following his death. The *Letters* are not very complimentary to women. In one letter, women are said to "have one object, this is their beauty; upon which, scarce any flattery is too gross for them to swallow" (London, Oct. 16, O.S. 1747). The letters also suggest that dissimulation is a key to social success.

194 *deceptious:* That is, deceptive.

LETTER LII

Page 195 *ult.:* Ultimo, of the previous month.

195 *Romeo and Juliet:* Shakespeare's *Romeo and Juliet* was probably the single most popular play in the colonies between the years 1763 and 1774; it was also the play most frequently performed from 1747 to 1776 at both the Covent Garden and Drury Lane theatres in London. During the entire colonial period, *Romeo and Juliet* is on record for having had twenty-nine performances, second only to Shakespeare's *Richard III.*

196 *Mr. Bowen's museum:* Museums were initiated in the post-Revolution era as places where heroes, victories, and memorable moments could be commemorated and where unusual artifacts could be displayed. The first museums were developed in Philadelphia, but within several decades, most eastern cities boasted at least one museum.

LETTER LIV

Page 198 *more in reversion:* That is, more money that will revert to her; reversions usually occur upon the death of one or both parents, although they can occur from relatives and friends.

198 *"Beauty soon grows familiar to the lover"*: This line, well known in Foster's day, was spoken by the character Juba, the central younger male character in *Cato. A Tragedy* (1713) by Joseph Addison (1672–1719). Juba is chiding his military commander, Syphax, for telling him that should Juba be unable to marry Marcia there are many women who could please him. (Marcia is the virtuous and dutiful daughter of the noble and stoic Cato.) The lines read: " 'Tis not a set of features, or complexion, / The tincture of a skin, that I admire. / Beauty soon grows familiar to the lover, / Fades in his eye and palls upon the sense" (*Cato* 1.4.143–46).

198 *"Fix'd like a plant, to one peculiar spot, / To draw nutrition, propagate, and rot"*: These are lines from *An Essay on Man* (1733–34) by Alexander Pope (1688–1744). Interestingly, Sanford seems to be one in whom self-love appears to predominate over the reason Pope speaks of: "*Self-Love,* the Spring of Motion, acts the Soul; / *Reason*'s comparing Balance rules the whole; / Man, but for that, no *Action* could attend, / And but for this, were active to no *End.* / Fix'd like a Plant on his peculiar Spot, / To draw nutrition, propagate, and rot; / Or Meteor-like flame lawless through the Void, / Destroying others, by himself destroy'd" (*An Essay on Man,* Epistle 2, lines 59–66).

LETTER LV

Page 199 *Millot's elements of history: The Elements of General History* was published in English in five volumes in London, 1778–79. French Jesuit Claude François Xavier Millot (1726–85) was considered so excellent a "modern" historian and this particular set of volumes so useful a historical guide that Millot was even incorporated into the traditionally classical curriculum by some colleges toward the end of the century. Harvard College added Millot to the curriculum after 1783; the College of New Jersey and then the University of North Carolina followed suit during the next decade. The reading of Millot by these women—as opposed to their reading novels, for instance—should be understood as a sign of the women's delight in rational rather than frivolous information and conversation.

LETTER LVI

Page 202 *a treaty of peace, and amity (but not of commerce,) is ratified:* Julia Granby is here playing on names given peace treaties during the eighteenth century. There were several treaties of peace in the era. The Treaty of Amity and Commerce of 1778 was a formal alliance between the Anglo-American colonies and France which assisted in securing for the colonies both their independence from (regardless of the outcome of the Revolutionary War) and their favorable trade relations with France.

LETTER LVIII

Page 205 *devotee . . . absolution:* Sanford here uses the language of religious devotion, blasphemously equating his request for Eliza's forgiveness with the

request of a penitent, someone who has sinned, to be formally granted forgiveness, or absolution, by a priest or minister.

206 *"The baseless fabric of a vision"*: The line comes from Shakespeare's *The Tempest* (1611), where the sprite Ariel has been conducting for his "master" Prospero a play within a play. Prospero concludes the scene: "Our revels are now ended. These our actors / (As I foretold you) were all spirits, and / Are melted into air, into thin air, / And like the baseless fabric of this vision, / The cloud-capp'd tow'rs, the gorgeous palaces, / The solemn temples, the great globe itself, / Yea, all which it inherit, shall dissolve, / And like this insubstantial pageant faded / Leave not a rack behind" (*The Tempest* 4.1.148–56).

LETTER LX

Page 209 *villain*: Printed as "villian" in the original, the typographical error has here been corrected.

LETTER LXII

Page 213 *doatingly*: Dotingly; here, exceedingly.

213 *"Happy the babe, who, privileged by fate . . . return to death"*: This quotation provides an interesting instance of the ways in which colonial authors might have found sources for their quotations. As quoted here, the lines are nearly a direct quotation (in an annotation) of four lines attributed to Matthew Prior's *Solomon* in "Meditations among the Tombs," published as part of *Meditations and Contemplations* brought out in two parts (1746–47) by James Hervey (1714–58). That is, Hervey's quotation is, except for variants in punctuation, exactly Foster's. The well-known and much admired poem, *Solomon on the Vanity of the World: A Poem in Three Books* (1718) by Matthew Prior (1664–1721)—clearly the origin of the Hervey redaction—included the lines: "Happy the Mortal Man, who now at last / Has thro' this doleful Vale of Mis'ry Past; . . . He happyer yet, who privileg'd by Fate / To shorter Labor, and a lighter Weight, / Receiv'd but Yesterday the Gift of Breath, / Order'd To-morrow to return to Death" (*Solomon* 2.225–26, 231–34).

LETTER LXIV

Page 216 *"like patience on a monument, smiling at grief!"*: This is a line from Shakespeare's *Twelfth Night* (1602). Viola is describing Olivia to the Duke: "She never told her love, / But let concealment like a worm i' th' bud / Feed on her damask cheek; she pined in thought, / And with a green and yellow melancholy / She sate like Patience on a monument, / Smiling at grief. Was this not love indeed?" (*Twelfth Night* 2.4.110–15).

LETTER LXV

Page 217 *"stolen waters are sweet, and bread eaten in secret is pleasant"*: A quotation from the Bible: "Stolen waters are sweet, and bread eaten in secret is

pleasant" (Proverbs 9.17). Perhaps Foster assumed her readers would know that the very next proverb in the Bible reads: "But he knoweth not that the dead are there: and that her guests are in the depths of hell."

217 *If it has reference . . . Yorick's sermon:* An allusion to *Tristram Shandy*, by Laurence Sterne (1713–68). Sterne's *Tristram Shandy* was published in separate volumes: volumes 1 and 2 (1760); 3 and 4, then 5 and 6 (1761); 7 and 8 (1765); and 9 (1767). The novel produced a sensation, first in England, then in all Europe, from the publication of its first volumes. Introduced in *Tristram Shandy*, Yorick "dies" at the conclusion of volume 1, chapter 12, where Tristram "buries" him in a page of black, quoting Shakespeare's Hamlet's words to Yorick's skull (*Hamlet* 5.1.179–80). When he published his first collection of his own sermons, Sterne called them *The Sermons of Mr. Yorick* (volumes 1 and 2, 1760: volumes 3 and 4, 1766).

217 *siege:* In describing the efforts he made against Eliza's chastity and fortitude, Sanford uses the language of a battle, calling their relations a siege, later referring to them as a combat. Eliza's virtue was thus "impregnable," that is, impenetrable or insurmountable, and Sanford speaks of her having "enter[ed] the lists," that is, taken up arms.

218 *An unlucky, but not a miraculous accident, has taken place:* Sanford is informing Deighton that Eliza is pregnant.

218 *ingrossed:* Engrossed, absorbed, occupied.

LETTER LXVI

Page 220 *harrows up:* Inflicts with distress, torments. The expression used here was a common one, probably drawn from Shakespeare's tragedy *Hamlet* (1601), in the scene in which the ghost of Hamlet's father first speaks to Hamlet: "But that I am forbid / To tell the secrets of my prison-house, / I could a tale unfold whose lightest word / Would harrow up thy soul, freeze thy young blood, / Make thy two eyes like stars start from their spheres, / Thy knotted and combined locks to part, / And each particular hair to stand on end, / Like quills upon the fearful porpentine [i.e., porcupine]" (*Hamlet* 1.5.13–20).

220 *will cause my sun to sit at noon:* The sun's setting at noon is a figurative way of saying that Sanford will cause Eliza an early death, a death while she is in her prime of life (her noonday).

220 *assiduous:* Here, constant and personal. The term *assiduous care* appeared in the lines on child rearing reflected in the quotation from the poem "Spring" in *The Seasons* (1730) by James Thomson (1700–48), in letter XLIII, where Mrs. Richman speaks about caring for her daughter.

220 *"where the wicked cease from troubling, and where the weary are at rest!":* A line from the book of Job in the Bible, where Job expresses a regret that he had ever been born: "Why died I not from the womb? why did I not give up the ghost when I came out of the belly? . . . For now should I have lain still and

been quiet, I should have slept: then had I been at rest. . . . There the wicked cease from troubling; and there the weary be at rest" (Job 3.11, 13, 17).

LETTER LXVII

Page 226 *"That I must die, it is my only comfort; . . . lay their burdens down!"*: These lines are those of Calista, the mournful central character in *The Fair Penitent* (1703), a tragedy by Nicholas Rowe (1674–1718): "That I must die— it is my only comfort; / Death is the privilege of human nature, / And life without it were not worth our taking; / Thither the poor, the pris'ner, and the mourner / Fly for relief and lay their burdens down" (*The Fair Penitent* 5.1.132–37).

LETTER LXX

Page 232 *lying in:* The expression given to what was then a woman's period of confinement during the final stages of her pregnancy before giving birth.

LETTER LXXI

Page 235 *a Boston paper:* Elizabeth Whitman's death was first announced in the *Salem Mercury*, July 29, 1788. After it became known that the "Mrs. Walker" who had checked in at the Bell Tavern in Danvers was Elizabeth Whitman, the story was picked up by many New England papers. Whitman's story became a "moral lecture to young ladies" by the time it was written up in Boston's *Independent Chronicle*, Sept. 11, 1788.

235 *It is the Lord; let him do what he will! Be still, O my soul, and know that he is God!:* The lines echo various psalms in the Bible, perhaps Psalm 46.10 most closely: "Be still, and know that I am God: I will be exalted among the heathen, I will be exalted in the earth."

236 *"But let no one reproach her memory. / Her life has paid the forfeit of her folly. / Let that suffice":* The source of this quotation has not been located.

LETTER LXXIV

Page 241 *unbedewed:* That is, without the dew, not moistened.

APPENDIX I

William Hill Brown's *The Power of Sympathy* makes explicit references to the *Advice from a Lady of Quality to Her Children, in the Last Stage of a Lingering Illness.** Members of the elite class were preoccupied with concerns about the conduct of young people and the ways in which young people's behaviors represented certain class-driven attitudes. Thus, novels like Brown's and advice books like the *Advice from a Lady of Quality* held a distinct interest for readers of the eighteenth century. Like many of the advice or conduct books written by the elite particularly for elite and bourgeois readers, *Advice from a Lady of Quality to Her Children* comes to us in the context of a long tradition notably established with the Renaissance Italian conduct book by Baldassare Castiglione called in English *The Book of the Courtier,* published in English translation in 1561 and said to have had a pervasive effect on the culture of Elizabethan England. Most eighteenth-century advice books, like the *Courtier,* tended to discuss society—whether they spoke of men's actions or politics or women's behaviors—in terms of the disposal of women's bodies and minds.

Attributed to Louis-Antoine de Caraccioli (1719–1803), the *Advice* originally appeared in French under the title *Derniers adieux de la maréchal de **** a ses enfants.* It was translated into English by Samuel Glasse, who dedicated the translation to Queen Charlotte Sophia. In the English translation, the volume is sometimes given the subheading "In a Series of Evening-Conferences on the Most Interesting Subjects." The English translation went through several editions in London and Boston beginning in 1778. The volume seems to have had great popularity in the Anglo-American colonies. Whether or not the work is a fiction is difficult to assess; the introductory chapter providing the "life" of the writer reads as if it were fiction. Indeed, the ways in which the woman speaker discusses her pursuit of pleasures during much of her life is strikingly similar to the ways in which Eliza Wharton in *The Coquette* describes herself, especially at the beginning of the novel, at the point where Foster would be establishing Eliza's "character." Many conduct books, whether or not they were fiction, included stories about the supposed "errors" of the authors' ways so that the authors would seem to be speaking, while writing about what comprises "proper" conduct, from their own experiences.

The two volumes of this conduct book provide "conferences" addressed primarily to two sons. "Conference X," however, is directed to a daughter. Pro-

* From *Advice from a Lady of Quality to Her Children*

vided below are two chapters: the introductory chapter, of the speaker's "History of Her Own Life," and "Conference X," the speaker's advice to her daughter. Interestingly, the conference to the daughter includes mention of the letters of Marie de Rabutin-Chantal, Marquise de Sevigne (1626–96). Sevigne's letters to her daughter, which include daily accounts recorded for the benefit of her daughter, were published in a number of editions during the eighteenth century, and they were frequently cited as sources of entertainment and edification for young women.

The text is a transcription, with an editorial addition in one place, of the edition of the *Advice* printed by S. Hall and published at Cornhill, Boston, 1796.

CONFERENCE I.

THE HISTORY OF HER OWN LIFE.

The very weak state of health, in which I have now been eighteen months, forbids me to hope for any long continuation of my life: I have determined therefore, my dear children, to call you together, as well to discharge my obligations, as to amuse my sufferings. By the loss of your father, my duties as a mother seem to be redoubled; I am called upon to supply to you the want of his excellent advice, and to labour to render you worthy inheritors of his glory and his virtues.

You are not insensible of the obligations laid upon you, to shew mankind from what ancestors you derive your origin. Their history you are sufficiently acquainted with, to know who they were, and how they distinguished themselves: but perhaps their example may less sensibly affect your minds, than my advice: especially if you consider, that it is your best friend, who is now conversing with you; one, whose instructions are the dictates of affection, and the result of a tender regard for your happiness. The only books, from which my precepts shall be drawn, are experience, a knowledge of the world, and the convictions of my own heart.

Descended from a family not less distinguished by its misfortunes than its honours, I was left an orphan at ten years of age. My education fell under the direction of my father's sister; whose inclination, as well as rank, drew her frequently to court. No time was lost in furnishing me with masters of every kind. I soon became an object of attention; and my friends took care to announce me possessed of a considerable fortune. The world presented itself to my view in the most brilliant colours; and with singular delight I indulged the deception. A succession of amusements served to stifle reflection; and I seemed to live for no other purpose than to pursue my pleasures.

Sometimes my soul, not quite as yet debased, seemed desirous to soar above these enchanting trifles; but vanity and dissipation soon hurried me away, and effaced the impressions of reflection. How far from real happiness is a life of subjection to prevailing fashions; from which it has neither opportunity, nor resolution to withdraw itself! In vain do we perceive the miseries, which intrude themselves amidst the pleasures of the world; in vain do we receive instructions, by which we might be both affected and improved: we still continue enslaved to our passions, and eagerly embrace the phantom of delusion. I resembled those

travellers, who, knowing the right way, yet thinking to shorten their journey, turn aside from it, and are lost.

All that were about me, conspired to fill my mind with false ideas; their language was that of flattery and deceit; they either concealed from me my faults, or they only corrected such as might serve to render me ridiculous. Scarce had I begun the day, when my attendants made it their business to inspire me with a love of idleness and pleasure: one part of it was spent in decorating my person with all the ornaments of dress; and the other, in receiving the rewards of my unprofitable industry. I was admired, in proportion to my external appearance; and this admiration served only to feed my vanity.

I never shall forget, that, being one evening quite overcome with that satiety, which destroys the satisfaction of the votaries of pleasure, I opened by chance a volume of moral essays, a few pages of which filled my soul with confusion and remorse: "*Either,*["] said I to myself, ["]*I am a dupe to the life which I now lead, or this writer is an egregious imposter.*"

These reflections began to disquiet me; when I was informed, that it was time for me to go a ball, to which I had been invited: my guardian, who took me with her in her coach, observed that I was unusually pensive; for which she seriously reproved me. Though she was in many respects an excellent woman, she was almost wholly engaged in the pursuit of amusements: she repeated her censures, when we entered the ball-room, in which every thing appeared truly magnificent; the elegant taste of the D——ss of —— had brought together persons of the most eminent rank, beauty, and accomplishments.

Too soon the instruments of music, and harmony of the voices, made me forget my Monitor, and all his reasoning: my heart, again seduced by pleasure, quickly persuaded me that such austere morality was calculated only to fill us with melancholy: I danced with some degree of elegance, and the praises bestowed upon me were excessive; in short, I returned home more enchanted than ever, with the world.

We crossed the park, which a judicious distribution of lamps had so illuminated, as to give it almost the glare of noon-day. The crowd of people about us, the variety of faces and dresses, an unrestrained festivity, which every where prevailed, all served to seduce my soul with stronger delusions. One needs no more than such a scene as this, to ruin one's taste forever. It fills the mind with the vast idea of the world and its pleasures; and when once the heart has received these first impressions, it is next to impossible to efface them.

Six years passed away in a continual round of pleasure and diversions; at the end of which, I was married to your much honoured father. Some circumstances, fortunate for me, gave HIM the preference in my regard to several young noblemen, who had professed the strongest attachment to me. Had any one of THESE succeeded in his addresses, I should have been wedded to folly and repentance; it was my happier lot to be connected with discretion and politeness.

We must needs appear with éclat on our marriage, and in this respect my natural turn of mind was of great service to me; it made me as splendid, as I was vain: And as our income was such as enabled me to indulge my taste for shew, I gave the reins to it without restraint. I kept a sort of court, in which I presided as a sovereign princess: My courtiers were lavish of their praises, they

were suppliant for favours, and my husband and I were considered as beings
superior to the rest of mankind in happiness and honours.

A WAR with the house of Austria deprived me of your father, for a time:
He parted from me with that heroic spirit, which distinguished his character to
the latest moment of his life; while in his absence I gave myself up to sorrow
and regret. His letters, however, comforted me; and no sooner was my peace of
mind restored, than my taste for pleasure returned. The opera of THETIS was
performed, at which I was present; and then it was, that my fondness for publick
diversions resumed its dominion in my heart. I now put myself forward to sit
in judgment on every new theatrical performance; and was the first to admire
the decorations of the stage. The world is like a troubled sea, whose waves
always carry us away much farther than we at first intended to go.

However, notwithstanding my allowed taste for whatever might gratify the
senses, or encourage vanity; I was generally considered as a pattern of prudence
and discretion: People were astonished to see a young woman, only twenty years
old, with any other passion than a love for dress, and shew, and diversions. The
world cannot conceive it possible, that while we are gliding down the stream of
luxury and pleasure, we are, in the eye of reason, objects of pity.

The hints, which I had received from my friendly Monitor, whose writings I
had only cursorily dipt into, were perpetually obtruding themselves; but, like
those gentle breezes, which ruffle the surface of the waters, they only served to
glance upon my heart. What surprized me was, that a very discreet relation of
mine, to whom I had mentioned this author, strictly forbade me looking into it.
But this she did, as she many years afterwards declared, merely to excite my
eagerness to read it, and attach me more strongly to my book. She well knew,
that prohibition serves only to stimulate; and that to interdict, is often the surest
means of fixing our affections on that which is forbidden us. Her stratagem
succeeded; I was never at rest, 'till I became possessed of these essays, and 'till
I had read them again and again. His reflections gave me some uneasiness; but
I was so far from being amended by them, that I only compared this emotion
to the transient effect of a tragical representation on the stage. I was affected
for a moment, and that was all.

At length, your father returned from the war, covered with wounds and
laurels: The compliments which were paid to him at court, and the honours
which were heaped upon him, occasioned a second diversion of my thoughts,
which plunged me deeper than ever in the gulf of dissipation.

My first study was, to be distinguished by the elegance of my entertainments;
and in this I was very successful; my exquisite taste was generally admired, and
every one expressed the highest satisfaction. What an encouragement was this
to a woman, whose only ambition was to shine in her sphere, to please and be
applauded! You will not wonder, that our expences were excessive; and that, to
support our vanity, we diminished our substance, and consequently your inheri-
tance.

You see, my dear children, that I lay open to you, without reserve, all the
circumstances of my life; and that my language is that of one, whose heart
dictates nothing but tenderness and sincerity. Where my conduct has been faulty,
you will, I am sure, be the first to forgive: It may, perhaps, prove a fortunate
circumstance FOR YOU, that I, who have been first seduced into the ways of

vanity and folly, am the better enabled to point out to you that path, which it will be your wisdom and happiness to pursue.

Certain it is, that this abridgment of our fortune wrought some change in my manner of life: Your father again left me in obedience to the orders of the court, which sent him into ITALY; and I endeavoured to amuse myself in his absence by reading our best historians.

There with delight I found the name, which you bear, mentioned with honour in the French and English history; where saw I those virtues displayed by your ancestors, which I hope it will be the study of your lives to imitate.

About this time, my friendship commenced with the Countess of S——, an excellent lady, of whom the hand of death has lately deprived the world; in which she seemed to live for no other purpose, than to do good. Her conversation charmed me; her prudence delighted me; there was no opportunity of instruction, which she did not improve; and this she did with so much ease and affability, and in a manner so natural and agreeable, that the most inconsiderate could not but attend to her: She often urged to me the necessity of uniting in the same character the Philosopher and the Christian. Here I must acknowledge, not without taking shame to myself, that the pleasures of the world left me nothing more than a fruitless desire of being what I ought to be. It was continually interposing itself between the conviction of my judgment, and the propensities of my will, 'till my mind was utterly distracted: I would, and I would not; and my existence was nothing more than a life perpetually interrupted with doubt and perplexity.

In this strange situation did your father find me at his return. The King received him with that gracious air, which often serves instead of more substantial favours; and which is in fact equivalent to a recompense. Every one partook of my joy; and dragged me out, as it were, in spite of myself, into the midst of pleasures and diversions. Paris and Versailles, each in its turn, beheld me wholly engaged in doing honour to my husband on account of his good fortune. Pleasure and ambition are cruel tyrants; they leave us not a moment to ourselves; and when they have filled us with hope, they almost always abandon us to disappointment.

Your father, though much engaged in the business of the world, had his intervals of solitude and retirement: He sometimes pleaded indisposition, that he might apply himself to the study of his profession; and, as I imagined, to amuse himself by a change of employment. He found, that the world has every thing that is good in it, except true wisdom.

The restless spirit of mankind renewed the war; and again obliged me to live in a state of separation from a husband, who was dearer to me than myself. His valour, which rendered him insensible of danger, procured him at the same time the honour—of being grievously wounded, and of being made a Lieutenant-General. Joy and solicitude by turns took possession of my heart; and in this anxious state I continued, 'till I was fully assured of his perfect recovery.

This advancement of my husband revived my passion for the vanities of the world: I now again felt myself inclined to taste largely of the pleasures of the court. I hired one house at Versailles, and another at Fontainbleau; and my taste for luxury, together with my natural vanity, led me to fit them up in the most expensive manner. I piqued myself on having more elegant furniture than any

woman of my rank, and on having my table more sumptuously supplied. I became proverbial for the magnificence of my entertainments; and happy was the man, who could be present at them. Persons of fashion assembled at my house with eagerness; and each endeavoured to distinguish himself by the utmost exertion of pleasantry and humour.

I never found myself so far removed from wisdom, as when I was surrounded by the most celebrated wits: I heard nothing from them but sallies of mirth, which interrupted all serious thoughts; and such flighty conversation, as served only to stifle reflection. Our decisions were peremptory on every subject, and were wholly influenced by fashion and by prejudice.

Thus was my mind entirely taken up in the pursuit of folly; instead of being employed, as it ought to have been, in attending to your education.

The prevalence of custom, my dear children, had taught me to think, that I ought not to have you with me more than a few days in a year; with which custom I could not comply, without doing violence to my tenderness and affection for you. Instead of endeavouring to inform myself, what school was under the best and wisest regulation, my inquiry was, which was the most genteel; and I was much more desirous that you should form honourable connexions, than that you should receive good instructions: Thus did I secretly encourage your vanity, while your IMPROVEMENT ought to have been my principal care. When we cannot amend our faults, the least we can do is to acknowledge them: And do not think that I offer any violence to myself in thus confessing my folly, and indiscretion: It is my greatest comfort, that I am giving you this surest evidence of my repentance. If my affection for you were less than it is, I should speak to you with less sincerity; it is the compunction I feel, for having listened more attentively to the voice of custom than to that of duty, which extorts from me this undisguised profession of my misconduct; in short, my extreme solicitude for you, banishes every selfish consideration from my mind.

The conduct of your father distinguished him now more than ever. He was deservedly esteemed a most accomplished soldier; insomuch that I dare venture to assert, without fearing the imputation of partiality or ostentation, that the dignity of Field-Marshal, to which he was advanced, was no more than a distinction due to his superior merit as an officer. He saw himself elevated to the highest point of honour in his profession; at a time of life, wherein he was very capable of enjoying the fruits of his promotion; being at that time not fifty years old.

I was too fond of gaiety and pleasure, not to surpass on this occasion all my former instances of luxury and expense. Balls, illuminations and entertainments of every kind, conspired to celebrate that happy event, which filled my heart with joy; and nothing was now to be seen around me, but trophies erected to my vanity: I was wholly taken up in going from one circle to another, eager to receive congratulation and applause from every quarter. But how inconstant is all earthly glory! alas! your father died within three years after his promotion to the honour of a Marshal: And my heart, overpowered by this dreadful stroke, seemed to go down with him even into the grave. He died like a Christian philosopher; full of loyalty to his King, full of tenderness for his wife and children; and most earnestly desiring to be admitted into the presence of GOD. He would have been better pleased, had his last breath been drawn in the service

of his country; and had he been permitted to make compensation with his life, for the honours which his sovereign had heaped upon him.

The first year of my widowhood was wholly given up to the effusions of grief; to an utter disrelish for every kind of satisfaction, and to an entire indifference about myself and every thing around me. I thought of nothing, but a most affectionate husband, who was now no more; and this sad idea served only to fill my soul with the most melancholy reflections.

I could then have readily answered for myself, that the world would never more take possession of my heart. But the world is not content with being a master only: It is a TYRANT, which holds its vassals in fetters of iron; from which in vain I endeavoured to release myself: My former habits resumed their empire in my heart; and though I did not forget my husband, I forgot all my resolutions. I now appeared a fashionable widow; wholly taken up by the pleasures of the world, and all its vanities. My greatest comfort in this moment of reflection is, that I never could be prevailed with to listen to any proposals of a second marriage. I had too much respect for the memory of your father, ever to consent to lose his name; and I had too much regard for you his children, ever to endanger your welfare and happiness by such a step. This double attachment was superior to every other consideration; I felt myself altogether devoted to my children; who I feared might be less the objects of my attention, if I transferred my affections to any other: This single circumstance was sufficient to determine me. Heaven grant, that you may make me the best return for this sacrifice, not merely by your thanks, but by the tenderest regard for my happiness. I have not a more sincere wish, than to excite your affection; and as I am truly sensible of the full extent of my own, no one surely can blame me for earnestly desiring, that our love for each other should be reciprocal.

Were I so unhappy as to discover in either of you an abatement of affection towards me, I should remind you, that there is not one of you, whose birth was not almost the occasion of my death; and that the more I suffered in bringing you into the world, the more closely is my heart attached to you: This only know, to what degree you have hitherto engaged its affections; and I can truly say, that, amidst the dissipations of a life of pleasure, I never felt any REAL satisfaction but in seeing you thus sitting round me. Happy moment! the only one which can afford me a gleam of consolation for a loss, which I can never cease to lament.

But, to return to the world; which continually enslaved my affections, and which, whilst I was engaged in the gratifications of my passion for pleasure, suffered me not to rest, day or night. I had sacrificed to it the best moments of my life; the hours destined to calm repose were devoted to it; and, on the return of every day, fresh snares were laid for me; and new temptations offered to engage me in its service. I found myself absolutely subject to its caprice; I was present at every publick assembly; I had a high opinion of its extravagancies; I studied all its refinements; I commended only what the world approved; I rejected only what the world condemned: I was, in short, as much a slave to its commands, as one who has no power to move or act, without the permission of his master.

Sometimes, quite wearied with its importunity, I wished to shake off the yoke; and to enter into a serious examination of my heart; of which it had too

long maintained an entire disposal: But such transient inclinations only served to convince me of my weakness. This sufficiently appeared, when after some days of strict retirement, which should have been the commencement of a new life, a slight invitation called me forth again, to put myself under the power of my tyrant; and made me foolishly repent of having ever wished to withdraw myself from his dominion.

In the mean time I began to perceive that the spring of my life was passed and gone; and that it was time to break the charm, which thus seduced me: However the lot was cast, and rather than have recourse to reason, I employed every artifice to supply the deficiency of blooming youth. Thus did I at once endeavour to impose on others, and delude myself; and nothing but the astonishing incident which I am going to relate, was capable of overcoming this dangerous illusion.

Having been informed that a new play was to be acted, I engaged to go with a party of friends to the theatre, and among the rest, with Lady ——, whom I loved with the tenderest affection. At the appointed hour, I called at the door of my friend. Surprised, at my arrival, not to find any of the servants ready to receive me, I immediately ran up into her bed-chamber; I went to her, and saluting her, I asked her the reason why she was not ready to go with me: Oh! Heaven! She was dead! Her countenance still retained its beauty; her flesh was yet warm, but her body was motionless and lifeless! Having shrieked so loud as to fill the whole house with my cries, I fell into a swoon, which lasted above an hour and a half. The domesticks, who in their consternation had fled different ways, re-assembled at the noise of my cries; and used every possible endeavour to bring me to my senses. After which, they informed me, that their mistress was just dead of a quinsy, that had choked her. Conceive, if you can, the horrors of my situation; I was almost suffocated with grief, which laboured to express itself; and in the utmost terror and amazement, I withdrew from this scene.

By this method it seemed that heaven thought fit to act upon my mind, to dissipate imposture and delusion. I returned to my house, wherein I saw nothing but emblems of pride and vanity. I now discovered for the first time, that those specious charms, with which the world had so long deceived me, were in reality no better than splendid miseries. I now reflected, that I had been only a dupe to my own pride, and the fashions of the world: That I had been running after a phantom of happiness, which had escaped me; that human life was most uncertain in its tenure; in short, that my essayest, who had distressed me, had told me the truth; and that one must be absolutely blind, not to see the force of his arguments.

As I had learnt from experience to distrust my own weakness, I felt no inclination to make a publick profession of my change of sentiments; especially, as I knew that it is not easy to support a consistency of character in extremes; that too great zeal is seldom lasting, and almost always indiscreet; and that to discharge the duties of Christianity, it was sufficient to be—a Christian.

However, I insensibly withdrew myself from the world and its pleasures; and under a pretence of taking care of my health, as my constitution had been always delicate, I begun with living very much alone, and no more mixing in large companies. I was considered as an invalid; and after a few censures from my acquaintance, the world as easily resigned me, as it had formerly solicited me.

There is nothing sooner forgotten, than a person, who wishes to be so: one's retirement from the world may afford a topic of conversation for a day, and to morrow nothing more is said about us.

My solitude being neither the affectation of singularity, nor the effect of ill humour, but the result of serious reflection; I continued to discharge the duties which I owed to society: I made my appearance at court, when it was thought necessary; I visited my acquaintance when civility required it: I paid that attention to the duties of my station, which it appeared to demand; and laid it down as a maxim, only to abstain from such things, as religion and reason forbade.

Very soon the pleasure of reading serious books, and of studying myself, convinced me, that true happiness consists in conformity to truth; and that they, who give themselves up to a life of dissipation, have in reality nothing more than the shadow of happiness.

That horrible spectacle before mentioned, continually presented itself to my mind. I never can forget, that, whilst I fancied I was embracing a living friend, I held in my arms only a lifeless corpse, on which GOD himself had already passed an irrevocable sentence! At midnight the image of my friend very frequently appeared to my disturbed imagination; whom I had been wishing to drag to the theatre, while heaven was pronouncing an irreversible decree either of life or death everlasting.

This it was, my children, which opened my eyes to a sight of my duty; this it was, which determined me to cultivate and improve your good dispositions, and to sow in your hearts the seeds of virtue and religion.

May heaven bless and prosper my design! Indeed it is with the greatest satisfaction I observe, that your sentiments appear to be such, as seem likely to do honour to the memory of your father; and that you want nothing but a little more knowledge and information, and a little more inclination to attain it. It is with a design to assist you herein, that I have determined to call you together every evening, when my health will permit; and to discourse with you on some of the most interesting subjects. Having now given you the history of my own life, I shall henceforth concern myself only about your's; and shall endeavour to furnish you with the best instructions in my power, that you may become acceptable to your GOD, useful to your Country, and worthy of the King whom you have the honour to serve.

CONFERENCE X.

On FEMALE CONDUCT.

I have long wished, my dear Daughter, for this opportunity of freely conversing with you on subjects of the utmost consequence to you. Your youth, the world into which you are going, the snares which it lays, and the few days which I have yet to live, all induce me to open my heart to you, and to give you some instructions relative to your dangerous situation.

If you could possibly entertain a doubt of my affection, the effort I am now making, when my soul is bowed down with sickness and sorrow, and sees nothing before it but the horrors of the grave, must needs convince you how earnestly I wish to secure your happiness. My wishes will never be realized, but while you

are careful to lay down proper rules for your conduct, and suffer nothing afterwards to tempt you to break through them.

If you are so unhappy as to give yourself up to the distraction of the world, you will no longer be able to maintain the dominion over your own heart: You will live an utter stranger to yourself; and there will not be a single day, which you will know how to dispose of in a proper manner. The world is never to be satisfied; the more we bestow upon it, the more unreasonable are its demands.

Your sex requires the utmost circumspection; what among MEN is reputed a venial fault, is an absolute crime with us. There are a thousand things said and done in their company, which a woman ought neither to hear nor see. I would wish that a young woman should be silent and modest; and the world, dissipated as it is, expects the same. Its judgment of us is very severe; and it often fixes our character for life.

If you are over-solicitous to please others, you will run into a ridiculous affectation: You must make yourself agreeable to every one you converse with, without letting them see that you are thinking about it. Nothing pleases which is not natural. A woman, who sets herself to draw the attention and admiration of all upon her, will soon become an arrant coquette, if she is not one already.

It is only a natural and virtuous behaviour, which will secure to you esteem and approbation: If this should not succeed, so much the worse for those you meet with. Whatever happens, this truth is indisputable; that one of the brightest ornaments of the sex is modesty. And that a young lady can never appear to greater advantage, than when she is utterly divested of affectation in her behaviour.

Do not confound the ideas of modesty and timidity: The one pleases, the other distresses; we cannot avoid being hurt, when we see a young person confused and disconcerted. There is such a thing as an ingenuous confidence, which should make you not unwilling to speak, when the subject requires it; and to sing or dance, when a proper opportunity presents itself. If you are not vain, you will not be timorous to a fault.

I shall be very sorry for you, if ever vanity takes possession of your heart; for then, instead of being agreeable and communicative, you will be always unhappy in yourself, and your boldness will only serve to make you ridiculous to others. A disdainful carriage is that of a person of mean talents, and a bad heart; people of quality are less apt to assume it, than those of an inferior rank. We seldom endeavour to set ourselves off by pride, but when we have no other means of distinguishing ourselves; this is a ridiculous affectation, which the world always laughs at, but never forgives: The more humiliating our behaviour is to others, the more pleasure do they take in letting us down.

Affability will supply the want of those qualities, which you do not possess: It is the best apology that I know for little imperfections. Great allowances are always made for one, who has no pride or pretensions to superior merit: But self-love naturally raises in us an opposition to arrogance and presumption. Many women have become the subjects of satire, only by their haughty behaviour. Your figure is not without its share of elegance; and the handsomer a lady is, the more ready people are to suspect that she is vain.

The education I have hitherto given you convinces me, that the toilet will not engage your chief attention; you ought to spend as much time at it, as is

necessary for your decent appearance in company. We must not fly in the face of fashion, or make ourselves remarkable by our singularity: But there are certain trifles in dress, which we ought to despise. Those which make a woman a slave to her dress, are fit only for such weak minds, as the present age, with all its attachment to trifles, hath not yet learnt to esteem.

Let your hours be properly regulated; and you will find time to worship GOD, and to pursue some useful study. You will then have no imaginary complaints; and will be an utter stranger to the miseries attendant upon idleness: A life well employed, is always an agreeable life.

Do not think of amusing yourself with reading romances: It is a real malady to have one's brain filled with such ideas as they furnish. We never see things in their true light; they give us a taste only for ridiculous extravagances, extraordinary adventures, and marvelous sentiments: We insensibly adopt the language of self-importance and affectation, and become ourselves the heroines of romance.

The books you read should be as pure as your heart, and be reduced within a narrow compass. It is a mistake, to pretend that our sex ought to STUDY. We have no offices of trust to fill, nor any dignities to be invested with; and therefore we have only need to learn what is necessary to form the mind, and improve the understanding. Almost every learned woman shews that the sciences do not belong to us: I have seldom seen one of them, that was not vain, decisive, and affected in her manner of thinking, speaking, and acting.

Your attention should be directed to works of ingenuity; and you should learn the best methods of regulating a family, whenever you shall be settled in the world. You may perhaps be told, that this is not the fashionable mode of education; but fashion must not be allowed to supersede duty. A woman, whose life is a perpetual round of trifles, is only fit to be made the subject of a comedy.

Pride persuades persons of a certain rank, that they live only to enjoy themselves. How should I be grieved, if you entertained such sentiments as these! Pleasure ought only to be considered as a relaxation from fatigue; and must always be regulated and approved by virtue. Observe this rule, and you will see what sentiments we ought to entertain of the generality of public diversions. I have so good an opinion of your understanding, as to think you would one day despise me, if I recommended them to you, as the means of giving you any solid satisfaction. If ONE innocent mind has been corrupted by them, that alone is sufficient to prove them dangerous; besides this, libertines speak highly enough of them, to make us suspect that they are rather of a mischievous, than useful tendency.

As to cards, played merely for amusement, and under the restrictions formerly mentioned, I see not why you should totally reject them. They ruin no one, they prevent idle conversation, they promote a social intercourse; and provided you use them with moderation, this is as allowable as any other relaxation. The same may be said of music; it is with great propriety considered as an accomplishment in a lady; and is often found of great use in those hours, wherein we wish for amusement.

Remember, my dear child, that an obliging behaviour is the very life of society. There is no one who is not pleased with a smiling countenance; a want of good humour would render you insupportable to yourself and every one

about you. A reasonable soul ought always to be under the guidance of reason; the behaviour of a capricious mistress is a great discouragement to her attendants: If you would secure their affection, endeavour to deserve it.

My weakness, which daily increases, will not allow me to hope that I shall live to see you settled in the world: But it is GOD's will that it should be so; and to his good Providence I submit. Yet let me previously observe to you, that an amiable and obliging wife may almost always insure to herself a kind and indulgent husband. Let your affection be confined to him, whom you have engaged to love: Seek only to please him, and peace shall dwell in your house. If, in spite of all your care and prudence, things should not always go smoothly on, you will find a conscience void of reproach, the greatest comfort in the world.

Keep yourself an utter stranger to intrigues; when we are faithful in the discharge of our duty, we have no need to have recourse to artifice and falsehood. The conduct of a virtuous woman never shuns the light: The more her character is inquired into, the better she is satisfied. It is a pitiable situation to live in a state of perpetual apprehension; and to have no better security against public shame than the prudence or fidelity of a domestic, whom one has made a confidant. Nothing is so dearly purchased, as the confidence of low and venal minds: Be connected only with women of the strictest virtue; it is our acquaintance, which fixes our reputation.

If you should have children; do not part with them at that time, when the light of reason begins to dawn in their minds. Then it is, that the soul is capable of impressions, which can never afterwards be effaced; then it is, that it must be filled with whatsoever can inspire it with the love of truth. How very imperfectly do they discharge the duty of a mother, who only see their children, either to admire, or to chide them! Reflect on the conduct of the fowls of the air; always engaged in the care of their young, they never leave them 'till they have taught them to fly. Are we less wise than these irrational creatures? One would think, by the difference in our conduct, that reason was inferior to instinct.

When you appear thoroughly impressed with a love of your duty, you will have fewer admirers of your person, than of your virtue. There is nothing more disgusting than the character of a woman, who listens only to fulsome compliments; who only lies in wait for flattery, and whose behaviour on obtaining it is truly ridiculous. A well disposed mind treats every one with proper respect; and never loses its dignity, even when it is most familiar.

Be always upon your guard against a professed wit: He is a critic, who often does us great mischief: If he is not satirical, he is at least very forward, and his repartees are to be dreaded. Modesty is no objection to any person: And few have ever yet complained of it. To give your own opinion with diffidence, to hear that of others with attention, and candidly to defend your neighbour's reputation where it may be defended, is a sure way to be loved and esteemed.

Abhor luxury and idleness; these two, which are the sources of many other vices, weaken and destroy the powers of the mind. Study nothing more than a delicacy of sentiment and behaviour; speak without affectation, and write without disguise; nothing is so pleasing as the truth. The letters of Madame DE SEVIGNE, which you cannot read too often, have never been without admirers,

from their being so exactly comfortable to nature; it is a sure sign of our want of wit, when we are always endeavouring to shew it.

Such is the advice, my dear daughter, which my own experience and my heart suggest; a knowledge of the world will supply the rest: This is a science, which never is forgotten, and which prevents our being deficient in any necessary point of behavior.

You are doubtless surprized that, in a series of instruction, which comprehends the whole life, I should have said nothing on the subject of religion. But you will cease to wonder, when I tell you, that I reserve a subject, so interesting to your brothers and yourself, for another conference; when I have an opportunity of speaking to you all together.

Your father, whom you scarce remember, charged me to be particularly attentive to YOUR education. Though he is no more, he ought to live continually in your heart, by a constant love of virtue; this is the best way of recalling him to your mind, and of shewing your respect for his memory.

The hour is at hand, when you will be an orphan; but you will be in the hands of GOD; he is more especially the protector of the fatherless. In other respects, you may depend on the goodness of your uncle, whose sentiments I well know. He loves you, and he is a man of the strictest integrity. He will consider you as his daughter;—and will settle you in the world, so as to make you happy. With all my heart I wish you to be so; for it is impossible to love your more tenderly than I do. But enough for the present, my dear child; it is time for you to retire; and I am too much agitated by talking thus tenderly with you. Your presence excites those tears, which my grief will not suffer to break forth:—I feel myself almost suffocated;—I would wish to recover my spirits, but I am not able:—Oh! amiable child!—Oh! mother, deeply afflicted!

APPENDIX II

As Annis Stockton's comments written to her daughter Julia Stockton Rush indicate, Mary Wollstonecraft's *A Vindication of the Rights of Woman* (1792) had a tremendous effect on the women of Stockton's generation and the generations to follow. While this letter provides a fascinating insight into an elite-class Anglo-American woman's response to European feminism, it also reveals the extent to which Annis Stockton, then in her fifties, felt a responsibility to her daughter in expressing her opinion of Wollstonecraft's book. The formal nature of the letter provides an index of the various kinds of letters women wrote each other during the era of the early Republic. The formal tone is at once a sign of Stockton's sense of decorum and propriety as it is of her self-conscious belief about her motherly responsibility. The characteristic self-effacement she used at the end of her letter—that Wollstonecraft was the philosopher and she only the novice—signals Stockton's belief about what a woman of good sense should say as she disagrees with another person. Such self-effacement does not suggest Stockton's deference to others; the letter too clearly shows Stockton's attempt to reason through her position much as a philosopher might.

Letters like this one provide us rare glimpses into a scene of early American "sisterhood" usually enacted orally among women, where they might comment on a text and on one another's responses to that text. The letter is, in other words, the sort of formal letter women wrote to one another out of the perception that they should assist their friends and relations in developing intellectual gifts and moral probity. Stockton's letter shows the ways in which women's networks operated both for sociability and for intellectual development. It is also an important reminder of the ways in which elite women's lives were being tested by the tensions between a growing interest in education for women and a clear anxiety that women might, in becoming educated, exceed their "proper sphere." In this regard, the letter gives us a rare glimpse of one elite-class woman's resolution to remain devotedly within the parameters of behavior regarded as appropriate for a woman of her social station. For Stockton, as for many of her generation, although women might be equal to men in all arenas, their function was to operate within a sphere separate from the one in which men operated.

If in *The Coquette* the letters between Lucy Freeman, Julia Granby, and Eliza

* Letter from Annis Boudinot Stockton to Julia Stockton Rush, on Mary Wollstonecraft's *A Vindication of the Rights of Woman* (1792)

Wharton seem tonally and morally harsh, and if those in *The Power of Sympathy* between Mrs. Holmes and Myra Harrington seem a bit stilted, they nonetheless provide fairly realistic portrayals of the formal and decorous letters women typically wrote to one another on concerns of education and morals. Just as the comments by the ministers in the novels (J. Boyer in *The Coquette*, and Rev. Mr. Holmes in *The Power of Sympathy*) reflect the station, education, and sentiment of those men characters, so the comments by the women characters aptly represent—as Stockton's letter to her daughter instances for us—what women of the day said to other women and the high seriousness of their endeavors, especially when speaking on women's issues.

Along with discussing Wollstonecraft, Stockton mentioned two other writers whose works were finding some influence in Anglo-America and who were of interest—so that she could refute them—to Mary Wollstonecraft. Wollstonecraft spent some time in her *Vindication* castigating the artificiality of European society. She cited the writings of Jean-Jacques Rousseau (1712–78) in this context, finding Rousseau a model man of sense and feeling. In Rousseau's view, the social structure, not God, was the author of evil in the world; it is a view Mary Wollstonecraft seemed to share. Yet Wollstonecraft, like Stockton here, found his comments about women and what might be expected of them reprehensible. The other man Stockton mentioned is Dr. John Gregory (1724–74), Scottish physician and author of *A Father's Legacy to His Daughters* (1774), which was having some favor in English North America. Gregory argued that women were not meant to be mere domestics, and he considered that some women might have vast intellectual potential. But he urged nonetheless that too great development of these women would render them unable to find marital happiness, which he considered women's greatest goal. Stockton commented on Wollstonecraft's position that all the writers on women's education, from Rousseau to Gregory, tend to make women more weak and artificial than necessary, which thus would render them less capable as equal citizens.

The following letter—available in the Rush-Williams-Biddle Family Papers at the Rosenbach Museum and Library, Philadelphia—was probably written on March 22, 1793, from Annis Stockton's estate home in New Jersey.

[March 22, 1793]

My dear Julia

I have been engaged these two days with reading the rights of women, which I never could procure before, tho it has been much longer in the neighbourhood. I have been musing upon the subject over my solitary fire till I took up the resolution to give you my sentiments upon it tho I suppose it is an old thing with you— I wonder you never Sent me your Critique— I am much pleased with her strength of reasoning, and her sentiment in general—but think that She like many other great geniuses—establish an Hypothesis and lay such a weight upon it as to cause the superstructure to destroy the foundation.— and I am sorry to find a woman capable to write such strictures should Complement Roussaus nonesense so much as to make his Ideas of women the criterion of the rank they hold in Society.— I think we need go no farther, than his Confessions, to discover that he had some defect in his brain, or that he was a refined Idiot, rather than an enlightened philosopher. I have always Contended that the edu-

cation of women was not made a matter of that importance, which it ought to be—but we see that error daily Correcting— and in this Country, the Empire of reason, is not monopolized by men, there is great pains taken to improve our sex, and store their minds with that knowledge best adapted, to make them useful in the situation that their creator has placed them—and we do not often see those efforts opposed by the other sex, but rather disposed to asist them by every means in their power, and men of sense generally prefer such women, as Companions thro life— The state of society may be different in Europe from what it is in America—but from the observation I have been able to make in my own Country, I do not think any of that Slavish obedience exists, that She talks so much of—I think the women have their equal right of every thing, Latin and Greek excepted.— and I believe women of the most exalted minds, and the most improved understanding, will be most likly to practice that Conciliating mode of Conduct, which She seems to Condemn, as blind Obedience, and Slavish Submission, to the Caprice of an arbitrary tyrant, which character she seems to apply to men as a sex.— but certainly exercising the virtues of moderation and forbearence—and avoiding desputes as much as possible, can easily be distinguished from Slavish fear— and must certainly tend to strengthen the mind, and give it a degree of fortitude, in accomodating ourselves to our situation, that adds dignity to the human character.—because this is necessary, not only with a husband, that one has chosen for a Companion thro life—but with every other person, that we are obliged to be in the habits of strict intimacy—you know that it is a favourite tenet with me, that there is no sex in Soul— I believe it as firmly as I do my existance—but at the same time I do not think that the sexes were made to be independent of each other—I believe that our creator intended us for different walks in life—and that it takes equal powers of mind, and understanding, properly to fulfil the duties that he has marked out for us— as it does for the other sex, to gain a knowledge of the arts and Sciences, and if our education was the same, our improvement would be the same— but there is no occasion for exactly the same education. I think we may draw the Conclusion that there is no sex in Soul, from the following illustrations—that there are many men, that have been taught, and have *not* obtained any great degree of knowledge in the circle of the Sciences—and that there *have* been women who have excelled in every branch, when they have had an opportunity of instruction, and I have no doubt if those advantages were oftener to occur, we should see more instances.— one argument brought to prove the inferiority of the mind of a woman, is that the organs of her body are weaker than mens, and that her Constitution is not so strong—now I know a great number of women, who have much stronger organs of body, and twice the strength of Constitution, that as great a number of men, and men of genius too, can boast of—or that from their infancy, they ever did enjoy—and it does not follow, that their souls are inferior, or that they are women instead of men.

I am much pleased with her remarks upon Doctor Gregory—I have many a time drawn upon my self a sneer, for venturing to desent from that amiable man, for one of his sentiments—respecting the reserve, which a woman should treat her husband with on the Subject of her affection for him— I allway thought it a little art, and such a want of Confidence unbecoming a woman of Sense. I Confess I have a nobler opinion of men than our author appears to have— I

dare say there are many who answer her description—but happily for me, those that I have had an opportunity to risk my opinion on, have had as high Ideas of the rationality of women—and there equal right to the exertion of the immortal mind, as the most tenacious of our sex could be—

She has some most charming remarks on education and her observation on some of the faults of her sex are good, but her whole chapter on modesty is admirable, and has some marks of originallity. but I must Confess that not withstanding the appearance of piety in her ejaculatory addresses to the supreme being, interspersed thro the book—I am not pleased with the bold, indeed I may say, almost presumptious manner, in which She speaks of the Diety—it too much partakes of the spirit of the whole work— which I think is written in a style that does not accord with the nature of our intercourse with each other— or with the imperfection of our state.— we are all beings dependant on one another, and therefore must often expect the inconveniences that must necessarily arise from the weakness of human nature, and the imperfection of some of those with whom we are Connected. and we must make the best of it.— and some of her expressions are by far, too strong for my Ideas.— but *she* writes like a philosopher, and *I* think as a novice.— yet to sum up my poor Judgement upon this wonderful book, I do really think a great deal of instruction may be gathered from it— and I am sure that no one, can read it, but they may find something or other, that will Correct their Conduct and enlarge their Ideas.—

I am frightened at the length of my letter—and more when I look at the watch and see the hour of the night— it is past one oclock, and not a creature up in the house but my self—but you will say, it is my custon to keep the vigils of the night.

Adieu my love, may heaven bless you and yours and protect you this night, prays your ever affectionate

mother A Stockton—

FOR THE BEST IN PAPERBACKS, LOOK FOR THE

In every corner of the world, on every subject under the sun, Penguin represents quality and variety—the very best in publishing today.

For complete information about books available from Penguin—including Puffins, Penguin Classics, and Arkana—and how to order them, write to us at the appropriate address below. Please note that for copyright reasons the selection of books varies from country to country.

In the United Kingdom: Please write to *Dept. JC, Penguin Books Ltd, FREEPOST, West Drayton, Middlesex UB7 0BR.*

If you have any difficulty in obtaining a title, please send your order with the correct money, plus ten percent for postage and packaging, to *P.O. Box No. 11, West Drayton, Middlesex UB7 0BR*

In the United States: Please write to *Consumer Sales, Penguin USA, P.O. Box 999, Dept. 17109, Bergenfield, New Jersey 07621-0120.* VISA and MasterCard holders call 1-800-253-6476 to order all Penguin titles

In Canada: Please write to *Penguin Books Canada Ltd, 10 Alcorn Avenue, Suite 300, Toronto, Ontario M4V 3B2*

In Australia: Please write to *Penguin Books Australia Ltd, P.O. Box 257, Ringwood, Victoria 3134*

In New Zealand: Please write to *Penguin Books (NZ) Ltd, Private Bag 102902, North Shore Mail Centre, Auckland 10*

In India: Please write to *Penguin Books India Pvt Ltd, 706 Eros Apartments, 56 Nehru Place, New Delhi 110 019*

In the Netherlands: Please write to *Penguin Books Netherlands bv, Postbus 3507, NL-1001 AH Amsterdam*

In Germany: Please write to *Penguin Books Deutschland GmbH, Metzlerstrasse 26, 60594 Frankfurt am Main*

In Spain: Please write to *Penguin Books S.A., Bravo Murillo 19, 1° B, 28015 Madrid*

In Italy: Please write to *Penguin Italia s.r.l., Via Felice Casati 20, I-20124 Milano*

In France: Please write to *Penguin France S.A., 17 rue Lejeune, F-31000 Toulouse*

In Japan: Please write to *Penguin Books Japan, Ishikiribashi Building, 2-5-4, Suido, Bunkyo-ku, Tokyo 112*

In Greece: Please write to *Penguin Hellas Ltd, Dimocritou 3, GR-106 71 Athens*

In South Africa: Please write to *Longman Penguin Southern Africa (Pty) Ltd, Private Bag X08, Bertsham 2013*